Adventure Stories for Boys

Edited by
John Canning

octopus

CONTENTS

HOW I WON THE WORLD TITLE

Muhammad Ali

Muhammad Ali is said to be the most famous man in the world. Put him in the middle of Teheran or Tokyo and he would be immediately recognized. He is that rare article, a genuine original who has brought a new dimension to the sport of boxing. Allied to the highest skill in the ring, he has the uncanny ability of being able to 'psych' an opponent out of a fight. Both these talents are well illustrated in his own account of his fight with Sonny Liston in 1964—the fight which first made him heavyweight champion of the world.

Of all the controversies surrounding my first war against Liston, the weigh-in ceremony will be the least understood. I'll be labelled as 'frightened to death' or 'hysterical' or 'terrified'. The truth of the matter is I've rehearsed and planned every move I make that day. Usually, weigh-in ceremonies are dull, routine little affairs in the Commissioners' office, but Liston has announced that he will annihilate me in the first round and I've decided I won't wait for the first round. I'll attack at the weigh-in. I'll act totally crazy and so will Bundini, who is an expert on craziness. 'I'll jump him, and when I do, you hold me back,' I tell my brother and Ronnie, and we march into the weigh-in room to play our part. Sugar Ray has flown down to be by my side, but he knows nothing of the plan and is embarrassed by the whole act.

We burst in through three hundred photographers and reporters, scuffling and pushing and shovelling to get close to us. 'We're ready to rumble! We're ready to rumble!' we scream. 'Float like a butterfly, sting like a bee!' we shout together. 'This is it, you big ugly bear!' I shake my fist at Liston when he comes up to the scale in his white terry cloth robe. 'It's all over! You'll be mine tomorrow night. I'm through playing with you. It's all over now.'

Liston turns a stone face to mine. I lunge at him, but my crew holds me back. I make a mighty effort to break through. 'Let's get it on!' I scream. 'Let's get it on right now!' I'm surprised to see a confused look cross his face. He speaks very low, for only me to hear: 'Don't let everyone know what a fool you are.' I'm delighted. He actually believes I'm a fool.

When I move up to the scale, I continue to shout. And then we face each other eye to eye. For ten seconds there's nothing but silence. Reporters and photographers back away as though they expect a fight. Finally, I break the silence. 'Would you look at this big ugly bear?' Liston steps back. 'You're not the champ, you're the chump. Tomorrow night is your last night.' Bundini's screaming along with me, Ronnie's laughing and shouting.

It's my turn on the scale. I weigh two-ten and when the doctor checks my blood pressure and pulse, his eyes widen in surprise. 'Your pulse rate is one-twenty,' he says, 'more than twice your normal rate.'

Jimmy Cannon, whose column appears in the Miami *Herald Reporter*, steps in with his pencil and pad. 'Does that mean he's frightened, doctor?'

The doctor nods. 'He's in mortal fear or he's emotional. We'll have to call the fight off if his pressure doesn't come down before he goes into that ring.'

My crew march out of the room shouting and screaming, and I go back to my house. It's hard to stop laughing. I have a tape of the words of the Honourable Elijah Muhammad, and finally I turn it on and play it and lay back relaxed and thinking. I'm resting quietly when Dr Pacheco comes in. He takes my blood pressure and finds it normal. He looked amazed. 'Liston has been boasting he's afraid of no man alive,' I tell him. 'But Liston means no sane man. Liston's got to be afraid of a crazy man.' With that, I go to sleep.

They've got me in my dressing-room nearly an hour before the fight. Over the loudspeaker the announcer is saying Rudolph Clay is about to fight, and I throw my robe around me and dash out. Angelo[1] tries to stop me, but I snatch away. My brother's fighting, I've got to see it. I'm always worried about Rudy when he fights.

8   [1]Angelo Dundee, Ali's trainer.

I rush up to the bleachers, stand next to a woman who says to me, 'Young man, shouldn't you be down in the dressing-room getting ready? We came here to see you fight Liston.' But I'm yelling encouragement down to Rudy, hollering at the top of my voice. 'Jab him! Jab him! Keep moving, Rudy! Keep moving!' The sweat is pouring off me. I feel Dr Pacheco tugging at my arm. 'Champ, you need all the rest you can get. For God sakes, you go on in thirty minutes.'

Rudy wins the fight by a split decision, and I hear the boos. They're booing him because he's been announced as my brother and they want to take it out on him. I want to call to Rudy, 'Come on out of that ring, little brother, you don't have to fight no more. I'll do the fighting.' And when he gets in my dressing-room I put my arms around him and I say, 'You're through fighting. I'm going to be The Champ tonight. You're not going to have to fight any more.' But it will be a long time before he listens to me.

Now they're calling for me to come out. There's a roar going up and through the stadium. They want to see if I can live up to all the boasting and predictions. They want to see someone kill the predictor. Of all the fights that I will have, of all the crossroads I have come through, this will be the most crucial and even months after the fight, after the storm has raged and subsided, I find I still try to put the pieces together.

I'm with Angelo and Bundini at the home of Dr Pacheco, who's saying, 'What always puzzled me is why you were so suspicious of your white friends that night. We were all together—you, me, Angelo, Rudy, Bundini. We were in that room and the doors were locked, waiting for the fight to start. No one could get in, no one could get out. That's how much suspiciousness was in the atmosphere. And all your water bottles were taped, as they should have been. You told Rudy not to take his eyes off the water. When you'd ask him, "Have you been watching the water bottles?" and Rudy would admit that he had left them alone for a few minutes, you'd say, "Take the tape off, throw the water out. Put fresh water in and tape it up again." And I kept thinking to myself, how is anyone going to get in the room to put anything in the bottle? What was going on? What was happening?'

I look back on that night and I see Pacheco and all of us sitting in that room, and it isn't only Liston that I feel on guard against. 'The truth is,' I tell Pacheco, 'I wasn't trusting Angelo at the time. I wasn't trusting

9

you, Dr Pacheco. I trusted only my brother and the Muslim Captain
Sam. All week I had been getting phone calls at my house saying,
"Nigger, you'll not win that Sonny Liston fight." That morning of the
fight I'd gotten calls saying, "You'll be lucky if you make it in the ring,
you loud-mouthed bastard." Then the caller would hang up and
another caller would say, "If Liston don't get you, we're gonna get you!
You'll never be the world heavyweight champion." At first I didn't
pay any attention, but Captain Samuels said, "The White Power structure wants you whipped. You were up in New York with Malcolm X
a couple of days before the fight, and it's out that you're a follower of
the Honourable Elijah Muhammad. You're a 'Black Muslim'. It's all
in the press now. We'll get Rudy to watch everything, especially your
water." I knew that only a few months earlier it had been published that
Harold Johnson, the fighter, had been given a doped orange by someone and he was groggy in the ring. The Kefauver Committee had exposed how corrupt and treacherous the Syndicate operations had been
inside boxing. It was my first big fight and I knew I was hated more
than Johnson.'

'Then I sting him with left jabs . . .'

'But why wouldn't you trust a man like Angelo, who had been with you since the first days?'

'Why? Because history shows people change. People in my own family had turned against me when I became a Muslim. Other people's families had turned against me. Why is it necessary for me to trust a white man just because he worked in my corner? I was twenty-two years old then. The only ones I could trust would be those closest to me. All I wanted that night was to make sure I got in that ring without being doped. I wanted the security of being satisfied. My insurance was to have only my brother, my blood brother, watch the water. No one else. I never thought Angelo was a crook. The only thing that could hurt me, I thought, was something coming through the water. And in the fifth round, when I was blinded, at first I felt again it was something coming in through the water.

'The first round was exactly as I had planned it. I could see my strategy paying off. Liston's coming at me like a bull, throwing wild punches. He wants to do me in the way he did Floyd Patterson, and I lean back and dance away. He tries to catch me on the ropes, but I duck

under his punches and spin around. I wait until I'm halfway through the round before I even open up on him. Then I sting him with left jabs, right crosses to the head. And when that round ended, I knew I had him.

'I remember the middle of the third round. In the clinches, I can feel the pace is telling on him. His face is swelling up from my jabs. I throw more right crosses and I open a cut under his left eye. I see he's shocked, confused, bewildered. He had never been cut in his entire career. Now his own blood is spilling into the ring for the first time. I see him come at me like a wounded animal, throwing hard shots to my body, but I catch most of them on my elbow, and when the bell rings I put my hand on his shoulder and push him away.

'And on into the fourth. I keep sticking him, moving and sticking him. Then the fifth round comes up. I felt at ease and relaxed, he was still doing everything I thought he would do. But in the fifth round, I would later find out he had been having some shoulder trouble and they had been rubbing him down with a liniment, and by brushing up against me and trading punches, some of the liniment got on my forehead, and when Angelo sponged my face between rounds, it dripped down into my eyes. "I can't see!" I cried out when I came back. "My eyes are burning! I can't see!" And I couldn't see. It's like if you put a drop of hot liniment in your eye, for a while it will burn and burn. Angelo was trying to rinse my eyes with the sponge, but that didn't help. That's when I said, "Cut the gloves off. Show the world there's wrong-doing going on."

'I was whipping Liston from the first round on. His eye was cut and bleeding. I knew what the press would say, that I got scared and quit. But why would I get scared and quit when I was winning the fight so easy? I started to quit because I couldn't see. They'd want to say I quit because I was getting slaughtered. They'd say I was using that for an excuse. Then Angelo said, "This is the big one. This is for the title shot. You gotta go back out there. You're winning."

'When the bell rang, Angelo pushed me back out into the ring, only ten seconds before the referee was about to give the fight to Liston. I could hear Bundini yelling, "Don't let him knock us out! Use the yardstick on him! Yardstick 'em, champ!" I went out with my right eye closed. Liston was lunging at me, throwing wild hooks that just

12

missed me. I could barely make out his image, but I ducked, pedalled and danced away.

'I wiped my eyes as Liston charged, trying to catch me with vicious punches that barely missed. He was going all out. Whenever he got within range, I reached out and put my hand on his head. My arms were longer than his and I knew he couldn't hit me as long as I kept him an arm's length away.

'Then I heard somebody scream from the ringside: "Beat that nigger's ass, Sonny! Beat that nigger's ass!" Somehow that stimulated me, and it made me more determined to hold on. And by the end of the round my eyes started to clear, and I went back on attack, snapping his head back with sharp jabs.

'When I got back to the corner, I knew everything would be all right. In the sixth, I went out and Liston was a changed man. He'd thrown his best stuff and he hadn't been able to do his damage. I felt his breathing. He was tired and I was still strong, and he knew he had no protection against my lefts or rights.

'When the bell rang for the start of the seventh round, he stayed in his corner. He sat limp on the stool, staring blankly across at us. Angelo and Bundini were screaming at me: "You the champion! You the champion!" I leaped into their arms. The long campaign was over. I had come into my own. I had fulfilled my prediction.'

In weeks ahead, things would happen which I could never have foreseen: I would fall in love and marry the most beautiful woman I'd ever met, and while my new marriage was being torn by religious quarrels, I would prepare for my return match with Liston.

I would learn how narrowly Angelo came to being roughed up when the fight was over: 'I thought your guys were going to kill me,' he said, speaking of Ronnie and Archie. 'They thought I had done something to the water. I saved myself by grabbing the bucket and drinking some of the water and rubbing it in my eyes to show them that my water was all right.'

When it's all over, there's one final talk I want to make—to the press. When they gather in front of me, it's hard to forget that nearly all of them had considered me a hoax. They start to shoot questions at me, but I cut them off: 'Hold it! Hold it!' I say. 'You've all had a chance to say

13

what you thought before the fight. Now it's my turn. You all said Sonny Liston would kill me. You said he was better than Jack Johnson or Jack Dempsey, even Joe Louis, and you ranked them the best heavy-weights of all time. You kept writing how Liston whipped Floyd Patterson twice, and when I told you I would get Liston in eight, you wouldn't believe it. Now I want all of you to tell the whole world while all the cameras are on us, tell the world that "I'm the greatest".'

There's a silence. 'Who's the greatest?' I ask them. Nobody answers. They look down at their pads and microphones. 'Who's the greatest?' I say again. They look up with solemn faces, but the room is still silent.

'For the *last time*!' I shout. 'All the eyes of the world on us. You just a bunch of hypocrites. I told you I was gonna get Liston and I got him. All the gamblers had me booked eight-to-one underdog. I proved all of you wrong. I shook up the world! Tell me who's the greatest! *Who is the greatest?*'

They hesitate for a minute, and finally in a dull tone they all answer: 'You are.'

THE TALKING HEAD

Gerald Durrell

In his book, Birds, Beasts and Relatives *the famous naturalist Gerald Durrell describes a holiday spent on the Greek island of Corfu with his family, comprising mother, brothers Lawrence and Leslie and his sister Margo. Gerald's interest was, as always, centred on the wildlife and one day he was fascinated to meet a gypsy and his performing bear, named Pavlo. He and Pavlo quickly became friends. The gypsy then began to talk mysteriously of 'my little talking head' which he kept with a pile of goods under a tarpaulin. Durrell was intrigued . . .*

'I have a Head,' he said jerking his thumb towards his pile of belongings, 'a living Head. It talks and answers questions. It is without doubt the most remarkable thing in the world.'

I was puzzled. Did he mean, I asked, a head without a body?

'Of course without a body. Just a Head,' and he cupped his hands in front of him, as though holding a coconut. 'It sits on a little stick and talks to you. Nothing like it has ever been seen in the world.'

But how, I inquired, if the head were a disembodied head, could it live?

'Magic,' said the man solemnly. 'Magic that my great-great-grandfather passed down to me.'

I felt sure that he was pulling my leg, but, intriguing though the discussion on talking heads was, I felt we were wandering away from my main objective, which was to acquire the immediate freehold of Pavlo, now sucking in through his muzzle, with wheezy sighs of satisfaction, my last bit of chocolate. I studied the man carefully as he squatted dreamy-eyed, his head enveloped in a cloud of smoke. I decided that with him the bold approach was the best. I asked him

15

bluntly whether he would consider selling the bear and for how much?

'Sell Pavlo?' he said. 'Never! He's like my own son.'

Surely, I said, if he went to a good home? Somewhere where he was loved and allowed to dance, surely then he might be tempted to sell? The man looked at me meditatively puffing on his cigarette.

'Twenty million drachmas?' he inquired, and then laughed at my look of consternation. 'Men who have fields must have donkeys to work them,' he said. 'They don't part with them easily. Pavlo is my donkey. He dances for his living and he dances for mine, and until he is too old to dance, I will not part with him.'

I was bitterly disappointed, but I could see that he was adamant. I rose from my recumbent position on the broad, warm, faintly snoring back of Pavlo and dusted myself down. Well, I said, there was nothing more I could do. I understood his wanting to keep the bear, but if he changed his mind, would he get in touch with me? He nodded gravely. And if he was performing in town, could he possibly let me know where, so that I could attend?

'Of course,' he said, 'but I think people will tell you where I am, for my Head is extraordinary.'

I nodded and shook his hand. Pavlo got to his feet and I patted his head.

When I reached the top of the valley I looked back. They were both standing side by side. The man waved briefly and Pavlo, swaying on his hind legs, had his muzzle in the air, questing after me with his nose. I liked to feel it was a gesture of farewell.

I walked slowly home thinking about the man and his talking Head and the wonderful Pavlo. Would it be possible, I wondered, for me to get a bear cub from somewhere and rear it? Perhaps if I advertised in a newspaper in Athens it might bring results?

The family were in the drawing-room having tea and I decided to put my problem to them. As I entered the room, however, a startling change came over what had been a placid scene. Margo uttered a piercing scream, Larry dropped a cup full of tea into his lap and then leapt up and took refuge behind the table, while Leslie picked up a chair and Mother gaped at me with a look of horror on her face. I had never known my presence to provoke quite such a positive reaction on the part of the family.

16

'Get it out of here,' roared Larry.

'Yes, get the bloody thing out,' said Leslie.

'It'll kill us all!' screamed Margo.

'Get a gun,' said Mother faintly. 'Get a gun and save Gerry.'

I couldn't, for the life of me, think what was the matter with them. They were all staring at something behind me. I turned and looked and there, standing in the doorway, sniffing hopefully towards the tea table, was Pavlo. I went up to him and caught hold of his muzzle. He nuzzled at me affectionately. I explained to the family that it was only Pavlo.

'I am not *having* it,' said Larry throatily. 'I am not *having* it. Birds and dogs and hedgehogs all over the house and now a bear. What does he think this is, for Christ's sake? A bloody Roman arena?'

'Gerry, dear, do be careful,' said Mother quaveringly. 'It looks rather fierce.'

'It will kill us all,' quavered Margo with conviction.

'I can't get past it to get to my guns,' said Leslie.

'You are *not* going to have it. I forbid it,' said Larry. 'I will *not* have the place turned into a bear pit.'

'Where did you get it, dear?' asked Mother.

'I don't care where he got it,' said Larry. 'He's to take it back this instant, quickly, before it rips us to pieces. The boy's got no sense of responsibility. I am not going to be turned into an early Christian martyr at my time of life.'

Pavlo got up on to his hind legs and uttered a long wheezing moan which I took to mean that he desired to join us in whatever delicacies were on the tea table. The family interpreted it differently.

'Ow!' screeched Margo, as though she had been bitten.

'Gerry, do be careful,' said Mother.

'I'll not be responsible for what I do to that boy,' said Larry.

'If you survive,' said Leslie. 'Do shut up Margo, you're only making matters worse. You'll provoke the bloody thing.'

'I can scream if I want to,' said Margo indignantly.

So raucous in their fear were the family that they had not given me a chance to explain. Now I attempted to. I said that, first of all, Pavlo was not mine, and secondly he was as tame as a dog and would not hurt a fly.

17

'Two statements I refuse to believe,' said Larry. 'You pinched it from some flaming circus. Not only are we to be disembowelled, but arrested for harbouring stolen goods as well.'

'Now, now, dear,' said Mother, 'let Gerry explain.'

'Explain?' said Larry. 'Explain? How do you explain a bloody great bear in the drawing-room?'

I said that the bear belonged to a gypsy who had a talking Head.

'What do you mean, a talking head?' asked Margo.

I said that it was a disembodied head that talked.

'The boy's mad,' said Larry with conviction. 'The sooner we have him certified the better.'

The family had now all backed away to the farthest corner of the room in a trembling group. I said, indignantly, that my story was perfectly true and that, to prove it, I'd make Pavlo dance. I seized a piece of cake from the table, hooked my finger into the ring on his muzzle and uttered the same commands as his master had done. His eyes fixed greedily on the cake, Pavlo reared up and danced with me.

'Oo, look!' said Margo. 'Look! It's dancing!'

'I don't care if it's behaving like a whole *corps de ballet*,' said Larry. 'I want the damn' thing out of here.'

I shovelled the cake in through Pavlo's muzzle and he sucked it down greedily.

'He really is rather sweet,' said Mother, adjusting her spectacles and staring at him with interest. 'I remember my brother had a bear in India once. She was a very nice pet.'

'No!' said Larry and Leslie simultaneously. 'He's not having it.'

I said I could not have it any way, because the man did not want to sell it.

'A jolly good thing too,' said Larry.

'Why don't you now return it to him, if you have quite finished doing a cabaret act all over the tea table?'

Getting another slice of cake as a bribe, I hooked my finger once more in the ring on Pavlo's muzzle and led him out of the house. Halfway back to the olive grove, I met the distraught owner.

'There he is! There he is! The wicked one. I couldn't think where he had got to. He never leaves my side normally, that's why I don't keep him tied up. He must have taken a great fancy to you.'

Honesty made me admit that I thought the only reason Pavlo had followed me was because he viewed me in the light of a purveyor of chocolates.

'Phew!' said the man. 'It is a relief to me. I thought he might have gone down to the village and that would have got me into trouble with the police.'

Reluctantly, I handed Pavlo over to his owner and watched them make their way back to their camp under the trees. And then, in some trepidation, I went back to face the family. Although it had not been my fault that Pavlo had followed me, my activities in the past stood against me and the family took a lot of convincing that, on this occasion, the guilt was not mine.

The following morning, my head still filled with thoughts of Pavlo, I dutifully went into town—as I did every morning—to the house of my tutor, Richard Kralefsky. Kralefsky was a little gnome of a man with a slightly humped back and great, earnest amber eyes who suffered from real tortures in his unsuccessful attempts to educate me. He had two most endearing qualities; one, a deep love for natural history (the whole attic of his house was devoted to an enormous variety of canaries and other birds), the other that, for at least a part of the time, he lived in a dream world where he was always the hero. These adventures he would relate to me. He was inevitably accompanied in them by a heroine who was never named, but known simply as 'a Lady'.

The first half of the morning was devoted to mathematics and, with my head full of thoughts of Pavlo, I proved to be even duller than usual, to the consternation of Kralefsky who had hitherto been under the impression that he had plumbed the depths of my ignorance.

'My dear boy, you simply aren't concentrating this morning,' he said earnestly. 'You don't seem able to grasp the simplest fact. Perhaps you are a trifle overtired? We'll have a short rest from it, shall we?'

Kralefsky enjoyed these short rests as much as I did. He would potter out into the kitchen and bring back two cups of coffee and some biscuits, and we would sit companionably while he told me highly coloured stories of his imaginary adventures. But this particular morning he did not get a chance. As soon as we were sitting comfortably, sipping our coffee, I told him all about Pavlo and the man with the talking Head and the bear.

19

'Quite extraordinary!' he said. 'Not the sort of thing that one expects to find in an olive grove. It must have surprised you, I'll be bound?'

Then his eyes glazed and he fell into a reverie, staring at the ceiling, tipping his cup of coffee so that it slopped into the saucer. It was obvious that my interest in the bear had set off a train of thought in his mind. It was several days since I had had an instalment of his memoirs and I waited eagerly to see what the result would be.

'When I was a young man,' began Kralefsky, glancing at me earnestly to see whether I was listening. 'When I was a young man I'm afraid I was a bit of a harum scarum. Always getting into trouble, you know.'

He chuckled reminiscently and brushed a few biscuit crumbs from his waistcoat. With his delicately manicured hands and his large, gentle eyes it was difficult to imagine him as a harum scarum, but I tried dutifully.

'I thought at one time I would even join a circus,' he said, with the air of one confessing to infanticide. 'I remember a large circus came to the village where we were living and I attended every performance. Every single performance. I got to know the circus folk quite well, and they even taught me some of their tricks. They said I was excellent on the trapeze.' He glanced at me, shyly, to see how I would take this. I nodded seriously, as though there was nothing ludicrous in the thought of Kralefsky, in a pair of spangled tights, on a trapeze.

'Have another biscuit?' he inquired. 'Yes! That's the ticket! I think I'll have one, too.'

Munching my biscuit, I waited patiently for him to resume.

'Well,' he continued, 'the week simply flew past and the evening came for the final performance. I wouldn't have missed it for the world. I was accompanied by a Lady, a young friend of mine, who was desirous of seeing the performance. How she laughed at the clowns! *And* admired the horses. She little knew of the horror that was soon to strike.'

He took out his delicately scented handkerchief and patted his moist brow with it. He always tended to get a trifle over-excited as he reached the climax of a story.

'The final act,' he said, 'was the lion tamer.' He paused so that the full portent of this statement could sink in. 'Five beasts he had. Huge

20

Nubian lions with black manes, fresh from the jungle so he told me. The Lady and I were sitting in the front row where we could obtain the best possible view of the ring. You know the sort of cage affair that they put up in the ring for the lion act? Well, in the middle of the act, one of the sections, which had not been securely bolted, fell inwards. To our horror, we saw it fall on the lion tamer, knocking him unconscious.' He paused, took a nervous sip of coffee, and wiped his brow once more.

'What was to be done?' he inquired, rhetorically. 'There were five huge, snarling lions and I had a Lady by my side. My thoughts worked fast. If the Lady was to be saved, there was only one thing I could do. Seizing my walking-stick, I leapt into the ring and marched into the cage.'

I made just audible sounds, indicative of admiration.

'During the week when I had been visiting the circus, I had studied the lion tamer's method with great care, and now I thanked my lucky stars for it. The snarling beasts on their pedestals towered over me, but I looked them straight in the eye. The human eye, you know, has great power over the animal world. Slowly, fixing them with a piercing gaze and pointing my walking-stick at them, I got them under control and drove them inch by inch out of the ring and back into their cage. A dreadful tragedy had been averted.'

I said that the Lady must have been grateful to him.

'She was indeed. She was indeed,' said Kralefsky, pleasedly. 'She even went so far as to say that I gave a better performance than the lion tamer himself.'

Had he, I wondered, during his circus days, ever had anything to do with dancing bears?

'All sorts of animals.' said Kralefsky lavishly. 'Elephants, seals, performing dogs, bears. They were all there.'

In that case, I said tentatively, would he not like to come and see the dancing bear. It was only just down the road and, although it was not exactly a circus, I felt it might interest him.

'By Jove, that's an idea,' said Kralefsky. He pulled his watch out of his waistcoat pocket and consulted it. 'Ten minutes, eh? It'll help blow the cobwebs away.'

He got his hat and stick and together we made our way eagerly

21

through the narrow, crowded streets of the town, redolent with the smell of fruit and vegetables, drains and freshly baked bread. By dint of questioning several small boys, we discovered where Pavlo's owner was holding his show. It was a large, dim barn at the back of a shop in the centre of town. On the way there I borrowed some money off Kralefsky and purchased a bar of sticky nougat, for I felt I could not go to see Pavlo without taking him a present.

'Ah, Pavlo's friend! Welcome,' said the gypsy as we appeared in the doorway of the barn.

To my delight, Pavlo recognized me and came shuffling forward, uttering little grunts, and then reared up on his hind legs in front of me. Kralefsky backed away, rather hurriedly, I thought, for one of his circus training, and took a firmer grip on his stick.

'Do be careful, my boy,' he said.

I fed the nougat to Pavlo and when finally he had squelched the last sticky lump off his back teeth and swallowed it, he gave a contented sigh and lay down with his head between his paws.

'Do you want to see the Head?' asked the gypsy. He gestured towards the back of the barn where there was a plain deal table on which was a square box, apparently made out of cloth.

'Wait,' he said, 'and I'll light the candles.'

He had a dozen or so large candles soldered to the top of a box in their own wax, and these he now lit so that they flickered and quivered and made the shadows dance. Then he went forward to the table and rapped on it with his bear stick.

'Head, are you ready?' he asked.

I waited with a delicate prickle of apprehension in my spine. Then from the interior of the cloth box a clear treble voice said,

'Yes, I'm ready.'

The man lifted the cloth at one side of the box and I saw that the box was formed of slender laths on which thin cloth had been loosely tacked. The box was about three feet square. In the centre of it was a small pedestal with a flattened top and on it, looking macabre in the flickering light of the candles, was the head of a seven-year-old boy.

'By Jove!' said Kralefsky in admiration. 'That is clever!'

What astonished me was that the head was alive. It was obviously the head of a young gypsy lad, made up rather crudely with black

22

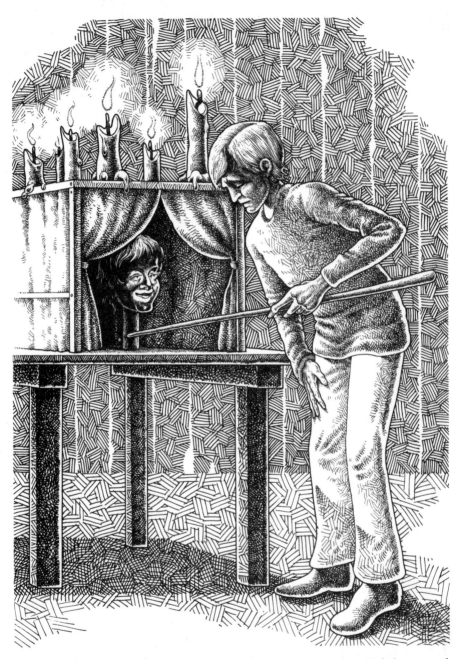

'*I poked around the pedestal and the Head watched me with a slightly amused expression.*'

23

grease paint to look like a Negro. It stared at us and blinked its eyes.

'Are you ready to answer questions now?' said the gypsy, looking, with obvious satisfaction at the entranced Kralefsky. The Head licked its lips and then said, 'Yes, I am ready.'

'How old are you?' asked the gypsy.

'Over a thousand years old,' said the Head.

'Where do you come from?'

'I come from Africa and my name is Ngo.'

The gypsy droned on with his questions and the Head answered them, but I was not interested in that. What I wanted to know was how the trick was done. When he at first told me about the Head, I had expected something carved out of wood or plaster which, by ventriloquism, could be made to speak, but this was a living head perched on a little wooden pedestal, the circumference of a candle. I had no doubt that the Head was alive for its eyes wandered to and fro as it answered the questions automatically, and once, when Pavlo got up and shook himself, a look of apprehension came over its face.

'There,' said the gypsy proudly, when he had finished his questioning. 'I told you, didn't I? It's the most remarkable thing in the world.'

I asked him whether I could examine the whole thing more closely. I had suddenly remembered that Theodore had told me of a similar illusion which was created with the aid of mirrors. I did not see where it was possible to conceal the body that obviously belonged to the Head, but I felt that the table and the box needed investigation.

'Certainly,' said the gypsy, somewhat to my surprise. 'Here, take my stick. But all I ask is that you don't touch the Head itself.'

Carefully, with the aid of the stick I poked all round the pedestal to see if there were any concealed mirrors or wires, and the Head watched me with a slightly amused expression in its black eyes. The sides of the box were definitely only of cloth and the floor of the box was, in fact, the top of the table on which it stood. I walked round the back of it and I could see nothing. I even crawled under the table, but there was nothing there and certainly no room to conceal a body. I was completely mystified.

'Ah,' said the gypsy in triumph. 'You didn't expect that, did you? You thought I had a boy concealed in there, didn't you?'

I admitted the charge and begged him to tell me how it was done.

'Oh, no. I can't tell you,' he said. 'It's magic. If I told you, the Head would disappear in a puff of smoke.'

I examined both the box and the table for a second time, but, even bringing a candle closer to aid my investigations, I still could not see how it was possible.

'Come,' said the gypsy. 'Enough of the Head. Come and dance with Pavlo.'

He hooked the stick into the bear's muzzle and Pavlo rose on to his hind legs. The gypsy handed the stick to me and then picked up a small wooden flute and started to play and Pavlo and I did a solemn dance together.

'Excellent, by Jove! Excellent!' said Kralefsky, clapping his hands with enthusiasm. I suggested that he might like to dance with Pavlo too, since he had such vast circus experience.

'Well, now,' said Kralefsky. 'I wonder whether it would be altogether wise? The animal, you see, is not familiar with me.'

'Oh, he'll be all right,' said the gypsy. 'He's tame with anyone.'

'Well,' said Kralefsky reluctantly, 'if you're sure. If you insist.'

He took the bear stick gingerly from me and stood facing Pavlo, looking extremely apprehensive.

'And now,' said the gypsy, 'you will dance.'

And he started to play a lilting little tune on his pipe.

I stood enchanted by the sight. The yellow, flickering light of the candles showing the shadows of Kralefsky's little hump-backed figure and the shaggy form of the bear on the wall as they pirouetted round and round and, squatting on its pedestal in the box, the Head watched them, grinning and chuckling to itself.

THE HUNTING OF TARKA

Henry Williamson

In one of the greatest of all animal books, Tarka the Otter, *author Henry Williamson describes Tarka's 'joyful water-life and death in the country of the two rivers', which is Devonshire. During the last year of his life Tarka had been spending some time sleeping among rushes at the shallow end of a lake. Then one morning he crossed woods and fields until he came to a stream where there was a rock in one of the banks with a wide opening half under water. Tarka slipped under the rock, intending to hide during the hours of sunlight.*

He was awakened by the tremendous baying of hounds. He saw feet splashing in the shallow water, a row of noses, and many flacking tongues. The entrance was too small for any head to enter. He crouched a yard away, against the cold rock. The noise hurt the fine drums of his ears.

Hob-nailed boots scraped on the brown shillets of the water-bed, and iron-tipped hunting poles tapped the rocks.

Go'r'n leave it! Leave it! Go'r'n leave it! Deadlock! Harper! Go'r'n leave it!

Tarka heard the horn and the low opening became lighter.

Go'r'n leave it! Captain! Deadlock! Go'r'n leave it!

The horn twanged fainter as the pack was taken away. Then a pole was thrust into the holt and prodded about blindly. It slid out again. Tarka saw boots and hands and the face of a terrier. A voice whispered, *Leu in there, Sammy, leu in there!* The small ragged brown animal crept out of the hands. Sammy smelled Tarka, saw him, and began to sidle towards him. *Waugh-waugh-waugh-wa-waugh.* As the otter did not move, the terrier crept nearer, yapping with head stretched forward.

After a minute Tarka could bear the irritating noises no more. Tissing, with open mouth, he moved past the terrier, whose snarly yapping changed to a high-pitched yelping. The men on the opposite bank stood silent and still. They saw Tarka's head in sunlight, which came through the trees behind them and turned the brown shillets a warm yellow. The water ran clear and cold. Tarka saw three men in blue coats; they did not move and he slipped into the water. It did not cover his back, and he returned to the bankside roots. He moved in the shadows and under the ferns at his ordinary travelling pace. One of three watching men declared that an otter had no sense of fear.

No hound spoke, but the reason of the silence was not considered by Tarka, who could not reason such things. He had been awakened with a shock, he had been tormented by a noise, he had left a dangerous place, and he was escaping from human enemies. As he walked upstream, with raised head, his senses of smell, sight, and hearing were alert for his greatest enemies, the hounds.

The stream being narrow and shallow, the otter was given four minutes' law. Four minutes after Tarka had left he heard behind him the short and long notes of the horn, and the huntsman crying amidst the tongues of hounds, *Ol-ol-ol-ol-ol-ol-over! Get on to 'm! Ol-ol-ol-ol-over!* as the pack returned in full cry to the water. Hounds splashed into the water around the rock, wedging themselves at its opening and breaking into couples and half-couples, leaping through the water after the wet and shivering terrier, throwing their tongues and dipping their noses to the wash of scent coming down.

Deadlock plunged at the lead, with Coraline, Sailoress, Captain and Playboy. They passed the terrier, and Deadlock was so eager that he knocked him down. Sammy picked up his shivery body and followed.

Tarka sank all but his nostrils in a pool and waited. He lay in the sunlit water like a brown log slanting to the stones on which his rudder rested. The hunstman saw him. Tarka lifted his whiskered head out of the water, and stared at the hunstman. Hounds were speaking just below. From the pool the stream flowed for six feet down the smooth slide up which he had crept. When Deadlock jumped into the pool and lapped the scent lying on the water, Tarka put down his head with hardly a ripple, and like a skin of brown oil moved under the hound's belly. Soundlessly he emerged, and the sun glistened on his water-

27

sleeked coat as he walked down on the algae-smeared rock. He seemed to walk under their muzzles slowly, and to be treading on their feet.

Let hounds hunt him! Don't help hounds or they'll chop him!

The pack was confused. Every hound owned the scent, which was like a tangled line, the end of which was sought for unravelling. But soon Deadlock pushed through the pack and told the way the otter had gone.

As Tarka was running over shillets, with water scarcely deep enough to cover his rudder, Deadlock saw him and with stiff stern ran straight at him. Tarka quitted the water. The dead twigs and leaves at the hedge-bottom crackled and rustled as he pushed through to the meadow. While he was running over the grass, he could hear the voice of Deadlock raging as the bigger black-and-white hound struggled through the hazel twigs and brambles and honeysuckle bines. He crossed fifty yards of meadow, climbed the bank, and ran down again on to a tarred road. The surface burned his pads, but he ran on, and even when an immense crimson creature bore down upon him he did not go back into the meadow across which hounds were streaming. With a series of shudders the crimson creature slowed to a standstill, while human figures rose out of it, and pointed. He ran under the motor-coach, and came out into brown sunshine, hearing above the shouts of men the clamour of hounds trying to scramble up the high bank and pulling each other down in their eagerness.

He ran in the shade of the ditch, among bits of newspaper, banana and orange skins, cigarette ends and crushed chocolate boxes. A long yellow creature grew bigger and bigger before him, and women rose out of it and peered down at him as he passed it. With smarting eyes he ran two hundred yards of the road, which for him was a place of choking stinks and hurtful noises. Pausing in the ditch, he harkened to the clamour changing its tone as hounds leaped down into the road. He ran on for another two hundred yards, then climbed the bank, pushed through dusty leaves and grasses and briars that would hold him, and down the sloping meadow to the stream. He splashed into the water and swam until rocks and boulders rose before him. He climbed and walked over them. His rudder drawn on mosses and lichens left a strong scent behind him. Deadlock, racing over the green-shadowed grassland, threw his tongue before the pack.

In the water, through shallow and pool, his pace was steady, but not hurried; he moved faster than the stream; he insinuated himself from slide to pool, from pool to boulder, leaving his scent in the wet marks of his pads and rudder.

People were running through the meadow, and in the near distance arose the notes of the horn and hoarse cries. Hounds' tongues broke out united and firm, and Tarka knew that they had reached the stream. The sun-laden water of the pools was spun into eddies by the thrusts of his webbed hindlegs. He passed through shadow and dapple, through runnel and plash. The water sparkled amber in the sunbeams, and his brown sleek pelt glistened whenever his back made ripples. His movements in water were unhurried, like an eel's. The hounds came nearer.

The stream after a bend flowed near the roadway, where more motor-cars were drawn up. Some men and women, holding notched poles, were watching from the cars—sportsmen on wheels.

Beggars' Roost Bridge was below. With hounds so near Tarka was heedless of the men that leaned over the stone parapet, watching for him. They shouted, waved hats, and cheered the hounds. There were ducks above the bridge, quacking loudly as they left the stream and waddled to the yard, and when Tarka came to where they had been, he left the water and ran after them. They beat their wings as they tried to fly from him, but he reached the file and scattered them, running through them and disappearing. Nearer and nearer came Deadlock, with Captain and Waterwitch leading the pack. Huntsman, whippers-in and field were left behind, struggling through hedges and over banks.

Hounds were bewildered when they reached the yard. They ran with noses to ground in puzzled excitement. Captain's shrill voice told that Tarka had gone under a gate. Waterwitch followed the wet seals in the dust, but turned off along a track of larger webs. The line was tangled again. Deadlock threw his belving tongue. Other hounds followed, but the scent led only to a duck that beat its wings and quacked in terror before them. A man with a rake drove them off, shouting and threatening to strike them. Dewdrop spoke across the yard and the hounds galloped to her, but the line led to a gate which they tried to leap, hurling themselves up and falling from the top bar. A duck had gone under the gate, but not Tarka.

All scent was gone. Hounds rolled in the dust or trotted up to men and

29

women, sniffing their pockets for food. Rufus found a rabbit skin and ate it; Render fought with Sandboy—but not seriously, as they feared each other; Deadlock went off alone. And hounds were waiting for a lead when the sweating huntsman, grey pot-hat pushed back from his red brow, ran up with the two whippers-in and called them into a pack again. The thick scent of the Muscovy ducks had checked the hunt.

Tarka had run through a drain back to the stream, and now he rested in the water that carried him every moment nearer to the murmurous glooms of the glen below. He saw the coloured blur of a kingfisher perching on a twig as it eyed the water for beetle or loach. The kingfisher saw him moving under the surface, as his shadow broke the net of ripple shadows that drifted in meshes of pale gold on the stony bed beneath him.

While he was walking past the roots of a willow under the bank, he heard the yapping of the terrier. Sammy had crept through the drain, and was looking out at the end, covered with black filth, and eagerly telling his big friends to follow him downstream. As he yapped, Deadlock threw his tongue. The stallion hound was below the drain, and had re-found the line where Tarka had last touched the shillets. Tarka saw him, ten yards away, and slipping back into the water, swam with all webs down the current, pushing from his nose a ream whose shadow beneath was an arrow of gold pointing down to the sea.

Again he quitted the water and ran on land to wear away his scent. He had gone twenty yards when Deadlock scrambled up the bank with Render and Sandboy, breathing the scent which was as high as their muzzles. Tarka reached the waterside trees again a length ahead of Deadlock, and fell into the water like a sodden log. Deadlock leapt after him and snapped at his head; but the water was friendly to the otter, who rolled in smooth and graceful movement away from the jaws, a straight bite of which would have crushed his skull.

Here sunlight was shut out by the oaks, and the roar of the first fall was beating back from the leaves. The current ran faster, narrowing into a race with twirls and hollows marking the sunken rocks. The roar grew louder in a drifting spray. Tarka and Deadlock were carried to where a broad sunbeam came down through a break in the foliage and lit the mist above the fall. Tarka went over in the heavy white folds of the torrent and Deadlock was hurled over after him. They were lost

Deadlock leapt into the water after Tarka . . .

in the churn and pressure of the pool until a small brown head appeared and gazed for its enemy in the broken honeycomb of foam. A black and white body uprolled beside it, and the head of the hound was thrust up as he tried to tread away from the current that would draw him under. Tarka was master of whirlpools; they were his playthings. He rocked in the surge with delight; then high above he heard the note of the horn. He yielded himself to the water and let it take him away down the gorge into a pool where rocks were piled above. He searched under the dripping ferny clitter for a hiding-place.

Under the water he saw two legs, joined to two wavering and inverted images of legs, and above them the blurred shapes of a man's head and shoulders. He turned away from the fisherman into the current again, and as he breathed he heard the horn again. On the road above the glen the pack was trotting between huntsman and whippers-in, and before them men were running with poles at the trail, hurrying down the hill to the bridge, to make a stickle to stop Tarka reaching the sea.

Tarka left Deadlock far behind. The hound was feeble and bruised, and breathing harshly, his head battered and his sight dazed, but still following. Tarka passed another fisherman, and by chance the tiny feathered hook lodged in his ear. The reel spun against the check, *re-re-re* continuously, until all the silken line had run through the snake-rings of the rod, which bent into a circle, and whipped back straight again as the gut trace snapped.

Tarka saw the bridge, the figure of a man below it, and a row of faces above. He heard shouts. The man standing on a rock took off his hat, scooped the air, and holla'd to the huntsman, who was running and slipping with the pack on the loose stones of the steep red road. Tarka walked out of the last pool above the bridge, ran over a mossy rock, merged with the water again, and pushed through the legs of the man.

Tally-ho!

Tarka had gone under the bridge when Harper splashed into the water. The pack poured through the gap between the end of the parapet and the hillside earth, and their tongues rang under the bridge and down the walls of the houses built on the rock above the river.

Among rotting motor tyres, broken bottles, tins, pails, shoes, and other castaway rubbish lying in the bright water, hounds made their plunging leaps. Once Tarka turned back; often he was splashed and trodden on. The stream was seldom deep enough to cover him, and always shallow enough for the hounds to move at double his speed. Sometimes he was under the pack, and then, while hounds were massing for the worry, his small head would look out beside a rock ten yards below them.

Between boulders and rocks crusted with shellfish and shaggy with seaweed, past worm-channered posts that marked the fairway for fishing boats at high water, the pack hunted the otter. Off each post a gull launched itself, cackling angrily as it looked down at the animals. Tarka reached the sea. He walked slowly into the surge of a wavelet, and sank away from the chop of old Harper's jaws, just as Deadlock ran through the pack. Hounds swam beyond the line of waves, while people stood at the sea-lap and watched the huntsman wading to his waist. It was said that the otter was dead-beat, and probably floating stiffly in the shallow water. After a few minutes the huntsman shook his head, and withdrew the horn from his waistcoat. He filled his lungs and stopped his breath and was tightening his lips for the four long notes of the call-off, when a brown head with hard dark eyes was thrust out of the water a yard from Deadlock. Tarka stared into the hound's face and cried *Ic-yang!*

The head sank. Swimming under Deadlock, Tarka bit on to the loose skin of the flews and pulled the hound's head underwater. Deadlock tried to twist round and crush the otter's skull in his jaws, but he struggled vainly. Bubbles blew out of his mouth. Soon he was choking. The hounds did not know what was happening. Deadlock's hindlegs kicked the air weakly. The huntsman waded out and pulled him in-shore, but Tarka loosened his bite only when he needed new air in his lungs; and then he swam under and gripped Deadlock again. Only when hounds were upon him did Tarka let go. He vanished in a wave.

Long after the water had been emptied out of Deadlock's lungs, and the pack had trotted off for the long uphill climb to the railway station, the gulls were flying over something in the sea beyond the mouth of the little estuary. Sometimes one dropped its yellow webs to alight on the water; always it flew up again into the restless, wailing throng, startled by the snaps of white teeth. A cargo steamer was passing up the Severn Sea, leaving a long smudge of smoke on the horizon, where a low line of clouds billowed over the coast of Wales. The regular thumps of its screw in the windless blue calm were borne to where Tarka lay, drowsy and content, but watching the pale yellow eyes of the nearest bird. At last the gulls grew tired of seeing only his eyes, and flew back to their posts; and turning on his back, Tarka yawned and stretched himself, and floated at his ease.

PICKING UP TERRIBLE COMPANY

Amelia B. Edwards

I am a Frenchman by birth, and my name is François Thierry. I need not weary you with my early history. Enough that I committed a political offence—that I was sent to the galleys for it—that I am an exile for it to this day. The brand was not abolished in my time. If I chose, I could show you the fiery letters on my shoulder.

I was arrested, tried, and sentened in Paris. I went out of the court with my condemnation ringing in my ears. The rumbling wheels of the prison-van repeated it all the way from Paris to Bicêtre that evening, and all the next day, and the next, and the next, along the weary road from Bicêtre to Toulon. When I look back upon that time, I think I must have been stupefied by the unexpected severity of my sentence; for I remember nothing of the journey, nor of the places where we stopped—nothing but the eternal repetition of 'travaux forcés—travaux forcés—travaux forcés à perpétuité,'[1] over and over and over again. Late in the afternoon of the third day, the van stopped, the door was thrown open, and I was conducted across a stone yard, through a stone corridor, into a huge stone hall, dimly lit from above. Here I was interrogated by a military superintendent, and entered by name in a

[1]'hard labour—hard labour—hard labour for life.'

ponderous ledger bound and clasped with iron, like a book in fetters.

'Number two hundred and seven,' said the superintendent. 'Green.'

They took me into an adjoining room, searched and stripped me, and plunged me into a cold bath. When I came out of the bath, I put on the livery of the galleys—a coarse canvas shirt, trousers of tawny serge, a red serge blouse, and heavy shoes clamped with iron. Last of all, a green woollen cap. On each leg of the trousers, and on the breast and back of the blouse, were printed the fatal letters 'T.F'. On a brass label in the front of the cap were engraved the figures '207'. From that moment I lost my individuality. I was no longer François Thierry. I was number two hundred and seven. The superintendent stood by and looked on.

'Come, be quick,' said he, twirling his long moustache between his thumb and forefinger. 'It grows late, and you must be married before supper.'

'Married!' I repeated.

The superintendent laughed, and lit a cigar, and his laugh was echoed by the guards and jailers.

Down another stone corridor, across another yard, into another gloomy hall, the very counterpart of the last, but filled with squalid figures, noisy with the clank of fetters, and pierced at each end with a circular opening, through which a cannon's mouth showed grimly.

'Bring number two hundred and six,' said the superintendent, 'and call the priest.'

Number two hundred and six came from a farther corner of the hall, dragging a heavy chain, and along with him a blacksmith, bare-armed and leather-aproned.

'Lie down,' said the blacksmith, with an insulting spurn of the foot.

I lay down. A heavy iron ring attached to a chain of eighteen links was then fitted to my ankle, and riveted with a single stroke of the hammer. A second ring next received the disengaged ends of my companion's chain and mine, and was secured in the same manner. The echo of each blow resounded through the vaulted roof like a hollow laugh.

'Good,' said the superintendent, drawing a small red book from his pocket. 'Number two hundred and seven, attend to the prison code. If you attempt to escape without succeeding, you will be bastinadoed[2]. If you succeed in getting beyond the port, and are then taken, you will

[2]beaten on the soles of the feet with a stick or baton.

receive three years of double-chaining. As soon as you are missed, three cannon shots will be fired, and alarm flags will be hoisted on every bastion. Signals will be telegraphed to the maritime guards, and to the police of the ten neighbouring districts. A price will be set upon your head. Placards will be posted upon the gates of Toulon, and sent to every town throughout the empire. It will be lawful to fire upon you, if you cannot be captured alive.'

Having read this with grim complacency, the superintendent resumed his cigar, replaced the book in his pocket, and walked away.

All was over now—all the incredulous wonder, the dreamy dullness, the smouldering hope, of the past three days. I was a felon, and (slavery in slavery!) chained to a fellow felon. I looked up, and found his eyes upon me. He was a swart, heavy-browed, sullen-jawed man of about forty; not much taller than myself, but of immensely powerful build.

'So,' said he, 'you're for life, are you? So am I.'

'How do you know I am for life?' I asked, wearily.

'By that.' And he touched my cap roughly with the back of his hand. 'Green, for life. Red, for a term of years. What are you in for?'

'I conspired against the government.'

He shrugged his shoulders contemptuously. 'Devil's mass! Then you're a gentleman-convict, I suppose! Pity you've not a berth to yourselves—we poor hard-labourers hate such fine company.'

'Are there many political prisoners?' I asked, after a moment's pause.

'None, in this department.'

Then, as if detecting my unspoken thought, 'I am no innocent,' he added with an oath. 'This is the fourth time I have been here. Did you ever hear of Gasparo?'

'Gasparo the forger?'

He nodded.

'Who escaped three or four months since, and ——'

'And flung the sentry over the ramparts, just as he was going to give the alarm. I'm the man.'

I had heard of him, as a man who, early in his career, had been sentenced to a long solitary imprisonment in a gloomy cell, and who had come forth from his solitude hardened into an absolute wild beast. I shuddered, and found his evil eye taking vindictive note of me. From that moment he hated me. From that moment I loathed him.

A bell rang, and a detachment of convicts came in from labour. They were immediately searched by the guard, and chained up, two and two, to a wooden platform that reached all down the centre of the hall. Our afternoon meal was then served out, consisting of a mess of beans, an allowance of bread and ship-biscuit, and a measure of thin wine. I drank the wine; but I could eat nothing. Gasparo took what he chose from my untouched allowance, and those who were nearest scrambled for the rest. The supper over, a shrill whistle echoed down the hall, each man took his narrow mattress from under the platform which made our common bedstead, rolled himself in a piece of seaweed matting, and lay down for the night. In less than five minutes, all was profoundly silent. Now and then I heard the blacksmith going round with his hammer, testing the gratings, and trying the locks, in all the corridors. Now and then, the guard stalked past with his musket on his shoulder. Sometimes a convict moaned, or shook his fetters in his sleep. Thus the weary hours went by. My companion slept heavily, and even I lost consciousness at last.

I was sentenced to hard labour. At Toulon the hard labour is of various kinds: such as quarrying, mining, pumping in the docks, loading and unloading vessels, transporting ammunition, and so forth. Gasparo and I were employed with about two hundred other convicts in a quarry a little beyond the port. Day after day, week after week, from seven in the morning until seven at night, the rocks echoed with our blows. At every blow, our chains rang and rebounded on the stony soil. In that fierce climate, terrible tempests and tropical droughts succeed each other throughout the summer and autumn. Often, after toiling for hours under a burning sky, have I gone back to prison and to my pallet, drenched to the skin. Thus the last days of the dreary spring ebbed slowly past; and then the more dreary summer, and then the autumn, came round.

My fellow convict was a Piedmontese. He had been a burglar, a forger, an incendiary. In his last escape he had committed manslaughter. Heaven alone knows how my sufferings were multiplied by that abhorred companionship—how I shrank from the touch of his hand—how I sickened if his breath came over me as we lay side by side at night. I strove to disguise my loathing; but in vain. He knew it as well as I knew it, and he revenged himself upon me by every means that a vindictive

37

nature could devise. That he should tyrannize over me was not wonderful; for his physical strength was gigantic, and he was looked upon as an authorized despot throughout the port; but simple tyranny was the least part of what I had to endure. I had been fastidiously nurtured; he purposely and continually offended my sense of delicacy.

I was unaccustomed to bodily labour; he imposed on me the largest share of our daily work. When I needed rest, he would insist on walking. When my limbs were cramped, he would lie down obstinately and refuse to stir. He delighted to sing blasphemous songs, and relate hideous stories of what he had thought and resolved on in his solitude. He would even twist the chain in ways that would gall me at every step. I was at that time just twenty-two years of age, and had been sickly from boyhood. To retaliate, or to defend myself, would have been alike impossible. To complain to the superintendent would only have been to provoke my tyrant.

There came a day, at length, when his hatred seemed to abate. He allowed me to rest when our hour of repose came round. He abstained from singing the songs I abhorred, and fell into long fits of abstraction. The next morning, shortly after we had begun work, he drew near enough to speak to me in a whisper.

'François, have you a mind to escape?'

I felt the blood rush to my face. I clasped my hands. I could not speak.

'Can you keep a secret?'

'To the death.'

'Listen, then. Tomorrow, a renowned marshal will visit the port. He will inspect the docks, the prisons, the quarries. There will be plenty of cannonading from the forts and the shipping, and if two convicts escape, a volley more or less will attract no attention round about Toulon. Do you understand?'

'You mean that no one will recognize the signals?'

'Not even the sentries at the town gates—not even the guards in the next quarry. Devil's mass! What can be easier than to strike off each other's fetters with the pickaxe when the superintendent is not looking, and the salutes are firing? Will you venture?'

'With my life!'

'A bargain. Shake hands on it.'

I had never touched his hand in fellowship before, and I felt as if my own were blood-stained by the contact. I knew by the sullen fire in his glance that he interpreted my faltering touch aright.

We were roused an hour earlier than usual the following morning, and went through a general inspection in the prison yard. Before going to work, we were served with a double allowance of wine. At one o'clock we heard the first far-off salutes from the ships of war in the harbour. The sound ran through me like a galvanic shock. One by one, the forts took up the signal. It was repeated by the gunboats closer in shore. Discharge followed discharge, all along the batteries on both sides of the port, and the air grew thick with smoke.

'As the first shot is fired yonder,' whispered Gasparo, pointing to the barracks behind the prison, 'strike at the first link of my chain, close to the ankle.'

A rapid suspicion flashed across me.

'If I do, how can I be sure that you will free me afterwards? No, Gasparo; you must deal the first blow.'

'As you please,' he replied, with a laugh.

At the same instant came a flash from the battlements of the barrack close by, and then a thunderous reverberation, multiplied again and again by the rocks around. As the roar burst over our heads I saw him strike and felt the fetters fall. Scarcely had the echo of the first gun died away, when the second was fired. It was now Gasparo's turn to be free. I struck; but less skilfully, and had twice to repeat the blow before breaking the stubborn link. We then went on, apparently, with our work, standing somewhat close together, with the chain huddled up between us. No one had observed us, and no one, at first sight, could have detected what we had done.

At the third shot, a party of officers and gentlemen made their appearance at the bend of the road leading up to the quarry. In an instant, every head was turned in their direction; every felon paused in his work; every guard presented arms. At that moment we flung away our caps and pickaxes, scaled the rugged bit of cliff on which we had been toiling, dropped into the ravine below, and made for the mountain passes that lead into the valley. Encumbered still with the iron anklets to which our chains had been fastened, we could not run very swiftly. To add to our difficulties, the road was uneven, strewn with flints and blocks of fallen granite, and tortuous as the windings of a snake. Suddenly, on turning a sharp angle of projecting cliff, we came upon a little guard-house and a couple of sentries. To retreat was impossible. The soldiers were within a few yards of us. They presented their pieces, and called to us to surrender. Gasparo turned upon me like a wolf at bay.

'Curse you!' said he, dealing me a tremendous blow, 'stay and be taken! I have always hated you!'

I fell as if struck down by a sledge-hammer, and, as I fell, saw him dash one soldier to the ground, dart past the other, heard a shot, and then . . . all became dark, and I knew no more.

When I next opened my eyes, I found myself lying on the floor of a small unfurnished room, dimly lit by a tiny window close against the ceiling. It seemed as if weeks had gone by since I lost consciousness. I had scarcely strength to rise, and, having risen, kept my feet with difficulty. Where my head had lain, the floor was wet with blood. Giddy and perplexed, I leaned against the wall, and tried to think.

In the first place, where was I? Evidently in no part of the prison from which I had escaped. There, all was solid stone and iron grating; here, was only whitewashed wood and plaster. I must be in a chamber of the little guard-house: probably in an upper chamber. Where, then, were the soldiers? Where was Gasparo? Had I strength to clamber up to that window, and if so, in what direction did that window look out? I stole to the door, and found it locked. I listened, breathlessly, but could hear no sound either below or above.

My decision was taken at once. To stay was certain capture; to venture, at all hazards, would make matters no worse. Again I listened, and again all was quiet. I drew myself through the little casement, dropped as gently as I could upon the moist earth, and, crouching against the wall, asked myself what I should do next. To climb the cliff would be to offer myself as a target to the first soldier who saw me. To venture along the ravine would be, perhaps, to encounter Gasparo and his captors face to face. Besides, it was getting dusk, and, under cover of the night, if I could only conceal myself till then, I might yet escape. But where was that concealment to be found? Heaven be thanked for the thought! There was the ditch.

Only two windows looked out upon the garden from the back of the guard-house. From one of those windows I had just now let myself

'Curse you,' he said, dealing me a tremendous blow, 'stay and be taken!'

down, and the other was partly shuttered up. I did not dare, however, openly to cross the garden. I dropped upon my face, and crawled in the furrows between the rows of vegetables, until I came to the ditch. Here, the water rose nearly to my waist, but the banks on either side were considerably higher, and, by stooping, I found that I could walk without bringing my head to the level of the road. I thus followed the course of the ditch for some two or three hundred yards in the direction of Toulon, thinking that my pursuers would be less likely to suspect me of doubling back towards prison than of pushing forward towards the country. Half lying, half crouching under the rank grasses that fringed the bank above, I then watched the gathering shadows.

I suffered an hour to go by before I ventured to move again. By that time it was intensely dark, and had begun to rain heavily. The water in the ditch became a brawling torrent, through which I waded, unheard, past the very windows of the guard-house.

After toiling through the water for a mile or more, I ventured out upon the road again: and so, with the rain and wind beating in my face, and the scattered boulders tripping me up continually, I made my way through the whole length of the winding pass, and came out upon the more open country about midnight. With no other guide than the wind, which was blowing from the north-east, and without even a star to help me, I then struck off to the right, following what seemed to be a rough by-road, lying through a valley. After a while the rain abated, and I discerned the dark outlines of a chain of hills extending all along to the left of the road. These, I concluded, must be the Maures. All was well, so far. I had taken the right direction, and was on the way to Italy.

Excepting to sit down now and then for a few minutes by the way-side, I never paused in my flight the whole night through. Fatigue and want of food prevented me, it is true, from walking very fast; but the love of liberty was strong within me, and, by keeping steadily on, I succeeded in placing about eighteen miles between myself and Toulon. At five o'clock, just as the day began to dawn, I heard a peal of chimes, and found that I was approaching a large town. In order to avoid this town, I was forced to turn back for some distance, and take to the heights. The sun had now risen, and I dared go no farther; so, having pulled some turnips in a field as I went along, I took refuge in a little lonely copse in a hollow among the hills, and there lay all day in safety.

When night again closed in I resumed my journey, keeping always among the mountains, and coming now and then on grand glimpses of moonlit bays, and tranquil islands lying off the shore; now and then, on pastoral hamlets nestled up among the palmy heights; or on promontories overgrown with the cactus and the aloe. I rested all the second day in a ruined shed at the bottom of a deserted sandpit, and, in the evening, feeling that I could no longer sustain life without some fitting nourishment, made my way down towards a tiny fishing village on the coast below. It was quite dark by the time I reached the level ground. I walked boldly past the cottages of the fishermen, meeting only an old woman and a little child on the way, and knocked at the parish priest's door. He opened it himself. I told my story in half-a-dozen words. The good man believed and pitied me. He gave me food and wine, an old handkerchief to wrap about my head, an old coat to replace my convict's jacket, and two or three francs to help me on my way. I parted from him with tears.

I walked all that night again, and all the next, keeping somewhat close upon the coast, and hiding among the cliffs during the daytime. On the fifth morning, having left Antibes behind me during the night's march, I came to the banks of the Var; crossed the torrent about half a mile below the wooden bridge; plunged into the pine-woods on the other side of the frontier; and lay down to rest on Italian ground at last!

Though comparatively safe, I still pursued my journey by the least frequented ways; how I bought a file at the first hamlet to which I came, and freed myself from the iron anklet; how, having lurked about Nice till my hair and beard had grown, I begged my way on to Genoa; how, at Genoa, I hung about the port, earning a scanty livelihood by any chance work that I could get, and so struggled, somehow, through the inclement winter; how, towards the early spring, I worked my passage on board a small trader from Genoa to Fiumicino, touching at all the ports along the coast; and how, coming slowly up the Tiber in a barge laden with oil and wine, I landed one evening in March on the Ripetta quay in Rome. My object had been to get to Rome, and that object was at last attained. In so large a city, and at so great a distance from the scene of my imprisonment, I was personally safe. I might hope to turn my talents and education to account. I might even find friends among the strangers who would flock there to the Easter festivals. Full

43

of hope, therefore, I sought a humble lodging in the neighbourhood of the quay, gave up a day or two to the enjoyment of my liberty and of the sights of Rome, and then set myself to find regular employment.

Regular employment, or, indeed, employment of any kind, was not, however, so easily to be obtained. It was a season of distress. Day by day, my hopes faded and my prospects darkened. Day by day, the little money I had scraped together on the passage melted away. I had thought to obtain a clerkship, or a secretaryship, or a situation in some public library. Before three weeks were over, I would gladly have swept a studio. At length there came a day when I saw nothing before me but starvation—when my last bajocco was expended, when my landlord shut the door in my face, and I knew not where to turn for a meal or a shelter. All that afternoon, I wandered hopelessly about the streets. It was Good Friday, of all days in the year. The churches were hung with black; the bells were tolling; the thoroughfares were crowded with people in mourning. I went into the little church of Santa Martina. They were chanting the Miserere, probably with no great skill, but with a pathos that seemed to open up all the sources of my despair.

Outcast that I was, I slept that night under a dark arch near the theatre of Marcellus. The morning dawned upon a glorious day, and I crept out, shivering, into the sunshine. Once I asked for alms, and was repulsed. I followed mechanically in the stream of carriages and foot passengers, and found myself in the midst of the crowd that ebbs and flows continually about St Peter's during Easter week. Stupefied and weary, I turned aside into the vestibule of the Sagrestia, and cowered down in the shelter of a doorway. Two gentlemen were reading a printed paper wafered against a pillar close by.

'Good heavens!' said one to the other, 'that a man should risk his neck for a few pauls!'

'Ay, and with the knowledge that out of eighty workmen, six or eight are dashed to pieces every time,' added his companion.

'Shocking! Why, that's an average of ten per cent!'

'No less. It's a desperate service.'

'But a fine sight,' said the first speaker, philosophically; and with this they walked away.

I sprang to my feet and read the placard with avidity. It was headed 'Illumination of Saint Peter's', and announced that, eighty workmen being required for the lighting of the dome and cupola, and three hundred for the cornices, pillars, colonnade, and so forth, the amministratore was empowered, etc. etc. In conclusion, it stated that every workman employed on the dome and cupola should receive in payment a dinner and twenty-four pauls, the wages of the rest being less than a third of that sum.

A desperate service, it was true; but I was a desperate man. After all, I could but die, and I might as well die after a good dinner as from starvation. I went at once to the *amministratore*, was entered in his list, received a couple of pauls as earnest of the contract, and engaged to present myself punctually at eleven o'clock on the following morning. That evening I supped at a street stall, and, for a few bajocchi, obtained leave to sleep on some straw in a loft over a stable at the back of the Via del Arco.

At eleven o'clock on the morning of Easter Sunday, 16 April, I found myself, accordingly, in the midst of a crowd of poor fellows, most of whom, I dare say, were as wretched as myself, waiting at the door of the administrator's office. The piazza in front of the cathedral was like a moving mosaic of life and colour. The sun was shining, the fountains were playing, the flags were flying over St Angelo. It was a glorious sight; but I saw it for only a few moments. As the clocks struck the hour, the folding doors were thrown open, and we passed, in a crowd, into a hall, where two long tables were laid for our accommodation. A couple of sentinels stood at the door; an usher marshalled us, standing, round the tables; and a priest read grace.

As he began to read, a strange sensation came upon me. I felt impelled to look across to the opposite table, and there . . . yes, by heaven! there I saw Gasparo.

He was looking full at me, but his eyes dropped on meeting mine. I saw him turn lividly white. The recollection of all he had made me suffer, and of the dastardly blow that he had dealt me on the day of our flight, overpowered for the moment even my surprise at seeing him in this place. Oh that I might live to meet him yet, under the free sky, where no priest was praying, and no guards were by!

The grace over, we sat down and fell to. Not even anger had power to blunt the edge of my appetite just then. I ate like a famished wolf, and so did most of the others. We were allowed no wine, and the doors

45

were locked upon us, that we might not procure any elsewhere. It was a wise regulation, considering the task we had to perform; but it made us none the less noisy. In certain circumstances, danger intoxicates like wine; and on this Easter Sunday, we eighty *sanpietrini*, any one of whom might have his brains dashed about the leads before supper-time, ate, talked, jested, and laughed, with a wild gaiety that had in it something appalling.

The dinner lasted long, and when no one seemed disposed to eat more, the tables were cleared. Most of the men threw themselves on the floor and benches, and went to sleep; Gasparo among the number. Seeing this, I could refrain no longer. I went over, and stirred him roughly with my foot.

'Gasparo! You know me?'

He looked up, sullenly.

'Devil's mass! I thought you were at Toulon.'

'It is not your fault that I am not at Toulon! Listen to me. If you and I survive this night, you shall answer to me for your treachery!'

He glared at me from under his deep brows, and, without replying, turned over on his face again, as if to sleep.

'There's an accursed fellow!' said one of the others, with a significant shrug, as I came away.

'Do you know anything of him?' I asked, eagerly.

'Cospetto! I know nothing of him; but that solitude is said to have made him a wolf.'

I could learn no more, so I also stretched myself upon the floor, as far as possible from my enemy, and fell profoundly asleep.

At seven, the guards roused those who still slept, and served each man with a small mug of thin wine. We were then formed into a double file, marched round by the back of the cathedral, and conducted up an inclined plane to the roof below the dome. From this point, a long series of staircases and winding passages carried us up between the double walls of the dome; and, at different stages in the ascent, a certain number of us were detached and posted ready for work. I was detached about halfway up, and I saw Gasparo going higher still.

When we were all posted, the superintendents came round and gave us our instructions. At a given signal, every man was to pass out through the loophole or window before which he was placed, and seat himself astride upon a narrow shelf of wood hanging to a strong rope just below. This rope came through the window, was wound round a roller, and secured from within. At the next signal, a lighted torch would be put into his right hand, and he was to grasp the rope firmly with his left. At the third signal the rope was to be unwound from within by an assistant placed there for the purpose, he was to be allowed to slide rapidly down, over the curve of the dome, and, while thus sliding, was to apply his torch to every lamp he passed in his downward progress.

Having received these instructions, we waited, each man at his window, until the first signal should be given.

It was fast getting dark, and the silver illumination had been lit since seven. All the great ribs of the dome, as far as I could see; all the cornices and friezes of the façade below; all the columns and parapets of the great colonnade surrounding the piazza four hundred feet below, were traced out in lines of paper lanterns, the light from which, subdued by the paper, gleamed with a silvery fire which had a magical and wondrous look. Between and among these *lanternoni* were placed, at different intervals all over the cathedral on the side facing the piazza, iron cups called *padelle*, ready filled with tallow and turpentine. To light those on the dome and cupola was the perilous task of the *sanpietrini*; when they were all lit the golden illumination would be effected.

A few moments of intense suspense elapsed. At every second the evening grew darker, the *lanternoni* burned brighter, the surging hum of thousands in the piazza and streets below rose louder to our ears. I felt the quickening breath of the assistant at my shoulder—I could almost hear the beating of my heart. Suddenly, like the passing of an electric current, the first signal flew from lip to lip. I got out, and crossed my legs firmly round the board; with the second signal I seized the blazing torch; with the third, I felt myself launched, and, lighting every cup as I glided past, saw all the mountainous dome above and below me spring into lines of leaping flame. The clock was now striking eight, and when the last stroke sounded the whole cathedral was glowing in outlines of fire. A roar, like the roar of a great ocean, rose up from the multitude below, and seemed to shake the very dome against which I was clinging. I could even see the light upon the gazing faces, the crowd upon the bridge of St Angelo, and the boats swarming along the Tiber.

Having dropped safely to the full length of my rope, and lit my allotted share of lamps, I was now sitting in secure enjoyment of this amazing scene. All at once I felt the rope vibrate. I looked up, saw a man clinging by one hand to the iron rod supporting the *padelle*, and with the other . . . Merciful heaven! It was the Piedmontese firing the rope above me with his torch!

I had no time for thought—I acted upon instinct. It was done in one fearful moment. I clambered up like a cat, dashed my torch full in the solitary felon's face, and grasped the rope an inch or two above the spot where it was burning! Blinded and baffled, he uttered a terrible cry, and dropped like a stone. Through all the roar of the living ocean below I could hear the dull crash with which he came down upon the leaded roof—resounding through all the years that have gone by since that night, I hear it now!

I had scarcely drawn breath when I found myself being hauled up. The assistance came not a moment too soon, for I was sick and giddy with horror, and fainted as soon as I was safe in the corridor.

The next day I waited on the *amministratore*, and told him all that had happened. My statement was corroborated by the vacant rope from which Gasparo had descended and the burnt fragment by which I had been drawn up. The *amministratore* repeated my story to a prelate high in office; and while none, even of the *sanpietrini*, suspected that my enemy had come by his death in any unusual manner, the truth was whispered from palace to palace until it reached the Vatican. I received much sympathy, and such financial assistance as enabled me to confront the future without fear.

SECRET MISSION TO NORTH AFRICA

Frederick C. Painton

In his London headquarters General Dwight Eisenhower stared at the US War Department cablegram marked *Most secret*. It put up to him one of the gravest decisions of his career. In essence, it said this: *A group of pro-Allied French officers in Algeria suggest that five officers from General Eisenhower's staff come secretly and at once to a rendezvous near Algiers with information as to what the Allies will do to help them face a threatened Axis invasion.*

The General reflected. On 'D-day' at 'H-hour' (8 November 1942, at 1 a.m.) American and British troops would make amphibious landings in North Africa. A secret rendezvous with the French could get information that might save many lives among the youngsters even now beginning to file aboard transports. But there was a terrible risk involved. The secret mission might be discovered, thus warning both the pro-German Vichy High Command and the Nazis of what was afoot. In that case the great operation might end in horrible disaster.

General Eisenhower turned to the man across the desk, six-foot-three Major-General Mark Wayne Clark, his Deputy Commander. 'I think you can do it, Wayne,' he said quietly.

The decision made, Eisenhower and Clark went at once to 10 Downing Street. Over lunch Prime Minster Winston Churchill heard the plan and welcomed the idea. It was an adventure after his own heart, one he might well have gloriously lived himself a half century before.

'Done,' he said. 'You'll have our fullest cooperation.'

Whereupon Clark hastily departed to hand-pick the four men to go with him: Captain Jerauld Wright, US Navy, a crack shot; Colonel Julius Holmes, who spoke French and knew Algeria; Colonel Arch Hamblen, an expert on shipping problems; and Brigadier-General Lyman Lemnitzer of G-3, the operations branch of the US Army.

Each was instructed: 'Leave your office as if you would be away no more than an hour. Take what a musette bag will carry. No papers of any kind. We leave tonight.'

Besides the musette bags they carried Garand-type carbines, tommy guns and a small quantity of gold—not the $18,000 reported erroneously in later newspaper accounts, but about $600 to be used in case of trouble. At 7.30 a.m. on 18 October, two big planes roared into the air. The historic mission had started.

In the meantime, coded cables had flashed orders to Captain (S) at a British naval base to provide a submarine and four so-called kayaks— small boats made of wood and canvas, which would be used to put the passengers ashore. The commandos contributed the services of three officers who were expert in this kind of business: Captains G. B. (Jumbo) Courtney and R. P. Livingston, and Lieutenant J. P. Foote.

Late in the afternoon the Clark party arrived at the base. Captain (S) listened attentively as the scheme was outlined. Then he said bluntly: 'It's very dangerous. We can put you ashore, no trouble there. But the kayaks are cockleshells. If a sea springs up you can't launch them, can't get away.'

Clark nodded. This was a risk he had already considered and accepted.

Captain (S) continued: 'General, this sounds like an Oppenheim secret service thriller where the hero goes to a haunted farmhouse that shows a light at midnight.'

Clark grinned. 'How the devil did you know that?'

For a farmhouse *was* to show a light if the coast was clear to land.

The moon was rising as the five Americans and the three British commandos, led by the submarine's commander, Lieutenant N. L. A.

Jewell, boarded a little 750-ton undersea craft. With them they took blue flashlights—which would not throw beams observable from the side—to signal in Morse code after they landed; and a small portable 'walky-talky' wireless set which they could use to communicate with the submarine, secure in the knowledge that the Germans could not pick up what was said. The diesels rumbled and the submarine got under way.

At 4 a.m. on the second night they sighted the rendezvous signal light on the African shore. But it was too close to dawn to risk a landing. They submerged again to wait for evening. Through the periscope Clark could see the old Moorish-type farmhouse, perched on the edge of an abrupt slope. Behind the farmhouse was the main highway to Algiers. They could see no sign of life anywhere.

Colonel Holmes studied the scene with mixed emotions. 'The last time I saw that highway,' he remarked, 'was when my wife and I drove along it on our honeymoon.'

For fifteen hours the tiny submarine remained below the surface. The air became so foul a struck match would not ignite. The men found themselves gasping, gulping. Their heads pounded; the slightest exertion brought utter fatigue. But night fell at last, and the submarine surfaced. The men climbed to the conning tower, the night air clearing their heads, and waited for the signal light to gleam again.

Eight o'clock came, then nine o'clock. The farmhouse remained dark. There were a lot of praying words used in an unprayerful way. Would they have to take twenty-four hours more of this mechanized sewer-pipe? Lemnitzer groaned. 'Something's happened. There'll be no light.'

'There will be a light,' said Clark, 'and I'll bet ten dollars on it.'

All except Holmes accepted his wager. Clark went below for a brief nap. At 11.10 Holmes shook him awake. 'You win. The light's on.'

The crew got the kayaks through the torpedo hatch and launched them. Keeping close together, the party headed for shore through a choppy sea that drenched them with chill spray. Some five hundred yards from the beach they stopped. Suppose the Vichy-controlled police had been warned and were lurking in the bushes ashore? Were they about to walk into a trap? Somebody had to go first and make sure of the ground.

Julius Holmes spoke French the best and knew some of the people ashore, so he and commando Captain Livingston headed in. If all was clear the others would follow. Ten minutes later Holmes' boat grated on the gravel. Carbines ready, the two men got out and moved cautiously along the beach.

Suddenly they heard someone moving in the brush. They whirled, guns levelled.

A voice said in English, 'Who's there?'

'Who're you?' asked Holmes.

'I'm Ridgeway Knight.'

Ridgeway Knight was an American Vice-Consul who had taken part in the arrangements for the rendezvous.

'I'm Julius Holmes. Where's Bob Murphy?'

(Murphy, the American Consul-General in North Africa, had been instrumental in bringing about the meeting.)

'He'll be along in a minute. Everything's okay.'

Holmes turned to Livingston. 'Make the signal'.

Livingston blinked his blue flashlight seaward. The signals were, 'K' for 'kerrect' if all was well; 'F' for 'foney' if there was trouble. He made the 'K' signal in Morse, and presently the remaining kayaks came out of the night and the other six men stepped ashore. Then the signal 'All's well' was made to the submarine, and its diesel drone died away as it stood offshore.

To hide the boats the wet shivering men hauled them up to the farmhouse and piled them in the kitchen. Then they took off their clothes, spread them out to dry, and after a slight meal—excited men rarely get hungry—dozed until the French party arrived at 7 o'clock, and the conference began.

The information obtained was priceless. It included the tonnage capacity of the ports of Casablanca, Algiers, Oran and Tunis; the French Navy's plans for preventing a landing; a list of the places where French Army resistance would be tough, and where it would be only token. Special information on airport runways later proved to be of inestimable value.

The sun climbed the sky and started down, and still the men talked, and figured, and marked the maps.

But General Clark's luck was running out at last. Jerry Wright heard a sound that brought him quickly out of the house. The wind was whistling round the house's red-tiled roof. Waves as tall as a man were roaring against the shore. Wright knew that no kayak could ever be launched in that foaming tumult. He went gloomily back inside.

Meanwhile two Arab servants, who had that morning been dismissed by the owner of the farmhouse for safety's sake, had gone to a nearby town and visited the commissioner of police. They reported that they had seen strange men carry big bundles (the boats) to the farmhouse. The place had once been a smuggler's hide-out; perhaps it was being thus used again. So presently a police car was humming along the highway towards the rendezvous . . .

The sun dropped into the sea, and lights behind the shaded farmhouse windows lit up the conference room. The discussions had almost reached an end. Only one point remained to be settled.

One of the French officers said, 'It will be necessary to have some leader here whom we will all follow. I suggest General Henri Honoré Giraud.'

'But he's in France,' objected Clark, 'and practically a prisoner.'

'He must be rescued and brought here. He is the only officer who can gain the loyalty of the many conflicting factions.'

Clark agreed, and promised that Giraud should be rescued and brought to North Africa. (The promise was kept—but that is another story.)

Then, in the next room, the telephone jangled. The conferees jerked erect, looked at each other. The house owner answered the call, and a moment later came rushing into the conference room, his eyes wide with fright.

'The police! They'll be here in five minutes!'

Most of the French officers—the top ones—hurried out. To be discovered here in these circumstances meant being shot for treason. Motors roared, gears crashed, and they were gone.

Clark's men hastily stuffed maps and papers inside their undershirts. They were trapped between the Vichy police and the stormy sea. And now the police car roared up, its lights gleaming against the white walls of the farmhouse. Where could they hide?

Clark was all for taking literally to the woods. Murphy objected;

53

if the police got suspicious and made a search, the Americans were bound to be discovered.

'There's an empty wine cellar,' said Murphy. 'You go down there, I'll get rid of the police.'

Clark didn't like it: a cellar seemed like a rat-trap—no room to manoeuvre. But there was now no time for anything else. They could hear the gendarmes piling out of their car. Gripping carbines and tommy guns, the eight officers filed down into the wine cellar. Murphy pulled the doors down flat, put boxes over them, then turned to meet the police.

He had one stratagem that might work. The conference table was littered with half-empty wine bottles and cigarette stubs. Two French lieutenants in civilian clothes took their lives in their hands to pretend a drunken party with Murphy and Knight. They began singing snatches of drinking songs, laughing and talking loudly. That was the scene the commissioner of police walked in on a moment later.

Down in the cellar—it was only ten feet square—Clark disposed his party behind the stairway and along the walls so that casual observation from above might not discover them. But if the police did come down to take a look, then what? General Clark's whispered orders were blunt: his men were to shoot to kill. Upstairs the situation rapidly worsened. They could hear Bob Murphy arguing with the Commissioner. He and a few friends, Murphy protested, were having a little party. Since when was that a crime? What would Monsieur le Commissaire think if American police invaded the privacy of French citizens in New York? But the voices were coming closer until they seemed at the very cellar door.

And now the tense silence in the cellar was broken by choking gasps. Jumbo Courtney was trying to suppress a fit of coughing. The strangling sounds seemed to his companions loud enough to be heard in Algiers. Jumbo struggled desperately.

'By George!' he gasped. 'I'm afraid I'll choke.'

'I'm afraid you won't!' said Clark, grimly. 'But here, chew this gum.'

Jumbo fumbled for the gum, chewed desperately. The spasm passed. Silence settled on the cellar. The men could hear their own hearts thudding.

Above, Murphy was still arguing vociferously. Snatches of drunken song came from the gallant French lieutenants. A minute took a century to pass.

And then the voices upstairs changed tone. The Commissioner was not so brusque. Holmes heaved a sigh. 'Bob's got him,' he whispered.

The Commissioner had decided there was no smuggling going on. Nonetheless, he said, he'd have to report to his superior. And, yes, without a doubt his superior would return to look into the matter further.

Just then Jumbo started to have another spasm of coughing.

'Chew that gum,' Clark whispered tensely.

'I am sir, but all the sweetness has gone out of it.'

'I don't wonder,' whispered Clark. 'I chewed it for an hour myself before I gave it to you.'

This was considered very funny—but much later.

At last, however, the footsteps faded away, and they heard the police car leave. Clark and his party ascended, anxious to get to the submarine as soon as possible. But the surf still pounded on the beach.

Jerry Wright said, 'I'd hate to have to launch a whaleboat in that sea.'

Yet the mission was now a success—if they could only get away with the information.

Clark said, 'We'll try it.'

A wireless message was sent to the submarine: 'Stand in as close as possible. We're in trouble and will embark immediately.'

They carried the kayaks down to the wind-swept beach. It took a bold man even to consider going into that roaring sea with a fragile craft hardly bigger than a child's toy boat. Clark stripped to his underclothes and, carrying his outer garments, walked out into the breakers with Livingston. They managed to get into the heaving little boat, and drove their paddles deep. Then a huge wall of water broke over them, the kayak up-ended, and Clark and Livingston vanished into a white fury of foam.

A moment later, battered, turned end over end by the undertow, they came rolling along the beach, full of sand, salt water and artistic profanity. The others retrieved the kayak, but the paddles and the General's clothing were being carried away by the current.

Somebody yelled, 'Get his pants!'

Clark and Livingston vanished into a white fury of foam.

Wright shouted, 'The hell with his pants. Get those paddles!' They got the paddles. The pants are still somewhere in Africa.

Even Clark was forced to admit they couldn't launch a boat that night. And he realized that they might be stranded here for days if the wind continued. But he refused to return to the cellar, police or no police. They would take to the woods where a man had a chance to shoot his way out.

So they hid themselves and the kayaks among the palms, shivering men in underwear, bitterly cold.

The next day high-command officers did sentry-go in their shorts. The wind continued unabated, preventing escape.

The police returned at 11 that night. The group in the woods, guns ready, hid tightly. Murphy greeted the police again, smiling his charming smile, talking rapidly and smoothly. In the end the police did not search the woods. They were not satisfied; they said they would return in the morning; but for the moment they were staved off.

By 4 a.m. the wind seemed to have lessened somewhat, though the seas were still mountainous.

'We'll try it again,' said Clark. His wireless to the submarine this time was imperative: 'Stand in as close as you possibly can.'

Jumbo, Knight and the two French lieutenants steadied the first kayak. Clark and Wright climbed in. Cautiously the four walked the frail craft out into the pounding surf until Wright saw a comparatively smooth stretch. 'Now!' he yelled.

The four men heaved the boat forward; Clark and Wright paddled with all their strength. The light kayak climbed the side of an oncoming wave, hung for an endless space almost perpendicular—then suddenly went over the hooked crest and cleared the surf.

Captain Wright, steering for the submarine, swore hoarsely. 'By God, thirty years in the navy and I wind up in command of a kayak!'

Meanwhile, the others were trying to float their boats. General Lemnitzer and Lieutenant Foote used the same four-man system of launching, but their kayak capsized almost at once. Men and boat were hauled ashore. They tried again, and this time, miraculously, got clear.

Holmes and Livingston got off without accident, but Arch Hamblen and Jumbo Courtney overturned on their first attempt. They were the last to reach the submarine, and just as they did so a gigantic wave caught their kayak, lifted it high and swept it down on the submarine. Members of the crew snatched the men clear, held them while the water poured in a torrent off the submarine's back. The wave broke the kayak in two and swept it away.

The danger was instantly apparent. A broken boat ashore with its contents scattered along the beach—it had contained letters, uniforms and a musette bag holding the gold—would be a complete betrayal of the Americans' presence. They flashed Murphy a warning to clear the beach of all debris.

Murphy, Knight and the two French lieutenants searched the beach early in the morning, destroyed all the boat fragments and other debris.

The submarine turned her bow north at a painful four knots. Clark, anxious to get his information to London as soon as possible, decided to risk breaking radio silence.

He sent a message to the nearest British base, giving the submarine's course, speed and position, and asking that a plane be sent out.

At 3.20 p.m. a Catalina flying-boat droned low overhead. An hour and a half later Clark and his men landed at the base and flashed

57

the news of the great success. Then they boarded planes for England. The plane carrying Clark ran into every kind of difficulty, as though fate at the last minute was reluctant to see him through. For hours they were completely lost in fog. The plane iced up so badly that at one time it staggered along, barely aloft. The General calls this flight 'the biggest thrill of the trip'.

In England, where the other plane had arrived right on time, there was consternation. But Clark's plane finally nosed safely down through the fog. You could have bought all that remained of her petrol for a few coppers.

In his North African headquarters, where he commanded the American Fifth Army, I gave this manuscript to General Clark to check for accuracy, and asked, 'Just what did your risky mission accomplish?'

He considered a moment.

'Well,' he said, 'I'm convinced that the information we gained saved thousands of American and British lives. I won't name a figure, because nobody can say accurately. Furthermore, French troops are now fighting bravely and well in our front line because of plans made at that conference. So far as I'm concerned, these are ample rewards for the venture. It was worth the risk.'

THE RUUM

Arthur Parges

The cruiser *Ilkor* had just gone into her interstellar overdrive beyond the orbit of Pluto when a worried officer reported to the Commander.

'Excellency,' he said uneasily, 'I regret to inform you that because of a technician's carelessness a Type H-9 Ruum has been left behind on the third planet, together with anything it may have collected.'

The Commander's triangular eyes hooded momentarily, but when he spoke his voice was level.

'How was the ruum set?'

'For a maximum radius of thirty miles, and one hundred and sixty pounds plus or minus fifteen.'

There was silence for several seconds; then the Commander said: 'We cannot reverse course now. In a few weeks we'll be returning, and can pick up the ruum then. I do not care to have one of those costly, self-energizing models charged against my ship. You will see,' he ordered coldly, 'that the individual responsible is severely punished.'

But at the end of its run, in the neighbourhood of Rigel, the cruiser met a flat, ring-shaped raider; and when the inevitable fire-fight was over, both ships, semi-molten, radioactive, and laden with dead, were starting a billion-year orbit around the star.

And on the earth, it was the age of reptiles.

When the two men had unloaded the last of the supplies, Jim Irwin watched his partner climb into the little seaplane. He waved at Walt.

'Don't forget to mail that letter to my wife,' Jim shouted.

'The minute I land,' Walt Leonard called back, starting to rev the engine. 'And you find us some uranium—a strike is just what Cele needs. A fortune for your son and her, hey?' His white teeth flashed in a grin. 'Don't rub noses with any grizzlies—shoot 'em, but don't scare 'em to death!'

Jim thumbed his nose as the seaplane speeded up, leaving a frothy wake. He felt a queer chill as the amphibian took off. For three weeks he would be isolated in this remote valley of the Canadian Rockies. If for any reason the plane failed to return to the icy blue lake, he would surely die. Even with enough food, no man could surmount the frozen peaks and make his way on foot over hundreds of miles of almost virgin wilderness. But, of course, Walt Leonard would return on schedule, and it was up to Jim whether or not they lost their stake. If there was any uranium in the valley, he had twenty-one days to find it. To work then, and no gloomy forebodings.

Moving with the unhurried precision of an experienced woodsman, he built a lean-to in the shelter of a rocky overhang. For this three weeks of summer, nothing more permanent was needed. Perspiring in the strong morning sun, he piled his supplies back under the ledge, well covered by a waterproof tarpaulin, and protected from the larger animal prowlers. All but the dynamite; that he cached, also carefully wrapped against moisture, two hundred yards away. Only a fool shares his quarters with a box of high explosives.

The first two weeks went by all too swiftly, without any encouraging finds. There was only one good possibility left, and just enough time to explore it. So early one morning towards the end of his third week, Jim Irwin prepared for a last-ditch foray into the north-east part of the valley, a region he had not yet visited.

He took the Geiger counter, slipping on the earphones, reversed to keep the normal rattle from dulling his hearing, and reaching for the rifle, set out, telling himself it was now or never so far as this particular

THE RUUM

expedition was concerned. The bulky .30–06 was a nuisance and he had no enthusiasm for its weight, but the huge grizzlies of Canada are not intruded upon with impunity, and take a lot of killing. He'd already had to dispose of two, a hateful chore, since the big bears were vanishing all too fast. And the rifle had proved a great comfort on several ticklish occasions when actual firing had been avoided. The .22 pistol he left in its sheepskin holster in the lean-to.

He was whistling at the start, for the clear, frosty air, the bright sun on blue-white ice fields, and the heady smell of summer, all delighted his heart despite his bad luck as a prospector. He planned to go one day's journey to the new region, spend about thirty-six hours exploring it intensively, and be back in time to meet the plane at noon. Except for his emergency packet, he took no food or water. It would be easy enough to knock over a rabbit, and the streams were alive with firm-fleshed rainbow trout of the kind no longer common in the States.

All morning Jim walked, feeling an occasional surge of hope as the counter chattered. But its clatter always died down. The valley had nothing radioactive of value, only traces. Apparently they'd made a bad choice. His cheerfulness faded. They needed a strike badly, especially Walt. And his own wife, Cele, with a kid on the way. But there was still a chance. These last thirty-six hours—he'd snoop at night, if necessary—might be the pay-off. He reflected a little bitterly that it would help quite a bit if some of those birds he'd staked would make a strike and return his dough. Right this minute there were close to eight thousand bucks owing to him.

A wry smile touched his lips, and he abandoned unprofitable speculations for plans about lunch. The sun, as well as his stomach, said it was time. He had just decided to take out his line and fish a foaming brook, when he rounded a grassy knoll to come upon a sight that made him stiffen to a halt, his jaw dropping.

It was like some enterprising giant's outdoor butcher shop: a great assortment of animal bodies, neatly lined up in a triple row that extended almost as far as the eye could see. And what animals! To be sure, those nearest him were ordinary deer, bear, cougars, and mountain sheep—one of each, apparently—but down the line were strange, uncouth, half-formed, hairy beasts; and beyond them a nightmare conglomeration of reptiles. One of the latter, at the extreme end of the remarkable

61

display, he recognized at once. There had been a much larger specimen, fabricated about an incomplete skeleton, of course, in the museum at home.

No doubt about it—it was a small stegosaur, no bigger than a pony!

Fascinated, Jim walked down the line, glancing back over the immense array. Peering more closely at one scaly, dirty-yellow lizard, he saw an eyelid tremble. Then he realized the truth. The animals were not dead, but paralysed and miraculously preserved. Perspiration prickled his forehead. How long since stegosaurs had roamed this valley?

All at once he noticed another curious circumstance: the victims were roughly of a size. Nowhere, for example, was there a really large saurian. No tyrannosaurus. For that matter, no mammoth. Each specimen was about the size of a large sheep. He was pondering this odd fact when the underbrush rustled a warning behind him.

Jim Irwin had once worked with mercury, and for a second it seemed to him that a half-filled leather sack of the liquid metal had rolled into the clearing. For the quasi-spherical object moved with just such a weighty, fluid motion. But it was not leather; and what appeared at first a disgusting wartiness turned out on closer scrutiny to be more like the functional projections of some outlandish mechanism. Whatever the thing was, he had little time to study it, for after the spheroid had whipped out and retracted a number of metal rods with bulbous, lens-like structures at their tips, it rolled towards him at a speed of about five miles an hour. And from its purposeful advance, the man had no doubts that it meant to add him to the pathetic heap of living-dead specimens.

Uttering an incoherent exclamation, Jim sprang back a number of paces, unslinging his rifle. The ruum that had been left behind was still some thirty yards off, approaching at that moderate but invariable velocity, an advance more terrifying in its regularity than the headlong charge of a mere brute beast.

Jim's hand flew to the bolt, and with practised deftness he slammed a cartridge into the chamber. He snuggled the battered stock against his cheek, and using the peep sight, aimed squarely at the leathery bulk—a perfect target in the bright afternoon sun. A grim little smile touched his lips as he squeezed the trigger. He knew what one of those 180-grain, metal-jacketed, boat-tail slugs could do at 2700 feet per second. Probably at this close range it would keyhole and blow the foul thing into a mush.

Wham! The familiar kick against his shoulder. E-e-e-e! The whining screech of a ricochet. He sucked in his breath. There could be no doubt whatever. At a mere twenty yards, a bullet from this hard-hitting rifle had glanced from the ruum's surface.

Frantically Jim worked the bolt. He blasted two more rounds, then realized the utter futility of such tactics. When the ruum was six feet away, he saw gleaming finger-hooks flick from warty knobs, and a hollow, sting-like probe, dripping greenish liquid, poised snakily between them. The man turned and fled.

Jim Irwin weighed exactly one hundred and forty-nine pounds.

It was easy enough to pull ahead. The ruum seemed incapable of increasing its speed. But Jim had no illusions on that score. The steady five-mile-an-hour pace was something no organism on earth could maintain for more than a few hours. Before long, Jim guessed, the hunted animal had either turned on its implacable pursuer, or, in the case of more timid creatures, run itself to exhaustion in a circle out of sheer panic. Only the winged were safe. But for anything on the ground the result was inevitable: another specimen for the awesome array. And for whom the whole collection? Why? Why?

Coolly, as he ran, Jim began to shed all surplus weight. He glanced at the reddening sun, wondering about the coming night. He hesitated over the rifle; it had proved useless against the ruum, but his military training impelled him to keep the weapon to the last. Still, every pound raised the odds against him in the gruelling race he foresaw clearly. Logic told him that military reasoning did not apply to a contest like this; there would be no disgrace in abandoning a worthless rifle. And when weight became really vital, the .30-06 would go. But meanwhile he slung it over one shoulder. The Geiger counter he placed as gently as possible on a flat rock, hardly breaking his stride.

One thing was certain. This would be no rabbit run, a blind, panicky flight until exhausted, ending in squealing submission. This would be a fighting retreat, and he'd use every trick of survival he'd learned in his hazard-filled lifetime.

Taking deep, measured breaths, he loped along, watching with shrewd eyes for anything that might be used for his advantage in the weird contest. Luckily the valley was sparsely wooded; in brush or forest his straightway speed would be almost useless.

Suddenly he came upon a sight that made him pause. It was a point where a huge boulder overhung the trail, and Jim saw possibilities in the situation. He grinned as he remembered a Malay mantrap that had once saved his life. Springing to a hillock, he looked back over the grassy plain. The afternoon sun cast long shadows, but it was easy enough to spot the pursuing ruum, still oozing along on Jim's trail. He watched the thing with painful anxiety. Everything hinged upon this brief survey. He was right! Yes, although at most places the man's trail was neither the only route nor the best one, the ruum dogged the footsteps of his prey. The significance of that fact was immense, but Irwin had no more than twelve minutes to implement the knowledge.

Deliberately dragging his feet, Irwin made it a clear trail directly under the boulder. After going past it for about ten yards, he walked backwards in his own prints until just short of the overhang, and then jumped up clear of the track to a point behind the balanced rock.

Whipping out his heavy-duty belt knife, he began to dig, scientifically, but with furious haste, about the base of the boulder. Every few moments, sweating with apprehension and effort, he rammed it with one shoulder. At last, it teetered a little. He had just jammed the knife back into his sheath, and was crouching there, panting, when the ruum rolled into sight over a small ridge on his back trail.

He watched the grey spheroid moving towards him and fought to quiet his sobbing breath. There was no telling what other senses it might bring into play, even though the ruum seemed to prefer just to follow in his prints. But it certainly had a whole battery of instruments at its disposal. He crouched low behind the rock, every nerve a charged wire.

But there was no change of technique by the ruum; seemingly intent on the footprints of its prey, the strange sphere rippled along, passing directly under the great boulder. As it did so, Irwin gave a savage yell, and thrusting his whole muscular weight against the balanced mass, toppled it squarely on the ruum. Five tons of stone fell from a height of twelve feet.

Jim scrambled down. He stood there, staring at the huge lump and shaking his head dazedly. He gave the boulder a kick. 'Hah! Walt and I

Irwin gave a savage yell and thrust his weight against the balanced mass . . .

might clear a buck or two yet from your little meat market. Maybe this expedition won't be a total loss. Enjoy yourself in hell where you came from!'

Then he leaped back, his eyes wild. The giant rock was shifting! Slowly its five-ton bulk was sliding off the trail, raising a ridge of soil as it grated along. Even as he stared, the boulder tilted, and a grey protuberance appeared under the nearest edge. With a choked cry, Jim Irwin broke into a lurching run.

He ran a full mile down the trail. Then, finally, he stopped and looked back. He could just make out a dark dot moving away from the fallen rock. It progressed as slowly and as regularly and as inexorably as before, and in his direction. Jim sat down heavily, putting his head in his scratched, grimy hands.

But that despairing mood did not last. After all, he had gained a twenty-minute respite. Lying down, trying to relax as much as possible, he took the flat packet of emergency rations from his jacket, and eating quickly but without bolting, disposed of some pemmican, biscuit, and chocolate. A few sips of icy water from a stream, and he was almost ready to continue his fantastic struggle. But first he swallowed one of the three Benzedrine pills he carried for physical crises. When the ruum was still an estimated ten minutes away, Jim Irwin trotted off, much of his wiry strength back, and fresh courage to counter bone-deep weariness.

After running for fifteen minutes, he came to a sheer face of rock about thirty feet high. The terrain on either side was barely passable, consisting of choked gullies, spiky brush, and knife-edged rocks. If Jim could make the top of this little cliff, the ruum sure would have to detour, a circumstance that might put it many minutes behind him.

He looked up at the sun. Huge and crimson, it was almost touching the horizon. He would have to move fast. Irwin was no rock-climber, but he did know the fundamentals. Using every crevice, roughness, and minute ledge, he fought his way up the cliff. Somehow—unconsciously—he used that flowing climb of a natural mountaineer, which takes each foothold very briefly as an unstressed pivot-point in a series of rhythmic advances.

He had just reached the top when the ruum rolled up to the base of the cliff.

Jim knew very well that he ought to leave at once, taking advantage of the few precious remaining moments of daylight. Every second gained was of tremendous value; but curiosity and hope made him wait. He told himself that the instant his pursuer detoured he would get out of there all the faster. Besides, the thing might even give up and he could sleep right here.

Sleep! His body lusted for it.

But the ruum would not detour. It hesitated only a few seconds at the foot of the barrier. Then a number of knobs opened to extrude metallic wands. One of these, topped with lenses, waved in the air. Jim drew back too late—their uncanny gaze had found him as he lay atop the cliff, peering down. He cursed his idiocy.

Immediately all the wands retracted, and from a different knob a slender rod, blood-red in the setting sun, began to shoot straight up to the man. As he watched, frozen in place, its barbed tip gripped the cliff's edge almost under his nose.

Jim leaped to his feet. Already the rod was shortening as the ruum re-absorbed its shining length. And the leathery sphere was rising off the ground. Swearing loudly, Jim fixed his eyes on the tenacious hook, drawing back one heavy foot.

But experience restrained him. The mighty kick was never launched. He had seen too many rough-and-tumbles lost by an injudicious attempt at the boot. It wouldn't do at all to let any part of his body get within reach of the ruum's superb tools. Instead he seized a length of dry branch, and inserting one end under the metal hook, began to pry.

There was a sputtering flash, white and lacy, and even through the dry wood he felt the potent surge of power that splintered the end. He dropped the smouldering stick with a gasp of pain, and wringing his numb fingers, backed off several steps, full of impotent rage. For a moment he paused, half inclined to run again, but then his upper lip drew back and, snarling, he unslung his rifle. He knew he had been right to lug the damned thing all this way—even if it had beat a tattoo on his ribs. Now he had the ruum right where he wanted it!

Kneeling to steady his aim in the failing light, Jim sighted at the hook and fired. There was a soggy thud as the ruum fell. Jim shouted. The heavy slug had done a lot more than he expected. Not only had it blasted the metal claw loose, but it had smashed a big gap in the cliff's edge. It would be pretty damned hard for the ruum to use that part of the rock again!

He looked down. Sure enough, the ruum was back at the bottom. Jim Irwin grinned. Every time the thing clamped a hook over the bluff, he'd blow that hook loose. There was plenty of ammunition in his pocket and, until the moon rose, bringing a good light for shooting with it, he'd stick the gun's muzzle inches away if necessary. Besides, the thing —whatever it might be—was obviously too intelligent to keep up a hopeless struggle. Sooner or later it would accept the detour. And then, maybe the night would help to hide his trail.

Then—he choked and, for a brief moment, tears came to his eyes. Down below, in the dimness, the squat, phlegmatic spheroid was extruding three hooked rods simultaneously in a fanlike spread. In a perfectly coordinated movement, the rods snagged the cliff's edge at intervals of about four feet.

Jim Irwin whipped the rifle to his shoulder. All right—this was going to be just like the rapid fire for record back at Benning. Only at Benning they didn't expect good shooting in the dark!

But the first shot was a bull's-eye, smacking the left-hand hook loose in a puff of rock dust. His second shot did almost as well, knocking the gritty stuff loose so the centre barb slipped off. But even as he whirled to level at number three, Jim saw it was hopeless.

The first hook was back in place. No matter how well he shot, at least one rod would always be in position, pulling the ruum to the top.

Jim hung the useless rifle muzzle down from a stunted tree and ran into the deepening dark. The toughening of his body, a process of years, was paying off now. So what? Where was he going? What could he do now? Was there anything that could stop that damned thing behind him?

Then he remembered the dynamite.

Gradually changing his course, the weary man cut back towards his camp by the lake. Overhead the stars brightened, pointing the way. Jim lost all sense of time. He must have eaten as he wobbled along, for he wasn't hungry. Maybe he could eat at the lean-to . . . no, there wouldn't be time . . . take a Benzedrine pill. No, the pills were all gone and the moon was up and he could hear the ruum close behind. Close.

Quite often phosphorescent eyes peered at him from the underbrush and once, just at dawn, a grizzly whoofed with displeasure at his passage.

Sometimes during the night his wife, Cele, stood before him with outstretched arms. 'Go away!' he rasped, 'Go away! You can make it! It can't chase both of us!' So she turned and ran lightly alongside of him. But when Irwin panted across a tiny glade, Cele faded away into the moonlight and he realized she hadn't been there at all.

Shortly after sunrise Jim Irwin reached the lake. The ruum was close enough for him to hear the dull sounds of its passage. Jim staggered, his eyes closed. He hit himself feebly on the nose, his eyes jerked open and he saw the explosive. The sight of the greasy sticks of dynamite snapped him wide awake.

He forced himself to calmness and carefully considered what to do. Fuse? No. It would be impossible to leave fused dynamite in the trail and time the detonation with the absolute precision he needed. Sweat poured down his body, his clothes were sodden with it. It was hard to think. The explosion *must* be set off from a distance and at the exact moment the ruum was passing over it. But Irwin dared not use a long fuse. The rate of burning was not constant enough. Couldn't calibrate it perfectly with the ruum's advance. Jim Irwin's body sagged all over, his chin sank toward his heaving chest. He jerked his head up, stepped back—and saw the .22 pistol where he had left it in the lean-to.

His sunken eyes flashed.

Moving with frenetic haste, he took the half-filled case, piled all the remaining percussion caps among the loose sticks in a devil's mixture. Weaving out to the trail, he carefully placed box and contents directly on his earlier tracks some twenty yards from a rocky ledge. It was a risk—the stuff might go any time—but that didn't matter. He would far rather be blown to rags than end up living but paralysed in the ruum's outdoor butcher's stall.

The exhausted Irwin had barely hunched down behind the thin ledge of rock before his inexorable pursuer appeared over a slight rise five hundred yards away. Jim scrunched deeper into the hollow, then saw a vertical gap, a narrow crack between rocks. That was it, he thought vaguely. He could sight through the gap at the dynamite and still be shielded from the blast. If it was a shield . . . when that half-caste blew only twenty yards away. . .

He stretched out on his belly, watching the ruum roll forward. A hammer of exhaustion pounded his ballooning skull. When had he slept last? This was the first time he had lain down in hours. Hours? Ha! It was days. His muscles stiffened, locked into throbbing, burning knots. Then he felt the morning sun on his back, soothing, warming, easing . . . No! If he let go, if he slept now, it was the ruum's macabre collection for Jim Irwin! Stiff fingers tightened around the pistol. He'd stay awake! If he lost—if the ruum survived the blast—there'd still be time to put a bullet through his brain.

He looked down at the sleek pistol, then out at the innocent-seeming booby trap. If he timed this right—and he would—the ruum wouldn't survive. No. He relaxed a little, yielding just a bit to the gently insistent sun. A bird whistled softly somewhere above him and a fish splashed in the lake.

Suddenly he was wrenched to full awareness. Damn! Of all times for a grizzly to come snooping about! With the whole of Irwin's camp ready for greedy looting, a fool bear had to come sniffing around the dynamite! The furred monster smelled carefully at the box, nosed around, rumbled deep displeasure at the alien scent of man. Irwin held his breath. Just a touch would blow a cap. A single cap meant . . .

The grizzly lifted his head from the box and growled hoarsely. The box was ignored, the offensive odour of man was forgotten. Its wild little eyes focused on a plodding spheroid that was now only forty yards away. Jim Irwin snickered. Until he had met the ruum the grizzly bear of the North American continent was the only thing in the world he had ever feared. And now—why the hell was he so calm about it?— the two terrors of his existence were meeting head on and he was laughing. He shook his head and the great side muscles in his neck hurt abominably. He looked down at his pistol, then out at the dynamite. *These* were the only real things in his world.

About six feet from the bear, the ruum paused. Still in the grip of that almost idiotic detachment, Jim Irwin found himself wondering again what it was, where it had come from. The grizzly arose on its haunches, the embodiment of utter ferocity. Terrible teeth flashed white against red lips. The business-like ruum started to roll past. The bear closed in, roaring. It cuffed at the ruum. A mighty paw, armed with black claws sharper and stronger than scythes, made that cuff. It would have disembowelled a rhinoceros. Irwin cringed as that side-

70

There was a flash, swift and deadly. The roar of the king became a whimper.

swipe knocked dust from the leathery sphere. The ruum was hurled back several inches. It paused, recovered, and with the same dreadful casualness it rippled on, making a wider circle, ignoring the bear.

But the lord of the woods wasn't settling for any draw. Moving with that incredible agility which has terrified Indians, Spanish, French and Anglo-Americans since the first encounter of any of them with his species, the grizzly whirled, side-stepped beautifully and hugged the ruum. The terrible, shaggy forearms tightened, the slavering jaws champed at the grey surface. Irwin half rose. 'Go it!' he croaked. Even as he cheered the clumsy emperor of the wild, Jim thought it was an insane tableau: the village idiot wrestling with a beach ball.

Then silver metal gleamed bright against grey. There was a flash, swift and deadly. The roar of the king abruptly became a whimper, a gurgle and then there was nearly a ton of terror wallowing in death—its throat slashed open. Jim Irwin saw the bloody blade retract into the grey spheroid, leaving a bright-red smear on the thing's dusty hide.

And the ruum rolled forward past the giant corpse, implacable, still intent on the man's spoor, his footprints, his pathway. Okay, baby,

Jim giggled at the dead grizzly, this is for you, for Cele, for—lots of poor dumb animals like us—come to, you damned fool, he cursed at himself. And aimed at the dynamite. And very calmly, very carefully, Jim Irwin squeezed the trigger of his pistol.

Briefly, sound first. Then giant hands lifted his body from where he lay, then let go. He came down hard, face in a patch of nettles, but he was sick, he didn't care. He remembered that the birds were quiet. Then there was a fluid thump as something massive struck the grass a few yards away. Then there was quiet.

Irwin lifted his head . . . all men do in such a case. His body still ached. He lifted sore shoulders and saw . . . an enormous, smoking crater in the earth. He also saw, a dozen paces away, grey-white because it was covered now with powdered rock, the ruum.

It was under a tall, handsome pine tree. Even as Jim watched, wondering if the ringing in his ears would ever stop, the ruum rolled towards him.

Irwin fumbled for his pistol. It was gone. It had dropped somewhere, out of reach. He wanted to pray, then, but couldn't get properly started. Instead, he kept thinking, idiotically, 'My sister Ethel can't spell Nebuchadnezzar and never could. My sister Ethel——'

The ruum was a foot away now, and Jim closed his eyes. He felt cool, metallic fingers touch, grip, lift. His unresisting body was raised several inches, and juggled oddly. Shuddering, he waited for the terrible syringe with its green liquid, seeing the yellow, shrunken face of a lizard with one eyelid a-tremble.

Then, dispassionately, without either roughness or solicitude, the ruum put him back on the ground. When he opened his eyes, some seconds later, the sphere was rolling away. Watching it go, he sobbed dryly.

It seemed only a matter of moments before he heard the seaplane's engine, and opened his eyes to see Walt Leonard bending over him.

Later, in the plane, five thousand feet above the valley, Walt grinned suddenly, slapped him on the back, and cried: 'Jim, I can get a whirly-bird, a four-place job! Why, if we can snatch up just a few of those prehistoric lizards and things while the museum keeper's away, it's like you said—the scientists will pay us plenty.'

Jim's hollow eyes lit up. 'That's the idea,' he agreed. Then, bitterly; 'I might just as well have stayed in bed. Evidently the damned thing didn't want me at all. Maybe it wanted to know what I paid for these pants! Barely touched me, then let go. And how I ran!'

'Yeah,' Walt said. 'That was damned queer. And after that marathon. I admire your guts, boy.' He glanced sideways at Jim Irwin's haggard face. 'That night's run cost you plenty. I figure you lost over ten pounds.'

I ESCAPE FROM THE BOERS

Sir Winston Churchill

Sent in 1899 to cover the war in South Africa as correspondent for
The Morning Post, *the 24-year-old Winston Churchill was taken
prisoner by the Boers during a reconnaissance in an armoured train.
A few weeks later he escaped from a prison camp in the Boer capital
of Pretoria and was slowly making his way eastwards, hoping to reach
the frontier of Portuguese East Africa (modern Mozambique) when
one night, near to exhaustion, he knocked at the door of a house in a
coal-mining area. The owner, who turned out to be the English-born
manager, Mr Howard, gave Churchill shelter, promised to help him
on his way and meanwhile hid him, with food, bedding and candles,
at the bottom of a deep mine-shaft.*

I do not know how many hours I slept, but the following afternoon
must have been far advanced when I found myself thoroughly awake.
I put out my hand for the candle, but could feel it nowhere. I did not
know what pitfalls these mining-galleries might contain, so I thought
it better to lie quiet on my mattress and await developments. Several
hours passed before the faint gleam of a lantern showed that someone
was coming. It proved to be Mr Howard himself, armed with a chicken
and other good things. He also brought several books. He asked me
why I had not lighted my candle. I said I couldn't find it.

'Didn't you put it under the mattress?' he asked.

'No.'

'Then the rats must have got it.'

He told me there were swarms of rats in the mine, that some years
ago he had introduced a particular kind of white rat, which was an
excellent scavenger, and that these had multiplied and thrived exceedingly. He told me he had been to the house of an English doctor twenty
miles away to get the chicken. He was worried at the attitude of the two

Dutch servants, who were very inquisitive about the depredations upon the leg of mutton for which I had been responsible. If he could not get another chicken cooked for the next day, he would have to take double helpings on his own plate and slip the surplus into a parcel for me while the servant was out of the room. He said that inquiries were being made for me all over the district by the Boers, and that the Pretoria Government was making a tremendous fuss about my escape. The fact that there were a number of English remaining in the Middelburg mining region indicated it as a likely place for me to have turned to, and all persons of English origin were more or less suspect.

I again expressed my willingness to go on alone with a Kaffir guide and a pony, but this he utterly refused to entertain. It would take a lot of planning, he said, to get me out of the country, and I might have to stay in the mine for quite a long time.

'Here,' he said, 'you are absolutely safe. Mac' (by which he meant one of the Scottish miners) 'knows all the disused workings and places that no one else would dream of. There is one place here where the water actually touches the roof for a foot or two. If they searched the mine, Mac would dive under that with you into the workings cut off beyond the water. No one would ever think of looking there. We have frightened the Kaffirs with tales of ghosts, and anyhow, we are watching their movements continually.'

He stayed with me while I dined, and then departed, leaving me, among other things, half a dozen candles which, duly warned, I tucked under my pillow and mattress.

I slept again for a long time, and woke suddenly with a feeling of movement about me. Something seemed to be pulling at my pillow. I put out my hand quickly. There was a perfect scurry. The rats were at the candles. I rescued the candles in time, and lighted one. Luckily for me, I have no horror of rats as such, and being reassured by their evident timidity, I was not particularly uneasy. All the same, the three days I passed in the mine were not among the most pleasant which my memory reillumines. The patter of little feet and a perceptible sense of stir and scurry were continuous. Once I was woken up from a doze by one actually galloping across me. On the candle being lighted these beings became invisible.

The next day—if you can call it day—arrived in due course. This

75

was 14 December, and the third day since I had escaped from the State Model Schools. It was relieved by a visit from the two Scottish miners, with whom I had a long confabulation. I then learned, to my surprise, that the mine was only about two hundred feet deep.

There were parts of it, said Mac, where one could see the daylight up a disused shaft. Would I like to take a turn around the old workings and have a glimmer? We passed an hour or two wandering round and up and down these subterranean galleries, and spent a quarter of an hour near the bottom of the shaft, where, grey and faint, the light of the sun and of the upper world was discerned. On this promenade I saw numbers of rats. They seemed rather nice little beasts, quite white, with dark eyes which I was assured in the daylight were a bright pink. Three years afterwards a British officer on duty in the district wrote to me that he had heard my statement at a lecture about the white rats and their pink eyes, and thought it was the limit of mendacity. He had taken the trouble to visit the mine and see for himself, and he proceeded to apologize for having doubted my truthfulness.

On the 15th Mr Howard announced that the hue and cry seemed to be dying away. No trace of the fugitive had been discovered throughout the mining district. The talk among the Boer officials was now that I must be hiding at the house of some British sympathizer in Pretoria. They did not believe that it was possible I could have got out of the town. In these circumstances he thought that I might come up and have a walk on the veldt that night, and that if all was quiet the next morning I might shift my quarters to the back room of the office. On the one hand he seemed reassured, and on the other increasingly excited by the adventure. Accordingly, I had a fine stroll in the glorious fresh air and moonlight, and thereafter, anticipating slightly our programme, I took up my quarters behind packing-cases in the inner room of the office. Here I remained for three more days, walking each night on the endless plain with Mr Howard or his assistant.

On the 16th, the fifth day of escape, Mr Howard informed me he had made a plan to get me out of the country. The mine was connected with the railway by a branch line. In the neighbourhood of the mine there lived a Dutchman, Burgener by name, who was sending a consignment of wool to Delagoa Bay on the 19th. This gentleman was well disposed to the British. He had been approached by Mr Howard, had

76

been made a party to our secret, and was willing to assist. Mr Burgener's wool was packed in great bales and would fill two or three large trucks. These trucks were to be loaded at the mine's siding. The bales could be so packed as to leave a small place in the centre of the truck in which I could be concealed. A tarpaulin would be fastened over each truck after it had been loaded, and it was very unlikely indeed that, if the fastenings were found intact, it would be removed at the frontier. Did I agree to take this chance?

I was more worried about this than almost anything that had happened to me so far in my adventure. When by extraordinary chance one has gained some great advantage or prize and actually had it in one's possession and been enjoying it for several days, the idea of losing it becomes almost insupportable. I had really come to count upon freedom as a certainty, and the idea of having to put myself in a position in which I should be perfectly helpless, without a move of any kind, absolutely at the caprice of a searching party at the frontier, was profoundly harassing. Rather than face this ordeal I would much have preferred to start off on the veldt with a pony and a guide, and far from the haunts of man to make my way march by march beyond the wide territories of the Boer Republic. However, in the end I accepted the proposal of my generous rescuer, and arrangements were made accordingly.

I should have been still more anxious if I could have read some of the telegrams which were reaching English newspapers. For instance:

Pretoria, 13 December—Though Mr Churchill's escape was cleverly executed there is little chance of his being able to cross the border.

Pretoria, 14 December—It is reported that Mr Winston Churchill has been captured at the border railway station of Komati Poort.

Lourenço Marques, 16 December—It is reported that Mr Churchill has been captured at Waterval Boven.

London, 16 December—With reference to the escape from Pretoria of Mr Winston Churchill, fears are expressed that he may be captured again before long and if so may probably be shot.

—or if I had read the description of myself and the reward for my recapture which were now widely distributed or posted along the railway line.

I am glad I knew nothing of all this.

The afternoon of the 18th dragged slowly away. I remember that I spent the greater part of it reading Stevenson's *Kidnapped*. Those thrilling pages which describe the escape of David Balfour and Alan Breck in the glens awakened sensations with which I was only too familiar. To be a fugitive, to be a hunted man, to be 'wanted', is a mental experience by itself. The risks of the battlefield, the hazards of the bullet or the shell are one thing; having the police after you is another. The need for concealment and deception breeds an actual sense of guilt very undermining to morale. Feeling that at any moment the officers of the law may present themselves or any stranger may ask the questions, 'Who are you?' 'Where do you come from?' 'Where are you going?' —to which questions no satisfactory answer could be given—gnawed the structure of self-confidence. I dreaded in every fibre the ordeal which awaited me at Komati Poort and which I must impotently and passively endure if I was to make good my escape from the enemy.

In this mood I was startled by the sound of rifle shots close at hand, one after another at irregular intervals. A sinister explanation flashed through my mind. The Boers had come! Howard and his handful of Englishmen were in open rebellion in the heart of the enemy's country! I had been strictly enjoined upon no account to leave my hiding-place behind the packing-cases in any circumstances whatever, and I accordingly remained there in great anxiety. Presently it became clear that the worst had not happened. The sounds of voices and presently of laughter came from the office. Evidently a conversation amicable, sociable in its character was in progress. I resumed my companionship with Alan Breck. At last the voices died away, and then after an interval my door was opened and Mr Howard's pale, sombre face appeared, suffused by a broad grin. He relocked the door behind him and walked towards me.

'The Field Cornet has been here,' he said. 'No, he was not looking for you. He says they caught you at Waterval Boven yesterday. But I didn't want him messing about, so I challenged him to a rifle match at bottles. He won two pounds off me and has gone away delighted.

'It is all fixed up for tonight,' he added.

'What do I do?' I asked.

'Nothing. You simply follow me when I come for you.'

At two o'clock on the morning of the 19th I awaited, fully dressed, the signal. The door opened. My host appeared. He beckoned. Not a word was spoken on either side. He led the way through the front office to the siding where three large bogie trucks stood. Three figures, evidently Dewsnap and the miners, were strolling about in different directions in the moonlight. A gang of Kaffirs were busy lifting an enormous bale into the rearmost truck. Howard strolled along to the first truck and walked across the line past the end of it. As he did so he pointed with his left hand. I nipped on to the buffers and saw before me a hole between the wool-bales and the end of the truck, just wide enough to squeeze into. From this there led a narrow tunnel formed of wool-bales into the centre of the truck. Here was a space wide enough to lie in, high enough to sit up in. In this I took up my abode.

Three or four hours later, when gleams of daylight had reached me through the interstices of my shelter and through chinks in the boards of the flooring of the truck, the noise of an approaching engine was heard. Then came the bumping and banging of coupling up. And again, after a further pause, we started rumbling off on our journey into the unknown.

I now took stock of my new abode and of the resources in munitions and supplies with which it was furnished. First there was a revolver. This was a moral support, though it was not easy to see in what way it could helpfully be applied to any problem I was likely to have to solve. Secondly, there were two roast chickens, some slices of meat, a loaf of bread, a melon, and three bottles of cold tea. The journey to the sea was not expected to take more than sixteen hours, but no one could tell what delay might occur to ordinary commercial traffic in time of war.

There was plenty of light now in the recess in which I was confined. There were many crevices in the boards composing the sides and floor of the truck, and through these the light found its way between the wool-bales. Working along the tunnel to the end of the truck, I found a chink which must have been nearly an eighth of an inch in width, and through which it was possible to gain a partial view of the outer world. To check the progress of the journey I had learnt by heart beforehand the names of all the stations on the route. I can remember many of them today: Witbank, Middelburg, Bergendal, Belfast, Dalmanutha, Machadodorp, Waterval Boven, Waterval Onder, Elands, Nooidgedacht, and so on to Komati Poort. We had by now reached the first of these. At

79

this point the branch line from the mine joined the railway. Here, after two or three hours' delay and shunting, we were evidently coupled up to a regular train, and soon started off at a superior and very satisfactory pace.

All day long we travelled eastward through the Transvaal; when darkness fell we were laid up for the night at a station which, according to my reckoning, was Waterval Boven. We had accomplished nearly half our journey. But how long should we wait on this siding? It might be for days; it would certainly be until the next morning. During all the dragging hours of the day I had lain on the floor of the truck occupying my mind as best I could, painting bright pictures of the pleasures of freedom, of the excitement of rejoining the army, of the triumph of a successful escape—but haunted also perpetually by anxieties about the search at the frontier, an ordeal inevitable and constantly approaching. Now another apprehension laid hold upon me. I wanted to go to sleep. Indeed, I did not think I could possibly keep awake. But if I slept I might snore! And if I snored while the train was at rest in the silent siding, I might be heard. And if I were heard! I decided in principle that it was only prudent to abstain from sleep, and shortly afterwards fell into a blissful slumber from which I was awakened the next morning by the banging and jerking of the train as the engine was again coupled to it.

Between Waterval Boven and Waterval Onder there is a very steep descent which the locomotive accomplishes by means of a rack and pinion. We ground our way down this at three or four miles an hour, and this feature made my reckoning certain that the next station was, in fact, Waterval Onder. All this day, too, we rattled through the enemy's country, and late in the afternoon we reached the dreaded Komati Poort. Peeping through my chink, I could see this was a considerable place, with numerous tracks of rails and several trains standing on them. Numbers of people were moving about. There were many voices and much shouting and whistling. After a preliminary inspection of the scene I retreated, as the train pulled up, into the very centre of my fastness, and covering myself up with a piece of sacking lay flat on the floor of the truck and awaited developments with a beating heart.

Three or four hours passed, and I did not know whether we had been searched or not. Several times people had passed up and down the train, talking in Dutch. But the tarpaulins had not been removed, and no special examination seemed to have been made of the truck. Meanwhile darkness had come on, and I had to resign myself to an indefinite continuance of my uncertainties. It was tantalizing to be held so long in jeopardy after all these hundreds of miles had been accomplished, and I was now within a few hundred yards of the frontier. Again I wondered about the dangers of snoring. But in the end I slept without mishap.

We were still stationary when I awoke. Perhaps they were searching the train so thoroughly that there was consequently a great delay! Alternatively, perhaps we were forgotten on the siding and would be left there for days or weeks. I was greatly tempted to peer out, but I resisted. At last, at eleven o'clock, we were coupled up, and almost immediately started. If I had been right in thinking that the station in which we had passed the night was Komati Poort, I was already in Portuguese territory. But perhaps I had made a mistake. Perhaps I had miscounted. Perhaps there was still another station before the frontier. Perhaps the search still impended. But all these doubts were dispelled when the train arrived at the next station. I peered through my chink and saw the uniform caps of the Portuguese officials on the platform and the name Resana Garcia painted on a board. I restrained all expression of my joy until we moved on again. Then, as we rumbled and banged along, I pushed my head out of the tarpaulin and sang and shouted and crowed at the top of my voice. Indeed, I was so carried away by thankfulness and delight that I fired my revolver two or three times in the air as a *feu de joie*. None of these follies led to any evil results.

It was late in the afternoon when we reached Lourenço Marques. My train ran into a goods yard, and a crowd of Kaffirs advanced to unload it. I thought the moment had now come for me to quit my hiding-place, in which I had passed nearly three anxious and uncomfortable days. I had already thrown out every vestige of food and had removed all traces of my occupation. I now slipped out at the end of the truck between the couplings, and mingling unnoticed with the Kaffirs and loafers in the yard—which my slovenly and unkempt appearance well fitted me to do—I strolled my way towards the gates and found myself in the streets of Lourenço Marques.

Burgener was waiting outside the gates. We exchanged glances. He turned and walked off into the town, and I followed twenty yards behind. We walked through several streets and turned a number of

'I pushed my head out of the tarpaulin and sang and shouted and crowed at the top of my voice.'

corners. Presently he stopped and stood for a moment gazing up at the roof of the opposite house. I looked in the same direction, and there— blest vision!—I saw floating the gay colours of the Union Jack. It was the British Consulate.

The secretary of the British Consul evidently did not expect my arrival.

'Be off,' he said. 'The Consul cannot see you today. Come to his office at nine tomorrow, if you want anything.'

At this I became so angry, and repeated so loudly that I insisted on seeing the Consul personally at once, that that gentleman himself looked out of the window and finally came down to the door and asked me my name. From that moment every resource of hospitality and welcome was at my disposal. A hot bath, clean clothing, an excellent dinner, means of telegraphing—all I could want.

I devoured the file of newspapers which was placed before me. Great events had taken place since I had climbed the wall of the State Model Schools. The Black Week of the Boer War had descended on the British Army. General Gatacre at Stormberg, Lord Methuen at Magersfontein, and Sir Redvers Buller at Colenso, had all suffered staggering defeats, and casualties on a scale unknown to England since the Crimean War. All this made me eager to rejoin the army, and the Consul himself was no less anxious to get me out of Lourenço Marques, which was full of Boers and Boer sympathizers. Happily the weekly steamer was leaving for Durban that very evening; in fact, it might almost be said it ran in connection with my train. On this steamer I decided to embark.

The news of my arrival had spread like wildfire through the town, and while we were at dinner the Consul was at first disturbed to see a group of strange figures in the garden. These, however, turned out to be Englishmen fully armed who had hurried up to the Consulate determined to resist any attempt at my recapture. Under the escort of these patriotic gentlemen I marched safely through the streets to the quay, and at about ten o'clock was on salt water in the steamship *Induna*.

I reached Durban to find myself a popular hero. I was received as if I had won a great victory. The harbour was decorated with flags. Bands and crowds thronged the quays. The admiral, the general, the mayor pressed on board to grasp my hand. I was nearly torn to pieces by enthusiastic kindness. Whirled along on the shoulders of the crowd, I was

83

carried to the steps of the town hall, where nothing would content them but a speech, which after a becoming reluctance I was induced to deliver. Sheaves of telegrams from all parts of the world poured in upon me, and I started that night for the army in a blaze of triumph.

Here, too, I was received with the greatest goodwill. I took up my quarters in the very platelayer's hut within one hundred yards of which I had a little more than a month before been taken prisoner, and there with the rude plenty of the Natal campaign celebrated by a dinner to many friends my good fortune and Christmas Eve.

DEATH'S HEAD

Gordon Roddick

As Tommy and Les—used to the bush their entire lives—usually snored all night without interruption, the Englishman picked up his blanket, skirted the tangled heap of dogs that lay in front of the fire, and chose himself a patch of ground beneath a big white gum tree. With his already battered hat, he smacked the dust off his jeans and shirt, took off his spurs, scooped out a small hollow in the hard red earth to accommodate his hip bones, wrapped his blanket loosely round him and flopped down on to the ground.

This was the moment of the day that he really savoured. All days were hard and today had been no exception. After eleven or twelve hours in the saddle he was pleased to get off his horse, fill his belly and roll up in his blanket. It had been three weeks since he had slept in a bed; now they were only twenty miles from their destination and this promised to be his last night under the stars. With the bonus they would get tomorrow for bringing the cattle in on schedule, and the money he had already saved, he could afford to leave Queensland and divert himself in Sydney for a while. After which he was due to return to England to take over the management of his father's farm. As these thoughts ran through his mind he smiled, in the fading light, with the confidence of a man, who, even at the age of twenty-three, knows what he is doing.

He rolled over on to his back and watched the flickering spasms of the dying fire. He drank in the still night, its peace more underlined than disturbed by the harmonic snoring of dogs and men. He was thinking idly about a hot bath and clean clothes when suddenly he saw it, silhouetted darkly somewhere between him and the fire: a thin swaying band of death, a snake.

He should have moved, rolled away, but he was paralysed by its hypnotic menace. In the half-light he could not estimate clearly the distance between them, but he was sure it could not be more than three feet. He watched, with mingled fascination and terror, the liquid, almost gentle rhythm as the creature swung in its ghastly dance, forked tongue flickering in unison with the flames. It dropped its head and he could no longer see it. He thought it had glided off, but his sigh of relief was cut to a strangled gasp as he felt it slipping over his feet and, worse still, moving firmly but leisurely towards his head, with a strong ripple of muscle. His whole body, caught in fear and revulsion, froze as the snake moved relentlessly upward, and he could hardly contain the hysterical scream that rose in his throat as the forked tongue tickled feather-like over his face.

The snake turned, coil after coil, and slithered under his blanket; when he opened his eyes it was to see the tail give a final derisive flick as it vanished under cover. Now he could feel it surging over the lower half of his body, and he prayed meaninglessly, frantically, 'God, no, no! God, oh God!' Then abruptly all movement ceased and he was aware that it had settled down in the hollow between his knees.

At first, the shock stupefied him. It was as if he had been hurled from a comfortable dream into an awakening so terrible that both his mind and his body utterly rejected it. In the crazy half-world of whirling, incoherent thought that followed, he almost managed to persuade himself that it *was* some kind of nightmare—until his returning wits, and the cold touch of the scaly body against his knees, forced him to accept the horrifying reality. Then, like a man coming round from an anaesthetic, he tried desperately to pull himself together, to adjust to the reality, to cut it down to size. To think.

He tried to hazard a guess at how long he had been lying there: was

His whole body froze as the snake moved relentlessly upward.

it minutes or hours? He decided at last that it was probably about half an hour. They had turned in at eleven o'clock, and now it must be at least half-past eleven. That meant another seven hours before sun-up. Could he keep still that long?

Already he was growing conscious of his body. Small aches were becoming manifest in several isolated regions, in his buttocks and thighs, in his midriff, and on the points of his shoulder-blades. The only parts of his body that he could move with any degree of safety were his head and his neck. How long would it be, he wondered, before these small aches grew into a massive pain too intense to be endured? How long before his limbs grew numb—before he cried out in pain and terror? And what would happen if he had an attack of cramp? Could he control the spasms?

He began to be conscious of every undulation in the ground beneath him. Each hollow was an abyss threatening to swallow him up, each hump a mountain boring into his back, and, to add to his discomfort, he had started to sweat. He thought vaguely of his mother. *Only horses sweat, dear; gentlemen perspire.* He started to cry silently in an orgy of

87

self-pity until the sobs almost shook his body. Then he remembered that, if he moved so much as a muscle, he would almost certainly die; so his weeping ceased abruptly.

The snake moved briefly, convulsively. He thought for a moment that it might emerge and leave him, but no, it settled again, nestling more firmly against the heat of his body. How could he escape? He considered and dismissed the idea of a sudden violent leap; the creature would almost certainly nail him before they parted company. Then how? He turned his head to look at Tommy and Les snoring peacefully twenty yards away. He did not dare shout out to them. The noise might rouse the snake, or it might be disturbed by the vibrations of his voice. He tried a loud whisper but fear had dried the saliva in his mouth and the only sound he could make was a frustrated croak. His vocal chords simply refused to function.

He kept on trying until he was exhausted, then just lay there. Poised in a hinterland between death and life, he thought of his home and his childhood, but irrationally and incoherently. For a time he relapsed into a near coma, then crept back to a painful reality in which he alternated between passive resignation and almost suicidal despair. He even contemplated ending his ordeal by moving, but directly the thought took shape he realized how much he wanted to live . . .

He began to search the sky for any hint of a let up in darkness, any faint sign that dawn would in the end stab its way over the horizon. He kept his ears alert to every variation of tone in the snoring of Tommy and Les, reminding himself that one or other of them must eventually wake up. But night seemed never-ending and by now he had lost all count of time. His body became an angry fire of blood unable to flow, of knotted muscles unable to relax. He had not known he could stand so much unrelenting pain. His legs had become so numb that he prayed he might not move them involuntarily.

Then one of the dogs moved, whimpering in its sleep. He wondered if it was his dog, and a new wave of terror swept over him. Suppose his blue cattle bitch woke up before Tommy or Les? Then, as she did every morning, she would come charging across to leap all over him and wash away his morning torpor. If that happened, he would indeed be finished. Why had he not listened to Les when he had warned him not to treat her like a 'bloody English lapdog'? The night breeze danced over his face and mocked silently at his impotence.

The hours dragged interminably on, with death's messenger lying in comfortable repose between his knees. Whyever had this happened to him? Why not to one of the others? Was it an act of God, or was it a natural biological occurrence? When would the snake leave? It might just have killed, then sought a warm place to digest its victim. So it would probably emerge when the sun rose, to bask in its heat. The night seemed longer than the whole of his life, and he relived every detail of it as, moment by moment, the hours crawled by.

At last all hope seeped out of him and he lay like a discarded doll, his unseeing eyes staring blankly into the limbs of the tree above him. Then slowly, unbelievably, he realized that he could see the branches and leaves a little more clearly. He turned his head and his eyes greedily drank in the line of the horizon: yes, it was true, the first slow beginnings of dawn were there. With the dawn came fresh hope that buoyed up inside him and threatened to burst out in a whoop of joy. Then he remembered his dog and looked anxiously over to where she lay curled up among the others. She showed no signs of stirring.

The night fled slowly, reluctantly, in the face of the day, but, with its receding, he turned his mind back to living. He started to moisten his lips and tongue with what little saliva he had left, and turned his head once more towards the two sleeping men. He whispered to them as loudly as he dared, hoarsely, desperately praying that one of them should waken, but neither moved. Every second brought more light flooding through the bush, and he gave up trying to call the others for fear of rousing the dogs.

The sun rolled just clear of the horizon, and as the morning light washed away the shadows before his eyes the whole landscape lay revealed in stark clarity. Then, suddenly, he was sure he felt the snake move again. Was it just another false alarm? But no, the movement was more definite this time. His terror reached a climax as he felt it uncoil and, with a long liquid thrust, weave its way once more towards his head. He closed his eyes so tight that it hurt them as the snake's endless length brushed past his cheek; then with a whip it was gone.

He rolled over, gave a strangled croak which woke the others. The undammed blood in his body ran riot, and the pain cut off sharply his incoherent babble of words. But, just before unconsciousness enshrouded him, he heard Les guffaw in the distance. 'Bloomin' pommy's gone raving mad or had a nightmare. Shouting something about snakes, wasn't he? Can't stand up to the sun—that's what's the matter with him.'

THE LOST MINES IN THE GREEN HELL

Lt.Colonel P. H. Fawcett

For long, Africa was regarded as the 'Dark Continent', but such a title could equally have been given to South America, with its fever-haunted jungles, thirty-foot anacondas, and savage tribes that hunted with poisoned arrows. Fawcett was drawn by those perilous, mysterious lands partly because of legends of ancient, abandoned cities, rich in the treasure of strange civilizations. He became a legend himself, for on his last expedition in 1925 he disappeared without trace in the wilds of Brazil. His fate remains a mystery to this day, in spite of various expeditions that searched for him. One legend current for a time was that he had been captured by an unknown Indian tribe who appointed him as their god. The story he tells here, based on old Portuguese documents, is an indication of the fascination he always felt for the dangerous haunts where eventually he, too, met his fate.

When Diego Alvarez struggled landwards through the Atlantic swell in a welter of wreckage from the disintegrating caravel, it was to land, exhausted, on a shore absolutely unknown to this sixteenth-century Portuguese. Only twenty-four years previously Columbus had discovered the New World and fired the imaginations of Iberian adventurers. The dawn of knowledge was only just breaking after the dark night of the Middle Ages; the world in its entirety was yet a mystery, and each venture to probe it disclosed new wonders. The border between myth and reality was not fixed, and the adventurer saw strange sights with an eye distorted by superstition.

Here, on the coast of Brazil where Bahia now stands, anything might exist. Behind the forest's edge on top of those cliffs were surely to be found wonderful things, and he—Diego Alvarez—would be the first of his race to set eyes on them. There might be dangers from the natives of the country—perhaps even those weird people, half human, half

91

monster, who, tradition had it, lived in this land—but they had to be faced if he was to find food and water. The spirit of the pioneer had driven him to join the ill-fated voyage; it spurred him on, and nothing short of death could stop him.

The place where he came ashore, sole survivor from the wreck, was in the territory of the cannibal Tupinambas. Perhaps he escaped being eaten by reason of his strangeness; perhaps his captors considered it a triumph over neighbouring tribes to display their captive alive. For his salvation the Portuguese had principally to thank an Indian girl named Paraguassu, the Pocahontas of South America, who took a fancy to him and became his wife—ultimately the favourite among several.

For many years the Portuguese mariner lived with the Indians. A number of his countrymen came to Brazil, and he was able to establish friendly relations between them and the savages. Finally he managed to bring Paraguassu into the fold of the Church, and a sister of hers married another Portuguese adventurer. The child of her sister's marriage, Melchoir Dias Moreyra, spent most of his life with the Indians, and was known by them as Muribeca. He discovered many mines, and accumulated vast quantities of silver, gold and precious stones, which were worked by the skilful Tapuya tribes into so wonderful a treasure that the early European colonists were filled with envy.

Muribeca had a son called Roberio Dias, who as a lad was familiar with the mines where his father's vast wealth originated. About 1610 Roberio Dias approached the Portuguese King, Dom Pedro II, with an offer to hand over the mines in exchange for the title of Marquis das Minas. He showed a rich specimen of silver-bearing ore and temptingly promised more silver than there was iron at Bilbao. He was only partly believed, but the royal greed for treasure was strong enough to cause a patent to be drawn up for the marquisate.

If Roberio Dias thought he would leave the court a marquis he was mistaken. Old Dom Pedro II was too cunning for that. The patent was sealed and delivered to a commission entrusted to hand it over only after the mines had been disclosed. But Dias in his turn had suspicions. He was not one to trust blindly to the King's faith. While the expedition was some distance from Bahia he managed to persuade the officer in command of the commission to open the envelope and allow him to see the patent. He found that he was down for a military commission as captain, and no more—not a word about the marquisate!

That settled it. Dias refused to hand over the mines, so the enraged officer took him back by force to Bahia, where he was flung into prison. Here he remained for two years, and then he was allowed to buy his freedom for 9,000 crowns. In 1622 he died, and the secret of the mines was never disclosed. Diego Alvarez had been dead for a long time; Muribeca himself had gone, no Indian would talk even under the most frightful tortures, so Dom Pedro was left to curse his ill-judged deceit and read over again and again the official reports of the assays made of Roberio Dias's specimens.

The secret of the mines was lost, but for years expeditions scoured the country in an effort to locate them. As failure succeeded failure, belief in their existence died away to survive only as myth, yet there were always some hardy souls ready to brave hostile savages and slow starvation for the chance of discovering a New Potosi.

The region beyond the São Francisco River was as unknown to the Portuguese colonists of those times as the forests of the Gongugy are to the Brazilians of today. Exploration was too difficult. Not only was it too much to contend with hordes of wild Indians shooting poisoned arrows from impenetrable cover, but food was not available to provide for an expedition large enough to protect itself from attack. Yet one after another ventured it, and more often than not was never heard of again. They called these expeditions *Bandeiras*, or Flags, for they were officially sponsored, accompanied by government troops, and usually by a contingent of missionaries. Occasionally civilians banded together for the purpose. armed a number of Negro slaves, enlisted tame Indians as guides, and disappeared into the Sertao (bush) for years at a time, if not for ever.

If you are romantically minded—and most of us are, I think—you have in the foregoing the background for a story so fascinating that I know none to compare. I myself came upon it in an old document still preserved at Rio de Janeiro, and, in the light of evidence gleaned from many quarters, believe it implicitly. I am not going to offer a literal translation of the strange account given in the document—the crabbed Portuguese script is broken in several places—but the story begins in

1753, when a native of Minas Gerais, whose name has not been preserved, decided to make a search for the Lost Mines of Muribeca.

Franciso Raposo—I must identify him by some name—was not to be deterred by wild beasts, venomous snakes, savages and insects from attempting to enrich himself and his followers as the Spaniards in Peru and Mexico had done only two centuries before. They were a hardy lot, those old pioneers—superstitious, perhaps, but when gold called all obstacles were forgotten.

It was always difficult to take cargo animals through the trackless hinterland. There were numerous rivers and bogs everywhere; pasture was coarse, and the continuous attacks of vampire bats soon finished the animals off. Climate ranged from very cold to extreme heat, and total drought would be followed by days of sheer deluge, so that a fair amount of equipment had to be carried. Yet Raposo and his band gave little consideration to such drawbacks, and set out hopefully into the wilds.

Exactly where they went I have only lately discovered. It was roughly northwards. There were no maps of the country in those days, and no member of the party knew anything about land navigation, so the clues in the record they left are entirely unreliable. Indians accompanied them from point to point and suggested the routes taken, otherwise they merely wandered into the unknown and left it to fortune to bring them to the coveted objective.

In the manner of all pioneers, they lived on what fish and game they could secure, and on fruit and vegetables pilfered from Indian plantations or begged from friendly tribes. It was thin living, for game is timid in the South American wilderness, but men lived more simply in those days and consequently their endurance was greater. Raposo, his compatriots, and their black slaves survived to continue their wanderings for ten years. Not counting the Indians who joined them from time to time and who would vanish when it suited them, the party was about eighteen strong. Perhaps that was the secret of their survival, for the usual *Bandeiras* numbered at least five hundred, and there is a record of one 1,400 strong, not a single member of which ever returned! Few might live where many would starve.

The time came when the party was travelling eastward again, towards the coast settlements, tired of this seemingly endless wandering, and disheartened by their failure to locate the lost mines. Raposo was almost ready to believe them a myth, and his companions had long ago decided that no such mines existed. They had come through swamp and bush country when jagged mountains showed up ahead, beyond a grassy plain broken by thin belts of green forest. Raposo in his narrative describes them poetically, 'They seemed to reach the ethereal regions and to serve as a throne for the wind and the stars themselves.' Anyone who has passed months on end in the monotonous flatness of the plains will appreciate his rhapsody.

These were no ordinary mountains. As the party came nearer, the side lit up in flame, for it had been raining and the setting sun was reflected from wet rocks rich in crystals and that slightly opaque quartz which is so common in this part of Brazil. To the eager explorers they seemed to be studded with gems. Streams leaped from rock to rock, and over the crest of the ridge a rainbow formed, as though to hint that treasure was to be found at its feet.

'An omen!' cried Raposo. 'See! We have found the treasure house of the great Muribeca!'

Night came down and forced them to camp before reaching the foot of those wonderful mountains; and next morning, when the sun came up from behind them, the crags appeared black and menacing. Enthusiasm waned; but there is always something fascinating about mountains for the explorer. Who knows what may be seen from the top-most ridge?

To the eyes of Raposo and his comrades their height was vast, and when they reached them it was to find sheer, unscalable precipices. All day they struggled over boulders and crevices, seeking a way up those glassy sides. Rattlesnakes abounded—and there is no remedy for the bite of the Brazilian species. Wearied by the hard going and constant vigilance to avoid these snakes, Raposo called a halt.

'Three leagues we have come and still no way up,' he said. 'It would be better to return to our old trail and find a way northwards. What do you say?'

'Camp!' was the reply. 'Let's camp. We've had enough for one day. Tomorrow we can return.'

'Very well,' answered the leader; and then to two of the men, 'You, José and Manoel—off you go to find wood for the fire!'

95

Camp was pitched and the party was resting when confused shouting and a crashing in the bush brought them to their feet, guns in hand. José and Manoel burst into view.

'*Patrao, Patrao!*' they cried. 'We've found it—the way up!'

Searching for firewood in the low scrub they had seen a dead tree at the edge of a small wooded creek. This was the best fuel to be had, and they were making their way towards it when a deer sprang up on the other side of the creek and disappeared beyond a corner of the cliff. Unslinging their guns the two men followed as quickly as they could, for here was meat enough to last them several days.

The animal had vanished, but beyond the outcropping of rock they came on a deep cleft in the face of the precipice, and saw that it was possible to climb up through it to the summit. Deer and firewood were forgotten in the excitement.

They broke camp at once, shouldered their packs, and set off with Manoel leading. With ejaculations of wonder they entered the crevice in single file, to find that it widened somewhat inside. It was rough going, but here and there were traces of what looked like old paving, and in places the sheer walls of the cleft seemed to bear the almost obliterated marks of tools. Clusters of rock crystals and frothy masses of quartz gave them the feeling of having entered a fairyland, and in the dim light filtering down through the tangled mass of creepers overhead all the magic of their first impressions returned.

The climb was so difficult that three hours passed before they emerged torn and breathless on a ledge high above the surrounding plain. From here to the ridge was clear ground, and soon they were standing shoulder to shoulder at the top, gazing, dumb with amazement, at the view spread out below them.

There at their feet, about four miles away, was a huge city.

Immediately they flung themselves down and edged back behind the cover of rocks, hoping that the inhabitants had not seen their distant figures against the sky, for this might be a colony of the hated Spaniards. Then again, it might be such a city as Cuzco, the ancient capital of the Incas in Peru, inhabited by a race of highly civilized people still holding out against the encroachments of the European invaders. Was it perhaps a Portuguese colony? It might be a stronghold of the Orizes Procazes, remnant of the mysterious Tapuyas, who showed unmistakable signs

There at their feet, about four miles away, was a huge city.

of having once been a highly civilized people.

Raposo wriggled up to the crest once more and, still lying flat, looked around him. The ridge stretched as far as he could see from south-east to north-west, and away over to the north, hazy with distance, was unbroken forest. In the immediate foreground was an extensive plain patched with green and brown, broken in places by shining pools of water. He could see where a continuation of the rocky trail they had ascended dropped down the side of the mountain to vanish below the range of vision, appearing again and winding over the plain to lose itself in the vegetation surrounding the city walls. No sign of life could he see. No smoke arose in the still air; no sound broke the utter silence.

He gave a quick sign to his followers, and one by one they crawled over the ridge and dropped down beyond the skyline to the shelter of scrub and rock. Then they made their way cautiously down the mountainside to the valley floor, and left the trail for a camp site near a small stream of clear water.

No fires were lit that night, and the men talked in whispers. They were awed by the sight of civilization after those long years in the wilds, and by no means confident of their safety. Two hours before nightfall Raposo had sent off two Portuguese and four Negroes to reconnoitre and find out what sort of people lived in this mysterious place. Nervously the rest of the party awaited their return, and every forest noise—every insect song and whisper of the foliage—was sinister. But the scouts had nothing to tell when they came back. Lack of cover had kept them from venturing too near the city, but no sign of occupation had they seen. The Indians of the party were as mystified as Raposo and his followers. By nature superstitious, certain parts of the country to them were taboo, and they were filled with alarm.

Raposo, however, was able to prevail on one of the Indians to scout forward single-handed after sunrise next morning. No one had slept much during the night, and their curiosity about the Indian's fate kept them from resting in the more comfortable light of day. At midday he crept back into camp, obviously terrified, and insisting that the city was uninhabited. It was too late to push forward that day, so they spent another restless night listening to the strange forest sounds around them, ready to face some unknown danger at any moment.

Early next morning Raposo sent ahead an advance guard of four Indians and followed towards the city with the rest of the party. As they came near the overgrown walls the Indians met them with the same story—the place was deserted—and so with less caution they followed the trail to an entrance under three arches formed of huge stone slabs. So impressive was this cyclopean structure—similar, probably, to much that can yet be seen at Sacsahuaman in Peru—that no man dared speak, but slipped by the blackened stones as stealthily as a cat.

High above the central arch characters of some sort were graven deeply into the weatherworn stone. Raposo, uneducated though he was, could see that this was no modern writing. A feeling of vast age brooded over everything, and it took a distinct effort for him to issue in a hoarse, unnatural voice the orders to advance.

The arches were still in a fair state of preservation, but one or two of the colossal uprights had twisted slightly on their bases. The men passed through and entered what had once been a wide street, but littered now with broken pillars and blocks of masonry rank with the parasitic vegetation of the tropics. On either side were two-storeyed houses built of great blocks fitting together with mortarless joins of almost incredible accuracy, the porticos, narrow above and wide below, decorated with elaborate carvings of what they took to be demons.

The descriptions, coming from men who had never seen Cuzco and Sacsahuaman, or the other wonder cities of old Peru—which were incredibly ancient when the Incas first came upon them—cannot be lightly dismissed. What they saw and related tallies closely with much that we can still see today. Uneducated adventurers could hardly invent an account so closely corroborated by the cyclopean remains now familiar to so many.

There was ruin everywhere, but many buildings were roofed with great slabs still in position. Those of the party who dared to enter the dark interiors and raise their voices ran out at the echoes flung back at them from walls and vaulted ceilings. It was impossible to say if any remnants of furnishings remained, for in most cases inner walls had collapsed, covering the floors with debris, and the bat droppings of centuries formed a thick carpet underfoot. So old was this place that perishables such as furniture and textiles must have disintegrated long ago.

Huddled together like a flock of frightened sheep, the men proceeded down the street and came to a vast square. Here in the centre was a huge column of black stone, and upon it the effigy, in perfect preservation, of a man with one hand on his hip and the other pointing towards the north. The majesty of this statue struck deep into the hearts of the Portuguese and they crossed themselves reverently. Carved obelisks of the same black stone, partially ruined, stood at each corner of the square, while running the length of one side was a building so magnificent in design and decoration that it must have been a palace. The walls and roof had collapsed in many places, but its great square columns were still intact. A broad flight of ruined stone steps led up and into a wide hall, where traces of colour still clung to the frescoes and carvings. Bats in countless thousands winged in circles through the dim chambers and the acrid reek of their droppings was suffocating.

The explorers were glad to get out into the clean air. The figure of a youth was carved over what seemed to be the principal doorway. It portrayed a beardless figure, naked from the waist up, with shield in hand and a band across one shoulder. The head was crowned with what looked to them like a wreath of laurel, judging by Grecian statuary they had seen in Portugal. Below were inscribed characters remarkably like those of ancient Greece. Raposo copied them on a tablet and reproduced them in his narrative.

Opposite the palace was the ruin of another huge building, evidently a temple. Eroded carvings of figures, animals and birds covered the walls that remained, and over the portal were more characters which again were copied as faithfully as Raposo or one of his followers was capable of doing.

Beyond the square and the main street the city lay in complete ruin, in some places actually buried under mounds of earth on which not a blade of grass or other vegetation grew. Here and there were gaping chasms, and when the explorers dropped rocks into these not a sound came up to indicate bottom. There was little doubt now what had devastated the place. The Portuguese knew what earthquakes were and what destruction they could do. Here whole buildings had been swallowed, leaving perhaps only a few carved blocks to show where they had stood. It was not difficult to imagine something of the awful cataclysm that had laid waste this glorious place, tumbled columns and

100

blocks weighing perhaps fifty tons and more, and that had destroyed in a matter of minutes the painstaking labour of a thousand years.

The far side of the square terminated in a river about thirty yards wide, flowing straight and easily from the north-west and vanishing in distant forest. At one time a fine promenade had bordered on the river, but the masonry was now broken up and much had subsided into the water. On the other side of the river were fields that were once cultivated, still covered with abundant coarse grass and a carpet of flowers. Rice had propagated and thrived in the shallow swamps all about, and here the waters were alive with duck.

Raposo and his party forded the river and crossed the swamps towards an isolated building about a quarter of a mile away, and the ducks scarcely troubled to move from their path. The building was approached by a flight of steps in stone of many colours, for it stood on a rise and its frontage extended for two hundred and fifty paces. The imposing entrance, behind a square monolith with deeply engraved characters, opened into a vast hall where carvings and decorations had resisted the depredations of time in an amazing manner. They found fifteen chambers opening off the great hall, and in each was a carved serpent's head with a thin stream of water still flowing from it into the open mouth of another stone serpent beneath. The place could have been the college of a priesthood.

Deserted and ruined the city was, but its environs of rice fields provided far more food for the explorers than they could find in the virgin forest. It is therefore not surprising that in spite of their awe of the place none of the men was anxious to leave it. Their fear gave way to a lust for treasure, and this increased when João Antonio—the only member of the party to be mentioned by name in the document—found a small gold coin in the rubble. On one face it bore the effigy of a youth on his knees, and on the other a bow, a crown and a musical instrument of some sort. The place must be full of gold, they told themselves; when the inhabitants fled they would have taken only the things most necessary for their survival.

The document hints at the finding of treasure, but no details are given. It may well be that the heavy aura of calamity hanging over the place was in the long run too much for the nerves of these superstitious pioneers. Perhaps the millions of bats deterred them. At any rate, it is

101

unlikely that they brought any quantity of it out with them, for they still had a formidable journey ahead if they were ever to see civilization again, and none of them would have been anxious to burden himself with more equipment than he already had.

Gathering rice from the swamps and hunting duck—if hunting it could be called—were perilous. Anacondas big enough to kill a man were common; and poisonous snakes, attracted by the game, swarmed everywhere, feeding not only on the birds but also on jerboas—'rats jumping like fleas', as the narrator describes them. Wild dogs, large grey brutes as big as wolves, haunted the plains, yet not a man would sleep within the city. Camp was pitched just beyond the gate where they first entered, and from here they watched at sunset the legions of bats emerging from the great buildings to disperse in the gloaming with a dry rustling of wings like the first breath of an approaching storm. By day the sky was black with swallows, greedy for the prolific insect life.

Franciso Raposo had no idea where they were, but at last decided to follow the river through the forest, hoping that his Indians would remember the landmarks when he returned with a properly equipped expedition to comb the wealth out of these ruins. Fifty miles down they came to a mighty waterfall, and in an adjoining cliff face were found distinct signs of mine workings. Here they tarried longer. Game was plentiful, several of the men were down with fever and the Indians were nervous about the possibility of hostile tribes in the vicinity. Below the fall the river broadened out into a series of swampy lagoons, as these South American rivers have a way of doing.

Investigation proved the suspected mineshafts to be holes they had no means of exploring, but at their mouths lay scattered about a quantity of rich silver ore. Here and there were caves hewn out of the cliff by hand, some of them sealed off by great stone slabs engraved with strange glyphs. The caves might have been tombs of the city's monarchs and high priests. The men tried in vain to move the stone slabs.

The adventurers pictured themselves as rich men and agreed to say nothing to anybody except the Viceroy, to whom Raposo owed a debt of gratitude. They would return here as soon as possible, take possession of the mines, and remove all treasure from the city.

In the meantime a scouting party had been sent out to explore farther down river. After traversing the lagoons and backwaters for nine days they caught a glimpse of a canoe paddled by two 'white people' with long black hair and dressed in some sort of clothing. They fired a shot to attract attention, but the canoe made off and vanished from view. Weary of the fatiguing business of making wide detours around the swamps, and afraid to continue farther down with so small a party, they returned to the fall.

Raposo felt the need of caution now that he and his followers had fortunes within their grasp. He had no wish to risk an encounter with hostile Indians and so he struck off eastwards. After some months of hard travel they reached the bank of the São Francisco River, crossed from there to the Paraguassu, and at length came to Bahia. From here he sent to the Viceroy, Don Luiz Peregrino de Carvalho Menezes de Athayde, the document from which this story is taken.

Nothing was done by the Viceroy, and one cannot say if Raposo returned to his discovery or not. At all events, he was never heard of again. For nearly a century the document was pigeon-holed at Rio de Janeiro, till the then State Government turned it up and commissioned a young priest to investigate. This exploration was entirely unsuccessful, apparently carried out with little intelligence.

It was difficult for an administration steeped in the narrow bigotry of an all-powerful Church to give much credence to such a thing as an old civilization. Egypt in those days was still a mystery, and the ecclesiastical spirit which wilfully destroyed the priceless records of Peru and Mexico was rife as ever.

I know that Raposo's lost city is not the only one of its kind. The late British Consul at Rio was taken to such a place in 1913 by a half-caste Indian; but it was a city far more easily reached, in non-mountainous country, and completely buried in forest. It too was distinguished by the remains of a statue on a great black pedestal in the middle of a square. Unfortunately a cloudburst carried away their cargo animal and they had to return immediately to avoid starvation.

There are other lost cities besides these two; and there exists another remnant of an old civilization, its people degenerate now, but still preserving records of a forgotten past in mummies, parchments and engraved metal plates. It is such a place as described in the story, but

103

far less ruined by earthquakes—and very difficult to reach. The Jesuits knew of it, and so did a Frenchman who in the present century made several unsuccessful attempts to reach it. So too did a certain Englishman, much travelled in the interior, who had learned of it from an old document in Jesuit keeping. He was a victim of advanced cancer, and either died of it or was lost.

I am probably the only other person who knows the secret.

THE RAILWAY RAID IN GEORGIA

John Buchan

The time is the spring of 1862, the second year of the American Civil War. The scene is the state of Tennessee; the Confederates are concentrating at Corinth, Mississippi, and the two Northern forces of Grant and Buell are moving on that spot. A month before Grant had won the important action of Fort Donelson. A month later he was to win the Battle of Shiloh.

In Buell's army was General O. M. Mitchel, commanding the Northern forces in middle Tennessee and protecting Nashville with a force of some seventeen thousand men. Now, President Lincoln especially desired that eastern Tennessee should be cleared of the enemy, since it was one of the latter's chief supply grounds. General Mitchel believed that Corinth would soon fall, and that the next movement would be eastward towards Chattanooga, that key point on the Tennessee River which was later the scene of one of Grant's most famous victories. He thought, rightly, that if he could press into the enemy's country and occupy strategic points ahead, he would pave the way for Grant's march eastward.

On 8 April the Northerners won the battle of Pittsburg Landing. Next day Mitchel marched south from Shelbyville into Alabama and seized Huntsville. From there he sent a detachment westward to open up communication with the Northern troops at Pittsburg Landing. On the same day he himself took another detachment seventy miles by rail and arrived without difficulty within thirty miles of Chattanooga, two hours from the key position in the west. There, however, he stuck fast, and the capture of Chattanooga was delayed for two years. He failed because another plan failed—the plan of this story.

Chattanooga at that moment was practically without a garrison; but in Georgia there were ample Confederate troops, and the Georgia

State Railway and the East Tennessee Railway could bring them up in great force at short notice. If Mitchel was to seize and hold Chattanooga these lines must be cut for long enough to enable him to consolidate his position. Now, in his army was a certain spy of the name of James J. Andrews, one of these daring adventurers who, in a civil war of volunteers, many of whom were as yet without regular uniforms, could perform exploits impossible in a normal campaign. Andrews conceived the idea of a raid on the Confederate railways, and Mitchel approved. Before he left Shelbyville he authorized Andrews to take twenty-four men, enter the enemy's territory and burn the bridges on the vital railways.

The men were selected from three Ohio regiments, and told only that they were required for secret and dangerous service. They exchanged their uniforms for the ordinary dress worn by civilians in the South, and carried no arms except revolvers. On 7 April, by the roadside a mile east of Shelbyville, in the late evening, they met Andrews, who told them his plan. In small detachments of three or four they were to go east into the Cumberland Mountains and work southward, and on the evening of the third day rendezvous with Andrews at Marietta in Georgia, more than two hundred miles distant. If anyone asked them questions they were to declare that they were Kentuckians going to join the Confederate army.

The weather was bad and the travellers were much delayed by swollen streams. This led Andrews to believe that Mitchel's column would also be delayed, so he sent secret word to the different groups that the attempt would be postponed one day, from Friday to Saturday, 12 April. Of the little party one lost his road and never arrived at the destination; two reached Marietta, but missed the rendezvous; and two were captured and forced into the Confederate army. Twenty, however, early on the morning of Saturday, 12 April, met in Andrews' room at the Marietta Hotel.

They had travelled from Chattanooga as ordinary passengers on the Georgia State Railway. The sight of that railway impressed them with the difficulties of their task, for it was crowded with trains and soldiers. In order to do their work they must capture an engine, but the station where the capture was to be made—Big Shanty—had recently been made a Confederate camp. Their job was, therefore, to seize an engine in a camp with soldiers all round them, to run it from one to two hundred miles through enemy country, and to dodge or overpower any trains they might meet—no small undertaking for a score of men. Some were in favour of abandoning the enterprise, but Andrews stuck stubbornly to his purpose. He gave his final instructions, and the twenty proceeded to the ticket office to purchase tickets for different stations on the line to Chattanooga.

For eight miles they rode in comfort as passengers, till at Big Shanty they saw the Confederate tents in the misty morning. It had been a drizzling April dawn, and a steady rain was now beginning. The train stopped at Big Shanty for breakfast, and this gave them their chance, for the conductor, the engine-driver, and most of the passengers descended for their meal, leaving the train unguarded.

Among the twenty were men who understood the stoking and driving of railway engines, and it did not take long to uncouple three empty vans, the locomotive, and the tender. Brown and Knight, the two engineers, and the fireman climbed into the cab, and the rest clambered into the rear goods van—no easy job, for the cars stood on a high bank. A sentry with rifle in hand stood not a dozen feet from the engine, watching the whole proceedings, but no move was made until it was too late. Andrews gave the signal, the wheels slipped at first on the greasy metals, and then the train moved forward; and before the uproar in the station behind began it had gathered speed.

The first and worst problem was the passing of trains coming from the north. There were two trains on the time-table which had to be passed at certain stations, and there was also a local goods train not scheduled, which might be anywhere. Andrews hoped to avoid the danger of collision by running according to the schedule of the train he had captured, until the goods train was passed, and then to increase to topmost speed till he reached the Oostenaula and Chickamauga bridges, burn them and pass on through Chattanooga to Mitchel as he moved up from Huntsville. He hoped to reach his chief early in the afternoon.

It was a perfectly feasible plan, and it would almost certainly have been carried out but for that fatal day's delay. On Friday, the day originally fixed, all the trains had been up to time, and the weather had been good; but on that Saturday, as luck would have it, the whole railway was in disorder, every train was late, and two 'extras' had been put on, of which the leader had no notion. Had he known this, even a man of his audacity would scarcely have started, and the world would have been the poorer by the loss of a stirring tale.

The party had to make frequent stops, particularly between stations, to tear up the track, cut the telegraph wires, and load on sleepers to be used for bridge burning; and also at wayside stations to take on wood and water. At the latter Andrews bluffed the officials by telling them that he was one of General Beauregard's officers, and was running a powder train through to Beauregard at Corinth. Unfortunately he had no proper instruments for pulling up the rails, and it was important to keep to the schedule of the captured train, so they tore light-heartedly past towns and villages, trusting to luck, and exhilarated by the successful start of their wild adventure.

At a station called Etowah they found the 'Yonah', an old engine owned by an iron company, standing with steam up; but their mind was all on the local goods train, so they left it untouched. Thirty miles on from Big Shanty they reached Kingston, where a branch line entered from the town of Rome. On the branch a train was waiting for the mail—that is to say, their captured train—and Andrews learned that the local goods was expected immediately; so he ran on to a side track, and waited for it.

Presently it arrived, and to the consternation of the little party it carried a red flag to show that another train was close behind it. Andrews marched boldly across to its conductor and asked what was the meaning of the railway being blocked in this fashion when he had orders to take the powder straight through to General Beauregard? In reply he was told that Mitchel had captured Huntsville and was said to be marching on Chattanooga, and that everything was being cleared out of that town. Andrews ordered him to move his train down the line out of the way, and he obeyed.

It seemed an eternity to the party before the 'extra' arrived, and to their dismay when it turned up they saw that it bore another red flag. The reason given was that it was too heavy for one engine and had therefore to be made up into two sections. So began another anxious wait. The little band—Andrews with the engine-drivers and fireman in the cab, and the rest taking the place of Beauregard's ammunition in the goods vans—had to preserve composure as best they could, with three trains clustered round them and every passenger in the three extremely curious about the mysterious powder train into which the morning mail had been transformed. For one hour and five minutes they waited at Kingston, the men in the goods vans being warned by Andrews to be ready to fight in case of need. He himself kept close to the station in case some mischief-maker should send an inquiring telegram down the line. At long last came the second half of the local, and as soon as it passed the end of their side track the adventurers moved on.

But the alarm had now been raised behind them. From the midst of the confusion at Big Shanty two men set out on foot along the track to make some effort to capture the Northerners. They were railwaymen— one the conductor of the train, W. A. Fuller, and the other a foreman of the Atlanta railway machine shops, called Anthony Murphy. They found a hand-car and pushed forward on it till they reached Etowah, where they realized that the line had been cut by pitching headforemost down the embankment into a ditch.

A little thing like this did not dismay them, and at Etowah they found the 'Yonah', the iron company's old locomotive which, as we know, was standing with steam up. They got on board, filled it up with soldiers who happened to be near, and started off at full speed for Kingston, where they were convinced they would catch the filibusters. The 'Yonah' actually entered Kingston station four minutes after Andrews had started, and was of course immediately confronted with the three long trains facing the wrong way. It would have taken too long to move them, so the 'Yonah' was abandoned, and Murphy uncoupled the engine and one coach of the Rome train, and continued the chase. It was now anyone's race. Andrews and his merry men were only a few minutes ahead.

Four miles north from Kingston the little party again stopped and cut the wires. They started to take up a rail and were pulling at the loosened end when to their consternation they heard behind them the whistle of an engine. They managed to break the rail and then clambered in and moved on. At the next station, Adairsville, they found a mixed goods and passenger train waiting, and learned that there was an express on the road. It was a crazy risk to take, but they dared not delay, so they started at a terrific speed for the next station, Calhoun, hoping to reach it before the express, which was late, could arrive.

They did the nine miles to Calhoun in less than nine minutes, and saw in front of them the express just starting. Hearing their whistle it backed, and enabled them to take a side track, but it stopped in such a manner as to close the other end of the switch. There stood the two trains side by side almost touching each other. Naturally questions were asked, and Andrews was hard put to it to explain. He told the powder story, and demanded in the name of General Beauregard that the other train should at once let him pass. With some difficulty its conductor was persuaded, and moved forward.

They were saved by the broken rail. The pursuit saw it in time and reversed their engine. Leaving the soldiers behind, Fuller and Murphy ran along the track till they met the train which Andrews had passed at Adairsville. They made it back in pursuit, and at Adairsville dropped the coaches and continued with only the locomotive and tender, both loaded with a further complement of armed soldiers. They thought that their quarry was safe at Calhoun, but they reached that place a minute or two after Andrews had moved out.

Everything now depended on whether the band of twenty could make another gap in the track in time, for if they could the road was clear before them to Chattanooga. A few minutes ahead of them was the Oostenaula bridge, and if that could be burned they would soon be safe in Mitchel's camp.

But the mischief was that they had no proper tools, and the taking up of the rails was terribly slow. Once again they heard the whistle of a locomotive behind them and saw their pursuer with armed men aboard. Another minute would have removed the rail, and their victory would have been assured; but they could do nothing more than bend it, and were compelled to hurry back to their engine.

Now began one of the most astounding hunts on record. At all costs Andrews must gain a little time so as to set fire to the Oostenaula bridge; so he dropped first one car and then another. The pursuing engine, however, simply picked them up and pushed them ahead of it. There was no time to do anything at the bridge. Over its high trestles they tore, with Fuller and his soldiers almost within rifle shot.

Soon it appeared that there was no difference in the pace of the two

On went the chase, mile after mile . . .

engines. The Confederates could not overtake the filibusters, and
Fuller's policy was therefore to keep close behind so as to prevent
Andrews damaging the track and taking on wood and water. Both
engines were driven to their last decimal of power, and Andrews
succeeded in keeping his distance. But he was constantly delayed, for
he was obliged to cut the telegraph wires after every station he passed,
in order that an alarm might not be sent ahead; and he could not stop
long enough to tear up rails.

All that man could do in the way of obstruction he did, for at all
costs he must gain enough ground to destroy the Chickamauga
bridges. He broke off the end of their last goods van and dropped it and
various sleepers behind him, and this sufficiently checked the pursuit
to enable him on two occasions to take in wood and water. More than
once his party almost succeeded in lifting a rail, but each time Fuller
got within rifle range before the work was completed. Through it all
it rained, a steady deluge. The day before had been clear, with a high
wind, and a fire would have been quick to start, but on that Saturday,
to burn a bridge would take time and much fuel.

On went the chase, mile after mile, past little forgotten stations and quiet villages, round perilous curves, and over culverts and embankments which had never before known such speed. Hope revived whenever the enemy was lost sight of behind a curve, but whenever the line straightened the smoke appeared again in the distance, and on their ears fell the ominous scream of his whistle. To the men, strung to a desperate tension, every minute seemed an hour.

If the Northerners' courage was superb, so also was the pursuit's. Several times Fuller only escaped wreck by a hair-breadth. At one point a rail placed across the track at a curve was not seen until the train was upon it, when, said Fuller, 'the engine seemed to bounce altogether off the track, and to alight again on the rails by a miracle.' A few of the soldiers lost their nerve and would have given up the chase, but the stubborn resolution of their leader constrained them.

Some of Andrews' party now proposed that they should turn and ambush the enemy, getting into close quarters so that their revolvers would be a match for his guns. This plan would probably have succeeded, but Andrews still hoped to gain sufficient ground to achieve his main purpose; and he feared, too, that the country ahead might have been warned by a telegram sent round to Chattanooga by way of Richmond. He thought his only chance was to stake everything on speed. Close to the town of Dalton he stopped again to cut wires and confuse the track. A Confederate regiment was encamped a hundred yards away, but, assuming that the train was part of the normal traffic, the men scarcely lifted their eyes to look at it. Fuller had written a telegram to Chattanooga and dropped a man with orders to send it. Part of the telegram got through before the wires were cut and created a panic in that town. Meantime, Andrews' supply of fuel was getting very low, and it was clear that unless he could delay the pursuit long enough to take in more, his journey would soon come to an end.

Beyond Dalton the adventurers made their last efforts to take up a rail, but, as they had no tools except an iron bar, the coming of the enemy compelled them to desist. Beyond that was a long tunnel which they made no attempt to damage. Andrews saw that the situation was getting desperate, and he played his last card.

He increased speed so that he gained some considerable distance. Then the side and end boards of the last goods van were broken up, fuel was piled upon it, and fire brought from the engine. A long covered bridge lay a little ahead, and by the time they reached it the van was fairly on fire. It was uncoupled in the middle of the bridge, and they awaited the issue. If this device was successful there was sufficient steam in their boiler to carry them to the next woodyard.

But the device did not succeed. Before the bridge had caught fire Fuller was upon them. He dashed right through the smoke and drove the burning car before him to the next side track.

Left with very little fuel and with no obstructions to drop on the track, the position of the adventurers was now hopeless. In a few minutes their engine would come to a standstill. Their only chance was to leave it and escape. The wisest plan would probably have been to desert the train in a body, move northward through the mountains by tracks which could not be followed by cavalry, and where there were no telegraphs. But Andrews thought that they should separate. He ordered the men to jump from the engine one by one and disperse in the woods. So ended in failure a most gallant enterprise.

Melancholy is the conclusion of the tale. Ignorant of the country and far from their friends, the fugitives were easily hunted down. Several were captured the same day, and all but two within the week. As the adventurers had been in civil dress inside the enemy's lines they were regarded as spies, court-martialled, and Andrews and seven others condemned and executed. The advance of the Northern forces prevented the trial of the rest and, of the remainder, eight succeeded in making their escape from Atlanta in broad daylight, ultimately reaching the North. The others, who also made the attempt, were recaptured and held captive till March 1863, when they were exchanged for Confederate prisoners.

I know of few stories where the enterprise was at once so audacious and so feasible, where success turned upon such an infinity of delicate chances, and where it was missed by so slender a margin.

THE MIRACLE OF THE BLACK CANYON

Morley Roberts

In that part of British Columbia called the Dry Belt, where rain is seldom and scanty, the whole landscape looks barren and desolate.

The Black Canyon itself is not terrible or imposing. It is but a narrower space where the steep iron-bound banks are set close together; the rocks are not perpendicular, nor does a tormented river run at unfathomable depths beyond the sunlight. But about it is the very horror of dry barrenness—it is an unspeakable place of thirst. Not a tree gives a moment's shadow in the hot noon.

But in the sullen depths lay the gold of a world's generations, and men hungered, as they have always done, on the barren edge of the impossible, desiring the rainbow gold of a river of death.

On the north side of the canyon's upper end was a mighty bluff some three hundred feet high. At the very base of this bluff was a layer of sandstone soft enough to scoop out with a knife; under that again was a thin line of semi-crystalline fracture. In one place close to the swirling stream was a little hollow cave, in which it could be seen how the strata sloped to the river. When the stream was high the cave was hidden, but at a low stage it appeared black to those who looked across from the southern side.

A month before the miracle two men sat on the opposing bank, staring sombrely into the waters. 'This place is accursed,' said the younger of the two, 'and I feel like a damned spirit myself. We are cast out of the borders of the earth.'

The elder man, Harry Payne, smoked quietly. Yet even he kicked his heels against the rock on which he sat, and his brows were drawn down; his teeth clenched his pipe's heavy wooden mouthpiece.

'It's no good wailing and gnashing your teeth,' he answered; 'I don't, and I've more to draw me away than you. We must put the survey through somehow, and trust that a paradise will open up for us when the work's done.'

But the young fellow made queer, ugly faces.

'And in the meantime we must grit our teeth on alkali dust, and dig prickly pear spines out of our hands and feet, and oil the blisters on our noses, and thank God for giving us our beautiful work. Oh, Lord, what a fool a man is. Is it natural to work this way? By thunder, no! We take it on as we would old rye—just to get blind and not care. Then it's tumble into the blankets and sleep the sleep of the drugged. And next day again and again.'

He sprang up excitedly and pointed down into the river.

'And look, Quin—here, here right underneath us, there's enough gold to buy ease and power and peace for a man's long lifetime!'

'Boy,' said Quin solemnly, 'don't butt your brains out on the impossible. It's easier to rob the biggest bank in the States or out of them than to burgle here.'

But Harry lay down on his stomach, and stared into the river.

'If it were only mine—a little of it! I can see the gold at the bottom,' said he.

'It's all mixed with mud and sand,' answered Quin literally. 'You can see nothing. You'll be having the worst kind of gold-fever if you watch it. This is no sort of a place to get kinks in your brain. You mind yourself, boy. Think of something else. Come, let's go back to the camp and grub.'

Harry grunted uneasily, for he could hardly take his eyes from the selfish water.

They stumbled over the rocks to their white tents, and after dinner

115

they slept, and woke feeling slimy all over and bad in their mouths; and then they smoked and growled and cursed the long hot day down into the west. For the misery of idleness was on them all, and the thoughts of far pleasure came to embitter them. Their day of rest was no boon. Even as they prayed for it to come so they were glad to see it go.

It was the same to them all; whether to Quin and Harry Payne, the bosses, or to Shaw and Liston and Willis, the men, the time was a burden.

'We've been here for years in this hell of dust,' growled Willis. And the others snarled at him and reduced his exaggeration to exact days. They quarrelled and spoke sick words, for the alkali in their throats dried up kindness. Even Quin was hard put to it not to jump on their necks.

'Damn you, men, what's the good of taking it so? Be men—not snarling cayoots! Did you come across the mountains to look for a soft seat? And did you reckon that the land of the Chinook was all roses? D'ye think I'm having a lovely time.'

'Do you really reckon there's much gold in this all-fired canyon, Mr Quin?' asked Shaw, the youngest of the crowd.

But Harry Payne answered him, and as he spoke in a high key the greed of wealth crept into the haggard lines of his young face, and avarice puckered his bloodshot eyes.

'Gold? Why, man, it's full of it! And away down to the end of the Fraser Canyon it's one long gold-trap—one almighty sluice-box!'

He rose and walked up and down like a caged bear. He took his hat off and threw it down to catch the cooler evening air upon his brow.

They were all sitting round the camp-fire; even the Chinese cooks were close by, and each squatted on a skillet or on an inverted empty tomato can. As their idle eyes followed Payne almost mechanically, the flames gleamed on lean, brown faces. Overhead the cool stars shone; there was a heavenly breath of air coming from the north. But Payne walked back and forth, back and forth, muttering. Presently he broke out again.

'Oh boys, but just think of it! Just to dam this river and turn the stream——'

'Where?' asked Quin sardonically.

116

'Where—where?' said Payne, with irritation. 'Why, it's just a dream! Turn it back through the hills, cut a tunnel for it, and run it into the Columbia.'

'Up-end it by hand,' cried Shaw, laughing—'shove it into the Peace River and capsize the stuff out!'

But Payne was set heavily in his fixed mind. He dreamed of it and spoke in his dreams. In his spare time he sneaked off to the river and sat opposite the great bluff. And now his child-like religion came back to him. He carried a Bible in his pocket, and read it at intervals. And a big notion was born in his brain. It grew marvellously, like a gourd—it overshadowed obstacles; he walked in foreseen triumph and prayed happily to God. It ran out of him in words—he talked to himself. And then a bitter revulsion came.

'I'm a weak, miserable, and sinful wretch! I hate myself and this place! And it holds me; but even when we shift further I shall be crawling down here again. I shall end in the river. It draws me; moth and flame—moth and fire. Gold in it, and ease and rest.'

He put his hand to his head and screamed. 'Oh, this awful, awful sun —it's in my brain and burns!' He crawled to the dangerous verge, and scooped up water in his hat and cooled his head.

On the bank he prayed. 'Oh, almighty God, be merciful unto me, and let me look into the bottomless pit of it, where I see the gold—the gold. Dry it up as thou didst the Red Sea, to let me pass through out of this bloody Egypt. Thrust the hills into it.'

And, looking up, he called in the noonday sun to the glaring northern bluff as if it were alive and aware, itself a god. He made a fetish of it— myths sprang in his rotting mind like toadstools on sick earth at hot midnight.

'Fall down, fall down, and stay the river!'

That night some teams camped close by. At one o'clock in the morning he went out and sneaked two boxes of dynamite from under the cover of a wagon. He cached his find carefully, and when he crawled into the open tent he laughed silently at Quin's peaceful face turned to the quiet moon.

In the morning before breakfast he wrote a letter to a store-keeper in Yale. He went out to work cheerfully, and spoke no more of the gold hidden in the canyon. But he never looked at Quin, and spoke

117

hardly at all. On the fifth or sixth day a small parcel came for him, which he opened in secret. He put its contents in his breast-pocket, and grinned with joy.

But he trembled very strangely, and his hands shook. In all his limbs came a fleeting aura, as though something breathed upon him.

That very night he stole out of the quiet moonlit camp, and finding the hidden boxes, he carried them, slung together, with great labour up the river bank. He shook so much and his limbs seemed so little under his control that he had to rest every hundred yards; but at last he came to a broader, quieter portion of the stream across which a taut rope was stretched. A crazy boat built by some man as a first attempt lay in a rocky recess. It was made fast to the rope by sliding rings, and could be pulled across the dangerous ferry by another rope that lay in the water, while a coil made fast to the shore from which it started paid itself out of the stern as it went.

Payne put his dynamite in the boat and pulled himself across the swirling stream. He sang and chattered and laughed as he pulled. When he came to the further shore he took his burden again and stumbled painfully down stream under the high, round moon, which gave him his own shadow for a companion to which he could talk. And soon the great bluff loomed up, and then it hung over him, and blotted out the moon, blinding him for a minute with opaque shadows that grew transparent once more for his trembling, doubtful feet. He laid down his heavy burden and sought for the little cave, which looked like a black patch at noon from the river's further bank.

When he found it he returned for his boxes, and on laying them down in the cave's mouth he prised off the lids with a heavy knife. The cartridges lay there packed in sawdust. He took them out one by one and touched them lovingly.

'If only Quin and the boys knew,' he said aloud, and above the low perpetual hiss of the waters his voice echoed with his very accent, and went whispering down the canyon's gap. He looked up suspiciously with his head on one side like a listening bird, and, being reassured, he screamed a high-pitched laughter that came back mixed and mingled in a chorus of discord, and ran off chuckling inaudibly. But Payne now took no note of aught but the dreadful strength under his hands. At last he emptied the boxes. Then one by one he packed the cartridges into

118

the recesses of the cavern. Yet he kept a single cartridge, and partly stripped off its covering.

'Now the fuse and the cap!' he muttered, and took from his pocket that which he had sent to Yale for. Pressing the end of the fuse in, he nipped the cap a little to make it hold, and, thrusting his fingers into the dynamite to make a deep hole, he put the cap in and squeezed the soft explosive about it again. He put the cartridge among the others, while the long length of fuse ran wormlike out of the cavern, the mouth of which he closed with broken rocks. He rose up and clasped his hands.

'Oh, God, be merciful to me—be merciful!'

As he turned, his quick mood changed; he laughed at the personal, hateful river, and then cursed it, laughing.

'I've done it! And now let them laugh. For the river shall be dry and the waters shall stand in a heap.'

He lay down on a flat rock which was under water in the early summer, and, rolling over like a caressed cat, he hugged himself with odd, choked chuckles. 'Tomorrow I'll do it. No; I'll keep it till Sunday— till Sunday; and all the week I will think what I shall do with the gold.'

He coiled up the loose end of the fuse, and hid it carefully from any man's sight, though he knew well that no man ever went there; and by three he was back in his camp-bed.

During the remainder of the working week he lived in concealed frenzy, cunning of look and speech. He calculated hugely the wealth that even one day's work in the dry canyon would make his. He saw the poor world at his feet, and trod on air.

When Quin woke on Sunday in the early dawn he saw the boy had gone. A note lay on the bed. 'What's this?' said Quin sleepily. As he deciphered it in the dusk he sprang up. The letter ran thus:

'Quin, mind what I say. For I know that the Lord ot Hosts is behind me. This is what I say. The river and its gold, from the great bluff down to the Fraser, is mine. It is all mine—the gold and the bed of the river. And when the bed runs dry, as it will today, all that is taken out is mine. At six there shall be a sign and a wonder, and the miracle will happen. I have prayed. The big bluff will fall into the river. And the water will stand in a heap. And the children of Israel will find the gold. For their day's pay I will give them a hundredth part. Each day the same till the water returns. Amen.'

119

Quin ran out. 'Willis—Liston—Shaw!' he called, and the men came half naked from their tents. 'Payne's gone raving mad,' cried Quin; 'he's away, and has left me a letter saying that the bluff is going to fall into the river, and that the gold in the dry bed is his. Hunt for him, you! I'll go to the river myself.'

And in a few minutes he was on the edge of the rocks at the bank. He called hopelessly in the dim dawn, but he was answered faintly.

'Is that you, Payne?' he shouted.

Then he saw a dark figure sitting on the other side. 'It is I. Who calls the chosen one of God?'

Quin stamped on the iron rock. 'Don't be an accursed fool!' he cried. 'Come back, man! What's gone wrong with you? What the hell are you doing there?'

Payne rose and rebuked him. 'Do not blaspheme God, or the works of God. I have prayed for the waters to be stayed, and he has put the power in my hands. The river will run dry, and the gold is mine.' He threw his hands up into the air, crying, 'Mine—mine!'

'He's mad—mad!' said Quin.

'As you have come I will wait no more,' cried Payne, and he stooped down. Yet he rose again. 'Quin'!

'What?'

'Get you under cover, or run, for the bluff will fall into the head of the canyon even now.'

And Quin saw him light a match. It spurted flame in the shadow of the cave's mouth, and then he saw Payne run like a goat along the hazardous edge of the river. As he went he signed with his open hand to Quin to lie down, to go, to hide.

Suddenly there was a mighty crash. To Quin it seemed that he was lying on something hollow that had been smitten from below by a giant's hammer, and for a moment he felt sick; then rocks and gravel flew past him or splintered on his shelter; the air was full of sand and dust that choked and blinded him. He rose and staggered and fell down.

And meantime Payne, blind and mad with furious excitement, his mind spurting flame, his brain overturned, went screaming hand over hand across the river in the creaking boat.

'The dry places shall be filled with water and the rivers shall be dry places. For the sea is in the hollow of his hand.'

He ran headlong for the camp. The other men were lying half stunned near the river. The blast had smitten them as they went running.

'By the holy frost, what's happened?' cried Shaw when he rose.

And Liston scrambled to his feet. They found Willis insensible with a cut on his head, and while they were attending him Quin came up.

But the great bluff stood yet in its ancient place, though Payne's god had torn away a buttress and dug a mighty hole into the dipping strata. Though the surface of the bluff was more concave, yet it had not fallen for all the awful blow dealt its foundations. And by now the river ran blue once more; the yellow patch of the fallen debris had been swept down.

And to the four men came Payne, singing.

But as they stared at him open-mouthed, awed and uncertain, he looked past and above them, and saw the great bluff gleam out in the arisen sun. His face went distorted, and his left hand twisted to his ear uncontrollably; his eyes turned into his head, and he fell grovelling. In the aspect of his stricken face was a curse on the works of God and his ways. And within an hour he was raving on his bed in the fevered horror of madness, and the men were hard put to it to hold him down.

Meanwhile, from this place and from that, camp and house and ranch, men came to their disturbed camp to inquire as to the reason of the sound which had run across the plateau at dawn. They came galloping, and at noon there were thirty men with Quin opposite the rent and splintered bluff.

'Dynamite, for sure,' said one man, 'for the sound of it was like a sudden clap, not the lifting roar of powder, and powder would have hoisted the bluff off its roots.'

'Where did he get it?' asked Quin, who was bewildered. But none answered, and the various talk ran on.

'Did he reckon—the madman—that the river would be dammed by the bluff even if he had fetched it down?'

Quin nodded.

'By the powers,' cried an old miner, 'but it's an almighty notion, and only a crazy lunatic could have tried it!'

They argued hotly in the rising heat whether enough could come down to block the river, and, granted that were possible, how long the dam would hold against the increasing waters. Though some took one side and some the other, the very imagined chance of robbing the river-bed inflamed their minds, and the desire of wealth got hold of them all alike; and they stood for unnoticed hours in the burning sun, with the heat coming doubly from the rocks beneath, and from the mighty bluff opposing them.

'Hark!' cried one man suddenly.

'It is nothing,' said his neighbour.

'It is distant thunder,' said a third.

Suddenly the very earth beneath them shook like an ill-built house, and there came a crack like a heavy rifle-shot, and after it a great grinding noise, that stayed their blood and made them pallid.

'Look! Look!' cried Quin—'it moves—it moves!'

The man next him cried 'No, no,' but even as he spoke the overhung edge of the bluff split and fell roaring into the torrent, beating it into spray that blinded them, and in the spray were a million wild rainbows.

But when the spray died slowly down there was an increasing roar, in which shouted words were dumb gestures, and the whole mighty bluff moved.

'Run, run!' they mouthed, and some ran and stayed again, and some stood petrified.

And with a grinding noise that was a terror of itself, the whole higher half of the bluff and hill behind it went steadily into the river. Thrusting the water aside, it strove like a decree of God, strong of accomplishment, even to the shadowed rocks of the hither side. Through the narrowing gate the water foamed turbidly; but at last the gap closed, and the calm river stayed against the silent obstacle.

The men sighed, awe-struck, and again held their breaths. But then the desire of gold took them, and they ran all ways for all things that might help them to the riches under the sinking waters.

It laid hold of Quin too. 'Quick,' he cried to his men—'all our things —pots or pans or skillets—anything that will hold water or scoop mud! Quick, or these others will sweep the camp clean!'

They ran to their tents like wolves after a deer. They were the first back to the west end of the canyon, and they found the river empty save for pools. It was a ghastly, weedy chasm, difficult of access, slimy, hideous with crawling insects in the holes and crannies. Here and there a stranded bewildered fish flapped desperately. They dropped a rope and lariat in the gap, and slid down.

'It's share and share alike here!' cried Liston.

They agreed on the word spoken.

'Then let Shaw stay here and hoist the buckets.'

He went down and stripped there, throwing his shirt and jacket away.

'Is the most gold here?' asked Willis.

But they worked where they stood.

Then the men who had been with them galloped back with buckets and scoops and all things they could find. The news ran like fire in dry grass; women and children drove up in carts with their household utensils; each moment others dropped into the canyon; in half an hour the black banks hummed. The Siwashes and their Klootchmen came with the whites; Chinamen worked with them. And as the drying river told those down below, buggies came furiously driven to the richest place. All along to the Fraser, men were in the river-bed, greedy of sudden wealth.

And he who had wrought this, and accomplished the impossible hopes of toiling men, lay parched and fevered and all alone. His lips cracked and bled, and he yelled in a narrow tent of a great world opened to him.

'It's all mine—mine!' and the tent fly flapped idly in the heated air.

He sang the hymn, 'Praise God, from whom all blessings flow.'

But in the canyon they cursed awfully; and were afraid, toiling under the dam against which the waters rose and rose still. On its edge one more fearful than the rest had stationed his old mother, and she was shaken with terror for her son. She watched the water as one would watch fire at sea. 'See if it breaks out under. Say when it reaches the top,' they had told her.

As each increased his pile of the drift which held gold, suspicion grew, and with it fear. Men doubted their partners, and glared angrily at each other on slight provocations. But the greater fear above them of the rising water cooled most contentions. And yet in the midst of them was panic crouching, known, hidden and unseen. A chance palsied motion of the grey-haired woman on the dam sent them flying more than once. They returned, worked, and some prayed.

123

'Oh, God! Oh, God, how long?'

Then on the height of the piled earth there sprang a white figure naked to the bitter sun.

'It is mine—mine, and all the wealth of it from here down even to the river's mouth!'

And the mad hero of the slidden mountain chanted dreadful joy of his riches, urging his men beneath to labour. In their ears he was as the buzz of a fly. But behind him, and against the barriers, the very quiet waters rose inch by inch; each distant hill sent aid. For nature was outraged and robbed—her secrets laid bare. As the madman sang, the pressed waters penetrated into every crevice, seeking every way, while a white naked insect yelled articulate blasphemy against the making of the world and the laws that hold matter in space.

'It is mine, and strong for ever!'

But now the backed-up waters began to spread on the lower terrace above the natural river. Every moment brought more power to bear upon the unnatural barrier. Even the old woman saw it. She turned and clambered down to the ancient rocks, for the man whose fair flesh was scorching in the sun terrified her. 'My son! my son!' she wailed.

But her boy down below strove desperately as the others strove. Not a man but left bloody finger-prints on the rocks; some paddled in blood, who, cursing for want of things to carry the river drift away, had stripped off their long boots in desperation. The lust for gold sent them wild: some cheered, some sang.

But others looked up and said, 'How long?'

For themselves they worked, but for none other than their own, and natural mercy left them. At one rich ledge two tramps fought unnoticed. The stronger beat out the brains of the weaker, and robbed him of his stolen bucket.

And the white genius of this sudden black inferno yelled congratulations to the burning skies, praising the Lord with fevered incantations.

Once again the workers fled and returned, and fled again, to come back once more. But down below Quin and his fellows toiled unmoved.

'Oh, there's millions—millions here!'

They spat blood and sweat, and worked blackly grimed and half naked. But at the dam's dry foot the waters began to chuckle, and

On the height of the piled earth there sprang a white figure naked to the bitter sun. 'It's mine, mine!' he yelled.

turbid springs spurted suddenly. The mad boy looked not behind. 'It's mine—it's mine. Oh, God! Oh, God!'

Then he turned and saw the gleaming lake behind him. Thrusting his hands against the hot air, he cursed and commanded the encroaching waters, that rose even to the dam's height and began to pour over. The word ran like thunder in the echoing chasm, and the men fled, stricken with white fear. Some cried, 'No, no—not yet!' even as they ran.

And the miracle-worker cursed his God at the motion under his feet, at the fear of poverty returning, at the loss of unmeasured hope.

'It moves—it moves!' piped the idiot woman, who had lived out her mind's life in that awful hour; and she picked idly at the withered flesh of her dry hands.

But he who was above her heard, and shook his clenched hand at the clear sky. 'No, no, no!' he cried, as the canyon edge was crowded with his men.

They clambered up the hanging ropes; they fought desperately for foothold, and pulled down those who had advantage. Only the brained man lay motionless in the slime, while his slayer, fearful of some terrible return of sane justice, grinned sickly on the bank.

The the great dam moved and surged with a grating noise, while the rivulets below gushed dreadfully, and after one long-drawn moment of expectation it gave way, and, with a roar that drowned the cries of the maddened crowd, it yielded wholly to the river that swept back into its ancient channel for ever, or till the end of long generations yet unborn.

But in the bitter surge and lifted crest of it he who had wrought the miracle was borne down like a foam bubble unregarded.

And then the order of the natural world returned.

RESCUE OF THE COMORIN'S CREW

Commander John Kerans

It was as the destroyer *Broke* soared on the crest of a mountainous sea that her lookouts first sighted the burning merchant cruiser *Comorin*, eight miles distant. Then *HMS Broke* plunged down, down, down into a watery chasm sixty feet deep.

The conditions were enough to frighten even the most intrepid seaman. A roaring south-easterly gale had piled up the North Atlantic into foam-capped mountains from which in its utter ferocity it was tearing off long hissing streamers of spray. Out there, hundreds of miles south of Iceland, the ocean was a howling waste of tempestuous waters where the great waves ran a thousand feet long and in the troughs between whole rows of giant buildings could have been lost. It had been in the midst of a fight for her own life that the *Broke* had picked up the call for help, and had answered without hesitation.

It was 6 April 1941, and the stricken *Comorin* was a converted P & O vessel of some 15,000 tons with a crew of around four hundred. She was one of the hastily-armed merchantmen pressed into service early in the war to patrol shipping routes. How the fire had started no one knew; it could have been a leaking fuel-pipe, it could have been many things.

But, fanned by the furious wind, it so swiftly took a hold on the ship that soon it was hard to distinguish the roar of the tempest from the roar of the flames. Members of the crew, particularly in the engine-room, had fought with desperate courage to control the inferno, but to no avail.

The British destroyer was battling through the awesome seas down wind of the position given in the *Comorin*'s SOS. Despite the almost unbelievable conditions of wave and wind there was a remarkable air of cool purposefulness about the crew of the *Broke*. It so happened they were specialists in hazardous rescues for, although the Second World War was but eighteen months old, they had already saved survivors from five torpedoed or bombed vessels. Already her mess decks were prepared to receive casualties, scrambling nets draped her sides, and ready to be thrown to men struggling in the seas were lifebelts, oil drums and ropes.

The *Comorin* was just a small angry red glow against the storm-black sky when first she was sighted. Even from afar she glowered like a mass of red-hot metal. As the destroyer topped one great, green foaming wall of water after another each brief glimpse of the burning vessel gradually built up a more detailed picture. The *Comorin* was wallowing beam on to the huge running seas with the wild wind streaming black billowing smoke away from her. Over the ship the smoke was under-flushed with the red of the inferno, while the smoke that belched from her single funnel was livid with flames. The stricken vessel, and those aboard her, could not hope to survive much longer.

Commander Scholfield, the commanding officer of the *Broke*, learned by radio that the work of rescue had already commenced. Pitching and careering near the stricken *Comorin* were the steamship *Glenartny* and *HMS Lincoln*, an ex-American destroyer of First World War vintage. They had taken off about two hundred men, some having fought through the towering seas in ship's boats, others having been ferried across to the *Lincoln* on Carley rafts attached to a line. In such hazardous conditions the ferrying was desperately slow and it was quite obvious the men still aboard the *Comorin*, nearly two hundred in number, stood little chance unless a swifter method could be devised. Night would soon be upon them, quite apart from the ever-swelling volume of flames devouring the doomed vessel.

The men still awaiting rescue were huddled together after with the fire steadily eating towards them. The vessel was being driven sideways on by the gale, all the time plunging and rearing. One moment her stern would be high up out of the water with screws and rudder bared, the next it would crash down in cascades of spray into the uprising wall of the next wave. Were a small ship, such as the destroyer *Broke*, to be caught beneath a gigantic down-blow, it must be smashed beneath the sea. Yet Commander Scholfield did not hesitate to go alongside to the rescue.

By this time it was night, a black night a'roar with wind furiously flinging massive walls of water at the floundering ships. The only light was the glare of the burning vessel. It was a ghastly incandescence that spread over the faces of the waiting men with an eerie glow and reddened the flying flakes of foam like the slaverings of hell hounds lurking in the outer darkness.

On decks that rolled and bucked furiously the *Broke*'s crew secured all the ship's fenders over the port side. They brought up from the mess decks locker cushions, hammocks and anything else soft enough to break a man's fall. They padded the deck of the forecastle in readiness for the *Comorin*'s men to leap to safety, leaps which could be made by only a few at a time as the destroyer came in on brief precarious runs alongside the blazing vessel. As towering wave crest was followed by abysmal trough it would be impossible to gauge the exact relative position of the two ships at the crucial moment of jumping—sometimes the *Broke* might be fifty feet below the *Comorin*, at others ten or twenty feet above. It was the only way, however, and the *Broke* would have to keep dashing in and backing away until all were off. Lieutenant Peter Scott, the destroyer's 'No. 1' and later the noted naturalist, who was in charge of the jumping operations, had stretcher parties standing by in case of injuries.

On her first run in the destroyer scraped alongside the blazing vessel's leeside. One moment she soared high above the glowering deck, the next she was plunging deep down amidst the smoke and the boiling waters. Yet somehow the nine men who made the first jump landed safely and unhurt. They were fortunate in that the pitching waves had dropped the *Broke* only a few feet below the *Comorin* at the moment of leaping.

Commander Scholfield backed his vessel away, lined up for a new approach, then went in again. The stretcher-bearers were needed this time. The *Comorin* suddenly bucked up and away from the rescue ship as it came alongside. Three of the six men who hurled themselves out from the blazing vessel fell heavily and lay twisted and groaning. Standing poised on the crazily pitching deck ready to snatch injured men out from beneath the next jumpers, the stretcher-bearers leaped to their aid. Speed was vital, for each time the *Broke* came briefly alongside it must be every jumper for himself, and no time to assess what had happened to the man before.

There were two reasons why Commander Scholfield backed away each time. The first and obvious one was that the longer they remained alongside the wind-driven, blazing vessel in such tempestuous seas the greater the risk of a giant blow from the 15,000-ton *Comorin* crushing and submerging the destroyer. The second was that the Commander wanted to have the *Broke*'s lean, grey hull examined for damage after each clash against the *Comorin*. Such collisions were inevitable and if damage became too bad the rescue attempt would have to be abandoned rather than risk the *Broke* sinking with all hands, including the rescued already aboard. The destroyer's very next run in did, in fact, produce a fearsome crash. Fortunately, however, the *Broke* was scarred but undamaged as she scraped down the *Comorin*'s side when plunged dizzyingly down below the blazing ship.

To the glowering of the flames was now added the intermittent illumination of the *Lincoln*'s searchlight. *Broke*, too, brought into play a group of lights shining down on to the forecastle jumping deck from the yardarms. Courageous men had struggled aloft in the teeth of the howling wind to rig these lights. Now the crew of the *Comorin* could see better where they were jumping, and judge their jumps with more certainty. The ship's doctor stood under the lights ready to deal immediately with casualties. Only a few hours before the *Comorin*'s SOS was picked up he had been declared a casualty himself and had been ordered to bed with a high temperature. But he shrugged off his fever in the emergency and was bracing himself out there in the storm ready to play his part.

By magnificent seamanship *Broke*'s Commander contrived a routine rescue manoeuvre amidst the maelstrom of roaring waters, smoke and crackling flames. Time and again he ran her in close alongside so that as her forecastle passed the *Comorin's* stern men could jump to safety. Time and again he reversed her out so that more men had a chance to leap as the forecastle once more slid by. Sometimes the *Broke* was too far down for a jump to be possible, sometimes the destroyer reared up on a wave crest too high above. But most runs produced at least a few men on the destroyer's padded deck. On the average a third of them sprawled out where they fell and had to be carried off to the sick bay by the stretcher party of brawny stokers. Meanwhile the shipwright's hasty inspection of damage to the *Broke's* hull revealed bent guard-rails and splinter shields and a long, jagged gash in the hull.

Often, as the great stern of the *Comorin* loomed over them and plunged sickeningly down in the giant seas, the *Broke* was narrowly missed. The destroyer's crew were alternately drenched by the cascades of spray flung out by the stricken vessel and seared by the inferno that raged aboard. Although broken legs and arms were the usual injuries to jumpers, some sustained internal and other more serious damage. The *Broke's* medical officer had more than he could handle and the cry went out for the *Comorin's* doctor if he were still aboard. 'Is there a doctor in the house?' one of *Broke's* stokers bawled in a great voice which could even be heard above the fury of storm and fire. There was a wave of acknowledgement from above and then the *Comorin's* surgeon lieutenant-commander appeared at the rails. As he poised to jump everyone knew that this jump, above all others, must succeed. The need for this doctor, fit and able to operate, was desperate.

Anxiously watched by all eyes, the MO poised, teetered on the edge, then launched himself out into the clutching wind. Down, down, down to the *Broke*, twenty feet beneath, he tumbled and in the last split second the watchers gasped in agony—he was going to miss the padded deck! He fell, flat on his back with a sickening crash, on the iron-hard deck beyond. The doctor lay motionless and silent as the dead. A stretcher party went staggering across the pitching deck towards him. Then suddenly he sat up and said: 'What happened?' A stoker, grinning over him in his relief, answered: 'You must have caught your foot in the funnel, sir.' The MO was helped to his feet, decided he was only bruised and shaken, and within ten minutes was tending the injured on the mess deck.

131

Again and yet again *Broke* thrust in beside the burning ship. Again and again she was damaged in the inevitable collision of hulls. The thin steel wall of the destroyer's port side was now a mass of jagged splits and tears. Water cascaded in each time she plunged into a wave so that it swirled around the men's feet. Continuous pumping and baling was imperative if she were to survive. But *Broke* kept careering in on her rescue dashes until she had taken off 130 survivors. There remained 50 men, 35 of them officers, aboard the *Comorin*.

Captain J. I. Hallett, RN, the stricken vessel's commanding officer, now gave orders for each man to take the first opportunity of jumping. Little time remained; it must be every man for himself. Yet they persisted in doing it in an orderly manner and more than one man stepped back for a comrade and said: 'No, after you, old boy.' And as so often in such a desperate situation there was much wit and laughter in the midst of the dreadful danger. One man, poised on the rail to leap, looked back over his shoulder and complained: 'I don't mind jumping into the sea, but there's a damn great ship in the way and I'm sure to hit it!' Then he launched himself out as the destroyer's forecastle rose

The MO poised, teetered, then launched himself out into the clutching wind . . .

lift-like from the depths, and sustained nothing worse than bruises in a crash-landing from twenty feet. By contrast, a steward folded his rain-coat neatly over his arm, casually drew on a cigarette in his other hand, and stepped nonchalantly over the *Comorin*'s rails on to the deck of the *Broke* as a wave lifted it to exactly the right height.

It was miraculous that no man had yet been lost overboard. Not only was there the danger of missing *Broke*'s wildly careering deck, but the surging sea constantly reached out for them. As she manoeuvred tortuously amidst the mountainous waves, the destroyer was repeatedly swept by swirling water. Even though men somehow managed to cling on, depth charges, towing tackles, cables and ropes were plucked from the decks. A long length of rope ensnared the port screw but fortunately did not stop it turning. Each time *Broke*'s engines raced full astern to drag her back from the great burning hulk, she was subjected to periods of such intense vibration that men's senses became numbed.

Broke was ground in once more against the *Comorin*, tortured throughout her whole length by the dragging collision. Screws threshed as engines were switched to hard astern and, at the very moment she gathered way backing out, two men jumped. They missed and disappeared into the angry seas. Peter Scott scrambled across the tilted, swirling decks to look for them, but all he saw was the turmoil of green waters and boiling foam. 'They've had it, poor devils!' muttered a sailor who had witnessed the tragedy.

Realizing there was nothing more he or any other man could do, Scott fought his way aft to make an inspection of the damage. He feared a split had been opened in the upper deck. If it had, and were it to extend under the stress and strain, then the future of the ship would be precarious indeed. Finding the worst had not happened he turned to go back to the forecastle, when he thought he caught the sound of a distant cry. Again through the roar of the tempest he heard it—a feeble shout of 'Help'. Scott looked over the side and there, immediately below him, was one of the men who had disappeared. He was desperately clinging to a scrambling net draped from the vessel's side. Willing hands hauled him to safety to find that, although he had lapsed into unconsciousness, his fingers crooked into the net had refused to let go. The other man was never seen again.

Ominously there came a sustained crackling explosion from deep

133

within the *Comorin*. A great rushing sound followed and then there flung skywards from the inferno a galaxy of sparkling rockets. Red Very lights added further colour to a fireworks display which briefly added a peculiarly light-hearted regatta atmosphere to an otherwise desperate situation. Hardly had this died out when a series of staccato explosions erupted within the blazing vessel as the flames reached the small arms ammunition store. These explosions increased to deep detonations in rapid succession until they became a continuous crackling roar. The violent disruptive power of all these explosions in the very heart of the doomed ship could mean only a swift acceleration of her inevitable end.

At the height of the firework display, with its background of deeper thunder, the livid sky illuminated an agonizing personal drama. One of the *Comorin's* officers leaped outwards, but a split second too late, for the *Broke* lurched and dropped away deep down into a foaming trough. He missed the destroyer's forecastle, but his frantically clutching fingers somehow managed to grasp the bottom guard-rail and hang on. That he had not plunged to his doom was not immediately apparent, for he was beyond the circle of light, but two of the *Broke's* men instinctively ran to the rails and reached down to grip him. At that moment the destroyer, once more coming up like an express lift, lurched in towards the burning ship. The sailors at the rail, although they also faced death by crushing, did not flinch from their task but kept hauling frantically at the officer.

At the very moment when it seemed the two steel walls must converge and crush the three men to pulp, a great wave surged in and rolled them apart. But their ordeal was not over. Exerting all their strength though they were, with the wild wind clutching them, the two rescuers had pulled the *Comorin's* officer little more than halfway up when once more the two vessels rolled together. Yet again a wave rushed in at the very last second, and death missed them by a fraction. Then a final desperate effort completed the rescue and the exhausted officer and his rescuers sprawled on the destroyer's deck. Even as they did so the ships plunged towards each other again and this time their hulls ground together sickeningly.

One of the *Comorin's* men was less fortunate. He misjudged his jump and disappeared with a wild cry between the two vessels, a cry hideously stifled as the sides clashed together. The experiences of two others caused all who saw them to wince—one of the men landed astride the guard-rail and the other astride the barrel of 'B' gun. Yet miraculously neither was injured. So it went on, minute by minute, hour by hour, until it was past midnight. Until at last there were only two men left on the *Comorin*, the Commander and the Captain.

Plunging, wallowing, soaring, tilting, the gallant *Broke* came in on her last run. *Comorin* was now an utterly terrifying inferno. From end to end she roared with flames, and the small section right aft where the last two survivors stood was the only place where a man could hope to remain alive. Then the *Broke*'s padded forecastle was up beneath the *Comorin*'s stern once more and the Commander jumped. He landed safely. Just one man to go—the Captain. Then he was out in mid-air, hurtling down towards the *Broke*. At that very moment a loose rope flapping and whipping from the burning vessel's deck caught him in a tentacle and spun him round so that he faced the *Comorin*. At the same time the *Broke* dropped precipitously and rolled violently outwards. Off balance, flailing the air helplessly, the Captain seemed certain to fall outside the guard-rail down into the thunderous seas below.

But there was one last miracle to be enacted. Whether the destroyer checked in her roll, or whether the Captain twisted towards safety in his fall no one could say, but he landed squarely astride the rail. For a breathless moment he teetered on the brink, swung this way and that and then rolled backwards to safety. He completed a neat back somersault on the padded deck, climbed to his feet with an air of dignity, brushed himself down, screwed his monocle into his eye and stepped smartly down on to the deck. He was the 180th man to land on the *Broke*. With the *SS Glenarty* having taken off 104 and *HMS Lincoln* 121, only 21 men of *Comorin*'s crew had been lost. Yet in the beginning it had seemed that from a fire so terrible in so dreadful a storm all aboard *Comorin* were doomed.

A DREAM OF DEATH

James Hogg

Not very long ago, one William Laidlaw, a sturdy Borderer, went on an excursion to a remote district in the Highlands of Scotland. He was a tall and very athletic man, remarkably active, and matchless at cudgel-playing, running, wrestling, and other exercises for which the Borderers have been noted from time immemorial. To his other accomplishments he added an excellent temper, was full of good humour, and a most capital bottle-companion.

Most of our modern travellers would have performed the greater part of the journey he undertook in a steam-boat, a stage-coach, or some such convenience; but he preferred going on foot, without any companion excepting an old oaken cudgel, which had been handed down to him from several generations, and which, by way of fancy, had been christened 'Knock-him-down'.

With this trusty friend in his hand, and fifty pounds sterling in his pocket, he found himself, by the fourth day, in one of the most dismal glens of the highlands. It was by this time nightfall, and both William's appetite and limbs told him it was high time to look about for a place of repose, having, since six in the morning, walked nearly fifty miles.

Now, the question which employed his thoughts at this moment was whether he should proceed, at the risk of losing his way among the bogs and morasses for which this district is famed, or remain till daybreak where he was? Both expedients were unpleasant, and it is difficult to say which he would have adopted, when, about a mile to the left, a glimmering among the darkness attracted his notice.

It might have been a 'Will-o'-the-wisp', or the light of some evil spirit at its midnight orgies; but whatever the cause might be, it decided Mr Laidlaw as to his further operations. He did not reflect a moment upon the matter, but exercising 'Knock-him-down' in its usual capacity of walking assistant, he found himself in a few minutes alongside the spot from which the light proceeded. It was a highland cottage, built after the usual fashion, partly of stone and partly of turf; but without examining too minutely the exterior of the building, he applied the stick to the door with such a degree of force as he conceived necessary to arouse the inmates.

'Wha's there?' cried a shrill voice, like that of an old woman; 'what want ye at this hour of the night?'

'I want lodging, honest woman, if such a thing is to be got.'

'Na, na,' replied the inmate, 'you can get nae lodging here. Neither gentle nor simple shall enter my house this night. Gang on your ways, you're no aboon five miles frae the clachan of Ballacher.'

'Five deevils!' exclaimed the Borderer; 'I tell you I have walked fifty miles already, and could as soon find out Johnny Groat's as the clachan.'

'Walk fifty more, then,' cried the obstinate portress; 'but here you downa enter, while I can keep you out.'

'If you come to that, my woman,' said William, 'we shall soon settle the point. In plain language, if you do not let me in wi' your gude-will I shall enter without it,' and with that he laid his shoulder to the door, with the full intention of storming the fortress. A whispering within made him pause a moment.

'And must I let him in?' murmured the old woman to someone who seemed in the interior.

'Yes,' answered a half-suppressed voice; 'he may enter—he is but one, and we are three—a lowland tup, I suppose.'

The door was slowly opened. The person who performed this unwilling act was a woman apparently above seventy, haggard and bent by an accumulation of infirmity and years. Her face was pale, malignant, and wrinkled, and her little sharp peering eyes seemed, like those of the adder, to shoot forth evil upon whomsoever she gazed. As William entered, he encountered this aged crone, her natural hideousness exposed full to his gaze by the little rush-light she held up above her head, the better to view the tall Borderer.

'You want a night's lodging, say you? Ay, nae doubt, like many others frae the south, come to trouble honest folks.'

'There's nae need to talk about troubling,' said Laidlaw. 'If you have trouble you shall be paid for it; and since you are pleased, my auld lady, to talk about the south, let me say a word of the north. I have got money in my pouch to pay my way wherever I go, and this is mair than some of your bonnie highland lairds can say. Here it lies, my lady!' and he struck with the palm of his hand the large and well-replenished pocket-book which bulged out from his side.

'I want nane of your money,' said the old crone, her eyes nevertheless sparkling with a malicious joy; 'walk in; you will have the company of strangers for the night.'

He followed her advice, and went to the end of the cottage, near which, upon the floor, blazed a large fire of peat. There was no grate, and for chimney a hole in the roof sufficed, through which the smoke ascended in large volumes. Here he saw the company mentioned by the crone. It consisted of three men, of the most fierce and savage aspect. Two of them were dressed as sailors, the third in a sort of highland garb.

He had never seen any persons who had so completely the air of desperadoes. The two first were dark in their complexions, their black bushy beards apparently unshorn for many weeks. Their expressions were dark and ominous, and bespoke spirits within which had been trained up in crime. Nor were the red locks of the third, and his fiery countenance, and sharp, cruel eyes, less appalling, and less indicative of evil.

So near an intercourse with such people, and under those circumstances, would have thrown a chill over most hearts; but William Laidlaw was naturally a stranger to fear, and, at any rate, his great strength gave him a confidence which it was very difficult to shake;

138

he had, besides, a most unbounded confidence in scientific cudgel-playing, and in the virtues of 'Knock-him-down'.

These three men were seated around the fire; and when our traveller came alongside of them, and saluted them, not one returned his salutation. Each sat in dogged silence. If they deigned to recognize him, it was by looks of ferocious sternness, and these looks were momentary, for they instantly relapsed into their former state of sullen apathy.

William was at this time beset by two most unfortunate indinations. He had an incorrigible desire, first, to speak, and secondly, to eat; and never had any propensities come upon so inappropriate a man. He sat for a few minutes absolutely nonplussed about the method of gratifying them. At length, after revolving the matter deeply in his mind, he contrived to get out with the following words:

'I have been thinking, gudewife, that something to eat is very agreeable when a body is hungry.' No answer.

'I have been thinking, mistress, that when a man is hungry he is the better of something to eat.' No answer.

'Did you hear what I was saying, mistress?'

'Perfectly weel.'

'And what is your opinion of the matter?'

'My opinion is, that a hungry man is the better of being fed.' Such was the old dame's reply; and he thought he could perceive a smile of bitter ridicule curl up the savage lips of his three neighbours.

'Was there ever such an auld hag?' thought the yeoman to himself. 'There she sits at her wheel, and cares nae mair for a fellow-creature than I would for a dead sheep.'

'Mistress,' continued he, 'I see you will not tak' hints. I maun then tell you plainly that I am the next door to starvation, and that I will thank you for something to eat.'

This produced the desired effect, for she instantly got up from her wheel, went to a cupboard, and produced a plentiful supply of cold venison, bread and cheese, together with a large bottle full of the finest whisky.

William now felt quite at his ease. Putting 'Knock-him-down' beside him, and planting himself at the table, he commenced operations in a style that would have done honour to Friar Tuck himself. Venison, bread and cheese disappeared like magic. So intently did he keep to his

139

occupation that he neither thought nor cared about any other object.

Everything which came under the heading of eatable having disappeared from the table, he proceeded to discuss the contents of the black bottle which stood by. He probably indulged rather freely in this respect, for shortly after commencing he became very talkative, and seemed resolved, at all risks, to extract conversation from his mute companions.

'You will be in the smuggling trade, frien'?' said he, slapping the shoulder of one of his dark-complexioned neighbours. The fellow started from his seat, and looked upon the Borderer with an expression of anger and menace, but he was suddenly quieted by one of his companions, who whispered into his ear, 'Hush, Roderick; never mind him; the time is not yet come.'

'I was saying, frien',' reiterated Laidlaw, without perceiving this interruption, 'that you will be in the smuggling trade?'

'Maybe I am,' was the fellow's answer.

'And you are a fish of the same water?' continued William to the second, who nodded assent.

'And you, frien', wi' the red hair, what are ye?'

'Humph!'

'Humph!' cried the Borderer; 'that is one way of answering questions—humph, ay humph, very good; ha, ha, your health, Mr Humph!' and he straightway swallowed another glass of the potent spirit.

These three personages, during the whole of his various harangues, preserved the same unchanged silence, replying to his broken and unconnected questions by nods and monosyllables. They even held no verbal communication with one another, but each continued apparently within himself the thread of his own gloomy meditations. The night by this time waxed late; the spirit began to riot a little in the Borderer's head; and concluding that there was no sociality among persons who would neither drink nor speak, he quaffed a final glass and dropped back on his chair.

How long he remained in this state cannot be known. Certain it is, he was rather suddenly awakened from it by a hand working its way cautiously and gently into his bosom. At first he did not know what to make of this: his ideas were as yet unrallied, and by a sort of instinct he merely pressed his left hand against the spot by way of resistance. The same force continuing, however, to operate as formerly, he opened his eyes, and saw himself surrounded by the three strangers. The red-haired ruffian was the person who had aroused him—the two others, one of them armed with a cutlass, stood by. William was so astonished at this scene that he could form no opinion on the subject. His brain still rang with the strange visions that had crossed it, and with the influence of intoxication.

'I am thinking, honest man, that you are stealing my pocket-book,' was the first ejaculation he came out with, gazing at the same time with a bewildered look on the plunderer.

'Down with the villain!' thundered one of these worthies at the same instant; 'and you, sir,' brandishing his cutlass over the Borderer's head, 'resist, and I will cleave you to the collar.'

This exclamation acted like magic upon Laidlaw; it seemed to sober him in an instant, and point out his perilous situation.

The trio had rushed upon him, and attempted to hold him down. Now or never was the period to put his immense strength to the trial. Collecting all his energies, he bounded from their grasp, and his herculean fist falling like a sledge-hammer upon the forehead of him who carried the cutlass, the ruffian tumbled headlong to the earth. In a moment more he stood in the centre of the cottage, whirling 'Knock-him-down' around his head in the attitude of defiance. Such was now his appearance of determined courage and strength that the two ruffians opposed to him, although powerful men, and armed with bludgeons, did not dare advance, but recoiled several paces from their opponent.

He had escaped thus far, but his situation was still very hazardous, for the men, though baffled, kept their eyes intently fixed upon him, and seemed only to wait an opportunity when they could rush on with most advantage. Besides, the one he had floored had just got up, and with his cutlass joined the others. If they had made an attack upon him, his great skill and vigour would in all probability have brought one of them to the ground, but then he would have been assailed by the two others; and the issue of such a contest, armed as one of them was, could not but be highly dangerous.

Meanwhile the men, although none of them ventured to rush singly upon the Borderer, began to advance in a body, as if for the purpose of getting behind him.

141

'Now,' thought William, 'if I can but keep you quiet till I get opposite the door, I may show you a trick that will astonish you.'

So planning his scheme, he continued retreating before his assailants, and holding up his cudgel in the true scientific position till he came within a foot of the door; most fortunately it stood wide open. One step aside, and the threshold was gained—another, and it was passed.

In the twinkling of an eye, swift like a thunderbolt, fell 'Knock-him-down' upon the head of the most forward opponent and in another out bolted William Laidlaw from the cottage. The whole was the work of an instant. He who received the blow fell stunned and bleeding to the ground, and his companions were so confounded that they stood mute and gazing at each other for several seconds. Their resolution was soon taken, and in a mood between shame and revenge, they sallied out after the fugitive. Their speed was, however, employed in vain against the fleetest runner of the Cheviots, and they were afraid to separate, lest each might encounter singly this formidable adversary, who perhaps might have dealt with them in the same manner as Horatius did with the Curiatii of old. The pursuit continued but a short way, as the yeoman more than double distanced his pursuers in the first two minutes, and left them no chance of coming up with him.

It was by this time three in the morning. The intense darkness of midnight had worn away, and though the sun was yet beneath the horizon, a sort of reflected light so far prevailed as to render near objects visible. In the course of an hour the hill tops became exposed above the misty wreaths which hung heavily upon their sides, and which began to dissolve away and float slowly down the glen in pale columns.

In a short time a hue like that of twilight rendered distinctly visible the mountain boundaries of the vale. William walked onward with his usual speed. Such at last was his prodigious rapidity of movement that he utterly lost the use of his senses. He appeared to himself to fly rather than walk over the earth; his head became giddy, and it is difficult to say where his flight might have ended, when 'Knock-him-down' was suddenly swept from his hand. This in a moment arrested his speed, for such was his sympathy with this companion that he could not possibly get on, or even live without it.

'Knock-him-down, whare are ye?' was his first exclamation at the departure of his favourite. 'I say, Knock-him-down—whare are ye?' Here honest William sat down upon the heath to bemoan his misfortune. Now for the first time in his life he parted with all recollection. A strange, mysterious, indescribable ringing took place in his ears—the hills reeled—his head nodded once, twice, and again—and in a few seconds he dropped into a profound sleep.

This may be considered an epoch in the yeoman's life, for here he, for the first time, according to his own account, was visited by a dream. Out of the pale mist of the glen he imagined he saw approach him the very person to whose house he was bound. The aspect of this man was melancholy—his face deadly pale—and as he stood opposite to the Borderer and said, 'William Laidlaw,' the latter felt his flesh creep with an unutterable dread.

'William Laidlaw,' continued he, 'you are going to my house, but you will not find me at home. I have gone to a far country—Neil McKinnon and his two cousins sent me there. You will find my body in the pit near the Cairn of Dalgulish. The money you are bringing to me give to my poor family, and may God bless you!' Having pronounced these words the figure vanished, nor had the Borderer the power to recall it. He did not, however, awake, but lay in the same restless state till the sun, shining in all the splendour of an August morning, burst upon him.

William awoke a sober man. The morning was indeed beautiful. The sun shone in his strength, lighting up the vale with a flood of radiance. On the summits of the hills not a cloud rested—all was clear and lucid as crystal, and the untainted sky hung like a vault of pure sapphire over the thousand rocks and glens beneath.

The object which first arrested our friend's attention was 'Knock-him-down' stuck up in the middle of a gorse bush, and his immediate impulse was to relieve it from this inglorious situation. Having done this, stretched his limbs, and examined his pocket-book, which he found 'tight and well', he proceeded on his journey. He was naturally the reverse of superstitious, but somehow or other a train of unpleasant thoughts came over him, which he could not get rid of. His mind was so unaccustomed to thinking of any kind, and above all, to gloomy thinking, that he knew not what to make of the matter. He whistled and sang in vain to dispel the feeling. The same load hung upon his

The aspect of this man was melancholy, his face deadly pale . . .

mind, and oppressed it grievously.

In this train he found himself at length in front of the clachan of
Ballacher. This small village was in possession of the individual to
whom he was journeying. His dwelling, a large farmhouse, was in the
centre; the cottages which surrounded it were occupied by his servants
and tenants.

It was about midday when he entered the village. It was deserted,
while a strange and subduing melancholy seemed to hang over it. He
strode slowly on, but no human being made his appearance. At length
a funeral procession, followed by many women and children, came
silently up the middle avenue of the village. It might be a deception
of his fancy, but he thought the looks of the mourners were more sad
and more profoundly interesting than he had ever witnessed on any
previous occasion. He followed the convoy to the cemetery, which was
not far distant, and when the last shovelful of earth was thrown upon
the grave, he inquired whose funeral it was.

'It is that of Allaster Wilson, our master,' was the reply.

'Good heaven! and how did he die?' cried William, deeply agitated.

'That no one knows,' answered an old man who stood by; 'he was
found murdered; but a day will come when the Lord will cause his
blood to be requited on his murderers.'

'And where was his body found?' said the astonished Borderer.

'In the chalkpit near the Cairn of Dalgulish,' replied the senior, and
he wiped his aged eyes and walked slowly away.

William started back with horror and instantly recollected his
dream. It was indeed the very individual to whose house he was
journeying that he now saw laid in his grave. His first duty was to go
to the bereaved family of his departed friend, and to comfort the
widow and the fatherless. A tear rolled from his manly eye as he entered
the mansion of sorrow; and when he saw the relict and the weeping
family of his friend he thought his heart would have died within him.
Having paid into their hands the money he owed them, and performed
various offices of kindness, he bade them for the present adieu, and went
to Inverness.

He had no business to transact there; his only object was to obtain
the aid of justice in pursuit of the three men whom he supposed to be
the murderers. Neil McKinnon was apprehended at the house where

145

Laidlaw first saw him; but though his guilt was strongly suspected, no positive proof could be adduced against him, and he was dismissed. The two other men were never heard of. It was supposed that they had gone on board a smuggling cutter which left Fort William, and afterwards perished, with all its crew, in the Sound of Mull.

The dream still continued to agitate the yeoman's mind to a great degree, and from being the gayest farmer of the Borders, he returned as thoughtful as a philosopher.

THE BOY SPY
Alphonse Daudet

From the sunny stories of Lettres de mon Moulin, *for which Daudet is best known, it is a far cry to this tragic tale of the Franco-Prussian War of 1870–71, in which the lure of a few francs helps turn a young boy traitor to his country.*

He was called Stenne: Little Stenne. He was a boy of Paris, sickly looking and pallid, who could have been ten years old—or perhaps even fifteen. With midgets like that you can never tell. His mother was dead; his father, an ex-marine, was caretaker of a garden square in the Temple quarter. The children, the nursemaids, the old ladies in deck-chairs, the poor mothers—all the people who took refuge from the traffic among those flower-bordered walks—they all knew old Papa Stenne, and adored him.

They knew that beneath the shaggy moustache there lurked a generous, almost maternal smile—and that to provoke that smile they had only to ask the dear old fellow: 'How's your little son?' The old man was so very fond of that boy of his! He was never so happy as in the evenings, when the boy came for him after school, and the pair of them strolled along the paths, halting at every seat and bench to have a word with the regulars.

But when the Prussians besieged Paris, everything changed utterly. Papa Stenne's square was closed and taken over as an oil-store. The poor old fellow spent all his time on guard, not even able to smoke—

and only getting a glimpse of his boy late at night. As for the Prussians, the old man's moustache used positively to bristle when he talked of *them*. But Little Stenne, on the other hand, didn't find all that much to grumble about in the changed conditions.

A siege! It was a great lark for the kids! No more school! No more homework! One long holiday, and the streets like a fairground.

The boy was out of doors playing the whole day. He used to accompany the local battalions whenever they marched off to the ramparts—preferably any battalion that had a good band, a subject on which Little Stenne was an expert. He could tell you emphatically that the band of the 98th wasn't much good, but that the 55th had a pretty good one. At other times, he would cast an eye at the reserves doing their drill, and there were always the queues to join.

With a shopping basket on his arm, he would tag on to those long queues outside the butcher's or the baker's and there, scuffling his feet in the gutter, he would meet people and earnestly discuss the situation—for being the son of Papa Stenne his opinion was always sought. Best of all were the games of *galoche*—a game in which you had to bowl over a cork with money on it and which the Breton reservists had made popular during the siege.

Whenever Little Stenne wasn't on the ramparts or queueing at the baker's, you could be sure of finding him at some *galoche* tournament in Water-Tower Square. He didn't take part—that would have needed too much money. He just looked on, and he particularly admired one of the players, a big lad in a blue coat who invariably gambled with five-franc pieces and nothing else. When that boy ran you could hear the money jingling in his coat pockets.

One day, as Little Stenne retrieved a coin that had rolled near the boy, the big fellow muttered to him: 'That makes you stare, eh? If you like, I'll show you where to find some more.'

At the end of the game he strolled away with Little Stenne and asked him if he'd like to go with him and sell newspapers to the Prussians, who would pay anyone thirty francs for the trouble. To begin with, Little Stenne refused indignantly—and he was so upset by the offer that he kept away from the game for several days. Terrible days they were—he couldn't eat or sleep for thinking about it all.

At night in bed he could see nothing but heaps of corks and glittering five-franc pieces. He couldn't resist the temptation. On the fourth day he went back to Water-Tower Square, spoke to the big lad again, and this time was easily persuaded.

One snowy morning the two of them started out with sacks over their shoulders and newspapers hidden in their clothes. Dawn had scarcely broken when they arrived at a place called the Pâte de Flandres on the outskirts of the city. The big boy took Little Stenne by the hand and approached the kindly looking, red-nosed French sentry.

'Here, mister,' he said in a whining tone, 'can we go on? Mother's ill and our old man's dead. My kid brother and I want to see if we can find some spuds in the fields out there.'

He started blubbering—and Little Stenne drooped his head in shame. The sentry eyed them for a moment, then glanced down the deserted, snow-covered road.

'All right, off with you,' he said, dismissing them—and straight away they were on the road to Aubervilliers. The older boy nearly laughed himself silly.

Bewildered, as if in a dream, Little Stenne caught sight of factories that had been taken over as barracks, ramshackle barricades, towering chimneys that pierced the mist and groped into the sky. Here and there were more sentries, officers surveying the distance through telescopes, little tents wet from melted snow near half-hearted fires.

The big lad knew all the roads and short cuts, but even so it wasn't his fault that they ran into a platoon of light infantry crouching in a trench alongside the Soissons railway. Although he told his story all over again the soldiers wouldn't let them pass. The big lad put up a show of crying again, and a sergeant, grizzled and white-haired, rather like old Papa Stenne, emerged from the level-crossing keeper's house to see what was going on.

'All right, kids,' he said, when he had listened to their story, 'stop all that noise. You can go and get your potatoes. But come in and warm yourselves first—that little fellow looks frozen!'

But it wasn't with cold that Little Stenne was shivering, it was with shame and fear. In the guardhouse, more soldiers were squatting round a miserable fire, trying to thaw out their bone-hard biscuits on the point of their bayonets. They moved over to make room for the boys, and gave them a mouthful of coffee. While they were drinking, an officer stuck his head in the door and beckoned to the sergeant with whom he had a rapid, whispered conversation.

'Well, lads!' the sergeant cried, rubbing his hands. 'We're going to have some fun tonight. They've got hold of the Prussian password and, if you ask me, we're going to recapture blessed old Bourget again, where we've had so many scraps in the past.'

The place echoed with cheers and exultant laughter. The soldiers began to polish their bayonets, singing and dancing as they did so, and in the midst of the tumult the boys took themselves off.

Beyond the trench lay nothing but the empty plain and in the distance a long white wall pierced with loop-holes. Pretending to be gathering potatoes, they made their way towards this wall. All the time Little Stenne kept urging the big lad to go back, but he only shrugged his shoulders and pressed on. All at once they heard the rattle of a rifle being cocked.

'Down!' said the big lad, flinging himself to the ground.

Lying there, he whistled. An answering whistle came across the snow. They crawled forward on hands and knees. In front of the wall, at ground level, a pair of yellow moustaches under a crumpled cap appeared. The big lad jumped down into the trench alongside the Prussian.

'This kid's my brother,' he said, jerking a thumb at Little Stenne.

Little Stenne was so small that the Prussian laughed at him—and had to take him in his arms to help him in.

On the other side of the breastwork there were strong earth ramparts reinforced with tree-trunks and in between them, foxholes, occupied by more yellow-moustached German soldiers in their crumpled caps.

In one corner of the fortification was a gardener's lodge, also supported with tree-trunks. On the ground floor more soldiers were playing cards or making soup on a blazing fire. The boiled cabbage and lard smelt good—very different from the poverty-stricken cooking-fire of the French infantrymen. Upstairs the officers could be heard strumming at a piano amid the popping of champagne corks.

When the two boys from Paris entered the room they were greeted with shouts of glee. They delivered their newspapers and were given drinks and encouraged to talk. All the officers looked haughty and formidable, but the big lad kept them amused with his cheeky ways and gutter slang. They roared with laughter, imitated his words, and revelled in the tittle-tattle he had brought from Paris.

Little Stenne would have liked to join in the talk, to show them he wasn't stupid either, but something held him back. Before him sat a Prussian who seemed more serious than the rest of them, and though he was pretending to read, his eyes never left Little Stenne. There was a kind of reproachful tenderness in those eyes, as if the man had a boy of his own at home and was thinking to himself: 'I'd rather be dead than see a son of mine acting like this.'

From that moment, Little Stenne felt as if a hand was pressing against his heart and preventing it from beating.

In order to get away from this pain, he gulped down his drink. Before long everything seemed to be whirling round him. He heard vaguely, to the accompaniment of laughter, his comrade mocking the French National Guard; giving an imitation of a call to arms in the Marais quarter of Paris; a night alarm on the ramparts. Eventually the big lad dropped his voice and the officers bent towards him with faces suddenly stern. The wretched youth was in the act of warning them of the infantrymen's intended attack.

At this Little Stenne leapt to his feet, angry and clear-headed: 'Not that, you great fool!' he cried. 'I won't let you ...'

But the other simply guffawed and continued his story. Before he had completed it, all the officers were standing up. One of them ushered the boys to the door.

'Off with you, out of the camp!' he ordered them, and the officers began to talk rapidly among themselves in German. The big lad strode out, proud of himself and clinking his money. Little Stenne followed him, shamefaced, and as he passed the Prussian officer whose gaze had distressed him, he heard him saying mournfully: 'Not good, that . . . not good,' and the tears came into young Stenne's eyes.

Out on the plain the boys started to run and quickly made their way back. Their sacks were full of potatoes the Prussians had given them and they got past the infantrymen's trench without difficulty. The men were getting ready for the attack that night. Troops were coming up under cover and massing near the railway. The old sergeant was there, busy giving orders with a keen air of anticipation. He recognized the boys as they passed and gave them a friendly grin.

151

Little Stenne leapt to his feet. 'Not that, you great fool!' he cried.

That grin hurt Little Stenne deeply. For a moment he was minded to cry out in warning: 'Don't carry out the attack . . . we've given you away.' But the big lad had said to him: 'If you say anything now they'd shoot us,' and fear prevented him from acting.

At Corneneuve they entered a deserted house and divided the money. It must be admitted that once he could hear those fine five-franc pieces jingling in his pockets, Little Stenne no longer felt so bad.

But later, when he was on his own, misery swept over him. When, inside the city gates, the big lad had left him, then his pockets seemed to grow terribly heavy . . . and that hand which gripped his heart was tighter than ever. Paris was no longer the same city in his eyes. The passers-by seemed to look at him harshly as if they knew where he had been. Spy—spy—spy! He could hear the word everywhere about him, in the sound of passing wheels, in the beating of drums being played along the canal. At last he reached home. Relieved to find that his father had not yet come back, he went swiftly upstairs to their room and hid under his pillow the money that weighed so ponderously on his conscience.

Papa Stenne had never been so warm-hearted and jolly as he was that evening. News had arrived from the provinces that things had taken a turn for the better. While he ate, the old marine glanced at his musket hanging on the wall, and remarked with a laugh: 'Well, my boy, you'd go for those Prussians right enough if you were older, eh?'

Towards eight o'clock there was the sound of cannon-fire.

'Hello? That's Aubervilliers. There's fighting at Bourget,' said the old fellow, for he knew all the forts.

Little Stenne grew pale and, pretending he was very tired, took himself off to bed. But he couldn't sleep. The guns thundered on and on. He saw in his mind's eye the French infantrymen setting out under cover of darkness to surprise the Prussians—and themselves falling into an ambush. He remembered the old sergeant who had grinned at him . . . and he could see him spread-eagled on the snow and many others with him . . . and the price of their blood was hidden there, under his very pillow. It was he, the son of Papa Stenne, ex-marine, who had betrayed them.

He was choked by tears. He heard his father moving about in the next room, opening a window. Down below in the square a call to arms rang out. A battalion of reservists was mustering urgently. Obviously a real battle was going on. The miserable boy could not contain his sobbing.

'What's it all about, then?' Papa Stenne demanded, entering the bedroom.

Little Stenne could bear it no longer. He leapt out of bed and flung himself at his father's feet. As he did so some of the money rolled to the floor.

'Hello? What's this? Have you been thieving?' the old man asked sharply, beginning to tremble.

Then, breathlessly, Little Stenne recounted how he had visited the Prussians, and what had happened there. As he uttered the words he felt his heart grow lighter. His confession made things easier to bear.

With a fearful expression Papa Stenne listened to the confession. At the end of it he bowed his head in his hands and wept silently.

'Father . . . father . . .' began the boy. But the old man repulsed him without a word and slowly gathered up the coins.

'Is this all?' was his only question.

153

Little Stenne nodded. The old man reached down his gun and his bandolier and put the money in his pocket. 'Ah, well,' he said, 'I am going to return it to them.'

Without speaking another word, without even a backward glance, he went down to the street to join the reservists who were setting off that night. He was never seen again.

THE SMASHING OF THE DAMS

Wing-Commander Guy Gibson

This account was written between May 1943 and September 1944, when Wing-Commander Guy Gibson, leader of the famous dambusting raid, was killed in action. At that time a vital aspect of the raid was still secret, namely the special ball-shaped bomb, invented for the operation by scientist Dr Barnes Wallis, which bounced over the water towards the target and then sank to the base of the dam wall. Further details of the daring raid and its preparation are given in The Dam-Busters, *by Paul Brickhill.*

In March 1943, after I had done 173 sorties and was pretty tired, the AOC, Air Vice-Marshal the Hon. Ralph Cochrane, sent for me and said: 'How would you like the idea of doing one more trip? It will be a pretty important one, perhaps one of the most devastating of all time, but I can't tell you any more now. Do you want to do it?' I said I thought I did.

Nothing happened for two days. On the third he sent for me and said: 'I have got to warn you that this is no ordinary sortie; in fact it can't be done for at least two months. Moreover, the training is of such importance that the Commander-in-Chief has decided that a special squadron is to be formed for the job. I want you to form that squadron. As far as air crews are concerned, I want the best—you choose them. Now there's a lot of urgency. I want your aircraft flying in four days' time. And not a word to anyone. Secrecy is vital.'

It took me an hour to pick my pilots. I picked them because I honestly believed that they were the best bomber pilots available.

By the end of two days the squadron was formed. There were 21 crews, which means 147 men—nearly all under 24, but all veterans.

Then I met a man whom I'm not going to try to describe in detail; I know he wouldn't like it. But I'm going to call him Jeff, a scientist[1].

He said to me: 'I'm glad you've come. I don't suppose you know what for?'

'No idea, I'm afraid.'

'Do you mean to say you don't know the target?' he asked.

'Not the faintest idea.'

'That makes it awkward, very awkward. But it can't be helped—I'll tell you as much as I dare. There are certain enemy objectives which are very vulnerable to air attack, and which are themselves very important military objectives. However, these need a very high amount of explosive placed very accurately to shift them or blow them out. The explosive would have to take the form of either a very large bomb or a very large mine to be dropped within a few yards of the right spot from below 300 feet. If they're dropped above that height then accuracy falls off and the job can't be done. Other snags are flak, balloons, and the difficulty of flying over water at low level.'

'Over water?' I queried.

'Yes, over water at night or early morning, with a lot of haze or fog all round. We've been working hard—very hard—on a certain theory of mine. I'll show you.'

The lights went out and a small screen lit up with a flickering motion picture. The title was 'Most Secret Trial No. 1'.

Then a plane came into view, diving very fast towards the sea. At about 200 feet it levelled out, and then a huge cylindrical object dropped out and fell rather slowly towards the water. When the object hit the water there was a great splash while the plane flew serenely on.

'You see it works,' said Jeff. 'That's my special mine. But I'm afraid it's only one-quarter size of the real thing required to do the job. Now what I want to know from you is this: can you fly to the limits I want? These are roughly a speed of 240 miles an hour at 150 feet above smooth water, having pulled out of a dive from 2,000 feet, and then be able to drop a bomb accurately within a few yards?'

I said I thought it was a bit difficult but worth trying.

The next day the AOC sent for me, and I noticed three large packing cases in his office. 'These are models of your targets,' he said. 'Now I'm not going to tell you where they are, but Jeff has told me that you won't

'Jeff' was in fact Barnes Wallis.

be able to train your squadron unless you know. You have got to be the only man in the squadron who can possibly know the target until the day before the attack is made.'

The three models were of three very large dams—perfect to the smallest detail.

Professor Jeff seemed pleased as I came in. 'How did you get on with the trials?' he asked. I told him how it was easy by day, but that flying level over water at 150 feet was very nearly impossible.

'But you could see the end all right?'

'Yes.'

'Good. Now to work. As you know, the Ruhr Valley is the most highly industrialized area in the whole of Germany.

'One great snag is the lack of water supply. So in 1911 the Germans built a mighty barrage dam blocking the Mohne Valley through which the Ruhr flowed. The Germans are very proud of this dam. It is rather beautifully built, Gothic and all that. It is some 850 yards long and 140 feet thick and as high as it is thick, and the lake it holds back is about 12 miles long, holding 140 million tons of water. At the same time they built another dam nearby called the Sorpe, very much smaller and of earthen construction.

'If they were to be breached the resultant shortage of water for both drinking and industrial purposes might be disastrous. Of course, the floods would result in more damage than has ever happened in this war. The third dam is the Eder, some 60 miles away, which supplies a lot of hydro-electric power. This holds back 202 million tons of water.

'But to breach these things is not so easy as it looks. You'll have to plan a special method of attack—inside a month.'

'But why the urgency?'

'Because dams can only be attacked when they are full of water. At the moment the water is twelve feet from the top, but we can only attack them when the water is four feet. Your projectiles will have to fall so that they sink into the water, actually touching the dam wall itself about 40 feet down: if they are not touching it'll be useless.'

Back at the squadron our great problem was the height. By now we had realized that we would have to get some method of flying accurately at 150 feet or else the whole project would have to be called off. Many methods were tried in vain.

Then one day it was solved. Mr Lockspeiser, of MAP, thought an old idea would work: spotlights placed on either wing pointing towards the water where they would converge at 150 feet. The pilot could see these spots, and when they merged into one he would then know his exact height. It all seemed simple now.

So two Aldis lights were fitted into each plane, one in the nose and one in the tail. Night after night, dawn after dawn, the boys flew around the Wash and the nearby lakes, and within a week everyone could fly to within two feet with amazing consistency.

One day I was flown for an urgent conference with Jeff. He began: 'Look, the best height to suit your aircraft is at the 60-foot level at 232 miles an hour. Can you fly at 60 feet above the water? If you can't the whole thing will have to be called off.'

I thought for a second. At 60 feet you would only have to hiccough and you would be in the drink. But I said, 'We'll have a crack tonight.'

Back at Scampton we altered the spotlights so that they converged at 60 feet, and we made our first trials. By 1 May, I rang up Jeff and told him we could do it.

On 16 May, reconnaissance aircraft reported that the water level of the dam was just right for the attack. It was a great moment when the public address system on the station said: 'All crews of 617 Squadron report to the briefing rooms immediately.'

The boys came in hushed. I let the scientist tell them all about it.

I shall never forget the final briefing. Jeff was very worried, because he felt personally responsible for their lives. He said to me: 'I hope they all come back.'

'It won't be your fault if they don't,' I said.

The AOC gave a pep talk. Then I explained the attack again, although they knew it backwards. I spoke for just over an hour.

Standing around before the take-off everyone was tense and no one said very much. Then someone at the control caravan waved a flag. I opened the throttles and we were off for Germany.

Out of the haze ahead appeared the Ruhr hills. 'We're there,' said Spam, the bomb aimer.

'Thank God,' said I feelingly.

As we came over the hill we saw the Mohne Lake, and then the dam itself. Squat and heavy and unconquerable it looked; grey and solid in the moonlight.

A structure like a battleship was showering out flak all along its length. It was light flak, mostly green, yellow and red, and the colours reflected on the dead calm of the black water so that, to us, it seemed there was twice as much as there really was.

We circled around stealthily. Every time we came within range of those bloody-minded flak gunners they let us have it.

I spoke to my crew. 'Well, boys, I suppose we had better start the ball rolling'—this with no enthusiasm whatsoever.

'Hello, all Cooler aircraft. I am going to attack. Stand by to come in to attack in your order when I tell you.'

Then to Hoppy: 'Hello, "M for Mother", stand by to take over if anything happens.'

Hoppy's clear and casual voice came back. 'Okay, Leader. Good luck.'

Then the boys dispersed to the prearranged hiding spots in the hills. Straightening up, we began to dive towards the flat, ominous water two miles away.

'Good show,' said Spam. 'This is wizard.' But as we came in over the tall fir trees his voice came up again rather quickly. 'You're going to hit them. You're going to hit those trees.'

'That's all right, Spam. I'm just getting my height.'

To Terry: 'Check height, Terry.'

To Pulford: 'Speed control, flight engineer.'

To Trevor: 'All guns ready, gunners.'

To Spam: 'Coming up, Spam.'

Terry turned on the spotlight and began: 'Down—down—down—steady—steady.' We were then at exactly 60 feet.

Pulford began working the speed to get the indicator exactly against the red mark. Spam began lining up his sights against the towers.

The gunners had seen us coming, with our spotlights on, from over two miles away. Now their tracers began swirling towards us. This was a horrible moment: we were being dragged along at four miles a minute, almost against our will, towards the thing we were going to destroy.

I think at that moment the boys didn't want to go. I know I didn't

159

want to go. I thought to myself, 'In another minute we will all be dead—so what?' I thought again, 'This is terrible, this feeling of fear—if it is fear.'

We were a few hundred yards away and I said to Pulford, under my breath: 'Better leave the throttles open now and stand by to pull me out of the seat if I get hit.' He looked a little glum on hearing this.

I began looking through the special sight on my windscreen. Spam had his eyes glued to the bomb-sight, his hand on his button. Terry was checking the height. Joe and Trevor began to raise their guns.

The flak could see us quite clearly now. I have been through far worse flak; but we were very low. There was something sinister and slightly unnerving about the whole operation. My aircraft was so small and the dam was so large, so thick and solid, and now it was angry.

We skimmed the surface of the lake, and my gunner was firing into the defences. Their shells were whistling past us, but we were not being hit.

Spam said, 'Left—little more left—steady—steady—steady—coming up.'

The next few seconds seemed a series of kaleidoscopic incidents:

The chatter from Joe's front guns . . . Pulford crouching beside me . . . the smell of burned cordite . . . the cold sweat underneath my oxygen mask . . . the tracers whisking past the windows . . . the closeness of the dam wall . . . Spam's exultant. 'mine gone!' . . . the speed of the whole thing . . . someone saying over the RT, 'Good show, Leader. Nice work!'

Then there came over us all, I think, an immense feeling of relief and confidence. As we circled round we could see a great thousand-foot column of whiteness where our mine had exploded. We could see with satisfaction that Spam's aim had been good.

The explosion had caused a great disturbance on the surface of the lake. Our mines could only be dropped in calm water, and we would have to wait until all became still again.

We waited about ten minutes. It seemed hours to us—but it must have seemed longer than that to Hoppy, who was the next to attack.

At last—'Hello, "M for Mother". You may attack now. Good luck.'

'Okay. Attacking.'

We saw him approach. Then the flak let him have it. When he was about 100 yards away someone said hoarsely, over the RT: 'Hell, he's been hit!'

'M for Mother' was on fire. A long jet of flame was beginning to stream out. I saw him drop his mine, but his bomb-aimer must have been wounded, because it fell straight on to the power house.

Hoppy staggered on, trying to gain altitude. When he had got up to about 500 feet there was a flash in the sky. His aircraft disintegrated and fell in flaming fragments. Then it burned quite gently in a field three miles beyond the dam.

Someone said: 'Poor old Hoppy.'

A furious rage surged up inside my own crew, and Trevor said: 'Let's go in and murder those gunners for this.'

Many minutes later I told Mickey to attack. Bob Hay, Mickey's bomb-aimer, did a good job, and his mine dropped in exactly the right place. There was again a gigantic explosion as the whole surface of the lake shook, then spewed forth its cascade of white water. Mickey was all right; he got through.

Once again we watched for the water to calm down—then in came Melvyn Young in 'D for Dog'. I yelled to him: 'Be careful of the flak. It's pretty hot.'

He said: 'Okay.'

I yelled again: 'Trevor's going to beat them up on the other side. He'll take most of it off you.' Melvyn's mine went in, again in exactly the right spot, and this time a colossal wall of water swept right over the dam.

Melvyn said, 'I think I've done it. I've broken it!' But we were in a better position to see and it had not rolled down yet.

All the while I had been in contact with Scampton—with the Air Officer Commanding and the Commander-in-Chief of Bomber Command, and with Jeff. He was sitting there, in the operations room, with his head in his hands, listening as one by one we announced the various aircraft had attacked, but that the wall had not yet broken.

I called up No. 5—David Maltby—and told him to attack. He came in fast, and I saw his mine fall within feet of the right spot.

Time was getting short, so I called Dave Shannon and told him to come in, but as he turned I got close to the dam wall and then saw what had happened. It had rolled over, but I could not believe my eyes. I heard someone shout, 'I think she's gone, I think she's gone,' and other voices took up the call and quickly I said: 'Stand by until I make a recce.'

I told Dave to turn away. We had a closer look. Now there was no doubt about it: there was a great breach, 100 yards across, and the water, looking like stirred porridge in the moonlight, was gushing out and rolling towards the industrial centres of Germany's Third Reich.

The other boys came down from the hills to have a closer look. There was no doubt about it at all—the Mohne Dam had been breached!

Then we began to shout and scream and act like madmen over the RT for this was a tremendous sight, a sight which probably no man will ever see again.

Quickly I told Hutch to tap out the code word for success, 'Nigger', to my base, and there was great excitement in the operations room. The scientist leaped up and danced and shouted.

Then I looked again at the dam. It was the most amazing sight. The whole valley was beginning to fill with fog from the steam of the gushing water, and down in the foggy valley we saw cars speeding along the roads in front of this great wave of water which was chasing

'There was no doubt about it—the Mohne Dam had been breached!'

them. I saw their headlights burning, and I saw water overtake them, wave by wave, and then the colour of the headlights underneath the water changing from light blue to green, from green to dark purple, until there was no longer anything except the water bouncing down in great waves.

The floods raced on, carrying with them as they went viaducts, railways, bridges. And three miles beyond the dam the remains of Hoppy's aircraft were still burning gently. I felt solemn and then pleased. Hoppy had been avenged.

I circled round there for about three minutes. Then I called up all aircraft and told Mickey and David Maltby to go home and the rest to follow me to Eder.

The Eder Dam took some finding because fog was already beginning to form in the valleys.

We rendezvous'd over the target. The time was getting short now; the glow in the north had begun to get brighter.

'Okay, Dave. You begin your attack.'

The dam was situated in a deep valley with high hills all around densely covered with fir trees. It involved a much higher degree of skill in flying than the Mohne Valley.

Dave dived down rather too steeply and he had to pull out at full boost to avoid hitting the mountain on the north side.

'Sorry, Leader. I made a mess of that. I'll try again.'

He tried again. He tried five times, but each time he was not satisfied and would not allow his bomb-aimer to drop his mine. He spoke again on the RT: 'I think I had better circle round a bit to try to get used to this place.'

'Okay, Dave. Hello "Z for Zebra" (this was Henry Maudslay). You can go in now.'

Henry made two attempts. He said he found it very difficult. We could see him running in. Suddenly he pulled away; but he turned quickly, climbed up over the mountain and put his nose right down, flinging his machine into the valley. This time he was running straight and true for the middle of the wall. We saw his spotlights together, so he must have been at 60 feet. We knew he had dropped his weapon.

A split-second later we saw something else; Henry had dropped his mine too late. It had hit the top of the parapet and had exploded immediately on impact with a slow, yellow, vivid flame which lit up the whole valley for just a few seconds. Someone said: 'He's blown himself up.'

Trevor: 'Bomb-aimer must have been wounded.'

I spoke quickly: 'Henry—Henry! Are you okay?' No answer. I called again.

But Henry had disappeared. There was no burning wreckage on the ground; there was no aircraft on fire in the air. There was nothing. Henry had disappeared. He never came back.

Once more we all had to wait for the smoke to clear.

At last to Dave: 'Okay. Attack now, David. Good luck!'

Dave went in and managed to put his mine up against the wall, more or less in the middle, but the wall of the dam did not move. Meanwhile Les Knight had been circling very patiently, not saying a word. When the water had calmed down he began his attack.

I saw him run in. I crossed my fingers. But Les was a good pilot and he made as perfect a run as ever seen that night. We saw his mine hit the water. We saw where it sank. We saw the tremendous earthquake which shook the base of the dam, and then, as if a gigantic hand had punched a hole through cardboard, the whole thing collapsed.

A great mass of water began running down the valley into Kassel. We watched it swirling and slopping in a 30-foot wall as it tore round the steep bends of the countryside. We saw it crash down in six great waves, swiping off power stations and roads as it went.

We saw it extinguish all the lights in the neighbourhood as though a great black shadow had been drawn across the earth.

We turned for home.

Then to Terry: 'I think we had better go the shortest way home. We're the last one and they'll probably try to get us if we lag behind.'

Down went the Lanc until we were a few feet off the ground, for this was the only way to survive. And we wanted to survive. We wanted to get home—quickly.

Back at the base they would be waiting for us. We did not know that when they received the code word 'Dinghy', which meant that the Eder had gone, there was a scene in the operations room such as the WAAF ops. clerks had never seen before.

The Air Officer Commanding had jumped up and had shaken Jeff by the hand and had almost embraced him. The Commander-in-Chief had picked up the phone and asked for Washington, where Sir Charles Portal was giving a dinner party. The C-in-C yelled, 'Downwood successful—yes.' Members of the dinner party heard the CAS say quietly, 'Good show,' and the dinner party was a roaring success.

Out of the 16 aircraft which had crossed the coast to carry out this mission, eight had been shot down. Only one man escaped to become a prisoner of war. Only one out of 56, for there is not much chance at 60 feet.

'North Sea ahead, boys,' said Spam.

And there it was. It looked beautiful to us then—perhaps the most wonderful thing in the world.

We were free. We had got through the gap.

ANNAPURNA
Maurice Herzog

The Annapurna Expedition of 1950 was a triumph for the French-men, led by Maurice Herzog, but it was one which cost them dear. Without either the solid organization and massive numbers which made Sir John Hunt's Everest climb outstanding, or the meticulous care which brought the British contingent safely home, Herzog's party raced, just before the monsoon broke, up a lesser-known and almost equally perilous mountain; they lost their tinted glasses and suffered from snow-blindness; they dropped their gloves looking for them, and were severely frost-bitten. The climb to the summit was bad enough, but the descent was even worse.

I was clear-headed and delirious by turns, and had the queer feeling that my eyes were glazed. Schatz[1] looked after me like a mother, and while the others were shouting with joy, he put his rope round me. The sky was blue—the deep blue of extreme altitude, so dark that one can almost see the stars—and we were bathed in the warm rays of the sun. Schatz spoke gently: 'We'll be moving now, Maurice, old man.'

I could not help obeying him with a good grace, and with his assistance I succeeded in getting up and standing in balance. He moved on gradually, pulling me after him. I seemed to make contact with the snow by means of two strange stilt-like objects—my legs. I could no longer see the others; I did not dare to turn round for fear of losing my balance, and I was dazzled by the reflection of the sun's rays.

Having walked about a couple of hundred yards, and skirted round an ice wall, without any sort of warning we came upon a tent. We had bivouacked two hundred yards from the camp. Couzy[2] got up as I appeared, and without speaking held me close and embraced me.

[1]Marcel Schatz, then aged 29—manager of a tailoring establishment.
[2]Jean Couzy, the 'baby' of the expedition, aged 27—an aeronautical engineer.

166

Terray[3] threw himself down in the tent and took off his boots. His feet, too, were frostbitten; he massaged them and beat them unmercifully.

The will to live stirred again in me. I tried to take in the situation: there was not much that we could do—but we should have to do whatever was possible. Our only hope lay in Oudot[4]; only he could save our feet and hands by the proper treatment. I heartily agreed to Schatz's suggestion that we should go down immediately to the lower Camp IV, which the Sherpas had re-established. Terray wanted to remain in the tent, and as he flailed his feet with the energy of despair he cried out: 'Come and get me tomorrow if necessary. I want to be whole, or dead!'

Rébuffat's[5] feet were affected, too, but he preferred to go down to Oudot immediately. He started the descent with Lachenal[6] and Couzy, while Schatz continued to look after me, for which I was deeply grateful. He took the rope and propelled me gently along the track. The slope suddenly became very steep, and the thin layer of snow adhering to the surface of the ice gave no foothold; I slipped several times, but Schatz holding me on a tight rope, was able to check me.

Below there was a broad track: no doubt the others had let themselves slide straight down towards the lower Camp IV, but they had started an avalanche which had swept the slope clear of snow, and this hardly made things easier for me. As soon as we drew in sight of the camp the Sherpas came up to meet us. In their eyes I read such kindliness and such pity that I began to realize my dreadful plight. They were busy clearing the tents which the avalanche had covered with snow. Lachenal was in a corner massaging his feet; from time to time Pansy[7] comforted him, saying that the Doctor Sahib would cure him.

I hurried everyone up; we must get down—that was our first objective. As for the equipment, well, it could not be helped; we simply must be off the mountain before the next onslaught of the monsoon. For those of us with frostbitten limbs it was a matter of hours. I chose Aila and Sarki to escort Rébuffat, Lachenal and myself. I tried to make the two Sherpas understand that they must watch me very closely and hold me on a short rope. For some unknown reason, neither Lachenal nor Rébuffat wished to rope.

[3]Lionel Terray, a guide from Chamonix.
[4]Jacques Oudot, the medical officer of the expedition.
[5]Gaston Rébuffat, an indefatigable mountaineer—born at the seaside.
[6]Louis Lachenal, an instructor in skiing and mountaineering.
[7]One of the Sherpas.

While we started down, Schatz, with Angtharkay and Pansy, went up to fetch Terray, who had remained on the glacier above. Schatz was master of the situation—none of the others were capable of taking the slightest initiative. After a hard struggle, he found Terray:

'You can get ready in a minute,' he said.

'I'm beginning to feel my feet again,' replied Terray, now more amenable to reason.

'I'm going to have a look in the crevasse. Herzog[8] couldn't find the camera and it's got all the shots he took high up.'

Terray made no reply; he had not really understood, and it was only several days later that we fully realized Schatz's heroism. He spent a long time searching the snow at the bottom of the cavern, while Terray began to get anxious; at last he returned triumphantly carrying the camera which contained the views taken from the summit. He also found my ice-axe and various other things, but no ciné-camera, so our last film shots would stop at 23,000 feet.

Then the descent began. Angtharkay was magnificent, going first and cutting comfortable steps for Terray. Schatz, coming down last, carefully safeguarded the whole party.

Our first group was advancing slowly. The snow was soft and we sank in up to our knees. Lachenal grew worse: he frequently stopped and moaned about his feet. Rébuffat was a few yards behind me.

I was concerned at the abnormal heat, and feared that bad weather would put an end here and now to the epic of Annapurna. It is said that mountaineers have a sixth sense that warns them of danger—suddenly I became aware of danger through every pore of my body. There was a feeling in the atmosphere that could not be ignored. Yesterday it had snowed heavily, and the heat was now working on these great masses of snow which were on the point of sliding off. Nothing in Europe can give any idea of the force of these avalanches. They roll down over a distance of miles and are preceded by a blast that destroys everything in its path.

The glare was so terrific that without glasses it would have been impossible to keep one's eyes open. By good luck we were fairly well spaced out, so that the risk was diminished. The Sherpas no longer remembered the different pitches, and, often with great difficulty, I had to take the lead and be let down on the end of the rope to find the

[8]Herzog, leader of the expedition and author of this account.

right way. I had no crampons and I could not grasp an axe. We lost height far too slowly for my liking, and it worried me to see my Sherpas going so slowly and carefully and at the same time so insecurely. In actual fact they went very well, but I was so impatient I could no longer judge their performance fairly.

Lachenal was a long way behind us and every time I turned round he was sitting down in the track. He, too, was affected by snow-blindness, though not as badly as Terray and Rébuffat, and found difficulty in seeing his way. Rébuffat went ahead by guesswork, with agony in his face, but he kept on. We crossed the couloir[9] without incident, and I congratulated myself that we had passed the danger zone.

The sun was at its height, the weather brilliant and the colours magnificent. Never had the mountains appeared to me so majestic as in this moment of extreme danger.

All at once a crack appeared in the snow under the feet of the Sherpas, and grew longer and wider. A mad notion flashed into my head—to climb up the slope at speed and reach solid ground. Then I was lifted up by a superhuman force, and as the Sherpas disappeared before my eyes, I went head over heels. I could not see what was happening. My head hit the ice. In spite of my efforts I could no longer breathe, and a violent blow on my left thigh caused me acute pain. I turned round and round like a puppet. In a flash I saw the blinding light of the sun through the snow which was pouring past my eyes. The rope joining me to Sarki and Aila curled round my neck—the Sherpas shooting down the slope beneath would shortly strangle me, and the pain was unbearable. Again and again I crashed into solid ice as I went hurtling from one *sérac*[10] to another, and the snow crushed me down. The rope tightened round my neck and brought me to a stop. Before I had recovered my wits I began to pass water, violently and uncontrollably.

I opened my eyes to find myself hanging head downwards, with the rope round my neck and my left leg, in a sort of hatchway of blue ice. I put out my elbows towards the walls in an attempt to stop the unbearable pendulum motion which sent me from one side to the other, and I caught a glimpse of the final slopes of the couloir beneath me. My breathing steadied, and I blessed the rope which had stood the strain of the shock.

I simply *had* to try to get myself out. My feet and hands were numb,

---

[9]steep gully.   [10]one of the pillar-like masses into which a glacier breaks on a steep incline.   169

'Again and again I crashed into solid ice . . .'

but I was able to make use of some little nicks in the wall. There was room for at least the edges of my boots. By frenzied, jerky movements I succeeded in freeing my left leg from the rope, and then managed to right myself and to climb up a yard or two. After every move I stopped, convinced that I had come to the end of my physical strength, and that in a second I should have to let go.

One more desperate effort, and I gained a few inches—I pulled on the rope and felt something give at the other end—no doubt the bodies of the Sherpas. I called, but hardly a whisper issued from my lips. There was a death-like silence. Where was Gaston?

Conscious of a shadow, as from a passing cloud, I looked up instinctively; and lo and behold, two scared black faces were framed against the circle of blue sky! Aila and Sarki! They were safe and sound, and at once set to work to rescue me. I was incapable of giving them the slightest advice. Aila disappeared, leaving Sarki alone at the edge of the hole; they began to pull on the rope, slowly, so as not to hurt me, and I was hauled up with a power and steadiness that gave me fresh courage. At last I was out. I collapsed on the snow.

The rope had caught over a ridge of ice and we had been suspended on either side; by good luck the weight of the two Sherpas and my own had balanced. If we had not been checked like this we should have hurtled down another fifteen hundred feet. There was chaos all around us. Where was Rébuffat? I was mortally anxious, for he was unroped. Looking up I caught sight of him less than a hundred yards away.

'Anything broken?' he called out to me.

I was greatly relieved, but I had no strength to reply. Lying flat, and semi-conscious, I gazed at the wreckage about me with unseeing eyes. We had been carried down for about five hundred feet. It was not a healthy place to linger in—suppose another avalanche should fall! I instructed the Sherpas:

'Now—Doctor Sahib. Quick, very quick!'

By gestures I tried to make them understand that they must hold me very firmly. In doing this I found that my left arm was practically useless. I could not move it at all; the elbow had seized up—was it broken? We should see later. Now we must push on to Oudot.

Rébuffat started down to join us, moving slowly; he had to place his feet by feel alone, and seeing him walk like this made my heart ache; he, too, had fallen, and must have struck something with his jaw, for blood was oozing from the corners of his mouth. Like me, he had lost his glasses and we were forced to shut our eyes. Aila had an old spare pair which did very well for me, and without a second's hesitation Sarki gave his own to Rébuffat.

We had to get down at once. The Sherpas helped me up, and I advanced as best I could, reeling about in the most alarming fashion, but they realized now that they must hold me from behind. I skirted round the avalanche to our old track which started again a little farther on.

We now came to the first wall. How on earth should we get down? Again, I asked the Sherpas to hold me firmly:

'*Hold me well because . . .*' And I showed them my hands.

'Yes, sir,' they replied together, like good pupils. I came to the piton[11]; the fixed rope attached to it hung down the wall and I had to hold on to it—there was no other way. It was terrible; my wooden feet kept slipping on the ice wall, and I could not grasp the thin line in my hands. Without letting go I endeavoured to wind it round them, but they were swollen and the skin broke in several places. Great strips of it

[11]iron peg or stanchion

171

came away and stuck to the rope and the flesh was laid bare. Yet I had to go on down; I could not give up half way.

'Aila! *Pay attention! Pay attention!*'

To save my hands I now let the rope slide over my good forearm and lowered myself like this in jerks. On reaching the bottom I fell about three feet, and the rope wrenched my forearm and wrists. The jolt was severe and affected my feet. I heard a queer crack and supposed I must have broken something—no doubt it was the frostbite that prevented me from feeling any pain.

Rébuffat and the Sherpas came down and we went on, but it all seemed to take an unconscionably long time, and the plateau of Camp II seemed a long way off. I was just about at the limit of my strength. Every minute I felt like giving up; and why, anyway, should I go on when for me everything was over? My conscience was quite easy; everyone was safe, and the others would all get down. Far away below I could see the tents. Just one more hour—I gave myself one more hour and then, wherever I was, I would lie down in the snow. I would let myself go. I would be through with it all, and could sleep content.

Setting this limit somehow cheered me on. I kept slipping, and on the steep slope the Sherpas could hardly hold me—it was miraculous that they did. The track stopped above a drop—the second and bigger of the walls we had equipped with a fixed rope. I tried to make up my mind, but I could not begin to see how I was going to get down. I pulled off the glove I had on one hand, and the red silk scarf that hid the other, which was covered in blood. This time everything was at stake—and my fingers could look after themselves. I placed Sarki and Aila on the stance from which I had been accustomed to belay them, and where the two of them would be able to take the strain of my rope by standing firmly braced against each other. I tried to take hold of the fixed rope; both my hands were bleeding, but I had no pity to spare for myself and I took the rope between my thumb and forefinger, and started off. At the first move I was faced at once with a painful decision: if I let go, we should all fall to the bottom: if I held on, what would remain of my hands? I decided to hold on.

Every inch was a torture I was resolved to ignore. The sight of my hands made me feel sick; the flesh was laid bare and red, and the rope was covered with blood. I tried not to tear the strips right off: other

172

accidents had taught me that one must preserve these bits to hasten the healing process later on. I tried to save my hands by braking with my stomach, my shoulders, and every other possible point of contact. When would this agony come to an end?

I came down to the nose of ice which I myself had cut away with my axe on the ascent. I felt about with my legs—it was all hard. There was no snow beneath. I was not yet down. In panic I called up to the Sherpas:

'Quick . . . Aila . . . Sarki . . . !'

They let my rope out more quickly and the friction on the fixed rope increased.

My hands were in a ghastly state. It felt as though all the flesh was being torn off. At last I was aware of something beneath my feet—the ledge. I had made it! I had to go along it now, always held by the rope; only three yards, but they were the trickiest of all. It was over. I collapsed, up to the waist in snow, and no longer conscious of time.

When I half-opened my eyes Rébuffat and the Sherpas were beside me, and I could distinctly see black dots moving about near the tents of Camp II. Sarki spoke to me, and pointed out two Sherpas coming up to meet us. They were a long way off, but all the same it cheered me up.

I had to rouse myself; things were getting worse and worse. The frostbite seemed to be gaining ground—up to my calves and my elbows. Sarki put my glasses on for me again, although the weather had turned grey. He put one glove on as best he could; but my left hand was in such a frightful state that it made him sick to look at it, and he tried to hide it in my red scarf.

The fantastic descent continued and I was sure that every step would be my last. Through the swirling mist I sometimes caught glimpses of the two Sherpas coming up. They had already reached the base of the avalanche cone, and when, from the little platform I had just reached, I saw them stop there, it sapped all my courage.

Snow began to fall, and we now had to make a long traverse over very unsafe ground where it was difficult to safeguard anyone; then, fifty yards farther, we came to the avalanche cone. I recognized Phutharkay and Angdawa mounting rapidly towards us. Evidently they expected bad news, and Angdawa must have been thinking of his two brothers, Aila and Pansy. The former was with us all right—he could see him in the flesh—but what about Pansy? Even at this distance they started up a conversation, and by the time we reached them they knew everything. I heaved a deep sigh of relief. I felt now as if I had laid down a burden so heavy that I had nearly given way beneath it. Phutharkay was beside me, smiling affectionately. How can anyone call such people 'primitive', or say that the rigours of their existence take away all sense of pity? The Sherpas rushed towards me, put down their sacks, uncorked their flasks. Ah, just to drink a few mouthfuls! Nothing more. It had all been such a long time . . .

Phutharkay lowered his eyes to my hands and lifted them again, almost with embarrassment. With infinite sorrow, he whispered: 'Poor Bara Sahib[12]—Ah . . .'

These reinforcements gave me a fresh access of courage, and Camp II was near. Phutharkay supported me, and Angdawa safeguarded us both. Phutharkay was smaller than I, and I hung on round his neck and leant on his shoulders, gripping him close. This contact comforted me and his warmth gave me strength. I staggered down with little jerky steps, leaning more and more on Phutharkay. Would I ever have the strength to make it even with his help? Summoning what seemed my very last ounce of energy, I begged Phutharkay to give me yet more help. He took my glasses off and I could see better then. Just a few more steps—the very last . . .

We were now quite near the tents of Camp II and Ichac, Noyelle and Oudot rushed up to meet us. I was in a fever to tell them the good news.

'We're back from Annapurna!' I shouted. 'We got to the top yesterday. Lachenal and I.' Then, after a pause: 'My feet and hands are frostbitten.'

They all helped me; Ichac held something out to me, and Noyelle supported me, while Oudot was examining my injuries. My responsibility was now at an end. We had succeeded, and I knew that the others would all be with us in a few minutes. We were saved! We had conquered Annapurna, and we had retreated in order. It was now for the others to take the initiative, above all Oudot, in whom lay our only hope. I would put myself entirely in their hands; I would trust myself to their devotion. Henceforth only one thing would count—the victory that we had brought back, that would remain for ever with us as an ecstatic happiness and a miraculous consolation. The others must organize our retreat and bring us back as best they could to the soil of France.

174   [12]big chief or master.

THE CENTURION'S ESCAPE

Anonymous

'How cursedly hot it is,' muttered the Centurion Septimius to his lieutenant, grave old Lepidus, as he lay half stripped in the shade of his tent, longing for the northern wind.

And he might well say so. The place was Syene, the time the month of August, and the almost vertical sun was pouring down his rays with a fierceness such as the Roman officer had never felt before.

Septimius and his cohort had been marched up to Syene to hold in check the inhabitants of the neighbourhood, who, servile in general, and little caring then as now who was their master, provided the taxes were not too heavy, had been stirred up by the priests to a state of most unwonted agitation, in consequence of some insult offered by the Roman soldiery to the sacred animals of the district.

The palm trees were standing motionless, not a breath stirring their long hanging branches; the broad, swollen Nile was glittering like molten metal as he rolled majestically to the sea. In the background the steep sandy ridges and black crags were baking in the sun, and the only sound that broke the silence was the roar of the distant cataract.

'Curse these Egyptians and their gods,' muttered poor Septimius.

175

'Hush, hush, Septimius,' answered Lepidus, his second-in-command, 'you shouldn't ventilate those free-thinking opinions of yours so openly. Whatever you *think*, keep a check on your tongue, for the old priesthood is jealous and powerful even yet, and strange stories are told of their secret doings.'

'A fig for the priesthood!' quoth Septimius. 'What care I for Apis or Osiris either? I am a Roman citizen and a Roman soldier. I fear no man but my superior officer, and I know no god but the Emperor.'

'Mark my words,' was the reply. 'Antony was a greater man than you, Septimius, and *he* bowed the knee to Apis and Osiris too; why, they say he was consecrated himself, and stood high in the priestly ranks, and yet he crouched like a beaten hound to old Petamon, the priest of Isis, and obeyed his very nod. I have heard strange things of that Petamon; men say he knew the old Egyptian secrets, and could raise the very dead from their long sleep to answer him. And his grandson and successor is a mightier enchanter than his sire. It was he that stirred up these poor Egyptian slaves almost to rebellion not ten days ago, because one of the legionaries broke the head of a dirty ape that he caught stealing the stores. They say he is at Philae just now concocting some new plot; so, my good fellow, keep your eyes open and your mouth shut—if you can.'

Septimius laughed, half good-naturedly, half contemptuously; and, humming a stave of Horace, turned in to take a nap, while Lepidus went round the sentries to see that none was sleeping at his post.

It was evening, the sun had set some half-hour before; and the sky, after melting through all the hues of the rainbow, had merged in one delicious violet, in which the pure clear moon and the planet Venus were shining with a glorious light such as they never attain in duller climes. Septimius, shaking off his drowsiness, left his tent to saunter through the village and see how his troops were faring.

The beauty and stillness of the night tempted him to extend his ramble. The outskirts of the town were soon passed, the few dogs he met shrank cowering from before his tall form and the clank of his good sword at his side, and in a few moments he was alone in the desert. He had more than once followed the same track towards the now silent quarries, where the old Egyptians once hewed those blocks of granite which are a wonder to all succeeding ages. It was the same scene, yet how different! When he had marched over the ground once before at the head of his legionaries to check an incursion of one of the marauding desert tribes, the sky seemed brass, the earth iron, the sun was blazing overhead like a ball of molten metal, and scorching all colour and life out of the landscape; the heat, reflected from the black basalt and red syenite rocks, had beaten on his armour almost beyond endurance, while his stout soldiers could barely struggle on through the heavy sand, sighing and groaning for one drop of water where none was to be had.

How different it was now; the moon, hanging low in the heavens, threw the long black shadows of the craggy rocks over the silvered sand; and the air was deliciously cool and fresh after the extreme heat of the day.

So he wandered on till he reached a huge boulder, on which some old Pharaoh, now forgotten, had carved the record of his marches and victories.

Suddenly from behind the boulder an old man advanced to him, and bowing low, with the cringing servility to which the lower classes of the Egyptians had been reduced by long ages of tyranny, prostrated himself at the feet of the Centurion, and in broken Greek craved a hearing.

'My lord Centurion,' said the beggar, 'I have followed your steps for days in the hope of obtaining a hearing. My tongue is Greek, but my heart is true. You have heard of the Egyptian priesthood and their wiles; not long ago one of your nation, a Centurion like yourself, fell into their hands, and they hold him captive in the neighbourhood. If you would deliver him come here tomorrow night, and come alone; I will tell you then what must be done, but I cannot now—meanwhile farewell.'

And before the Centurion could utter a word he had vanished behind the rocks.

'By Castor and Pollux,' muttered Septimius, 'was ever a decent fellow—not that I am a particularly decent fellow—in such a fix before? It may be a trap set for me; yet surely they dare not touch a soldier of the Emperor's—a Centurion too,' he said. 'Ay, poor Claudius vanished a month ago; they said it was a crocodile, but none saw it—yes, it

177

must be Claudius; go I will, let Lepidus say what he likes. But wait, if I tell Lepidus he will have my steps dogged, or some such nonsense. I'll keep my own counsel; I'll go, and go alone.' With a brisk step he turned on his heel and made his way back to his quarters.

The beggar stood behind the rock, his keen black eyes glittering with the light of triumph; his long white beard fell off, and the rags dropped from his shoulders as he joined his companion, who was lying hidden behind the rock. He drew himself up to his full stature, and his haughty step and proud port marked Petamon, the son of Osorkon, and grandson of Petamon, the High Priest of Isis at Philae.

'Hey, Sheshonk,' he laughed to his subordinate, with a snort of scorn, 'I have baited the trap for my eagle right daintily, and the noble bird shall have his wings clipped 'ere long. He mocks the divine Apis, does he, and blasphemes the Ape of Thoth!'

'Well done, Petamon,' quoth Sheshonk, the assistant priest, whose low forehead, heavy brow, and sensual lips were in strange contrast to his companion's face. 'What a pity there is nobody here to listen to you, and that such eloquence should be thrown away upon me, who knows, as well as you do yourself, if the truth were told, that Apis is only a bull after all, and Thoth's ape is a very dirty troublesome ape;

at least the one I had charge of at Hermopolis was.'

'Peace, fool,' replied Petamon, with an angry glare of his eye. The beasts are but beasts, that *I* know as well as you; but the beast is only the type of the divinity, whom the vulgar may not know. Enough.'

The rest of their conversation was lost in the distance as they slowly wended their way to the south.

Next day Septimius was somewhat thoughtful; he retired early to his tent on the pretence of weariness, and when all was still he stole out of the town as before. The hour was the same, but how different this night was from the last. A tornado had been blowing from the south all day, raising the sand in huge clouds, which obscured everything and nearly choked man and beast with a fine, penetrating dust. Even now the air was hot and depressing, the sand felt heavy under foot, and the Centurion's heart was so full of foreboding that more than once he had almost turned back.

At last he reached the granite boulder, and, crouching in its shade as

The four mysterious phantoms raised the litter and bore it across the sands.

before, sat the beggar. He rose as the Centurion approached, and beckoned him silently to proceed. Somewhat puzzled, Septimius obeyed and followed in silence, plodding wearily through the deep sand. At last the beggar turned.

'Sir Centurion,' he said, 'the night is hot and the way heavy; let me ease you of your sword'; and before Septimius could argue or resist, his nimble hands had unstrapped the belt and slung the sword over his own shoulder. 'What men you Romans are!' he continued, slightly raising his voice as they passed along a narrow track between high rocks on either side. 'You fear nothing in heaven or on earth. I verily believe you would make beef-steaks of the divine Apis'; and he halted full in the way and seemed absolutely to grow before the Centurion's eyes, he loomed so large and majestic in the moonlight, while his eyes glared like blazing coals with hatred and revenge.

The Centurion recoiled, and at the same moment two from each side, four strange white figures, each with the head of a hawk, sur-mounted by the disc of the sun, glided forth and laid hands on him. Septimius struggled like a snared lion, but it was of no avail; he threatened them with the wrath of the Emperor, and they answered with a low mocking laugh. He made one furious rush at the former beggar who had betrayed him, and clutched him by the robe. Petamon quietly threw the sword far away over the sand and crossed his arms, while his ghostly allies advanced to the rescue. In another moment the prisoner was torn away, but not before he had rent off a fragment of the priest's robes, which fell upon the sand. His good sword was gone far beyond his reach, and after a few frantic plunges he was bound hand and foot and lashed to a rude litter which was brought from behind the rock. The four mysterious phantoms silently raised the litter and bore it swiftly across the sands, while Petamon, with a vigour remarkable in one so far advanced in years, led the way.

They had advanced along the sandy tract for some distance when suddenly the eye of Septimius, who could just raise his head and look forward by straining painfully against his bonds, caught the glimmer of the moonlight on the water, and before him rose perhaps the most unearthly, most beautiful scene that can meet the eyes of man.

Ruined as it now is, with its broken columns and shattered piers, marked at every turn by the hand of the destroyer, Philae, and Philae by moonlight, is wondrously lovely; what must it have been then?

In the midst of a quiet lagoon lay the Sacred Island, enclosed by hills, on whose rugged sides the black basalt rocks were piled in the most magnificent confusion—a green spot in the midst of a desert of stone—and, amid the grove of palms upon its shore, rose the roofs of temples and the tops of huge pyramidal gateways, while the solemn moonlight poured over all. A boat, manned by four more of the strange hawk-headed beings, was anchored at the shore. Silently the priest embarked, silently Septimius was lifted on board, silently the rowers bent to their oars, and in a few minutes they were passing along under the massy wall which rises sheer out of the water on the western side.

Suddenly the boat stopped and the priest struck the wall thrice, repeating each time, 'In the name of Him who sleeps at Philae.' Silently a portion of the apparently massy wall swung back and disclosed a narrow stair, up which they carried the Centurion; and by a side door entered the outer court. Before them rose the huge gateway, on each of whose towers was carved the giant semblance of a conqueror grasping with his left hand a group of captives by the hair, while he lifts the right to strike the death-blow. They hurried on through the great Hall of Pillars up a narrow stair, and. opening a small aperture, more like a window than a door, thrust in the Centurion, and left him, bound hand and foot, to his own reflections.

Next morning Lepidus was early astir, and, after going his rounds, entered the tent of Septimius. It was empty, the bed had not been slept on, and there were no signs whatever of the tenant. 'Mad boy,' muttered Lepidus; 'off on some frolic as usual. I must hush it up, or Septimius, great though his family interest be, will get but a rough welcome from the General on our return.'

Noonday and evening came and went, and still Septimius was absent; and next morning, Lepidus, blaming himself much for having delayed so long, gave the alarm that the Centurion had vanished or been spirited away, and instituted a regular inquiry. Little information could be elicited. One of the sentries had noticed Septimius wandering away towards the desert, but he was too much accustomed to his officer's little vagaries to take much note of the fact.

Towards evening one of the sergeants craved an audience with him, and when they were alone together produced the Centurion's sword and a piece of a heavy golden fringe. He had struck into the desert, come upon a spot where there were evident marks of a struggle, and picked up the sword and torn fringe lying on the ground. Sergeant and officer looked at each other, and the same fear clouded the faces of both.

'Petamon is at Philae?' inquired Lepidus.

'He is, sir.'

'Then may Jove the Preserver help the poor boy, for he will need all his help. I see it now: his foolish scoffs at the gods have reached the ears of the crafty priest, who has hated us Romans bitterly for long, and he has kidnapped the lad. We may be too late to save him not too late for revenge. Muster the men at once and let us to Philae—quick!'

In half an hour the cohort were tramping through the sand under the still moonlight, and an hour more brought them to the banks of the quiet river. There was no boat, and they had to halt till morning broke.

At sunrise a boat was brought from the neighbouring village, and Lepidus, embarking with a portion of his troop, was rowed over to the Sacred Island. He landed at a flight of steps on the northern side, and mounting them, halted for an instant, giving the quick imperative, 'In the name of the Emperor.' Ere many minutes elapsed a band of priests, headed by Petamon himself, appeared at the great gateway, and the Centurion, advancing, briefly demanded to speak with their High Priest.

Petamon, with the rising sun flashing on his leopard-skin cloak and the golden fringe of his girdle, with his head and beard close-shaven, in his pure linen garments and papyrus sandals, stepped forward.

'I am Petamon, the grandson of Petamon, High Priest of Isis. Roman soldier, speak on.'

'I seek——' commenced Lepidus; but he stopped abruptly. His eye had caught the glitter of the golden fringe, and he saw that at one side a piece had been torn away. He sprung forward like a tiger and grasped the priest's throat. 'Petamon, Priest of Isis, I arrest you on the charge of kidnapping a Roman citizen. In the name of Caesar Domitian; soldiers, secure him!'

Priests and soldiers stood for a moment transfixed with amazement

182

while Lepidus slowly released his grasp on the priest's throat, and they stood face to face till the Roman almost flinched before the fierce glare of the Egyptian's eye. The other priests began to press forward with threatening gestures; they outnumbered the Romans three times, and, though the strength and discipline of the latter would doubtless have proved victorious in the end, might have offered a stout resistance; but Petamon motioned them back. 'Fear not, children,' he said, speaking in the Greek tongue, so that both parties might understand him, 'the gods can protect their own, and you, Sir Roman, that have laid hands on the servant of Isis, tremble!' He walked forward and surrendered himself to two of the soldiers.

'Rather him than me,' muttered Sheshonk. 'The gods are all very well to fool the people with, but I doubt if Isis herself will save him under the Roman rods.'

Petamon raised his eyes and met those of Sheshonk. A few words in the Egyptian tongue and a few secret signals passed between them, and Sheshonk, with a deep reverence, retired into the temple and disappeared.

The soldiers were despatched to search the island, and poor Septimius heard them several times pass the very door of his prison, but his gaolers had had time to thrust a gag into his mouth, so he could give no alarm. He lay there sick at heart, for he was stiff and weary, and even his cheerful spirits felt nearly broken.

The search was fruitless, as Lepidus had fully expected; and he commanded Petamon again to be brought before him. 'Sir Priest,' he said, 'I seek Septimius the Centurion, who is or was in your hands; unless he is restored before tomorrow's sun sinks in the west you die the death.'

'It is well,' said the priest, while the mock submission of his attitude was belied by the sinister fire of his eye; 'the gods can protect their own.'

Towards evening Petamon requested an audience of Lepidus, and when they were again together addressed him with more civility than he had hitherto condescended to use. He explained that it was the practice that the High Priest should, at certain seasons, sleep in the sacred recesses of the temple, and have the decrees of the goddess revealed to him in visions; he humbly craved permission to perform

183

this sacred duty, as it might be for the last time. Lepidus mused for a moment and then gave orders that the priest, chained between two soldiers, should have leave to sleep where he would.

The night closed in; the shrine of the goddess was illuminated; and the blaze of a hundred lamps flashed on the rich colours and quaint designs on the walls of the shrine. One picture especially, behind the altar, attracted the eye of Lepidus. It represented King Ptolemy trampling down an enemy, while Isis stood by his side, with her hand raised in blessing, and Osiris held out a huge blue falchion as if to bid him complete his task. Before the altar stood Sheshonk burning incense, while Petamon, chained between his guards, bowed for a time in prayer. By midnight the ceremony was over; Petamon, chained to a soldier on each side, lay down before the altar; the lights, all but one, were extinguished; the great door of the sacred chamber was closed. Lepidus lay down across it with his drawn sword in his hand, and, wearied with anxiety and care, soon fell fast asleep.

The sun was rising when he awoke, and, hastily rising, gave orders to change the guard upon the prisoner, and himself entered the chamber to see that the fetters were properly secured. The lamp was burning dimly, and there lay the two soldiers: but where was the prisoner? He was gone—utterly gone. The fetters were there, but Petamon had vanished. Half mad with vexation, Lepidus gave one of his soldiers an angry kick; the man neither stirred nor groaned; he snatched up the lamp and threw its rays upon the soldier's face. It was white and still, and a small stream of blood, which had flowed from a wound over the heart, told too plain a tale. It was the same with the other; the soldiers' last battle was fought, and they had gone to their long home.

Terrified and perplexed beyond measure Lepidus rushed out into the court, and hastily roused the cohort. It was some minutes ere he could get them to comprehend what had happened; and even then men followed him most unwillingly as he snatched up a torch and hurried back. To his amazement the corpses of the soldiers were gone, and in their place lay two rams, newly slaughtered and bound with palm ropes; the fetters had also vanished. He raised his eyes and now noticed what he had not seen before—the picture of Osiris and Isis was behind the altar still, but the blade of the falchion of the god was dyed red, and dripping with newly-shed gore. Shuddering and horror-stricken he

184

left the chamber, followed by the soldiers; and, as he passed out of the temple, met Sheshonk in his priestly robes going in to perform the morning services.

A panic seized the soldiery, in which Lepidus more than half concurred. They were men, they said; why fight against the gods? In half an hour they had left Philae and were marching through the desert to Syene, with drooping heads and weary steps, under the already scorching sun.

Terrified though he was at this awful tragedy, Lepidus was too honest and true to abandon the quest. The soldiers positively refused to assist further in the search, and he was left almost to his own resources. After much thought he published a proclamation in Egyptian and Greek offering a thousand pieces of gold for the Centurion, if alive; five hundred for the conviction of his murderers, if dead; and five hundred more for the head of the priest Petamon; and threatening the last penalty of the law on all men detaining the Roman a prisoner or sheltering his murderers.

His hopes were faint, but he could do no more; and having despatched a full report of the whole case to the Roman General at Alexandria, he waited, impatiently enough, his heart sickened with alternate hopes and fears.

During the next few days he was much disturbed by the sentiments of disaffection which he heard being muttered among the soldiers. Like all ignorant men they were superstitious, the events which had occurred at Philae had produced a deep impression on their minds, and they murmured almost openly at Lepidus for having taken them to such a fearful place, and even now for halting in so ill-omened a neighbourhood.

This feeling was much increased by an old beggar-man who constantly haunted the camp. He had attracted the attention of the soldiers by some ordinary tricks of magic, and was constantly telling fortunes and reciting prophecies, all foreboding evil to the cohort if it stayed in the neighbourhood; and, indeed, foretelling the speedy and utter downfall of Roman power.

Much grieved and perplexed, Lepidus ordered the beggar to be brought before him, and when he came taxed him with attempting to incite the soldiers to mutiny, and sternly reminded him that the punish-

185

ment for such an attempt was death. The old man listened quietly and calmly, crossing his arms and fixing his glittering eye, which seemed strangely familiar to Lepidus, on the Roman officer.

After a pause he spoke—'My lord,' and again the tone struck Lepidus as strangely familiar to his ear, 'I serve the gods, and you the Emperor: let us both serve our masters truly. You would have news of Septimius the Centurion? It may be that the gods will permit you to see a vision: shall it be so?'

A slight curl of contempt was on the Roman's lips as he answered: 'You know the proclamation. I am prepared to fulfil its terms.'

The old man shook himself like an awakening lion, and again the gesture struck Lepidus as familiar.

'I seek not gold,' he said; 'give me your attention, and keep the gold for those that need it.'

'It is well,' said Lepidus. 'Proceed.'

A small stove was burning in the tent; the old man cast upon the charcoal some drugs that raised a dense smoke and filled the tent with a heavy perfumed smell.

'Look!' said the old man, pointing to the smoke; and retiring behind Lepidus he crouched upon the ground.

A circle of light formed itself clearly and well defined among the smoke, and in its midst Lepidus suddenly saw the image of the bull Apis, as he had seen him once before at Memphis, with all his gorgeous scarlet and gold trappings, and the golden disc between his horns. A moment, and the image suddenly grew smaller and smaller, and vanished from the eyes of the wondering Roman.

Again the circle of light formed and he saw Osiris seated on his judgment throne, and the human soul being tried before him. There was the child Horus seated on a lotus flower, with his finger at his lips. There was the dog of the infernal regions, panting to devour the wicked; and there was the Ape of Thoth, watching the turn of the balance. Again the vision faded.

'These are our gods,' said the beggar. 'Now behold thine own.'

The circle formed again, and he saw the Emperor Domitian, his features bloated with intemperance, revelling among the degenerate senators and trembling patricians. The soldier sighed and the vision faded again.

Again the circle formed, and this time he saw the Centurion Septimius sitting at his tent door, as when we first saw him, and, stranger still, he saw himself in converse with him.

But suddenly, whether it was the perfumes or the excitement that overcame him he never knew, but the circle of light, the old man, the tent spun round and round, and he sank fainting to the ground.

When he awoke from his swoon the stove was burnt out, the old man was gone, and he hardly knew whether he had been dreaming or not. He felt dull and heavy and could scarcely rise. His servant entered with a light. He glanced at his finger, on which he wore his signet-ring, with which all important despatches must be sealed, and which marked their authenticity—it was gone. He felt in his bosom for the secret orders which the General had entrusted to him rather than to the headlong Septimius—they were gone too. His head still swum round; he could not think; he fell upon his bed, and sank into a heavy sleep.

We must now return to Philae—on the fifth day after Lepidus so hurriedly left it.

Septimius was still alive. A scanty allowance of bread and water was daily furnished him and his bonds had been somewhat loosed, but he had not seen the light of day since his capture, and his heart sank within him in hopeless despondency.

The news of Lepidus's proclamation had just reached the island of Philae. It was the turn of Sheshonk to officiate at the altar of Isis, and, while the incense was burning, he stood for a few moments wrapped in deep thought, then proceeded briskly about his accustomed duties.

The evening closed, the night was half spent, and Petamon, who had been away all day, had not returned, when Sheshonk stole silently up the stair with a bundle under his arm, and, touching the spring, entered the dungeon of Septimius. The weary-worn Centurion inquired in a languid voice who it was.

'A friend,' whispered Sheshonk. 'Hush, Sir Centurion, and hearken. Lepidus, your second in command, has offered a thousand pieces of gold for your safe return; do you confirm the offer?'

'Ay, and add a thousand to it,' answered the Centurion. 'I have an old father in Rome who values his son at that sum ten times fold, spendthrift youngster though he be.'

187

'Good,' said the priest. 'Petamon seeks your life, and in a few days will take it; you cannot be worse than you are, therefore you can lose nothing by trusting me—will you do so?'

'I will,' said the Centurion.

A knife was drawn gently across the cords which bound him, and he stretched his limbs here and there with a delicious sense of recovered freedom. Cautiously the priest struck a light with flint and steel and lighted a small lantern, after which he produced from his bundle a pair of huge hawks' heads, surmounted by the disc of the sun, with great glass eyes, and a pair of white disguises, such as the original captors of Septimius had worn. The Centurion eyed them with an amused smile, and muttering to himself, 'so much for the hawk demons,' proceeded to array himself in the disguise, while Sheshonk did the same. This accomplished, the priest opened the door and they cautiously descended the stairs. They met a young priest, but at a whispered word from Sheshonk he bowed and passed them by. They entered a small chamber on the west side; the priest touched a mark on the floor, and a trap-door opened at their feet, showing a long dark stair. Down this they slowly made their way, the priest stopping for a moment to draw a heavy bolt on the under side of the trap-door to impede pursuit.

After some time the Centurion heard a rushing of water above him, the passage grew damper and damper, and the priest in a whisper explained that they were passing under the bed of the river. In a little while they again ascended a high flight of steps, another trap-door opened at the touch of Sheshonk, and they emerged in a small temple on the Island of Snem, now called Biggeh. The priest silently opened the door, and they stole out. The fresh breeze was blowing from the north, and Septimius, raising for a moment the choking weight of the hawk's head, let the air play about his temples, and then, at a warning sign from his companion, replaced the mask.

The moon had set and the night was almost dark. Cautiously picking their steps they crossed the island, and found at the other side a small skiff lying at anchor, and two swarthy Nubian rowers in attendance; a few words passed between them and Sheshonk.

'We must wait,' he said, 'till the day breaks; they dare not pass the cataract by night. Sleep if you can, and I will watch.'

Septimius was too glad of the permission; he had slept but ill in his dungeon, and, taking off the heavy mask, he buried his head in his garments and fell fast asleep.

In a few hours the morning broke, and ere the sun was risen Sheshonk and Septimius were on board the boat. The rowers pulled stoutly at their oars, and they soon neared the cataract, whose roar became louder as they advanced. Before them lay a stretch of the river, fenced in on either hand with desolate rocky hills; here, there, everywhere, in the course of the stream jutted out the heads of cruel black rocks, round which the water foamed and raced like the stream of a mill-dam. On sped the boat. The Centurion shut his eyes and held his breath; the current caught them; they were hurried helplessly along for a moment, stern foremost, and were on the point of being dashed upon a rock, when a dextrous stroke of one of the oars righted them: a rush—a tumult of waters—dashing spray and the roar of the current for a moment, then the boat floated again in calm water and the danger was past.

In a few moments they reached the Roman encampment. The Nubians, at a word from Sheshonk, pulled away up the stream, while the two hawk-headed ones hurried through the camp, to the no small wonderment of several drowsy sentries.

Lepidus was just awakening with the weary disheartened feelings of one who dreads impending misfortune, when the flap of his tent-door was thrown back, and the sleepy officer fancied he must still be dreaming when he saw a hawk-headed phantom rush into the room.

It was no phantom, as he found to his cost, for it hugged him close in its arms, while its huge beak left a dint on his face that he bore till his dying day, and a voice—the voice of Septimius—issued forth, hollow sounding, from the depths of the mask:

'Dear, dear, old Lepidus. I never thought to see your sulky face again.'

There was little time for greeting and congratulations, Sheshonk was urgent on them to complete their work, and ere long the legionaries, their fears dispelled by the reappearance of the young Centurion, hastened again across the desert to Philae, burning so hotly to wipe out the insult that had been offered to the Roman name that they never felt the sun.

189

Several boats were lying at the shore, and while Lepidus with the main body of the men made for the stairs upon the northern side, Septimius and a few chosen followers, under the guidance of Sheshonk, crept along under the western wall in a small boat and reached the secret door. It opened, obedient to the touch of the priest, and silently they mounted the stair—they met the other party in the great Hall of Columns; the island seemed deserted—no living thing was to be seen.

Sheshonk's eye twinkled. 'Five hundred golden pieces for Petamon's head!'

'Ay, and five hundred more,' said Septimius.

The priest beckoned them on. They entered the sacred chamber where Petamon had kept his vigil on that memorable night, and Lepidus half shuddered as he looked round at the familiar paintings on the wall. The altar was prepared and the fire burning on it. The priest advanced and set his foot heavily on one side of the step in front. Suddenly altar and step, solid though they seemed, rolled away noiselessly to one side, disclosing a dark passage beneath. In a moment the Romans leapt down, Lepidus hastily lighting a torch at the altar fire as they did so. The passage led them to a small room in the thickness of the wall, and throwing in the light of his torch, he saw the arms and accoutrements of the two murdered soldiers, and the fetters that had bound Petamon lying in a corner. Here the passage apparently terminated abruptly, but the priest raised a stone in the roof with his hand, and they crept up through the narrow aperture thus opened. A strongly barred wooden door was on their left. They shot back the bolts and the door opened, revealing a small cell hewn out of one solid stone, with no aperture save the door for the admission of air; the light of day has never penetrated these gloomy recesses. The cell was untenanted, but a heap of human bones at one corner told of the uses to which it had been applied.

Shuddering they closed the door, and upon Sheshonk touching another spring, a square aperture opened, through which they glided, serpentwise, into another of the sacred chambers, and gladly hailed the light of day as it glimmered faintly through the door.

They searched the whole temple, but in vain; secret chambers they found more than one; even the dungeon of Septimius was opened, but nothing was discovered, and even the bloodhound sagacity of Sheshonk seemed for a moment at fault.

But his eye soon brightened, and muttering to himself 'five hundred pieces of gold,' he led them through the court under the high painted pillars, and opening a door in one of the sides of the pyramidal gateway, proceeded up a long narrow stair. Suddenly a rustle of garments was heard above them, and they caught sight of the robes of Petamon, his leopard-skin cloak and his golden fringe, as he fled before them. The two Romans dashed after him like greyhounds on a hare, but as they reached the top of the staircase Septimius stumbled and fell, and so checked the pursuit for an instant. In a moment he recovered himself, but in that instant Petamon, casting back on his pursuers a glance of baffled hatred, sprang from the tower, and in another moment lay, dashed upon the pavement of the hall, a shapeless mass, while his blood and brains were splashed over the gay painting of the pillars.

The soldiers and Sheshonk, horror-struck, hastened down, and were standing beside the body—Lepidus had just recovered from the finger of the priest the signet-ring that he had lost, and was in the act of drawing the roll of secret orders from his bosom—Sheshonk had raised his head-dress and was wiping the perspiration from his brow,

A sharp dagger was hurled with unerring aim . . .

191

when suddenly, from aloft—it almost seemed from heaven—a sharp dagger was hurled with unerring aim. It cleft the bald skull of the traitor, and he fell, with scarcely a groan, on the top of Petamon's corpse.

The Romans looked up: no one was to be seen. With a party of soldiers they searched the huge gateway towers, but without a guide such a quest was hopeless, and they never traced the hand from which the dagger came.

Their main object was accomplished. Petamon was dead, and with him expired all chances of a revolutionary outbreak. Sheshonk was dead too; but, as Lepidus said, that saved the good gold pieces.

The same evening they returned to Syene, and next day the camp was broken up, and the cohort embarked on the river and floated down to rejoin the garrison at Memphis.

THE HAUNTED TUCKSHOP
Frank Richards

Frank Richards, who died in 1961 at the age of eighty-six, was a writing phenomenon; his literary output is reckoned to have been the equivalent of a thousand full-length novels. His most memorable creation was Greyfriars School and its inhabitants. Generations of boys—and girls—enjoyed week by week the eternally youthful pranks of Billy Bunter, Harry Wharton, Bob Cherry and the rest through the pages of The Magnet. *The following is a story about Billy Bunter, 'The Fat Owl of the Remove', in a typical situation.*

'No, Master Bunter! I would not dream of it!'

Dame Mimble's tone was firm—and final.

Billy Bunter gave the tuckshop dame an appealing blink. But Dame Mimble was proof against appealing blinks. She had been proof, also, against Bunter's stream of eloquence. For the space of five minutes, the fat junior had begged, and entreated, and cajoled, but all to no purpose.

It was the old, old story. Billy Bunter was hungry, and he badly wanted some jam-tarts; but he lacked the wherewithal to procure them. He had therefore requested to be supplied with the tarts on credit—to be paid for as soon as his postal order turned up.

Mrs Mimble knew that postal order—and she knew Bunter! And she was not to be drawn. She pointed out to him, as she had done many a time and oft, that her establishment was a tuckshop, not a tick-shop.

Billy Bunter launched a last appeal.

'Oh, really, ma'am! If you realized how fearfully hungry I am— jolly nearly starving, in fact—you'd serve me without a moment's hesitation! It's nearly locking-up time, and I've had nothing to eat since tea. And I shall get nothing more for twelve hours! People have died of starvation in less time than that. You wouldn't like to see me starve, would you? You wouldn't like to attend the inquest, and to have to admit that you refused to serve me with the nourishment which would have saved me?

'Don't be dramatic, Master Bunter.'

'Six twopenny tarts!' pleaded Bunter. 'And you shall have the shilling first thing in the morning. My postal order's bound to arrive then. It's been in the post since——'

'The day you first came to Greyfriars,' suggested Dame Mimble sarcastically.

'Since the day before yesterday!' said Bunter desperately. 'But it's been hung up somewhere. These incompetent postal officials, you know——'

'Kindly leave my shop, Master Bunter. I am waiting to put up the shutters.'

Dame Mimble's tone showed clearly that the discussion was closed. But Billy Bunter lingered. Hope was dead in his breast; yet he could not tear himself away.

'Dame Mimble!'

The name was suddenly rapped out in a harsh voice—a voice that sounded strangely uncanny. It seemed to come from the ceiling, and Mrs Mimble gave a startled jump, and gazed upwards.

The tuckshop was in semi-darkness, and that voice had a most unnerving effect. Describing her sensations afterwards to her husband, the school gardener, Mrs Mimble admitted that she was 'all of a-tremble'.

'Dame Mimble!'

The name was repeated—more insistently this time; and again the voice seemed to come from the ceiling.

Dame Mimble stared upwards with starting eyes, but in the half-light she saw nothing—though she hardly knew what she had expected to see. 'Mercy me!' gasped the tuckshop dame, in great alarm. 'Who —who's calling?'

'I am the Ghost of Greyfriars!'

That alarming information was imparted in the same weird, uncanny voice.

Billy Bunter, still lingering in the shop, uttered a startled yelp.

'The—the Ghost of Greyfriars!' faltered Mrs Mimble.

'I have spoken!'

Dame Mimble shivered. Had it been broad daylight, she might have laughed at the idea of a ghost. She was a practical, matter-of-fact person who did not believe in such phenomena as 'ghosties and ghoulies, and things that go bump in the night.'

But the voice? It was not, apparently, the voice of any human being. It had scared Bunter, and it scared Dame Mimble. She decided to light the gas, with a view to locating the owner of the voice; but somehow her limbs refused to function, and she stood rooted to the floor.

'I—I say, ma'am——' faltered Billy Bunter.

'Be silent, varlet! I have nought to say to thee. I would fain hold converse with Dame Mimble. Dost hear me, dame?'

'Ye-e-s,' quavered Mrs Mimble. And she wondered whether she ought to add 'sir'. Not having conversed with spooks before, she could not be sure whether or not they were entitled to that respectful appellation.

'Listen!' went on the voice. 'This night, and for many nights to come, I will haunt thy premises!'

'G-g-good gracious!'

'I depart now, but at the witching hour of midnight I will return, to affright thee!'

Dame Mimble shuddered.

'As for that plump and scurvy knave——' continued the voice.

Billy Bunter did not wait to hear more. Panic appeared to seize him, and he fled precipitately from the tuckshop.

The Ghost of Greyfriars seemed to vanish at the same time; for Mrs Mimble, listening apprehensively for the voice to continue, heard no more.

When she had recovered the power of movement, the tuckshop dame put up her shutters and locked up. Then she hurried into the friendly light of her parlour, where she awaited the homecoming of her husband, eager to apprise Mr Mimble of the weird happenings which had disturbed the tranquillity of her mind.

Mr Mimble arrived at length, and listened to his wife's story. He was bluntly, almost brutally sceptical. He averred, emphatically, that

195

Panic appeared to seize Bunter, and he fled from the tuckshop.

there were no such things as ghosts, and that Dame Mimble had imagined it all. When she pointed out that Billy Bunter had also heard the voice, Mr Mimble was not impressed.

'Wot I says is this 'ere—you both imagined it!' he said, with a snort.

'Very well,' retorted Mrs Mimble. 'Just you wait till midnight, Joseph, and then p'r'aps you'll be convinced.'

Mr Joseph Mimble shook his head doggedly, and knocked out his pipe, and picked up the evening paper. He was not prepared to discuss the Ghost of Greyfriars any further; indeed, he was quite satisfied in his own mind, and in his own words, that 'there wasn't no sich person'.

Midnight came—and with it came the ghostly visitant, as per promise, or rather threat.

In their bedroom over the tuckshop, Mr and Mrs Mimble passed a very uncomfortable ten minutes. They saw nothing—not even when Mr Mimble rose reluctantly from his bed and lighted a candle; but they certainly heard something.

The weird, uncanny voice, which had startled Mrs Mimble in the twilight, now informed them that the Ghost of Greyfriars was present.

Mr Mimble had laughed at his wife's fears; but he didn't laugh now. He stood quaking and shaking, candlestick in hand, blinking round the room like a frightened owl.

'Joseph Mimble!' said the voice sternly. 'Tremble!'

The command was superfluous; Joseph Mimble was already trembling like an aspen leaf.

'I have come hither to haunt thee!' went on the voice. 'Canst thou see me?'

Mr Mimble directed a startled glance at the ceiling, from whence the voice seemed to come; then he blinked all round the room.

The candlelight cast strange shadows over the walls and ceiling. They might have been merely shadows; on the other hand, one of them might have been the outline of a ghostly form.

'Canst see me?' insisted the voice, which now seemed to come from beneath the bed.

'Nunno!' gasped Mr Mimble.

'Look under the bed, Joseph,' urged Mrs Mimble, with chattering teeth.

Very reluctantly, Mr Mimble dropped on all fours. In a state of abject terror, he grovelled on the floor, and nerved himself to lift up the counterpane which overlapped the bed. But the flickering light of the candle revealed no crouching, ghostly form.

Then the voice spoke again; and this time it seemed to come from inside the wardrobe.

'Joseph Mimble! Thou art a craven wight! Screw up thy courage, man, and investigate!'

'Look in the wardrobe, Joseph,' advised Mrs Mimble.

Mr Mimble picked himself up, and staggered across to the wardrobe. With his disengaged hand, he threw it open, half-expecting a grisly phantom to spring out at him.

But nothing happened.

'Joseph Mimble!' said the voice. 'I come to warn thee that some day thou shalt surely die!'

'Wow!' yelped Mr Mimble. And the perspiration stood out in beads on his forehead.

This time, the voice had seemed to come from the window.

'Go to the window, Joseph!' commanded Mrs Mimble.

And her husband tremblingly obeyed. He crossed to the little casement, and peered out into the blackness.

Greyfriars stood still and silent under the frowning midnight sky. There was no movement or motion in the dusky close.

Mr Mimble had more than expected to find a ghostly figure perched upon the outer window-sill. He was agreeably disappointed.

And then, just as he withdrew his nightcapped head, the voice sounded in his ear, at startlingly close quarters.

'Coward! Poltroon! Thou fearest me! Pah! I would fain strike thee with my spectral hand——'

'Yaroooo!'

With a wild yell of terror, Mr Mimble thrust the candlestick on to the nearest chair, and darted towards his bed. He scrambled in, and drew the bedclothes over his head, and lay there, trembling as if with the ague. Mr Mimble was no longer sceptical on the subject of ghosts. He would not be prepared to take an affidavit that he had seen one; but he had certainly heard one, and that was quite enough. In fact, it was more than enough!

The voice was not heard again, for which Joseph Mimble and his wife were truly thankful.

For over an hour they remained awake, expecting further molestation; but apparently the Ghost of Greyfriars had flitted away into the night. And Mr and Mrs Mimble fell into a troubled and uneasy slumber.

Morning came—a sunny spring morning—and the terrors of the night were dispersed like a flock of rooks at a farmer's gun.

It seemed difficult to believe, in broad daylight, that the Greyfriars tuckshop was haunted. But Dame Mimble and her husband knew only too well that it was. They had their alarming midnight experience as proof.

Probably nobody else would have accepted it as proof. The Greyfriars fellows would have laughed to scorn the notion of the tuckshop being haunted. They would have put the whole thing down to a vivid imagination on the part of the Mimbles—or possibly a nightmare. Certainly they would have discredited the story of the Ghost of Greyfriars.

'We'd better not mention this affair to any of the young gents, Joseph,' said Mrs Mimble, over the breakfast table. 'I hope Master Bunter hasn't done so. We should only be laughed at, and told that it was pure fancy on our part.'

Mr Mimble nodded. 'We won't say nothin' about it,' he agreed. 'But I'll tell you this, Jessie—I ain't goin' to sleep on these 'ere premises tonight, not if I knows it! That spook will be pretty certain to turn up again at midnight; an' my nerves wouldn't stand it! I ain't a timid man, by no means. I'd tackle anythin' in flesh an' blood. But when it comes to the soopernatural——'

'You didn't believe in ghosts last night,' Mrs Mimble reminded him.

'No; but I believes in 'em now—I believes in 'em implicit. An' I wouldn't sleep over this 'ere shop again, not if I was offered an 'undred pounds! Why, I'd as soon sleep in the chamber of 'orrors at Madam Two-swords! We must take rooms down in the village, my dear. I'll fix it up durin' the day.'

'But what about the shop, Joseph?' protested Mrs Mimble. 'Somebody will have to be on the premises. We can't leave the place unguarded.'

Mr Mimble stroked his chin thoughtfully. He saw the point clearly enough. It would not be good policy to leave the tuckshop to the mercy of a possible raider. Even with the shop shuttered, there were ways and means by which an agile person might gain access.

'Couldn't you take one of the young gents into your confidence, an' get 'im to come an' sleep over the shop? It would 'ave to be a secret arrangement, of course. The 'Ead wouldn't approve of such goings on.'

'I'll try Master Wharton,' said Mrs Mimble. 'He's a boy I can thoroughly trust, and he's got any amount of pluck.'

Mr Mimble signified his approval, and went off to his day's work in the Head's garden.

Billy Bunter rolled cheerfully into the little tuckshop.

'Good morning, ma'am!' he said genially, blinking at Dame Mimble through his big spectacles.

'Good morning, Master Bunter!'

Mrs Mimble beckoned confidentially to the fat junior, and lowered her voice. 'Have you told anybody about what happened last night?'

'Eh? About the Ghost of Greyfriars, do you mean? No, I haven't told a soul. Nobody would believe me if I did.'

Mrs Mimble looked relieved.

'I'm glad of that,' she said. 'I don't want this story to get about. Everybody would laugh at us.'

'Of course!' said Bunter. 'Hardly anybody at Greyfriars believes in ghosts. By the way, did the spook turn up again at midnight, as he threatened to?'

'Yes,' said Dame Mimble, with a shiver. 'It—it was terrible, Master Bunter! We could hear that voice coming from all parts of the room, but we couldn't actually see the ghost. And we didn't want to, either! We're not going to sleep here tonight. Mr Mimble intends to take rooms in the village.'

'A jolly good wheeze!' said Billy Bunter. 'But I suppose you'll have somebody on the premises, just to keep guard?'

'I have just been discussing that with Mr Mimble,' said the dame, with a worried look.

'You ought really to get somebody, you know. You need some

fearless, lion-hearted fellow, who would snap his fingers at a blessed ghost.'

Mrs Mimble nodded. 'I was thinking of asking Master Wharton——' she began.

'Wharton!' Billy Bunter's tone was scornful and contemptuous. 'Why, he hasn't the pluck of a rabbit! If Wharton saw a ghost, he'd turn up his toes!'

Dame Mimble smiled. 'You weren't exactly a hero yourself last night, Master Bunter,' she said. 'You soon bolted when you heard that voice!'

'I didn't!' he exclaimed in hot denial. 'I'll tell you why I buzzed off in such a hurry. I saw by your clock that it was time for calling-over, and I was afraid I should be late.'

'Oh!'

'Look here, ma'am. I shouldn't say a word to Wharton about this business, if I were you. He'd only laugh at you, and so would all his pals. Nobody believes in ghosts.'

Mrs Mimble felt that Bunter was right. She wrung her hands helplessly. 'But what am I to do?' she said. 'Somebody ought to be here tonight——'

'I'm your man!' said Bunter promptly.

'You!'

Dame Mimble's tone, and look, were expressive of blank amazement. She had never regarded Billy Bunter as being of the stuff of which heroes are made. She found it difficult to picture him enduring a lonely vigil in the room overhead, and defying the Ghost of Greyfriars, and denouncing him by bell, book, and candle, so to speak.

Billy Bunter nodded his head vigorously. 'I'm quite game to sleep over your shop tonight, ma'am. You wouldn't find another fellow, not in all Greyfriars, who'd be willing to do it. They wouldn't see any necessity for it. But I'll take on the job! When you close your shop tonight, leave the key of your private door with me; and after lights out I'll come along here and take up my post as night-watchman. Is that a go, ma'am?'

Dame Mimble hesitated. She had no great liking for Billy Bunter; and her opinion of his physical bravery was not very high.

But it was necessary to find somebody who would agree to guard

201

the premises; and, since Bunter had volunteered for that hazardous job, in defiance of the ghost and the 'voice', why not close with his offer?

It occurred to Dame Mimble, for a fleeting moment, that the provisions and foodstuffs in her shop would not be safe, with Billy Bunter in close proximity. But she quickly dismissed from her mind the notion that Bunter might tamper with her supplies. For the tuckshop was haunted; and the presence of the Ghost of Greyfriars on the premises would effectively check any attempt at a raid, even if Bunter dared to contemplate such a thing. With that uncanny voice close at hand, reproving and admonishing, it was extremely unlikely that Bunter would feel like helping himself to food from the tuckshop. Indeed, that weird and terrifying voice would probably have the effect of taking away his appetite.

'Are you really serious, Master Bunter?' asked Mrs Mimble, at length.

'Absolutely!'

'You're not afraid to spend the night in the room overhead?'

'A Bunter is never afraid, ma'am.'

'But supposing they find that you are absent from your dormitory?'

Billy Bunter shrugged his shoulders. 'Oh, I'll chance that, ma'am!' he said carelessly. 'I'll come here after lights out, and stay till daybreak. There won't be any ghosts after dawn; they always vanish at cock-crow, you know.'

'I hope you won't be dreadfully scared,' Master Bunter, when midnight comes, and you hear the voice!'

Billy Bunter scornfully repudiated that suggestion. 'It would take more than a voice to scare me!' he declared. 'I'm not a funk. I fear no foe in shining armour—or ghostly trappings!'

'It's good of you to help us in this way, Master Bunter,' said Dame Mimble gratefully.

'Yes, it is, isn't it?' said the fat junior, with whom modesty was not a cardinal virtue. 'Awfully decent of me, really; but then, I always was a generous and obliging sort of chap. Ahem! I wonder if you would let me have a few jam-tarts, ma'am! I'm expecting the postman at any moment, and I'll settle for them as soon as he comes.'

Dame Mimble promptly passed a dish of tarts across the counter, and Billy Bunter fell upon them like a ravenous wolf. Perched on a stool, he proceeded to enjoy himself. He felt that he needed a little snack, to whet his appetite for breakfast.

Dame Mimble did not begrudge the jam-tarts. She was only too relieved to have found someone who was willing to spend the night on her premises.

'You fellows awake?'

Billy Bunter sat up in bed, and peered through the gloom, and waited breathlessly for a response to his softly uttered query.

But there was no response. The members of the Greyfriars Remove, with the exception of William George Bunter, were in the arms of Morpheus. The only sound which broke the silence of the Remove dormitory was the booming snore of Bolsover major.

Billy Bunter slipped quietly out of bed, and dressed in the darkness. He donned a pair of rubber-soled shoes, and stole quietly from the dormitory.

The fat junior chuckled softly as he groped his way down the wide staircase. Jingling in his trousers pocket was a bunch of keys—the keys of the school tuckshop.

It had been one of Billy Bunter's most dearly cherished ambitions to become the custodian of those keys for a few hours. They were as precious to him as the keys of paradise, for they gave access to a glorious realm of unlimited tuck—a land flowing with milk and honey, as it were.

Even in his wildest dreams, Bunter had never seriously thought that he would ever obtain possession of the keys to the tuckshop, or be in a position to pass the night in that delightful establishment. But he had the keys now; and the tuckshop was at his mercy.

Strangely enough, he did not seem a bit perturbed at the prospect of receiving a midnight visit from the Ghost of Greyfriars. He was remarkably cheerful for a fellow who was about to undergo a nerve-racking ordeal. Perhaps the traditional bravery of the Bunters—of which William George was so fond of boasting—stood him in good stead now.

He stole through the shadows in the direction of the tuckshop. Standing in silent isolation, in a corner of the close, the building was in utter darkness, and its aspect was ghostly and forbidding. Braver hearts

203

than Bunter's might have quailed at the prospect of entering the place, knowing it to be haunted. Yet Bunter was chuckling quite gleefully as he made his way to Mrs Mimble's private entrance at the back.

He unlocked the door, let himself in, and passed through the little parlour into the shop.

If Billy Bunter had heard a ghostly voice, or felt the touch of a clammy spectral hand on his cheek, he would probably have jumped out of his skin. But he heard no voice, and he felt no icy touch. The only sound which broke the silence of the tuckshop was the scuttling of a mouse, which had been disturbed whilst having late supper in a biscuit tin, the lid of which Dame Mimble had inadvertently left off.

Billy Bunter lit the gas. Owing to the window being shuttered, there was no fear of the light being seen from without.

The sudden blaze of illumination flooded the tuckshop, and revealed a choice array of foodstuffs stacked upon the shelves.

Beneath glass covers, Billy Bunter had a vision of tempting jam-tarts, and doughnuts, and meringues, and maids-of-honour. In Mrs Mimble's safe was a large steak and kidney pie, recently baked. Affixed to the counter was a corpulent barrel of home-made ginger-beer.

Certainly there was no danger of Bunter starving in the midst of plenty! He smacked his lips, and blinked around the shop.

It was Bunter's intention to have the feed of his life, but he scarcely knew where to start. The tuckshop contained a vast and varied assort-ment of good things—'infinite riches in a little room', as the poet puts it—and it was difficult to decide which delicacy to sample first.

But Billy Bunter did not hesitate for long! He went from dish to dish, lifting the glass covers, taking a nibble here and a nibble there.

An hour passed—one crowded hour of glorious bliss, so far as Billy Bunter was concerned. And by the time the hour expired, the fat marauder had sampled not merely a little of everything, but quite a lot of everything!

Bunter had fairly let himself go, and he had done himself well—too well, in fact. Even Bunter's voracious appetite was satiated. Like the average London omnibus, he had 'no room inside'. He seemed in imminent peril of bursting, and it was some time before he could move.

At last he managed to summon enough energy to extinguish the gas, and heave himself upstairs.

The bedroom had been neatly prepared for him; but Bunter was in no state to notice that. He felt considerably the worse for food, having taken far too much cargo on board; and his one desire was for sleep.

Partially undressing, Billy Bunter crawled between the sheets, and was soon sound asleep.

Midnight came, and passed; but the Ghost of Greyfriars, apparently, was taking a night off!

When Dame Mimble arrived at the tuckshop next morning, it was to find Billy Bunter still in bed, and uttering heart-rending moans. His complexion was almost green, and he was obviously in the throes of a bilious attack.

Dame Mimble's next discovery was of an alarming depletion in her stock. She at once connected the depletion with Bunter's bilious attack, and she accused the fat junior, accordingly, of having raided her supplies during the night.

Billy Bunter indignantly denied the charge. If there was anything missing, he averred, the Ghost of Greyfriars must be held responsible.

By this time, Dame Mimble was seriously beginning to doubt whether the Ghost of Greyfriars was an existent entity. She began to suspect Bunter, not only of raiding her supplies, but of engineering the whole business.

A little later, when Mr Quelch, the Remove-master, came into the tuckshop for his morning glass of milk, Dame Mimble sent him upstairs to interview Bunter.

The interview was a painful one. Under Mr Quelch's stern and searching cross-examination, Billy Bunter floundered helplessly in a sea of denials and contradictions.

'I don't know anything about the grub being raided, sir!' he declared. 'I haven't budged from this bed all night, sir—honour bright!'

'You have no business to be in this bed at all, Bunter!' said Mr Quelch sternly.

'Oh, really, sir——. Mrs Mimble begged me to come and sleep here, because of the ghost. This tuckshop is haunted, sir, by a fearful apparition in white, with clanking chains——'

'Nonsense, Bunter!' Mr Quelch looked very grim. 'I think we shall find that the "ghost" is a very substantial one of flesh and blood!'

Billy Bunter quaked beneath the bed-clothes.

'I—I hope Mrs Mimble hasn't been making accusations against me, sir,' he said. 'It's quite wrong to say that the ghostly voice was due to my ventriloquism——'

'What!'

'And if Mrs Mimble suggests that I climbed up to the fanlight over her bedroom, the night before last, and scared her and her husband by throwing my voice all round the room, I can only say that it's an awful fib, sir!'

'Bunter!' The voice of Mr Quelch resembled the rumble of thunder. 'What you have just told me is tantamount to an admission that you have been scaring Mr and Mrs Mimble with your ventriloquial tricks! You succeeded, in fact, in scaring them off the premises.'

'Oh, really, sir——'

'I can clearly see what has occurred,' said the Remove-master. 'By means of ventriloquism, you deluded Mrs Mimble and her husband into believing that the place was haunted. You then volunteered to sleep on the premises, with the object of helping yourself to the supplies, and holding a disgusting orgy. Such conduct, Bunter, merits condign punishment. When you are sufficiently recovered from your revolting state of biliousness, I shall take you before the Headmaster!'

'But—but you've got it all wrong, sir!' protested Bunter. 'I used to be a jolly good ventriloquist, but I've given it up since I strained my larynx. As for raiding the tuck, sir, such an idea would never enter my head. I've always been taught to keep my hands from sticking and peeling—I mean, picking and stealing——'

'Be silent, Bunter!' snapped Mr Quelch. 'You cannot hope to impose upon my credulity by a tissue of falsehoods. As soon as you are well enough to rise and dress, you will report to me, and accompany me to Doctor Locke's study!'

So saying, Mr Quelch took his departure, leaving Billy Bunter to spend a melancholy morning, and an even more melancholy afternoon.

When the bilious attack had passed off, Bunter was arraigned before the Head; and there was weeping and gnashing of teeth. Those who happened to be in earshot surmised that pig-sticking was in progress.

William George Bunter was being made to realize—not for the first time in his chequered career—that the way of the transgressor is hard!

ASSIGNMENT WITH AN OCTOPUS

Arthur Grimble

I certainly should never have ventured out alone for pure sport, armed with nothing but a knife, to fight a tiger-shark in its own element. I am as little ashamed of that degree of discretion as the big-game hunter who takes care not to attack a rhinoceros with a shotgun. The fear I had for the larger kinds of octopus was quite different. It was a blind fear, sick with digust, unreasoned as a child's horror of darkness. Victor Hugo was the man who first brought it up to the level of my conscious thought. I still remember vividly the impression left on me as a boy of fourteen by that account in *Les Travailleurs de la Mer* of Gilliatt's fight with the monster that caught him among the rocks of The Douvres. For years after reading it, I tortured myself with wondering how ever I could behave with decent courage if faced with a giant at once so strong and so loathsome. My commonest nightmare of the period was of an octopus-like Presence poised motionless behind me, towards which I dared not turn, from which my limbs were too frozen to escape. But that phase did pass before I left school, and the Thing lay dormant inside me until a day at Tarawa.

Before I reached Tarawa, however, chance gave me a swift glimpse of what a biggish octopus can do to a man. I was wading at low tide one calm evening on the lip of the reef at Ocean Island when a Baanaban villager, back from fishing, brought his canoe to land within twenty yards of where I stood. There was no more than a show of breaking seas, but the water was only knee deep, and this obliged the fisherman to slide overboard and handle his lightened craft over the jagged edge. But no sooner were his feet upon the reef than he seemed to be tied where he stood. The canoe was washed shorewards ahead of him; while he stood with legs braced, tugging desperately away from something. I had just time to see a tapering, greyish-yellow rope curled around his right wrist before he broke away from it. He fell sprawling into the foam at the reef's edge. The fisherman picked himself up and nursed his right arm. I had reached him by then. The octopus had caught him with only the tip of one tentacle, but the terrible hold of the few suckers on his wrist had torn the skin whole from it as he wrenched himself adrift.

Possibly, if you can watch objectively, the sight of *Octopus Vulgaris* searching for crabs and crayfish on the floor of the lagoon may move you to something like admiration. You cannot usually see the dreadful eyes from a water-glass straight above its feeding-ground, and your feeling for crustaceans is too impersonal for horror at their fates between pouncing suckers and jaws. There is real beauty in the rich change of its colours as it moves from shadow to sunlight, and the gliding ease of its arms as they reach and flicker over the rough rocks fascinates the eye with its deadly grace. You feel that if only the creature would stick to its grubbing on the bottom the shocking ugliness of its shape might even win your sympathy, as for some poor Caliban in the enchanted garden of the lagoon.

But it is no honest grubber in the open. For every one of its kind that you see crawling below you, there are a dozen skulking in recesses of the reef that falls away like a cliff from the edge where you stand watching. When *Octopus Vulgaris* has eaten its fill of the teeming crabs and crayfish it seeks a dark cleft in the coral face and anchors itself there with a few of the large suckers nearest to its body. Thus shielded from attack in the rear, with tentacles gathered to pounce, it squats glaring from the shadows, alert for anything alive to swim within striking distance. It can hurl one or all of those whiplashes forward with the speed of dark lightning, and once its scores of suckers, rimmed with hooks for grip on slippery skins, are clamped about their prey, nothing but the brute's death will break their awful hold.

But that very quality of the octopus that most horrifies the imagination, its relentless tenacity, becomes its undoing when hungry man steps into the picture. The people of the Gilbert Islands happen to value certain parts of it as food, and their method of fighting it is coolly based upon the one fact that its arms never change their grip. They hunt for it in pairs. One man acts as the bait, his partner as the killer. First, they swim eyes-under at low tide just off the reef, and search the crannies of the submarine cliff for sight of any tentacle that may flicker out for a catch. When they have placed their quarry they land on the reef for the next stage. The human bait starts the real game. He dives and tempts the lurking brute by swimming a few strokes in front of its cranny, at first a little beyond striking range. Then he turns and makes straight for the cranny, to give himself into the embrace of those waiting arms. Sometimes nothing happens. The beast will not always respond to the lure. But usually it strikes.

The partner on the reef above stares down through the pellucid water, waiting for his moment. His teeth are his only weapon. His killing efficiency depends on his avoiding every one of those strangling arms. He must wait until his partner's body has been drawn right up to the entrance of the cleft. The monster inside is groping then with its horny mouth against the victim's flesh, and sees nothing beyond it. That point is reached in a matter of no more than thirty seconds after the decoy has plunged. The killer dives, lays hold of his pinioned friend at arms' length, and jerks him away from the cleft; the octopus is torn adrift from the anchorage of its proximal suckers, and clamps itself the more fiercely to its prey.

In the same second the human bait gives a kick which brings him, with quarry annexed, to the surface. He turns on his back, still holding his breath for better buoyancy, and this exposes the body of the beast for the kill. The killer closes in, grasps the evil head from behind, and wrenches it away from its meal. Turning the face up towards himself, he plunges his teeth between the bulging eyes, and bites down and in with all his strength. That is the end of it. It dies on the instant; the suckers release their hold; the arms fall away; the two fishers paddle with whoops of delighted laughter to the reef, where they string the catch to a pole before going to rout out the next one.

Any two boys of seventeen, any day of the week, will go out and get you half a dozen octopus like that for the mere fun of it. Here lies the whole point of this story. The hunt is, in the most literal sense, nothing but child's play to the Gilbertese.

As I was standing one day at the end of a jetty in Tarawa lagoon, I saw two boys from the near village shouldering a string of octopus slung on a pole between them. I started to wade out in their direction, but before I hailed them they had stopped, planted the carrying-pole upright in a fissure and, leaving it there, swam off the edge for a while with faces submerged, evidently searching for something under the water. I had only been a few months at Tarawa, and that was my first near view of an octopus-hunt. I watched every stage of it from the dive of the human bait to the landing of the dead catch. When it was over I went up to them. I could hardly believe that in those few seconds, with no more than a frivolous-looking splash or two on the surface, they could have found, caught, and killed the creature they were now stringing up before my eyes. They explained the amusing simplicity of the thing.

'There's only one trick the decoy-man must never forget,' they said, 'and that's not difficult to remember. If he is not wearing the water-spectacles of the Men of Matang he must cover his eyes with a hand as he comes close to the *kika* (octopus), or the suckers might blind him.' It appears that the ultimate fate of the eyes was not the thing to worry about; the immediate point was that the sudden pain of a sucker clamping itself to an eyeball might cause the bait to expel his breath and inhale sea-water; that would spoil his buoyancy, and he would fail then to give his friend the best chance of a kill.

Then they began whispering together. I knew in a curdling flash what they were saying to each other. Before they turned to speak to me again, a horrified conviction was upon me. My wretched curiosity had led me into a trap from which there was no escape. They were going to propose that I should take a turn at being the bait myself, just to see how delightfully easy it was. And that is what they did. It did not even occur to them that I might not leap at the offer. I was already known as a young Man of Matang who liked swimming, and fishing, and laughing with the villagers; I had just shown an interest in this particular

210

'I remember a dreadful sliminess with a herculean power behind it.'

form of hunting; naturally, I should enjoy the fun of it as much as they did. Without even waiting for my answer, they gleefully ducked off the edge of the reef to look for another octopus—a fine fat one—*mine*.

I was dressed in khaki slacks, canvas shoes, and a short-sleeved singlet. I took off the shoes and made up my mind to shed the singlet if told to do so; but I was wildly determined to stick to my trousers throughout. Dead or alive, said a voice within me, an official minus his pants is a preposterous object, and I felt I could not face that extra horror. However, nobody asked me to remove anything.

I hope I did not look as yellow as I felt when I stood to take the plunge; I have never been so sick with fear before or since. 'Remember, one hand for your eyes,' said someone from a thousand miles off, and I dived.

I do not suppose it is really true that the eyes of an octopus shine in the dark, and besides, it was clear daylight only six feet down in the limpid water; but I could have sworn the brute's eyes burned at me as I turned in towards his cranny. That dark glow—whatever may have been its origin—was the last thing I saw as I blacked out with my left hand and rose into his clutches. Then I remember chiefly a dreadful sliminess with a herculean power behind it. Something whipped round my left forearm and the back of my neck, binding the two together. In the same flash another something slapped itself high on my forehead, and I felt it crawling down inside the back of my singlet. My impulse was to tear at it with my right hand, but I felt the whole of that arm pinioned to my ribs.

In most emergencies the mind works with crystal-clear impersonality. This was not even an emergency, for I knew myself perfectly safe. But my boyhood's nightmare was upon me. When I felt the swift constriction of those disgusting arms jerk my head and shoulders in towards the reef, my mind went blank of every thought save the beastliness of contact with that squat head. A mouth began to nuzzle below my throat, at the junction of the collar-bones. I forgot there was anyone to save me. Yet something still directed me to hold my breath.

I was awakened from my cowardly trance by a quick, strong pull on my shoulders, back from the cranny. The cables around me tightened painfully, but I knew I was adrift from the reef. I gave a kick, rose to the surface, and turned on my back with the brute sticking out of my chest like a tumour. My mouth was smothered by some flabby moving horror. The suckers felt like hot rings pulling at my skin. It was only two seconds, I suppose, from then to the attack of my deliverer, but it seemed like a century of nausea.

My friend came up between me and the reef. He pounced, pulled, bit down, and the thing was over—for everyone but me. At the sudden relaxation of the tentacles, I let out a great breath, sank, and drew in the next under water. It took the united help of both boys to get me, coughing, heaving, and pretending to join in their delighted laughter, back to the reef. I had to submit there to a kind of war-dance round me, in which the dead beast was slung whizzing past my head from one to the other. I had a chance to observe then that it was not by any stretch of fancy a giant, but just plain average. That took the bulge out of my budding self-esteem. I left hurriedly for the cover of the jetty, and was sick.

212

THE VOYAGE TO SOUTH GEORGIA

Sir Ernest Shackleton

Sir Ernest Shackleton set out in 1913 for the Antarctic on a trans-polar expedition, but his plans were thwarted when his ship, the Endurance, *became trapped in the ice. After drifting for nine months, she was completely crushed, leaving Shackleton's party stranded on the ice. This was in October 1915, and after spending the summer sledging slowly across the ice, Shackleton decided on his desperate bid for help—an 800-mile boat voyage from Elephant Island to South Georgia Island in the South Atlantic, across some of the stormiest seas in the world.*

The weather was fine on 23 April, and we hurried forward our preparations. It was on this day I decided finally that the crew for the *James Caird* should consist of Worsley, Crean, McNeish, McCarthy, Vincent and myself. A storm came on about noon, with driving snow and heavy squalls. Occasionally the air would clear for a few minutes, and we could see a line of pack-ice, five miles out, driving across from west to east. This sight increased my anxiety to get away quickly. Winter was advancing, and soon the pack might close completely round the island and stay our departure for days or even weeks.

Worsley, Wild, and I climbed to the summit of the seaward rocks and examined the ice from a better vantage-point than the beach offered. The belt of pack outside appeared to be sufficiently broken for our purposes, and I decided that, unless the conditions forbade it, we would make a start in the *James Caird* the following morning. Obviously the pack might close at any time. This decision made, I spent the rest of the day looking over the boat, gear, and stores, and discussing plans with Worsley and Wild.

Our last night on the solid ground of Elephant Island was cold and

213

uncomfortable. We turned out at dawn and had breakfast. Then we launched the *Stancomb Wills* and loaded her with stores, gear, and ballast, which would be transferred to the *James Caird* when the heavier boat had been launched. The ballast consisted of bags made from blankets and filled with sand, making a total weight of about a thousand pounds. In addition we had gathered a number of boulders and about two hundred and fifty pounds of ice, which would supplement our two casks of water.

The stores taken in the *James Caird*, which would last six men for one month, were as follows:

30 boxes of matches	2 cases nut food
6½ gallons paraffin	2 cases biscuits
1 tin methylated spirit	1 case lump sugar
10 boxes of flamers	30 packets of Trumilk
1 box of blue lights	1 tin of Bovril cubes
2 Primus stoves with spare	1 tin of Cerebos salt
parts and prickers	36 gallons of water
1 Nansen aluminium	250 lb of ice
cooker	*Instruments*:
6 sleeping-bags	Sextant
A few spare socks	Binoculars
Few candles and some blubber-	Prismatic compass
oil in an oil bag	Sea-anchor
Food:	Charts
3 cases sledging rations	Aneroid

The swell was slight when the *Stancomb Wills* was launched and the boat got under way without any difficulty; but half an hour later, when we were pulling down the *James Caird*, the swell increased suddenly. Apparently the movement of the ice outside had made the opening and allowed the sea to run in without being blanketed by the line of pack. The swell made things difficult. Many of us got wet to the waist while dragging the boat out—a serious matter in that climate. When the *James Caird* was afloat in the surf she nearly capsized among the rocks before we could get her clear, and Vincent and the carpenter, who were on the deck, were thrown into the water. This was really bad luck, for the two men would have small chance of drying their clothes after we had got under way.

The *James Caird* was soon clear of the breakers. We used all the available ropes as a long painter to prevent her drifting away to the north-east, and then the *Stancomb Wills* came alongside, transferred her load, and went back to the shore for more. As she was being beached this time the sea took her stern and half filled it with water. She had to be turned over and emptied before the return journey could be made. Every member of the crew of the *Stancomb Wills* was wet to the skin. The water casks were towed behind the *Stancomb Wills* on this second journey, and the swell, which was increasing rapidly, drove the boat on to the rocks, where one of the casks was slightly damaged. This accident proved later to be a serious one, since some sea-water had entered the cask and the contents were now brackish.

By midday the *James Caird* was ready for the voyage. Vincent and the carpenter had secured some dry clothes by exchange with members of the shore party (I heard afterwards that it was a full fortnight before the soaked garments were finally dried), and the boat's crew was standing by waiting for the order to cast off. A moderate westerly breeze was blowing. I went ashore in the *Stancomb Wills* and had a last word with Wild, who was remaining in full command, with direction as to his course of action in the event of our failure to bring relief, but I practically left the whole situation and scope of action and decision to his own judgment, secure in the knowledge that he would act wisely. I told him that I trusted the party to him and said good-bye to the men.

Then we pushed off for the last time, and within a few minutes I was aboard the *James Caird*. The crew of the *Stancomb Wills* shook hands with us as the boats bumped together and offered us the last good wishes. Then, setting our jib, we cut the painter and moved away to the north-east. The men who were staying behind made a pathetic little group on the beach, with the grim heights of the island behind them and the sea seething at their feet, but they waved to us and gave three hearty cheers. There was hope in their hearts and they trusted us to bring the help that they needed.

I had all sails set, and the *James Caird* quickly dipped the beach and its line of dark figures. The westerly wind took us rapidly to the line of the pack, and as we entered it I stood up with my arm round the mast, directing the steering, so as to avoid the great lumps of ice that were flung about in the heave of the sea. The pack thickened and we were forced to turn almost due east, running before the wind towards a gap I had seen in the morning from the high ground. I could not see the gap now, but we had come out on its bearing and I was prepared to find that it had been influenced by the easterly drift.

At four o'clock in the afternoon we found the channel, much narrower than it had seemed in the morning but still navigable. Dropping sail, we rowed through without touching the ice anywhere, and by 5.30 p.m. we were clear of the pack with open water before us. We passed one more piece of ice in the darkness an hour later, but the pack lay behind, and with a fair wind swelling the sails we steered our little craft through the night, our hopes centred on our distant goal.

The tale of the next sixteen days is one of supreme strife amid heaving waters. The Antarctic Ocean lived up to its evil winter reputation. I decided to run north for at least two days while the wind held and so get into warmer weather before turning to the east and laying a course for South Georgia. We took two-hourly spells at the tiller. The men who were not on watch crawled into the sodden sleeping-bags and tried to forget their troubles for a period; but there was no comfort in the boat. The bags and cases seemed to be alive in the unfailing knack of presenting their most uncomfortable angles to our rest-seeking bodies. A man might imagine for a moment that he had found a position of ease, but always discovered quickly that some unyielding point was impinging on muscle or bone. The first night aboard the boat was one of acute discomfort for us all, and we were heartily glad when the dawn came and we could set about the preparation of a hot breakfast.

This record of the voyage to South Georgia is based on scanty notes made day by day. The notes dealt usually with the bare facts of distances, positions, and weather, but our memories retained the incidents of the passing days in a period never to be forgotten. By running north for the first two days I hoped to get warmer weather and also to avoid lines of pack-ice that might be extending beyond the main body. We needed all the advantage that we could obtain from the higher latitude for sailing on the great circle, but we had to be cautious regarding possible ice-streams.

216

Cramped in our narrow quarters and continually wet by the spray, we suffered severely from cold throughout the journey. We fought the seas and the winds and at the same time had a daily struggle to keep ourselves alive. At times we were in dire peril.

Generally we were upheld by the knowledge that we were making progress towards the land where we would be, but there were days and nights when we lay to, drifting across the storm-whitened seas and watching with eyes interested rather than apprehensive the uprearing masses of water, flung to and fro by nature in the pride of her strength. Deep seemed the valleys when we lay between the reeling seas. High were the hills when we perched momentarily on the tops of giant combers. Nearly always there were gales. So small was our boat and so great were the seas that often our sail flapped idly in the calm between the crests of two waves. Then we would climb the next slope and catch the full fury of the gale where the wool-whiteness of the breaking water surged around us. We had our moments of laughter—rare, it is true, but hearty enough. Even when cracked lips and swollen mouths checked the outward and visible signs of amusement we could see a joke of the primitive kind.

The wind came up strong and worked into a gale from the north-west on the third day out. We stood away to the east. The increasing seas discovered the weakness of our decking. The continuous blows shifted the box-lids and sledge-runners so that the canvas sagged down and accumulated water. Then icy trickles, distinct from the driving sprays, poured fore and aft into the boat. The nails that the carpenter had extracted from cases at Elephant Island and used to fasten down the battens were too short to make firm the decking. We did what we could to secure it, but our means were very limited, and the water continued to enter the boat at a dozen points. Much baling was necessary, and nothing that we could do prevented our gear from becoming sodden. The searching runnels from the canvas were really more unpleasant than the sudden definite douches of the sprays. Lying under the thwarts during watches below, we tried vainly to avoid them. There were no dry patches in the boat, and at last we simply covered our heads with our Burberrys and endured the all-pervading water.

The baling was work for the watch. Real rest we had none. The perpetual motion of the boat made repose impossible; we were cold,

217

sore and anxious. We moved on hands and knees in the semi-darkness of the day under the decking. The darkness was complete by 6 p.m., and not until 7 a.m. of the following day could we see one another under the thwarts. We had a few scraps of candle, and they were preserved carefully in order that we might have light at meal-times. There was one fairly dry spot in the boat, under the solid original decking at the bows, and we managed to protect some of our biscuits from the salt water; but I do not think any of us got the taste of salt out of our mouth during the voyage.

The difficulty of movement in the boat would have had its humorous side if it had not involved us in so many aches and pains. We had to crawl under the thwarts in order to move along the boat, and our knees suffered considerably. When a watch turned out it was necessary for me to direct each man by name when and where to move, since if all hands crawled about at the same time the result would have been dire confusion and many bruises. Then there was the trim of the boat to be considered. The order of the watch was four hours on and four hours off, three men to the watch. One man had the tiller-ropes, the second man attended to the sail, and the third baled for all he was worth. Sometimes when the water in the boat had been reduced to reasonable proportions, our home-made pump could be used.

While a new watch was shivering in the wind and spray, the men who had been relieved groped hurriedly among the soaked sleeping-bags and tried to steal a little of the warmth created by the last occupants; but it was not always possible for us to find even this comfort when we went off watch. The boulders that we had taken aboard for ballast had to be shifted continually in order to trim the boat and give access to the pump, which became choked with hairs from the moulting sleeping-bags and finnesko (reindeer-skin boots). The four reindeer-skin sleeping-bags shed their hair freely owing to the continuous wetting, and soon became quite bald in appearance.

The moving of the boulders was weary and painful work. We came to know every one of the stones by sight and touch, and I have vivid memories of their angular peculiarities even today. They might have been of considerable interest as geological specimens to a scientific man under happier conditions. As ballast they were simply appalling. They spared no portion of our poor bodies.

218

Another of our troubles worth mentioning here was the chafing of our legs by our wet clothes, which had not been changed now for seven months. The insides of our thighs were rubbed raw, and the one tube of Hazeline cream in our medicine chest did not go far in alleviating our pain, which was increased by the bite of the salt water.

We thought at the time that we never slept. The fact was that we would doze off uncomfortably, to be aroused quickly by some new ache or call to effort. My own share of the general unpleasantness was accentuated by a finely developed bout of sciatica. I had become possessor of this originally on the ice-floes several months earlier.

Our meals were regular, in spite of the gales. Attention to this point was essential, since the conditions of the voyage made increasing calls on our vitality. Breakfast, at 8 a.m., consisted of a pannikin of hot hoosh made from Bovril, sledging ration, two biscuits, and some lumps of sugar. Lunch came at 1 p.m., and comprised Bovril, sledging ration, eaten raw, and a pannikin of hot milk for each man. Tea, at 5 p.m., had the same menu. Then during the night we had a hot drink, generally of milk. The meals were the bright beacons on those cold and stormy days. The glow of warmth and comfort produced by the food and drink made optimists of us all.

A severe south-westerly gale on the fourth day out forced us to heave to. I would have liked to have run before the wind, but the sea was very high and the *James Caird* was in danger of broaching to and swamping. The delay was frustrating, since up to that time we had been making sixty or seventy miles a day, good going with our limited sail area. We hove to under double-reefed mainsail and our little jigger, and waited for the gale to blow itself out. During the afternoon we saw bits of wreckage, the remains probably of some unfortunate vessel that had failed to weather the strong gales south of Cape Horn. The weather conditions did not improve, and on the fifth day out the gale was so fierce that we were compelled to take in the double-reefed mainsail and hoist our small jib instead. We put out a sea-anchor to keep the *James Caird's* head up to the sea.

Even then the crests of the waves would often curl right over us and we shipped a great deal of water, which necessitated unceasing baling and pumping. Looking out abeam, we could see a hollow tunnel formed as the crest of a big wave toppled over on to the swelling body of

219

water. A thousand times it appeared as though the *James Caird* must be engulfed; but the boat lived. The south-westerly gale had its birth-place above the Antarctic continent, and its freezing breath lowered the temperature far toward zero. The sprays froze upon the boat and gave bows, sides, and decking a heavy coat of mail.

This accumulation of ice reduced the buoyancy of the boat, and to that extent was an added peril; but it possessed a notable advantage from one point of view. The water ceased to drop and trickle from the canvas, and the spray came in solely at the well in the after part of the boat. We would not allow the load of ice to grow beyond a certain point, and in turns we crawled about the decking forward, chipping and picking at it with the available tools.

When daylight came on the morning of the sixth day out we saw and felt that the *James Caird* had lost her resiliency She was not rising to the oncoming seas. The weight of the ice that had formed in her and on her during the night was having its effect, and she was becoming more like a log than a boat. The situation called for immediate action. We first broke away the spare oars, which were encased in ice and frozen to the side of the boat, and threw them overboard. We retained two oars for use when we got inshore. Two of the fur sleeping-bags went over the side; they were thoroughly wet, weighing probably forty pounds each, and they had frozen stiff during the night. Three men constituted the watch below, and when a man went down it was better to turn into the wet bag just vacated by another man than to thaw out a frozen bag with the heat of his unfortunate body. We now had four bags, three in use and one for emergency use in case a member of the party should break down permanently. The reduction of weight relieved the boat to some extent, and vigorous chipping and scraping did more. We had to be very careful not to put axe or knife through the frozen canvas of the decking as we crawled over it, but gradually we got rid of a lot of ice. The *James Caird* lifted to the endless waves as though she lived again.

At about 11 a.m. the boat suddenly fell off into the trough of the sea. The painter had parted and the sea-anchor had gone. This was serious. The *James Caird* went away to leeward, and we had no chance at all of recovering the anchor and our valuable rope, which had been our only means of keeping the boat's head up to the seas without the risk of hoisting a sail in a gale. Now we had to set the sail and trust to its holding. While the *James Caird* rolled heavily in the trough, we beat the frozen canvas until the bulk of the ice had cracked off it and then hoisted it. The frozen gear worked protestingly, but after a struggle our little craft came up to the wind again, and we breathed more freely. Skin frost-bites were troubling us, and we had developed large blisters on our fingers and hands. I shall always carry the scar of one of these frostbites on my left hand, which became badly inflamed after the skin had burst and the cold had bitten deeply.

We held the boat up to the gale during that day, enduring as best we could discomforts that amounted to pain. The boat tossed interminably on the big waves under grey, threatening skies. Our thoughts did not embrace much more than the necessities of the hour. Every surge of the sea was an enemy to be watched and circumvented. We ate our scanty meals, treated our frostbites, and hoped for the improved conditions that the morrow might bring. Night fell early, and in the lagging hours of darkness we were cheered by a change for the better in the weather. The wind dropped, the snow-squalls became less frequent, and the sea moderated.

When the morning of the seventh day dawned there was not much wind. We shook the reef out of the sail and laid our course once more for South Georgia. The sun came out bright and clear and presently Worsley got a snap for longitude. We hoped that the sky would remain clear until noon, so that we could get the latitude. We had been six days without an observation, and our dead reckoning naturally was uncertain. The boat must have presented a strange appearance that morning. All hands basked in the sun. We hung our sleeping-bags to the mast and spread our socks and other gear all over the deck.

We revelled in the warmth of the sun that day. Life was not so bad, after all. We felt we were well on our way. Our gear was drying, and we could have a hot meal in comparative comfort. The swell was still heavy, but it was not breaking and the boat rode easily. At noon Worsley balanced himself on the gunwale and clung with one hand to the stay of the mainmast while he got a snap of the sun. The result was more than encouraging. We had done over three hundred and eighty miles and were getting on for halfway to South Georgia. It looked as though we were going to get through.

The wind freshened to a good stiff breeze during the afternoon, and the *James Caird* made satisfactory progress. I had not realized until the sunlight came how small our boat really was. There was some influence in the light and warmth, some hint of happier days, that made us revive memories of other voyages, when we had stout decks beneath our feet, unlimited food at our command, and pleasant cabins for our ease. Now we clung to a battered little boat, 'alone, alone—all, all alone; alone on a wide, wide sea'. So low in the water were we that each succeeding swell cut off our view of the skyline. We were a tiny speck in the vast vista of the sea—the ocean that is open to all and merciful to none, that threatens even when it seems to yield, and that is pitiless always to weakness. For a moment the consciousness of the forces arrayed against us would be almost overwhelming. Then hope and confidence would rise again as our boat rose to a wave and tossed aside the crest in a sparkling shower like the play of prismatic colours at the foot of a waterfall.

The eighth, ninth and tenth days of the voyage had few features worthy of special note. The wind blew hard during those days, and the strain of navigating the boat was unceasing; but always we made some advance towards our goal. No bergs showed on our horizon, and we knew that we were clear of the ice-fields. Each day brought its little

round of troubles, but also compensation in the form of food and growing hope. We felt that we were going to succeed. The odds against us had been great, but we were winning through.

We still suffered severely from the cold, for, though the temperature was rising, our vitality was declining owing to the shortage of food, exposure, and the necessity of maintaining our cramped positions day and night. I found that it was now absolutely necessary to prepare hot milk for all hands during the night, in order to sustain life till dawn. This meant lighting the Primus lamp in darkness and involved an increased drain on our small store of matches. It was the rule that one match must serve when the Primus was being lit. We had no lamp for the compass and during the early days of the voyage we would strike a match when the steersman wanted to see the course at night; but later the necessity for strict economy impressed itself upon us, and the practice of striking matches at night was stopped.

On the tenth night Worsley could not straighten his body after his spell at the tiller. He was thoroughly cramped, and we had to drag

'We felt our boat lifted and flung forward like a cork in a breaking surf. We were in a seething chaos of tortured water.'

him beneath the decking and massage him before he could unbend himself and get into a sleeping-bag. A hard north-westerly gale came up on the eleventh day (5 May) and shifted to the south-west in the late afternoon. The sky was overcast and occasional snow-squalls added to the discomfort produced by the tremendous cross-sea—the worst, I thought, that we had experienced. At midnight I was at the tiller and suddenly noticed a line of clear sky between the south and south-west. I called to the other men that the sky was clearing, and then a moment later I realized that what I had seen was not a rift in the clouds but the white crest of an enormous wave. During twenty-six years' experience of the ocean in all its moods I had not encountered a wave so gigantic. It was a mighty upheaval of the ocean, a thing quite apart from the big white-capped seas that had been our tireless enemies for many days. I shouted, 'For God's sake, hold on! It's got us.'

Then came a moment of suspense that seemed drawn out into hours. White surged the foam of the breaking seas around us. We felt our boat lifted and flung forward like a cork in breaking surf. We were in a seething chaos of tortured water; but somehow the boat lived through it, half full of water sagging to the dead weight and shuddering under the blow. We baled with the energy of men fighting for life, flinging the water over the sides with every receptacle that came to our hands, and after ten minutes of uncertainty we felt the boat renew her life beneath us. She floated again and ceased to lurch drunkenly as though dazed by the attack of the sea. Earnestly we hoped that never again would we encounter such a wave.

The conditions in the boat, uncomfortable before, had been made worse by the deluge of water. All our gear was thoroughly wet again. Our cooking stove had been floating about in the bottom of the boat, and portions of our last hoosh seemed to have permeated everything. Not until 3 a.m., when we were all chilled almost to the limit of endurance, did we manage to get the stove alight and make ourselves hot drinks. The carpenter was suffering particularly, but he showed grit and spirit. Vincent had for the past week ceased to be an active member of the crew, and I could not easily account for his collapse. Physically he was one of the strongest men in the boat. He was a young man, he had served on North Sea trawlers, and he should have been able to bear hardships better than McCarthy, who, not strong, was always happy.

The weather was better on the following day (6 May), and we got a glimpse of the sun. Worsley's observation showed that we were not more than a hundred miles from the north-west corner of South Georgia. Two more days with a favourable wind and we would sight the promised land. I hoped that there would be no delay, for our supply of water was running very low. The hot drink at night was essential, but I decided that the daily allowance of water must be cut down to half a pint per man.

Thirst took possession of us. I dared not permit the allowance of water to be increased since an unfavourable wind might drive us away from the island and lengthen our voyage by many days. Lack of water is always the most severe privation that men can be condemned to endure, and we found, as during our earlier boat voyage, that the salt water in our clothing and the salt spray that lashed our faces made our thirst grow quickly to a burning pain. I had to be very firm in refusing to allow anyone to anticipate the next day's allowance, which I was sometimes begged to do.

We did the necessary work dully and hoped for the land. I had altered the course to the east so as to make sure of our striking the island, which would have been impossible to regain if we had run past the northern end. The course was laid on our scrap of chart for a point some thirty miles down the coat. That day and the following day passed for us in a sort of nightmare. Our mouths were dry and our tongues were swollen. The wind was still strong and the heavy sea forced us to navigate carefully, but any thoughts of our peril from the waves was buried beneath the consciousness of our raging thirst. The bright moments were those when we each received our one mug of hot milk during the long, bitter watches of the night. Things were bad for us in those days, but the end was coming.

The morning of 8 May broke thick and stormy, with squalls from the north-west. We searched the water ahead for a sign of land, and though we could see nothing than had met our eyes for many days, we were cheered by a sense that the goal was near at hand. About ten o'clock that morning we passed a little bit of kelp, a glad signal of the proximity of land. An hour later we saw two shags sitting on a big mass of kelp, and knew then that we must be within ten or fifteen miles of the shore. These birds are as sure an indication of the proximity of

225

land as a lighthouse is, for they never venture far to sea. We gazed ahead with increasing eagerness, and at 12.30 p.m., through a rift in the clouds, McCarthy caught a glimpse of the black cliffs of South Georgia, just fourteen days after our departure from Elephant Island. It was a glad moment. Thirst-ridden, chilled, and weak as we were, happiness irradiated us. The job was nearly done.

We stood in towards the shore to look for a landing-place, and presently we could see the green tussock-grass on the ledges above the surf-beaten rocks. Ahead of us and to the south, blind rollers showed the presence of uncharted reefs along the coast. Here and there the hungry rocks were close to the surface, and over them the great waves broke, swirling viciously and spouting thirty and forty feet into the air. The rocky coast appeared to descend sheer to the sea. Our need of water and rest was well-nigh desperate, but to have attempted a landing at that time would have been suicidal. Night was drawing near, and the weather indications were not favourable. There was nothing for it but to haul off until the following morning, so we stood away on the starboard tack until we had made what appeared to be a safe offing. Then we hove to in the high westerly swell.

The hours passed slowly as we waited the dawn, which would herald, we fondly hoped, the last stage of our journey. Our thirst was a torment and we could scarcely touch our food; the cold seemed to strike right through our weakened bodies. At 5 a.m. the wind shifted to the north-west and quickly increased to one of the worst hurricanes any of us had ever experienced. A great cross-sea was running, and the wind simply shrieked as it tore the tops off the waves and converted the whole seascape into a haze of driving spray. Down into valleys, up to tossing heights, straining until her seams opened, swung our little boat, brave still but labouring heavily. We knew that the wind and set of sea was driving us ashore, but we could do nothing.

The dawn showed us a storm-torn ocean, and the morning passed without bringing us a sight of the land; but at 1 p.m., through a rift in the flying mists, we got a glimpse of the huge crags of the island and I realized that our position had become desperate. We were on a dead lee shore, and we could gauge our approach to the unseen cliffs by the roar of the breakers against the sheer walls of rock. I ordered the double-reefed mainsail to be set in the hope that we might claw off, and this attempt increased the strain on the boat. The *James Caird* was bumping heavily, and the water was pouring in everywhere. Our thirst was forgotten in the realization of our imminent danger, as we baled unceasingly, and adjusted our weights from time to time; occasional glimpses showed that the shore was nearer.

I knew that Annewkow Island lay to the south of us, but our small and badly marked chart showed uncertain reefs in the passage between the island and the mainland, and I dared not trust it, though as a last resort we could try to lie under the lee of the island. The afternoon wore away as we edged down the coast, with the thunder of the breakers in our ears. The approach of evening found us still some distance from Annewkow Island, and, dimly in the twilight, we could see a snow-capped mountain looming above us. The chance of surviving the night, with the driving gale and the implacable sea forcing us on to the lee shore, seemed small. I think most of us had a feeling that the end was very near.

Just after 6 p.m., in the dark, as the boat was in the yeasty backwash from the seas flung from this iron-bound coast, just when things looked their worst, they changed for the best. I have marvelled often at the thin line that divides success from failure and the sudden turn that leads from apparently certain disaster to comparative safety. The wind suddenly shifted and we were free once more to make an offing. Almost as soon as the gale eased, the pin that locked the mast to the thwart fell out. It must have been on the point of doing this throughout the hurricane, and if it had gone nothing could have saved us; the mast would have snapped like a carrot. Our backstays had carried away once before when iced up and were not too strongly fastened now. We were thankful indeed for the mercy that had held the pin in its place throughout the hurricane.

We stood off-shore again, tired almost to the point of apathy. Our water had long been finished. The last was about a pint of hairy liquid, which we strained through a bit of gauze from the medicine chest. The pangs of thirst attacked us with redoubled intensity, and I felt that we must make a landing on the following day at almost any hazard. The night wore on. We were very tired. We longed for day.

When at last the dawn came on the morning of 10 May there was practically no wind, but a high cross-sea was running. We made slow progress towards the shore. About 8 a.m. the wind backed to the north-west and threatened another blow. We had sighted in the meantime a big indentation which I thought must be King Haakon Bay, and I decided that we must land there. We set the bows of the boat towards the bay and ran before the freshening gale. Soon we had angry reefs on either side. Great glaciers came down to the sea and offered no landing-place. The sea spouted on the reefs and thundered against the shore.

About noon we sighted a line of jagged reef, like blackened teeth, that seemed to bar the entrance to the bay. Inside, comparatively smooth water stretched eight or nine miles to the head of the bay. A gap in the reef appeared, and we made for it. But the fates had another rebuff for us. The wind shifted and blew from the east right out of the bay. We could see the way through the reef, but we could not approach it directly. That afternoon we bore up, tacking five times in the strong wind. The last tack enabled us to get through and at last we were in the wide mouth of the bay. Dusk was approaching. A small cove, with a boulder-strewn beach guarded by a reef, made a break in the cliffs on the south side of the bay and we turned in that direction. I stood in the bows directing the steering as we ran through the kelp and made the passage of the reef. The entrance was so narrow that we had to take in the oars, and the swell was piling itself right over the reef into the cove; but in a minute or two we were inside, and in the gathering darkness the *James Caird* ran in on a swell and touched the beach.

I sprang ashore with the short painter and held on when the boat went out with the backward surge. When the *James Caird* came in again three of the men got ashore, and they held the painter while I climbed some rocks with another line. A slip on the wet rocks twenty feet up nearly closed my part of the story just at the moment when we were achieving safety. A jagged piece of rock held and at the same time bruised me sorely. However, I made fast the line, and in a few minutes we were all safe on the beach with the boat floating in the surging water just off the shore. We heard a gurgling sound that was sweet music in our ears, and, peering around, found a stream of fresh water almost at our feet. A moment later we were down on our knees drinking the pure ice-cold water in long draughts that put new life into us. It was a splendid moment.

The boat party's adventures were by no means over. They had landed on the opposite side of the island to the Norwegian whaling station and Shackleton knew that neither boat nor crew would survive if they attempted to sail the remaining one hundred and fifty miles round the coast. The alternative was to cross the island climbing a five hundred-foot previously unexplored mountain range in the process. Somehow they made it. The journey took three days— and when they arrived at the whaling station they were unrecognizable scarecrows.

After this it took four attempts before the survivors on Elephant Island could be rescued; but without the incredible boat journey the whole party would undoubtedly have perished.

Shackleton's boat, the James Caird, *can be seen at the National Maritime Museum, Greenwich, London.*

ACCESSORY BEFORE THE FACT

Algernon Blackwood

At the moorland crossroads Martin stood examining the signpost for several minutes in some bewilderment. The names on the four arms were not what he expected, distances were not given, and his map, he concluded with impatience, must be hopelessly out of date. Spreading it against the post, he stooped to study it more closely. The wind blew the corners flapping against his face. The small print was almost indecipherable in the fading light. It appeared, however—as well as he could make out—that two miles back he must have taken the wrong turning.

He remembered that turning. The path had looked inviting; he had hesitated a moment, then followed it, caught by the usual lure of walkers that it 'might prove a short cut'. The short-cut snare is old as human nature. For some minutes he studied the signpost and the map alternately. Dusk was falling, and his knapsack had grown heavy. He could not make the two guides tally, however, and a feeling of uncertainty crept over his mind. He felt oddly baffled, frustrated. His thought grew thick. Decision was most difficult. 'I'm muddled,' he thought; 'I must be tired,' as at length he chose the most likely arm. 'Sooner or later it will bring me to an inn, though not the one I intended.' He accepted his walker's luck, and started briskly. The arm read 'Over Litacy Hill' in small, fine letters that danced and shifted every time he looked at them; but the name was not discoverable on the map. It was, however, inviting like the short cut. A similar impulse again directed his choice. Only this time it seemed more insistent, almost urgent.

And he became aware, then, of the exceeding loneliness of the country about him. The road for a hundred yards went straight, then curved like a white river running into space; the deep blue-green of heather lined the banks, spreading upwards through the twilight; and occasional small pines stood solitary here and there, all unexplained. The curious adjective, having made its appearance, haunted him. So many things that afternoon were similarly unexplained: the short cut, the darkened map, the names on the signpost, his own erratic impulses, and the growing strange confusion that crept upon his spirit. The entire countryside needed explanation, though perhaps 'interpretation' was the truer word. Those little lonely trees had made him see it. Why had he lost his way so easily? Why did he suffer vague impressions to influence his directions? Why was he *here*—exactly here? And why did he go now 'over Litacy Hill'?

Then, by a green field that shone like a thought of daylight amid the darkness of the moor, he saw a figure lying in the grass. It was a blot upon the landscape, a mere huddled patch of dirty rags, yet with a certain horrid picturesqueness too; and his mind—though his German was of the schoolroom order—at once picked out the German equivalents as against the English. *Lump* and *Lumpen* flashed across his brain most oddly. They seemed in that moment right, and so expressive, almost like onomatopoeic words, if that were possible of sight. Neither 'rags' nor 'rascal' would have fitted what he saw. The adequate description was in German.

Here was a clue tossed up by the part of him that did not reason. But it seems he missed it. And the next minute the tramp rose to a sitting posture and asked the time of evening. In German he asked it. And Martin, answering without a second's hesitation, gave it, also in German, *'halb sieben'*—half-past six. The instinctive guess was accurate. A glance at his watch when he looked a moment later proved it. He heard the man say, with the covert insolence of tramps, 'T'ank you;

231

much opliged.' For Martin had not shown his watch—another intuition subconsciously obeyed.

He quickened his pace along that lonely road, a curious jumble of thoughts and feelings surging through him. He had somehow known the question would come, and come in German. Yet it flustered and dismayed him. Another thing had also flustered and dismayed him. He had expected it in the same queer fashion: it was right. For when the ragged brown thing rose to ask the question, a part of it remained lying on the grass—another brown, dirty thing. There were two tramps. And he saw both faces clearly. Behind the untidy beards, and below the old slouch hats, he caught the look of unpleasant, clever faces that watched him closely while he passed. The eyes followed him. For a second he looked straight into those eyes, so that he could not fail to know them. And he understood, quite horridly, that both faces were too sleek, refined, and cunning for those of ordinary tramps. The men were not really tramps at all. They were disguised.

'How covertly they watched me!' was his thought, as he hurried along the darkening road, aware in dead earnestness now of the loneliness and desolation of the moorland all about him.

Uneasy and distressed, he increased his pace. Midway in thinking what an unnecessarily clanking noise his nailed boots made upon the hard white road, there came upon him with a rush together the company of these things that haunted him as 'unexplained'. They brought a single definite message: that all this business was not really meant for him at all, and hence his confusion and bewilderment; that he had intruded into some one else's scenery, and was trespassing upon another's map of life. By some wrong *inner* turning he had interpolated his person into a group of foreign forces which operated in the little world of someone else. Unwittingly, somewhere, he had crossed the threshold, and now was fairly in—a trespasser, an eavesdropper, a Peeping Tom. He was listening, peeping; overhearing things he had no right to know, because they were intended for another. Like a ship at sea he was intercepting wireless messages he could not properly interpret, because his receiver was not accurately tuned to their reception. And more—these messages were warnings!

Then fear dropped upon him like the night. He was caught in a net of delicate, deep forces he could not manage, knowing neither their origin nor purpose. He had walked into some huge psychic trap elaborately planned and baited, yet calculated for another man than himself. Something had lured him in, something in the landscape, the time of day, his mood. Owing to some undiscovered weakness in himself he had been easily caught. His fear slipped easily into terror.

What happened next occurred with such speed and concentration that it all seemed crammed into a moment. At once and in a heap it happened. It was quite inevitable. Down the white road to meet him a man came swaying from side to side in drunkenness quite obviously feigned—a tramp; and while Martin made room for him to pass, the lurch changed in a second to attack, and the fellow was upon him. The blow was sudden and terrific, yet even while it fell Martin was aware that behind him rushed a second man, who caught his legs from under him and bore him with a thud and crash to the ground. Blows rained then; he saw a gleam of something shining; a sudden deadly nausea plunged him into utter weakness where resistance was impossible. Something of fire entered his throat, and from his mouth poured a thick sweet thing that choked him. The world sank far away into darkness . . . Yet through all the horror and confusion ran the trail of two clear thoughts: he realized that the first tramp had sneaked at a fast double through the heather and so come down to meet him; and that something heavy was torn from the fastenings that clipped it tight and close beneath his clothes against his body . . .

Abruptly then the darkness lifted, passed utterly away. He found himself peering into the map against the signpost. The wind was flapping the corners against his cheek, and he was poring over names that now he saw quite clear. Upon the arms of the signpost above were those he had expected to find, and the map recorded them quite faithfully. All was accurate again and as it should be. He read the name of the village he had meant to make—it was plainly visible in the dusk, two miles the distance given. Bewildered, shaken, unable to think of anything, he stuffed the map into his pocket unfolded, and hurried forward like a man who has just awakened from an awful dream that had compressed into a single second all the detailed misery of some prolonged, oppressive nightmare.

He broke into a steady trot that soon became a run; the perspiration poured from him; his legs felt weak, and his breath was difficult to

233

manage. He was only conscious of the overpowering desire to get away as fast as possible from the signpost at the crossroads where the dreadful vision had flashed upon him. For Martin, accountant on a holiday, had never dreamed of any world of psychic possibilities. The entire thing was torture. It was worse than a 'cooked' balance of the books that some conspiracy of clerks and directors proved at his innocent door. He raced as though the countryside ran crying at his heels. And always still ran with him the incredible conviction that none of this was really meant for himself at all. He had overheard the secrets of another. He had taken the warning for another unto himself, and so altered its direction. He had thereby prevented its right delivery. It all shocked him beyond words. It dislocated the machinery of his just and accurate soul. The warning was intended for another, who could not—would not—now receive it.

The physical exertion, however, brought at length a more comfortable reaction and some measure of composure. With the lights in sight, he slowed down and entered the village at a reasonable pace. The inn was reached, a bedroom inspected and engaged, and supper ordered with the solid comfort of a large Bass to satisfy an unholy thirst and complete the restoration of balance. The unusual sensations largely passed away, and the odd feeling that anything in his simple, wholesome world required explanation was no longer present. Still with a vague uneasiness about him, though actual fear quite gone, he went into the bar to smoke an after-supper pipe and chat with the locals, as his pleasure was upon a holiday, and so saw two mean leaning upon the counter at the far end with their backs towards him. He saw their faces instantly in the glass, and the pipe nearly slipped from between his teeth. Clean-shaven, sleek, clever faces—and he caught a word or two as they talked over their drinks—German words. Well dressed they were, both men, with nothing about them calling for particular attention; they might have been two tourists holiday-making like himself in tweeds and walking-boots. And they presently paid for their drinks and went out. He never saw them face to face at all; but the sweat broke out afresh all over him, a feverish rush of heat and ice together ran about his body; beyond question he recognized the two tramps, this time not disguised—not *yet* disguised.

He remained in his corner without moving, puffing violently at

He saw their faces instantly in the glass, and his pipe nearly slipped . . .

an extinguished pipe, gripped helplessly by the return of that first vile terror. It came again to him with an absolute clarity of certainty that it was not with himself they had to do, these men, and, further, that he had no right in the world to interfere. He had no right to interfere; it would be immoral . . . even if the opportunity came. And the opportunity, he felt, would come. He had been an eavesdropper, and had come upon private information of a secret kind that he had no right to make use of, even that good might come—even to save life. He sat on in his corner, terrified and silent, waiting for the thing that should happen next.

But night came without explanation. Nothing happened. He slept soundly. There was no other guest at the inn but an elderly man, apparently a tourist like himself. He wore gold-rimmed glasses, and in the morning Martin overheard him asking the landlord what direction he should take for Litacy Hill. His teeth began then to chatter and a weakness came into his knees. 'You turn to the left at the crossroads,' Martin broke in before the landlord could reply. 'You'll see the signpost about two miles from here, and after that it's a matter of four miles

235

more.' How in the world did he know, flashed horribly through him. 'I'm going that way myself,' he was saying next. 'I'll go with you for a bit—if you don't mind!' The words came out impulsively and ill-considered; of their own accord they came. For his own direction was exactly opposite. *He did not want the man to go alone.* The stranger, however, easily evaded his offer of companionship. He thanked him with the remark that he was starting later in the day . . . They were standing, all three, beside the horse-trough, in front of the inn, when at that very moment a tramp, slouching along the road, looked up and asked the time of day. And it was the man with the gold-rimmed glasses who told him.

'T'ank you; much opliged,' the tramp replied, passing on with his slow, slouching gait, while the landlord, a talkative fellow, proceeded to remark upon the number of Germans that lived in England and were ready to swell the Teutonic invasion which *he*, for his part, deemed imminent.

But Martin heard it not. Before he had gone a mile upon his way he went into the woods to fight his conscience all alone. His feebleness, his cowardice, were surely criminal. Real anguish tortured him. A dozen times he decided to go back upon his steps, and a dozen times the singular authority that whispered he had no right to interfere prevented him. How could he act upon knowledge gained by eavesdropping? How interfere in the private business of another's hidden life merely because he had overheard, as at the telephone, its secret dangers? Some inner confusion prevented straight thinking altogether. The stranger would merely think him mad. He had no 'fact' to go upon. He smothered a hundred impulses . . . and finally went on his way with a shaking, troubled heart.

The last two days of his holiday were ruined by doubts and questions and alarms—all justified later when he read of the murder of a tourist upon Litacy Hill. The man wore gold-rimmed glasses, and carried in a belt about his person a large sum of money. His throat was cut. And the police were hard upon the trail of a mysterious pair of tramps, said to be—Germans.

CHICKAMAUGA
Thomas Wolfe

*The Civil War between the northern and southern states of America—
the Unionists and the Confederates—arose from the southerners'
determination to secede from the Union, do as they pleased in their
territory regardless of the central government and, in particular, maintain the institution of Negro slavery. The war, entailing enormous
losses on both sides, lasted from 1861 to 1865 and ended in victory for
the north, so preserving the unity of the United States. The battle described in this story took place in 1863 in Confederate country, General
William Rosencrans ('Old Rosey') leading the Union Army and
General Braxton Bragg the Confederates.*

All through the spring and summer of that year Old Rosey follered
us through Tennessee.

We had him stopped the year before, the time we whupped him at
Stone's River at the end of '62. We tard him out so bad he had to wait.
He waited thar six months at Murfreesboro. But we knowed he was
a-comin' all the time. Old Rosey started at the end of June and drove us
out of Shelbyville. We fell back on Tullahoma in rains the like of which
you never seed. The rains that fell the last week in June that year was
terrible. But Rosey kept a-comin' on.

He drove us out of Tullahoma too. We fell back across the Cumberland, we pulled back behind the mountain, but he follered us.

I reckon thar was fellers that was quicker when a fight was on, and
when they'd seed just what hit was they had to do. But when it came to
plannin' and a-figgerin', Old Rosey Rosencrans took the cake. Old
Rosey was a fox. Fer sheer natural cunnin' I never knowed the beat of
him.

While Bragg was watchin' him at Chattanooga to keep him from
gittin' across the Tennessee, he sent some fellers forty mile upstream.

237

And then he'd march 'em back and forth and round the hill and back in front of us again where we could look at 'em, until you'd a-thought that every Yankee in the world was there. But, law! All that was just a dodge! He had fellers a-sawin' and a-hammerin', a-buildin' boats, a-blowin' bugles and a-beatin' drums, makin' all the noise they could— you could hear 'em over yonder gittin' ready—and all the time Old Rosey was fifty mile or more downstream, ten mile *past* Chattanooga, a-fixin' to git over way down thar. That was the kind of feller he was.

We reached Chattanooga early in July and waited fer two months. Old Rosey hadn't caught up with us yet. He still had to cross the Cumberland, push his men and pull his trains across the ridges and through the gaps before he got to us. July went by, we had no news of him. 'O Lord!' said Jim, 'perhaps he ain't a-comin'!' I knowed he was a-comin', but I let Jim have his way.

Some of the fellers would git used to hit. A feller'd git into a frame of mind where he wouldn't let hit worry him. He'd let termorrer look out fer hitself. That was the way hit was with me.

With Jim hit was the other way around. Now that he knowed Martha Patton he was a different man. I think he hated the war and army life from the moment that he met her. From that time he was livin' only fer one thing—to go back home and marry that gal. When mail would come and some of us was gittin' letters he'd be the first in line; and if she wrote him why he'd walk away like someone in a dream. And if she failed to write he'd jest go off somers and set down by himself: he'd be in such a state of misery he didn't want to talk to no one. He got the reputation with the fellers fer bein' queer—unsociable— always a-broodin' and a-frettin' about somethin' and a-wantin' to be left alone. And so, after a time, they let him be. He wasn't popular with most of them—but they never knowed what was wrong, they never knowed that he wasn't really the way they thought he was at all. Hit was jest that he was hit so desperate hard, the worst-in-love man that I ever seed. But, law! I knowed! I knowed what was the trouble from the start.

Hit's funny how war took a feller. Before the war I was the serious one, and Jim had been the one to play. But then the war came and hit changed him so you wouldn't a-knowed he was the same man.

And, as I say, hit didn't happen all at once. Jim was the happiest man

I ever seed that mornin' that we started out from home. I reckon he thought of the war as we all did, as a big frolic. We gave hit jest about six months. We figgered we'd be back by then, and of course all that jest suited Jim. I reckon that suited all of us. It would give us all a chance to wear a uniform and to see the world, to shoot some Yankees and to run 'em north, and then to come back home and lord it over those who hadn't been and be a hero and court the gals.

That summer I been tellin' you about, Old Rosey drove us down through Tennessee. He drove us out of Shelbyville, and we fell back on Tullahoma, to the passes of the hills. When we pulled back across the Cumberland I said to Jim: 'Now we've got him. He'll have to cross the mountains now to git at us. And when he does, we'll have him. That's all that Bragg's been waitin' fer. We'll whup the daylights out of him this time,' I said, 'and after that thar'll be nothin' left of him. We'll be home by Christmas, Jim—you wait and see.'

And Jim just looked at me and shook his head and said: 'Lord, Lord, I don't believe this war'll ever end!'

Hit wasn't that he was afraid—or, if he was, hit made a wildcat of him in the fightin'. Jim could get fightin' mad like no one else I ever seed. He could do things, take chances no one else I ever knowed would take. But I reckon hit was jest because he was so desperate. He hated hit so much. He couldn't git used to hit the way the others could. He couldn't take hit as hit came. Hit wasn't so much that he was afraid to die. I guess hit was that he was still so full of livin'. He didn't want to die because he wanted to live. And he wanted to live so much because he was in love.

. . . So, like I say, Old Rosey finally pushed us back across the Cumberland. We was in Chattanooga in July, and fer a few weeks hit was quiet thar. But all the time I knowed that Rosey would keep comin' on. We got wind of him again long in August. He had started after us again. He pushed his trains across the Cumberland, with the roads so bad, what with the rains, his wagons sunk down to the axle hubs. But he got 'em over, came down in the valley, then across the ridge, and early in September he was on our heels again.

We cleared out of Chattanooga on the eighth. And our tail end was pullin' out at one end of the town as Rosey came in through the other. We dropped down around the mountain south of town and Rosey thought he had us on the run again.

But this time he was fooled. We was ready fer him now, a-pickin' out our spot and layin' low. Old Rosey follered us. He sent McCook around down towards the south to head us off. He thought he had us in retreat but when McCook got thar we wasn't thar at all. We'd come down south of town and taken our positions along Chickamauga Creek. McCook had gone too far. Thomas was follerin' us from the north and when McCook tried to git back to join Thomas, he couldn't pass us, fer we blocked the way. They had to fight us or be cut in two.

We was in position on the Chickamauga on the seventeenth. The Yankees streamed in on the eighteenth, and took their position in the woods a-facin' us. We had our backs to Lookout Mountain and the Chickamauga Creek. The Yankees had their line thar in the woods before us on a rise, with Missionary Ridge behind them to the east.

The Battle of Chickamauga was fought in a cedar thicket. That cedar thicket, from what I knowed of hit, was about three miles long and one mile wide. We fought fer two days all up and down that thicket and to and fro across hit. When the fight started that cedar thicket was so thick and dense you could a-took a butcher knife and drove hit in thar any-whereas and hit would a-stuck. And when that fight was over that cedar thicket had been so destroyed by shot and shell you could a-looked in thar anywheres with your naked eye and seed a black snake run a hundred yards away. If you'd a-looked at that cedar thicket the day after that fight was over you'd a -wondered how a hummin' bird the size of your thumb-nail could a-flown through thar without bein' torn into pieces by the fire. And yet more than half of us who went into that thicket came out of hit alive and told the tale. You wouldn't have thought that hit was possible. But I was thar and seed hit, and hit was.

A little after midnight—hit may have been about two o'clock that mornin', while we lay there waitin' for the fight we knowed was bound to come next day—Jim woke me up. I woke up like a flash—you got used to hit in those days—and though hit was so dark you could hardly see your hand a foot away, I knowed his face at once. He was white as a ghost and he had got thin as a rail in that last year's campaign. In the dark his face looked white as paper. He dug his hand into my arm so hard hit hurt. I roused up sharp like; then I seed him and knowed who hit was.

'John!' he said—'John!'—and he dug his fingers in my arm so hard he made hit ache—'John! I've seed him! He was here again!'

I tell you what, the way he said hit made my blood run cold. They say we Pentlands are a superstitious people, and perhaps we are. They told hit how they saw my brother George comin' up the hill one day at sunset, how they all went out upon the porch and waited fer him, how everyone, the childern and the grown-ups alike, all seed him as he clumb the hill, and how he passed behind a tree and disappeared as if the ground had swallered him—and how they got the news ten days later that he'd been killed at Chancellorsville on that very day and hour. I've heared these stories and I know the others all believe them, but I never put no stock in them myself. And yet, I tell you what! The sight of that white face and those black eyes a-burnin' at me in the dark—the way he said hit and the way hit was—fer I could feel the men around me and hear somethin' movin' in the wood—I heared a trace chain rattle and hit was enough to make your blood run cold! I grabbed hold of him—I shook him by the arm—I didn't want the rest of 'em to hear—I told him to hush up ——

'John, he was here!' he said.

I never asked him what he meant—I knowed too well to ask. It was the third time he'd seed hit in a month—a man upon a horse. I didn't want to hear no more—I told him that hit was a dream and I told him to go back to sleep.

'I tell you, John, hit was no dream!' he said. 'Oh, John, I heared hit—and I heared his horse—and I seed him sittin' thar as plain as day—and he never said a word to me—he jest sat thar lookin' down, and then he turned and rode away into the woods . . . John, John, I heared him and I don't know what hit means!'

Well, whether he seed hit or imagined hit or dreamed hit, I don't know. But the sight of his black eyes a burnin' holes through me in the dark made me feel almost as if I'd seed hit too. I told him to lay down by me—and still I seed his eyes a-blazin' thar. I know he didn't sleep a wink the rest of that whole night. I closed my eyes and tried to make him think that I was sleepin' but hit was no use—we lay thar wide awake. And both of us was glad when mornin' came.

The fight began upon our right at ten o'clock. We couldn't find out what was happenin': the woods thar was so close and thick we never

241

knowed fer two days what had happened, and we didn't know for
certain then. We never knowed how many we was fightin' or how
many we had lost. I've heard them say that even Old Rosey himself
didn't know jest what had happened when he rode back into town next
day, and didn't know that Thomas was still standin' like a rock. And if
Old Rosey didn't know no more than this about hit, what could a
common soldier know? We fought back and forth across that cedar
thicket fer two days, and thar was times when you would be right up
on top of them before you even knowed that they was thar. And that's
the way the fightin' went—the bloodiest fightin' that was ever knowed,
until that cedar thicket was soaked red with blood, and thar was hardly
a place left in thar where a sparrer could have perched.

And as I say, we heared 'em fightin' out upon our right at ten o'clock,
and then the fightin' came our way. I heared later that this fightin'
started when the Yanks come down to the creek and run into a bunch of
Forrest's men and drove 'em back. And then they had hit back and
forth until they got drove back themselves, and that's the way we had
hit all day long. We'd attack and then they'd throw us back, then they'd
attack and we'd beat them off. And that was the way hit went from
mornin' till night. We piled up there upon their left: they mowed us
down with canister and grape until the very grass was soakin' with our
blood, but we kept comin' on. We must have charged a dozen times
that day—I was in four of 'em myself. We fought back and forth across
that wood until there wasn't a piece of hit as big as the palm of your
hand we hadn't fought on. We busted through their right at two-thirty
in the afternoon and got way over past the Widder Glenn's where Rosey
had his quarters, and beat 'em back until we got the whole way cross the
Lafayette Road and took possession of the road. And then they drove
us out again. And we kept comin' on, and both sides were still at hit
after darkness fell.

We fought back and forth across that road all day with first one side
and then the tother holdin' hit until that road hitself was soaked in blood.
They called that road the Bloody Lane, and that was jest the name
for hit.

We kept fightin' fer an hour or more after hit had gotten dark, and
you could see the rifles flashin' in the woods, but then hit all died down.
I tell you what, that night was somethin' to remember and to marvel

at as long as you live. The fight had set the wood afire in places, and you could see the smoke and flames and hear the screamin' and the hollerin' of the wounded until hit made your blood run cold. We got as many as we could—but some we didn't even try to git—we jest let 'em lay. It was an awful thing to hear. I reckon many a wounded man was jest left to die or burn to death because we couldn't git 'em out.

You could see the nurses and the stretcher-bearers movin' through the woods, and each side huntin' fer hits dead. You could see them movin' in the smoke an' flames, an' you could see the dead men layin' there as thick as wheat, with their corpse-like faces an' black powder on their lips, an' a little bit of moonlight comin' through the trees, and all of hit more like a nightmare out of hell than anything I ever knowed before.

But we had other work to do. All through the night we could hear the Yanks a-choppin' and a-thrashin' round, and we knowed that they was fellin' trees to block us when we went fer them next mornin'. Fer we knowed the fight was only jest begun. We figgered that we'd had the best of hit, but we knowed no one had won the battle yet. We knowed the second day would beat the first.

Jim knowed hit too. Poor Jim, he didn't sleep that night—he never seed the man upon the horse that night—he jest sat there, a-grippin' his knees and starin', and a-sayin': 'Lord God, Lord God, when will hit ever end?'

Then mornin' came at last. This time we knowed jest where we was and what hit was we had to do. Our line was fixed by that time. Bragg knowed at last where Rosey had his line, and Rosey knowed where we was. So we waited there, both sides, till mornin' came. Hit was a foggy mornin' with mist upon the ground. Around ten o'clock when the mist began to rise, we got the order and we went chargin' through the wood again.

We knowed the fight was goin' to be upon the right—upon our right, that is—on Rosey's left. And we knowed that Thomas was in charge of Rosey's left. And we all knowed that hit was easier to crack a flint rock with your teeth than to make old Thomas budge. But we went after him, and I tell you what, that was a fight! The first day's fight had been like playin' marbles when compared to this.

We hit old Thomas on his left at half-past ten, and Breckenridge came sweepin' round and turned old Thomas's flank and came in at his back, and then we had hit hot and heavy. Old Thomas whupped his men around like he would crack a rawhide whup and drove Brecken-ridge back around the flank again, but we was back on top of him before you knowed the first attack was over.

The fight went ragin' down the flank, down to the center of Old Rosey's army and back and forth across the left, and all up and down old Thomas's line. We'd hit him right and left and in the middle, and he'd come back at us and throw us back again. And we went ragin' back and forth thar like two bloody lions with that cedar thicket so tore up, so bloody and so thick with dead by that time, that hit looked as if all hell had broken loose in thar.

Rosey kept a-whuppin' men around off of his right, to help old Thomas on the left to stave us off. And then we'd hit old Thomas left of centre and we'd bang him in the middle and we'd hit him on his left again, and he'd whup those Yankees back and forth off of the right into his flanks and middle as we went fer him, until we run those Yankees ragged. We had them gallopin' back and forth like kangaroos, and in the end that was the thing that cooked their goose.

The worst fightin' had been on the left, on Thomas's line, but to hold us thar they'd thinned their right out and had failed to close in on the centre of their line. And at two o'clock that afternoon when Longstreet seed the gap in Wood's position on the right, he took five brigades of us and poured us through. That whupped them. That broke their line and smashed their whole right all to smithereens. We went after them like a pack of ragin' devils. We killed 'em and we took 'em by the thousands, and those we didn't kill and take right thar went streamin' back across the Ridge as if all hell was at their heels.

That was a rout if ever I heared tell of one! They went streamin' back across the Ridge—hit was each man fer himself and the devil take the hindmost. They caught Rosey comin' up—he rode into them—he tried to check 'em, face 'em round, and get 'em to come on again—hit was like tryin' to swim the Mississippi upstream on a boneyard mule! They swept him back with them as if he'd been a wooden chip. They went streamin' into Rossville like the rag-tag of creation—the worst whupped army that you ever seed, and Old Rosey was along with all the rest!

He knowed hit was all up with h..m, or thought he knowed hit, for everybody told him the Army of the Cumberland had been blowed to smithereens and that hit was a general rout. And Old Rosey turned and rode to Chattanooga, and he was a beaten man. I've heard tell that when he rode up to his headquarters thar in Chattanooga they had to help him from his horse, and that he walked into the house all dazed and fuddled like, like he never knowed what had happened to him—and that he jest sat thar struck dumb and never spoke.

This was at four o'clock of that same afternoon. And then the news was brought to him that Thomas was still thar upon the field and wouldn't budge. Old Thomas stayed thar like a rock. We'd smashed the right, we'd sent it flyin' back across the Ridge, the whole Yankee right was broken into bits and streamin' back to Rossville for dear life. Then we bent old Thomas back upon his left. We thought we had him, he'd have to leave the field or else surrender. But old Thomas turned and fell back along the Ridge and put his back against the wall thar, and he wouldn't budge.

Longstreet pulled us back at three o'clock when we had broken up the right and sent them streamin' back across the Ridge. We thought that hit was over then. We moved back stumblin' like men walkin' in a dream. And I turned to Jim—I put my arm around him, and I said: 'Jim, what did I say? I knowed hit, we've licked 'em and this is the end!' I never even knowed if he heared me. He went stumblin' on beside me with his face as white as paper and his lips black with the powder of the cartridge bite, mumblin' and mutterin' to himself like someone talkin' in a dream. And we fell back to position, and they told us all to rest. And we leaned thar on our rifles like men who hardly knowed if they had come out of that hell alive or dead.

'Oh, Jim, we've got 'em and this is the end!' I said.

He leaned thar swayin' on his rifle, starin' through the wood. He jest leaned and swayed thar, and he never said a word, and those great eyes of his a-burnin' through the wood.

'Jim, don't you hear me?'—and I shook him by the arm. 'Hit's over, man! We've licked 'em and the fight is over!—Can't you understand?'

And then I heared them shoutin' on the right, the word came down the line again, and—Jim—poor Jim!—he raised his head and listened, and 'O God!' he said, 'we've got to go again!'

Well, hit was true. The word had come that Thomas had lined up

'Jim stumbled and spun round as if somethin' had whipped him like a top.

upon the Ridge, and we had to go fer him again. After that I never exactly knowed what happened. Hit was like fightin' in a bloody dream —like doin' somethin' in a nightmare—only the nightmare was like death and hell. Longstreet threw us up that hill five times, I think, before darkness came. We'd charge up to the very muzzles of their guns, and they'd mow us down like grass, and we'd come stumblin' back—or what was left of us—and form again at the foot of the hill, and then come on again. We'd charge right up the Ridge and drive 'em through the gap and fight 'em with cold steel, and they'd come back again and we'd brain each other with the butt end of our guns. Then they'd throw us back and we'd re-form and come on after 'em again.

The last charge happened jest at dark. We came along and stripped the ammunition off the dead—we took hit from the wounded—we had nothin' left ourselves. Then we hit the first line—and we drove them back. We hit the second and swept over them. We were goin' up to take the third and last—they waited till they saw the colour of our eyes before they let us have hit. Hit was like a river of red-hot lead had poured down on us: the line melted thar like snow. Jim stumbled and spun around as if somethin' had whupped him like a top. He fell right towards me, with his eyes wide open and the blood a-pourin' from his mouth. I took one look at him and then stepped over him like he was a log. Thar was no more to see or think of now—no more to reach— except that line. We reached hit and they let us have hit—and we stumbled back.

And yet we knowed that we had won a victory. That's what they told us later—and we knowed hit must be so because when daybreak came next mornin' the Yankees was all gone. They had all retreated into town, and we was left there by the creek at Chickamauga in possession of the field.

I don't know how many men got killed. I don't know which side lost the most. I only know you could have walked across the dead men without settin' foot upon the ground. I only know that cedar thicket which had been so dense and thick two days before you could've drove a knife into hit and hit would of stuck, had been so shot to pieces that you could've looked in thar on Monday mornin' with your naked eye and seed a black snake run a hundred yards away.

I don't know how many men we lost or how many of the Yankees

247

we may have killed. The generals on both sides can figger all that out to suit themselves. But I know that when that fight was over you could have looked in thar and wondered how a hummin' bird could've flown through that cedar thicket and come out alive. And yet that happened, yes, and something more than hummin' birds—fer men came out, alive.

And on that Monday mornin', when I went back up the Ridge to where Jim lay, thar just beside him on a little torn piece of bough, I heard a redbird sing. I turned Jim over and got his watch, his pocket-knife, and what few papers and belongin's that he had, and some letters that he'd had from Martha Patton. And I put them in my pocket.

And then I got up and looked around. It all seemed funny after hit had happened, like something that had happened in a dream. Fer Jim had wanted so desperate hard to live, and hit had never mattered half so much to me, and now I was a-standin' thar with Jim's watch and Martha Patton's letters in my pocket and a-listenin' to that little redbird sing.

And I would go all through the war and go back home and marry Martha later on, and fellers like poor Jim was layin' thar at Chicka-mauga Creek.

Hit's all so strange now when you think of hit. Hit all turned out so different from the way we thought. And that was long ago, and I'll be ninety-five years old if I am livin' on the seventh day of August, of this present year. Now that's goin' back a long ways, hain't hit? And yet hit all comes back to me as clear as if hit happened yesterday. And then hit all will go away and be as strange as if hit happened in a dream.

But I have been in some big battles, I can tell you. I've seen strange things and been in bloody fights. But the biggest fight that I was ever in—the bloodiest battle anyone has ever fought—was at Chickamauga in that cedar thicket—at Chickamauga Creek in that great war.

CRATERS OF FIRE

H. Tazieff

Haroun Tazieff is a trained geologist. In pursuance of his scientific studies, he has explored both caves, as a speleologist, and—as recorded in his first published book, Craters of Fire—*volcanoes. He created the term 'volcanologist' to describe this aspect of his professional work. The volcano of which he writes in this section of the book is in Africa.*

Standing on the summit of the growling cone, even before I got my breath back after the stiff climb, I peered down into the crater.

I was astonished. Two days previously the red lava had been boiling up to the level of the gigantic lip; now the funnel seemed to be empty. All that incandescent magma[1] had disappeared, drawn back into the depths by the reflex of some mysterious ebb and flow, a sort of breathing. But there, about fifty feet below where I was standing, was the glow and the almost animate fury of the great throat which volcanologists call the conduit or chimney. It was quite a while before I could tear my eyes away from that lurid, fiery centre, that weird palpitation of the abyss. At intervals of about a minute, heralded each time by a dry clacking, bursts of projectiles were flung up, running away up into the air, spreading out fanwise, all aglare, and then falling back, whistling, on the outer sides of the cone. I was rather tense, ready to leap aside at any moment, as I watched these showers, with their menacing trajectories.

Each outburst of rage was followed by a short lull. Then heavy rolls of brown and bluish fumes came puffing out, while a muffled grum-

[1] a crude, pasty sludge of mineral and organic matter.

bling, rather like that of some monstrous watchdog, set the whole bulk of the volcano quivering. There was not much chance for one's nerves to relax, so swiftly did each follow on the other—the sudden tremor, the burst, the momentary intensification of the incandescence, and the outbreak of a fresh salvo. The bombs went roaring up, the cone of fire opening out overhead, while I hung in suspense. Then came the hissing and sizzling, increasing in speed and intensity, each 'whoosh' ending up in a muffled thud as the bomb fell. On their black bed of scoriae[2], the clots of molten magma lay with the fire slowly dying out of them, one after the other growing dark and cold.

Some minutes of observation were all I needed. I noted that today, apart from three narrow zones to the west, north, and north-east, the edges of the crater had scarcely been damaged at all by the barrage from underground. The southern point where I stood was a mound rising some twelve or fifteen feet above the general level of the rim, that narrow, crumbling lip of scoriae nearer to the fire, where I had never risked setting foot. I looked at this rather alarming ledge all round the crater, and gradually felt an increasing desire to do something about it . . . It became irresistible. After all, as the level of the column of lava had dropped to such an exceptional degree, was this not the moment to try what I was so tempted to do and go right round the crater?

Still, I hesitated. This great maw, these jaws sending out heat that was like the heavy breathing of some living creature, thoroughly frightened me. Leaning forward over that hideous glow, I was no longer a geologist in search of information, but a terrified savage.

'If I lose my grip,' I said aloud, 'I shall simply run for it.'

The sound of my own voice restored me to normal awareness of myself. I got back my critical sense and began to think about what I could reasonably risk trying. '*De l'audace, encore de l'audace . . .*' That was all very well, of course, but one must also be careful. Past experience whispered a warning not to rush into anything blindly. Getting the upper hand of both anxiety and impatience, I spent several minutes considering, with the greatest care, the monster's manner of behaving. Solitude has got me into the habit of talking to myself, and so it was more or less aloud that I gave myself permission to go ahead.

'Right, then. It can be done.'

I turned up my collar and buttoned my canvas jacket tight at the

[2]fragments of lava.

throat—I didn't want a sly cinder down the back of my neck! Then I tucked what was left of my hair under an old felt hat that did service for a helmet. And now for it!

Very cautiously indeed, I approach the few yards of pretty steep slope separating the peak from the rim I am going to explore. I cross, in a gingerly manner, the first incandescent crevasse. It is intense orange in colour and quivering with heat, as though opening straight into a mass of glowing embers. The fraction of a second it takes me to cross it is just long enough for it to scorch the thick cord of my breeches. I get a strong whiff of burnt wool.

A promising start, I must say!

Here comes a second break in the ground. Damn it, a wide one, too! I can't just stride across this one: I'll have to jump it. The incline makes me thoughtful. Standing there, I consider the unstable slope of scoriae that will have to serve me for a landing-ground. If I don't manage to pull up . . . if I go rolling along down this funnel with the flames lurking at the bottom of it . . . My little expedition all at once strikes me as thoroughly rash, and I stay where I am, hesitating. But the heat under my feet is becoming unbearable. I can't endure it except by shifting ground. It only needs ten seconds of standing still on this enemy territory, with the burning gases slowly and steadily seeping through it, and the soles of my feet are already baking hot. From second to second the alternative becomes increasingly urgent: I must jump for it or retreat.

Here I am! I have landed some way down the fissure. The ashes slide underfoot, but I stop without too much trouble. As so often happens, the anxiety caused by the obstacle made me overestimate its importance.

Step by step, I set out on my way along the wide wall of the slag-like debris that forms a sort of fortification all round the precipice. The explosions are still going on at regular intervals of between sixty and eighty seconds. So far no projectile has come down on this side, and this cheers me up considerably. With marked satisfaction I note that it is pretty rare for two bombs of the same salvo to fall less than three yards apart: the average distance between them seems to be one of several paces. This is encouraging. One of the great advantages of this sort of bombardment, compared with one by artillery, lies in the relative slowness with which the projectiles fall, the eye being able to follow them quite easily. Furthermore, these shells don't burst. But what an uproar, what an enormous, prolonged bellowing accompanies their being hurled out of the bowels of the earth!

I make use of a brief respite in order to get quickly across the ticklish north-eastern sector. Then I stop for a few seconds, just long enough to see yet another burst gush up and come showering down a little ahead of me, after which I start out for the conquest of the northern sector. Here the crest narrows down so much that it becomes a mere ridge, where walking is so difficult and balancing so precarious that I find myself forced to go on along the outer slope, very slightly lower down. Little by little, as I advance through all this tumult, a feeling of enthusiasm is overtaking me. The immediate imperative necessity for action has driven panic far into the background. And under the hot, dry skin of my face, taut on forehead and cheekbones, I can feel my compressed lips parting, of their own accord, in a smile of sheer delight. But look out!

A sudden intensification of the light warns me that I am approaching a point right in the prolongation of the fiery chimney. In fact, the chimney is not vertical, but slightly inclined in a north-westerly direction, and from here one can look straight down into it. These terrestrial entrails, brilliantly yellow, seem to be surging with heat. The sight is so utterly amazing that I stand there, transfixed.

Suddenly, before I can make any move, the dazzling yellow changes to white, and in the same instant I feel a muffled tremor all through my body and there is a thunderous uproar in my ears. The burst of in-candescent blocks is already in full swing. My throat tightens as, motionless, I follow with my gaze the clusters of red lumps rising in slow, perfect curves. There is an instant of uncertainty. And then comes down the hail of fire.

This time the warning was too short: I am right in the middle of it all. With my shoulders hunched up, head drawn back, chin in air, buttocks as much tucked in as possible, I peer up into the vault of sinister whining and whizzing there above me. All around bombs are crashing down, still pasty and soft, making a succession of muffled *plops*. One dark mass seems to have singled me out and is making straight for my face. Instinctively I take a leap to one side, and *feel* the great lump flatten itself out a few inches from my left foot. I should like to have a look, but this is not the moment! Here comes another projectile. I take another leap to dodge it. It lands close beside me. Then suddenly the humming in the air begins to thin out. There are a few more whizzing sounds, and then the downpour is over.

Have you ever tried to imagine a snail's state of mind as it creeps out of its shell again, the danger past? That was the way my head, which had been drawn back between hunched-up shoulders, gradually began to rise up again on my neck, and my arched back began to straighten, my arms to loosen, my hands to unclench. Right, then—it's better not to hang about in this sector! So I set out again. By this time I have got round three-quarters of the crater, and am in the gap between the northern and western zones, which are those that get the worst pounding. From here I can get back on to the ridge proper.

I am now almost directly over the roaring chasm, and my gaze goes straight down into it like a stone dropping into the pit. After all, it's nothing but a tunnel. That's all. It's a vertical tunnel, ten or fifteen yards across, its walls heated to such a degree that they stretch and 'rise' like dough, and up from its depths every now and then enormous drops of liquid fire spurt forth, a great splashing sweat that falls and vanishes, golden flash upon flash, back into the dazzling gulf. Even the brownish vapours emanating from the pit cannot quite veil its splendour. It is nothing but a tunnel running down into viscous copper-coloured draperies; yet it opens into the very substance of another world. The sight is so extraordinary that I forget the insecurity of my position and the hellish burning under the soles of my feet. Quite mechanically, I go on lifting first the left foot, then the right. It is as though my mind were held fast in a trap by the sight of this burning well from which a terrifying snore continually rises, interrupted by sharp explosions and the rolling of thunder.

Suddenly I hurl myself backwards. The flight of projectiles has whizzed past my face. Hunched up again, instinctively trying to make as small a target of myself as I can, I once more go through the horrors that I am beginning to know. I am in the thick of this hair's breadth game of anticipation and dodging.

And now it's all over; I take a last glance into the marvellous and terrible abyss, and am just getting ready to start off on the last stage of this burning circumnavigation, all two hundred yards of it, when I get a sudden sharp blow in the back. A delayed-action bomb! With all the breath knocked out of me, I stand rigid.

A moment passes. I wonder why I am not dead. But nothing seems to have happened to me—no pain, no change of any sort. Slowly I risk turning my head, and at my feet I see a sort of huge red loaf with the glow dying out of it.

I stretch my arms and wriggle my back. Nothing hurts. Everything seems to be in its proper place. Later on, examining my jacket, I discovered a brownish scorch-mark with slightly charred edges, about the size of my hand, and I drew from it a conclusion of immense value to me in future explorations: so long as one is not straight in the line of fire, volcanic bombs, which fall in a still pasty state, but already covered with a kind of very thin elastic skin, graze one without having time to cause a deep burn.

I set off at a run, for I must be as quick as I can in crossing this part of the crater-edge, which is one of the most heavily bombarded. But I am assailed by an unexpected blast of suffocating fumes. My eyes close, full of smarting tears. I am caught in a cloud of gas forced down by the wind. I fight for breath. It feels as if I were swallowing lumps of dry, corrosive cotton-wool. My head swims, but I urge myself at all costs to get the upper hand. The main thing is not to breathe this poisoned air. Groping, I fumble in a pocket. Damn, not this one. How about this other one, then? No. At last I get a handkerchief out and, still with my eyes shut, cover my mouth with it.

Then, stumbling along, I try to get through the loathsome cloud. I no longer even bother to pay any attention to the series of bursts from the volcano, being too anxious to get out of this hell before I lose grip entirely. I am getting pretty exhausted, staggering . . . The air filtered through the handkerchief just about keeps me going, but it is still too poisonous, and there is too little of it for the effort involved in making this agonizing journey across rough and dangerous terrain. The gases are too concentrated, and the great maw that is belching them forth is too near.

A few steps ahead of me I catch a glimpse of the steep wall of the peak, or promontory, from the other side of which I started about a century ago, it seems to me now. The noxious mists are licking round the peak, which is almost vertical and twice the height of a man. It's so near! But

I realize at once that I shall never have the strength to clamber up it.

In less than a second, the few possible solutions to this life-and-death problem race through my mind. Shall I turn my back to the crater and rush away down the outer slope, which is bombarded by the thickest barrages? No. About face and back along the ledge? Whatever I do, I must turn back. And then make my escape. By sliding down the northern slope? That is also under too heavy bombardment. And the worst of it would be that in making a descent of that sort there would be no time to keep a watch for blocks of lava coming down on me.

Only one possibility is left: to make my way back all along the circular ridge, more than a hundred yards of it, till I reach the eastern rim, where neither gas nor projectiles are so concentrated as to be necessarily fatal.

I swing round. I stumble and collapse on all fours, uncovering my mouth for an instant. The gulp of gas that I swallow hurts my lungs, and leaves me gasping. Red-hot scoriae are embedded in the palms of my hands. I shall never get out of this!

The first fifteen or twenty steps of this journey back through the

'The first steps back through the acrid fumes were a slow nightmare.'

acrid fumes of sulphur and chlorine are a slow nightmare; no step means any progress and no breath brings any oxygen into the lungs. The threat of bombs no longer counts. Only these gases exist now. Air! Air!

I came to myself again on the eastern rim, gasping down the clean air borne by the wind, washing out my lungs with deep fresh gulps of it, as though I could never get enough. How wide and comfortable this ledge is! What a paradise compared with the suffocating, torrid hell from which I have at last escaped! And yet this is where I was so anxious and so tense less than a quarter of an hour ago.

Several draughts of the prevailing breeze have relieved my agony. All at once, life is again worth living! I no longer feel that desire to escape from here as swiftly as possible. On the contrary, I feel a new upsurge of explorer's curiosity. Once more my gaze turns towards the mouth, out of which sporadic bursts of grape-shot are still spurting forth. Now and then there are bigger explosions and I have to keep a look-out for what may come down on my head, which momentarily interrupts the dance I keep up from one foot to the other, that *tresca*[3] of which Dante speaks—the dance of the damned, harried by fire. True, I have come to the conclusion that the impact of these bombs is not necessarily fatal, but I am in no hurry to verify the observation.

The inner walls of the crater do not all incline at the same angle. To the north, west and south they are practically vertical, not to say over-hanging, but here on the east the slope drops away at an angle of no more than fifty degrees. So long as one moved along in a gingerly way, this might be an incline one could negotiate. It would mean going down into the very heart of the volcano. For an instant I am astounded by my own fool-hardiness. Still, it's really too tempting . . .

Cautiously, I take a step forward . . . then another . . . and another . . . seems all right . . . it *is* all right. I begin the climb down, digging my heels as deep as I can into the red-hot scoriae. Gradually, below me, the oval of the enormous maw comes nearer, growing bigger, and the terrifying uproar becomes more deafening. My eyes, open as wide as they will go are drunken with its monstrous glory. Here are those ponderous draperies of molten gold and copper, so near—so near that I feel as if I, human being that I am, had entered right into their fabulous world. The air is stiflingly hot. I am right in the fiery furnace.

256   [3]from *The Inferno*.

I linger before this fascinating spectacle. But then, by sheer effort, I tear myself away. It's time to get back to being 'scientific' and measure the temperatures of the ground, and of the atmosphere. I plunge the long spike of the thermometer into the shifting scoriae, and the steel of it glitters among these brownish and grey screes with their dull shimmer. At a depth of six inches the temperature is two hundred and twenty degrees centigrade. It's amusing to think that when I used to dream, it was always about polar exploration!

Suddenly, the monster vomits out another burst; so close that the noise deafens me. I bury my face in my arms. Fortunately almost every one of the projectiles comes down outside the crater . . .

Without a break the grim, steady growling continues to rise from the depths of that throat, only out-roared at intervals by the bellowing and belching of lava. It's too much; I can feel myself giving up. I turn my back on it, and try, on all fours, to scramble up the slope, which has now become incredibly steep and crumbles and gives way under my weight, which is dragging me down, down . . .

Little by little, by immense exertions, I regain control of my movements, as well as the mental steadiness I need. I persuade myself to climb *calmly* up this short slope which keeps crumbling away under my feet. When I reach the top, I stand upright for just a moment. Then, crossing the two glowing fissures that still intersect my course, I reach the part of the rim from where there is a way down to the world of ordinary peaceful things.

LAFFEY AND THE KAMIKAZES

Commander John Kerans

When the radar operator's urgent voice called out: 'Kamikazes—too many to count—coming in fast!' Commander Frederick Becton of the destroyer *USS Laffey* knew he and his men were in for a tough time.

The date was 16 April 1945, and the place fifty miles north of the Japanese fortress island of Okinawa. Since 1 April the 10th US Army, with massive fleet support, had been engaged in a desperate assault on Okinawa. From the bitterness of the Japanese resistance it was obvious this was going to be the most murderous battle of all the Pacific campaign. The enemy were fully aware that once Okinawa was captured the Americans would have a base only 325 miles from the Japanese mainland.

That the fanaticism already widespread among the Japanese fighting men flamed even more ferociously when their homeland was threatened with invasion, was already terribly apparent. The cult of the Kamikaze —the young men who gloried in sacrificing themselves in suicide attacks—was at its peak. Kamikaze pilots were diving their bomb-loaded planes squarely on to warships, supply ships and troop transports; suicide swimmers and boatmen were ramming contact-detonated high-explosive against ships; shore soldiers crouched in foxholes, clutching big bombs which they detonated when tanks or armoured carriers passed over them. At Okinawa there were more Japanese suicide attacks made by land, sea and air than on any other battlefield.

The reason why the *Laffey* was where she was, at station Roger Peter One, on this calm sunny April morning, was because she was operating as a radar picket ship to give warning of approaching Kamikazes. She was, in fact, the forward picket ship, nearly one hundred miles closer to Japan than the main force attacking Okinawa. Inevitably she would be the first of the hated enemy the Japanese would see as they flew out on their desperate one-way missions. And now the first wave was approaching: 'Range 17,000—still coming fast and impossible to count!' called the breathless voice of the radar operator.

Commander Becton, a quietly-spoken, intense man who became suddenly dynamic when action was required, sounded the general alarm. Down the voice-pipe to the chief engineer he called for speed: 'Henke, we want every turn you've got!' Although the *Laffey* had not been attacked or in action yet, her men had a good idea what happened when the Kamikazes came. In the Hagushi anchorage of Okinawa, seized in the opening assault and now thronged with the multitude of vessels of the invading force, there had been many victims of the power-diving suicide planes. Contorted metal, gaping holes in decks, smouldering wreckage, gruesome remains of what had been men and already ashore a cemetery which daily expanded . . . all was grim testimony to the fact that many a Japanese pilot had taken far more than one enemy with him when he died. While the *Laffey* was briefly in that graveyard anchorage being equipped with the complicated radar installation of an early-warning ship, they had been tersely advised by a gun captain from a battle-scarred destroyer: 'You guys will have a fighting chance —you'll knock a lot of them down and you'll think you're doing fine but they'll just keep on coming until one of them gets you!'

The *Laffey*, a powerfully-gunned destroyer of 2,200 tons, had been on extreme forward duty exactly twenty-four hours when the scanning radar first registered the swarming cluster of blips. The seas were calm, so that she gently rocked as she cruised beneath a sky smiling and blue by day and soft star-spangled velvet by night. Pacific seemed the right name for this ocean and there was nothing to indicate it would be different until the threshing propellers churned up the bloated body of a Japanese pilot and the charred wreckage of his plane.

Now the lean, grey destroyer was a'shudder with the pulse of her engines as the men below responded to the orders for full speed. Still the wide blue heavens were innocent of anything at all that could be deemed hostile. High-powered glasses on the bridge, intently scanning the sky to the north, searched for something that at first would look like a swarm of gnats. Although still invisible to the naked eye, the approaching Kamikazes were coming up bigger and bigger on the radar screen. Then: 'Seem to be opening out—but they're still coming on!' came the operator's report.

That suicide planes were heading her way did not necessarily mean the *Laffey* was their target. It was more likely they had been ordered to crash with their bomb-loads on to the decks of the huge American aircraft-carriers which were playing such a great part in the island-hopping advance on Japan. Other priority targets would be the battle-ships, cruisers and big transports whose destruction must bring death to large numbers of Americans. 'Most likely they'll go over us,' suggested one of the *Laffey*'s officers. 'Maybe they'll get shot down by our combat air patrols before they can do any damage.' But Lieutenant Challen McCune, the Executive Officer, reported that the American fighter patrol was at the moment being relieved; it would be some little time before the relieving fighters could get to the area.

Suddenly Captain Becton's binoculars picked out the planes! 'Bogies ahead—coming fast!' a sailor shouted from the look-out platform. The Kamikazes were coming! (Afterwards the survivors learned there were no fewer than 165 suicide planes in that approaching cloud!) 'Lieutenant Smith requests permission to fire', came in excited tones from the forward five-inch guns. 'Fire when ready!' rapped the Captain. The murmur of the approaching enemy could now be heard; with each second it swelled until it was an agry hornet-like drone. Suddenly the forward guns belched fire and smoke. The whole ship shuddered. 'Hard left rudder! All guns commence fire!' roared Captain Becton. And the azure morning erupted into one vast bellowing, flaming inferno.

The roar of the *Laffey*'s big guns was joined by insistent throbbing from forty millimetre guns and pulsing whip-cracks from twenty millimetre cannons. The sky ahead was full of Japanese planes. Crackling smoke puffs of the destroyer's first salvo were planted blackly in their path. Then four Aichi 99 dive bombers peeled off and power-dived at the *Laffey*. Engines bellowing they hurtled down, down, down like thunderbolts, two at the bows and two at the stern. Their fanatical pilots were giving every atom of engine power, every taut, strained fibre of their own dedicated beings. They dived to certain death for the destruction of their enemies.

A stream of smoke whirled back from one of the bombers forward. Suddenly it was a fire-streaked comet plunging straight into the sea. The five-inch guns had claimed their first victim. The water still frothed where it had vanished when the other bomber diving at the bows lurched, cartwheeled dramatically, shattered into fragments as it struck the sea. All around and above her now the *Laffey* was surrounded by the black smoke of her bursting shells. Then the red and white tracer streams of her close-range automatic weapons leaped out and up. Abruptly a billow of smoke and flame aft told the ending of another of the attackers: shells from number three turret had destroyed it. The tail of the fourth was spectacularly whipped away by a cannon-shell stream; it disintegrated in mid-air and was gone. Momentarily man looked at man in speechless wonderment at what they had done— then the next attack was coming in.

Two Kamikaze bombers streaked in headlong, then parted and peeled off left and right for flank attacks. Boiling the sea into foam behind her, flinging out great spumes of white water forward, the *Laffey* heeled to port and then to starboard as she dodged and weaved. One plane tearing in at two thousand yards range was suddenly the centre of shell bursts and criss-cross tracer streams. It had its wings torn off in mid-air, and a great waterspout climbed up where it vanished into the sea. The Kamikaze on the other side twisted frantically, got within fifty yards, then was caught by a salvo of the destroyer's big guns which blew it apart. Although the pilot was dead the big bomb he had intended to take with him to his death on the *Laffey*'s deck tumbled from the smoke cloud and burst alongside. The ship lurched violently at the concussion, her nearest escape yet, but although men were flung down none was wounded.

'God! How long can our luck hold!' gasped a gunner. The men of

They hurtled down, down, down like thunderbolts . . .

the *Laffey* were well aware that most of the savagely-torn ships they had seen in Hagushi Bay had each been victim of no more than one Kamikaze. Yet already the *Laffey* had survived six separate attacks and destroyed the attackers. The roar above them now was deafening; the Kamikaze swarm seemed to be milling round waiting to take it in turns to dive-bomb. Surely there could be no hope of surviving if the Kamikazes did not press on to other targets?

'Hard right!' By both voice and gesture Becton gave the order urgently. Another bomber was coming, skimming the sea on the port bow. The destroyer keeled over, steeper and steeper, until the frothing sea surged along her slanting deck, until she was round with the Kamikaze howling over her stern instead of attacking her broadside. The pilot missed his death crash but barely clipped the top of one of the five-inch guns, killing one of the crew instantly. The *Laffey* had suffered her first casualty. The ensuing lull was just long enough for the dead man to be dragged away, and hasty repairs to be made to the broken signal wires, then the eighth Kamikaze was coming at them.

This torpedo-bomber also dodged in at sea level, on the starboard beam. But a deadly concentration of tracer fastened on to it, its fuel tank exploded and it was a funeral pyre rushing toward the ship. Then the whole thing disintegrated and vanished, leaving only a sinister patch on the sea.

Without any respite the ninth attacker screamed down. Down, down, down it plunged then zoomed in a short shattering climb, levelled out, and was at them. Every gun that the twisting, turning *Laffey* could bring to bear thundered and cracked and rattled, but to no avail. As he hurtled towards the thunderous death he had chosen, the Kamikaze pilot bore a charmed life. Some men who glimpsed his face in the last split second swore it had a set, dedicated look, as though he were already not of this world; he wasn't an instant later, when the plane smashed into the destroyer amongst a nest of guns amidships. With a horrible 'whoof' a great tower of smoke and flame boiled up from the destroyer. 'Fire amidships!' the dread call went out. 'Damage control and fire-fighting parties needed topside on the double!'

With this pillar of smoke and fire standing up from the ocean to make the *Laffey* a target that could be seen for miles, the suicide pilots were spurred to an absolute frenzy. Despite all the variety of targets

263

beyond at Okinawa, all the great warships and transports whose destruction was so vital to the Japanese soldiers fanatically defending the island, the Kamikaze pilots seemed obsessed with a desire to obliterate this one American destroyer.

Perhaps it was because this warship was the closest enemy to their homeland; perhaps it was the unreasoning inflexibility which so often caused the Japs to squander fighting men on comparatively unimportant outposts which they should have by-passed. Whatever it was, the blind, furious persistence with which the Kamikazes kept attacking the *Laffey* undoubtedly saved countless American lives at Okinawa.

Weaving and writhing through the sea like an animal in extreme pain, the destroyer was now amid a swarm of plunging warplanes piloted by fanatics seeking death and glory. Fortunately there were still sufficient guns working, and men to serve them, to put up a formidable curtain of exploding steel. But the tenth Kamikaze also got home, and even more devastatingly than the previous one. Wave-hopping and jinking, it burst through the fire curtain and crashed terrifyingly on to the after five-inch gun mounting.

Almost immediately an eleventh, hot on its heels, shattered down near the same place. A huge billow of flame, like sudden engulfment by a prairie fire, enveloped the destroyer from end to end. One complete side of the turret had been blown out, great holes gaped in the main deck, and flaming fuel spewed through into the living space below. The *Laffey* shuddered as though in her death throes as the forty millimetre ammunition magazine took fire and shells began to explode deep down within her, blowing men there to bits.

As though that were not enough yet another attacker, the twelfth, glided in silently on the port side, masked by the billowing smoke. He dropped a bomb near the stern and it tore through the ship's side, exploded in a machine-gun magazine and jammed the rudder. Listing, blazing, crippled, the *Laffey* could now only circle on the one course. She was an absolute sitting target.

In the inferno below a damage control party worked heroically. Dr Mathew Darnell, Jr., the ship's MO, plucked live ammunition from amidst red hot metal and tossed it overboard. Commander Becton, still in complete control of an almost indescribably desperate situation, kept the destroyer flat out on its jammed circular course.

The thirteenth Kamikaze plunged down with the fourteenth right behind it. They crashed on to the after deckhouse almost simultaneously. The terrifying impact, coupled with the shattering explosion of the bombs, nearly power-punched the *Laffey* beneath the sea. But she rode up again, with yet another terrible fire adding to her shroud of black smoke and leaping flames. High-octane fuel released by the smashing of water-tight hatches added to the roaring conflagration.

A brave attempt was now made by Lieutenant Ted Runk and three enlisted men to repair the damaged steering. They fought their way through smoke and flame without breathing masks and struggled to clear the rudder. But the flames were licking closer all the time and they were forced back. On their way out they walked straight into an unexploded Japanese bomb ringed by flames and quickly rolled it overboard. Meanwhile, on a wrecked forty millimetre gun aft with flames leaping around him, Lieutenant Joe Youngquist tossed live hot ammunition into the sea.

The attacking bombers could now only be glimpsed through rifts in the pall of smoke that enveloped the destroyer. Suddenly the fifteenth Kamikaze was plunging down on them, but as they saw it they saw also there was a Corsair fighter of the US Navy tearing after it with guns blazing. The *Laffey*'s forward machine-guns opened up on the enemy and at the last minute its nose lifted and it howled over the ship instead of on to it, just clipping the radar mast. Seconds later it disintegrated, struck by a concentration of fire. The Corsair could not pull out and also hit the radar mast, rolled over as it zoomed, and the pilot bailed out.

Yet another Kamikaze roared in, this time to port, again with a Corsair hammering away on its tail. It burst into flames before reaching the destroyer but dropped a bomb which burst so close that splinters struck down some of the gunners still tirelessly serving the now nearly red-hot forty-millimetre and twenty-millimetre guns. It also destroyed the communications to the two five-inch guns still in action. The fate of the seventeenth Kamikaze proved that the destruction of communications had not put these guns out of action. One of them, now manually trained, blasted the suicide plane out of the sky as it came in head on.

The next two Kamikazes to attack were just too easy to be true.

They were two Nakajima army fighters fitted out with bombs. The destroyer's remaining big guns just blasted them out of the sky—one, two—at long range.

But the twentieth suicide bomber was far more formidable. Dropping down from a steep glide out of the sun, it twisted and turned to present the most difficult target possible, then opened up its engine and howled down on the ship. But yet again a Corsair came swooping in with all guns blazing, braving the curtain of fire put up by the destroyer's guns. Shots ripped the Japanese plane from above and below as it thundered over, so close as to clip off the one remaining yardarm. It plummeted into the water just beyond the *Laffey*'s stern.

Still the Kamikazes came! And still the half-sunken destroyer fought back! The twenty-first bomber was blasted out of the sky by the forward five-inch guns and the last remaining forty-millimetre gun. The twenty-second howled in through a hail of shell-fire and machine-gun bullets, then abruptly reeled, spun and disintegrated in a great puff of smoke.

Then suddenly all the brave men aboard the *Laffey* who could still listen stood stock still. Their eyes and ears strained out and upwards towards a new sound that was filling the sky. It was a crescendo of engine song of a great number of diving warplanes, pitched in a key they recognized as American. At last the combat air patrol had arrived! Squadrons of Marine-piloted Corsair fighters hurtled on the milling Kamikazes. Now the *Laffey* plunged clear of her smoke shroud—and high above her could be seen the downrush of the attacking fighters and the twisting, flaming downfall of their victims. It was as though a band of shining angels had suddenly rescued them from the hell that enveloped them. For a moment the men stood in bewilderment, as though they could hardly comprehend that they were going to live after all. Then cheer after cheer rose from the destroyer and the blood-stained, sweat-soaked, smoke-blackened men shouted exultingly: 'Get the bastards!—Rip 'em up!—Give 'em hell!'

A great silence descended upon the Pacific Ocean fifty miles north of Okinawa. The crippled, heroic *Laffey* wallowed there amidst the wreckage of the unbelievable battle through which she had just fought. For seventy-nine minutes non-stop she had been subjected to relentless Kamikaze attacks, no fewer than twenty-two of them pressed right home. Yet still she was afloat, still prepared to fight on. She had lost thirty-one killed, seventy-two wounded and was a mass of tortured, smoking wreckage; but she was still indomitable.

Early that afternoon another warship steamed up, warned of the *Laffey's* condition by the fighter-pilots who had terminated the battle. She took the gallant destroyer in tow, back to Hagushi Bay. In that harbour of Kamikaze victims the *Laffey* caused wonderment and admiration, for the minds of men who had experienced the terror of suicide bombers boggled at the thought of the *Laffey's* twenty-two attacks and could not imagine how she had still fought on and lived to tell the tale.

In due course the destroyer was patched up at Pearl Harbour, then moved back to be rebuilt in the great Todd shipyards at San Francisco. While there she was for five days put on display so that the American people could appreciate what their sailors had to face from the Kamikaze suicide attacks. Commander Frederick Becton was awarded the Navy Cross for his great heroism and devotion to duty. Many said he should have received America's highest award for valour, the Congressional Medal.

Captain Frank Manson, one of the Laffey's *surviving officers, is now known the world over as the man who thought up the idea of the Great White Fleet. This project envisages a 'mercy task force' of obsolete warships and other vessels not in use to take aid anywhere in the world that disease, hunger and disaster requires it. Britain's bomber hero Group Captain Leonard Cheshire, VC, is associated with Manson in this. The American officer was obsessed with the idea after becoming convinced of the futility of the slaughter he had witnessed. He determined that warships 'in their retirement' should be used to alleviate some of the world's misery.*

BEN BLOWER'S STORY

Charles Fenno Hoffman

'Are you sure that's the *Flame* over by the shore?'

'Cer*ting*, manny! I could tell her pipes acrost the Mazoura.'

'And you will overhaul her?'

'Won't we though! I tell ye, strannger, so sure as my name's Ben Blower, that that last tar-bar'l I hove in the furnace has put jist the smart chance of go-ahead into us to cut off the *Flame* from yonder pint, or send our boat to kingdom come.'

'The devil!' exclaimed a bystander who, intensely interested in the race, was leaning the while against the partitions of the boiler-room. 'I've chosen a nice place to see the fun, near this infernal powder-barrel.'

'Not so bad as if you were in it,' coolly observed Ben as the other walked rapidly away.

'As if he were in it! In what? In the boiler?'

'Cer*ting*! Don't folks sometimes go into bilers, manny?'

'I should think there'd be other parts of the boat more comfortable.'

'That's right; poking fun at me at once't: but wait till we get through this brush with the old *Flame* and I'll tell ye of a regular-fixin scrape that a man may get into. It's true, too, every word of it, as sure as my name's Ben Blower . . .'

'You have seen the *Flame* then afore, strannger? Six year ago, when new upon the river, she was a raal out and outer, I tell ye. I was at that time a hand aboard of her. Yes, I belonged to her at the time of her great race with the *Go-liar*. You've heern, mahap, of the blow-up by which we lost it. They made a great fuss about it; but it was nothing but a mere fiz of hot water after all. Only the springing of a few rivets, which loosened a biler-plate or two, and let out a thin spirting upon some niggers that hadn't sense enough to get out of the way. Well, the *Go-liar* took off our passengers, and we ran into Smasher's Landing to repair damages, and bury the poor fools that were killed. Here we laid for a matter of thirty hours or so, and got things to rights on board for a bran new start. There was some carpenters' work yet to be done, but the captain said that that might be fixed off jist as well when we were under way—we had worked hard—the weather was sour, and we needn't do anything more jist now—we might take that afternoon to ourselves, but the next morning he'd get up steam bright and airly, and we'd all come out *new*. There was no temperance society at Smasher's Landing, and I went ashore upon a lark with some of the hands.'

I omit the worthy Benjamin's adventures upon land, and, despairing of fully conveying his language in its original force, will not hesitate to give the rest of his singular narrative in my own words, save where, in a few instances, I can recall his precise phraseology, which the reader will easily recognize.

'The night was raw and sleety when I regained the deck of our boat. The officers, instead of leaving a watch above, had closed up everything, and shut themselves in the cabin. The fire-room only was open. The boards dashed from the outside by the explosion had not yet been replaced. The floor of the room was wet, and there was scarcely a corner which afforded a shelter from the driving storm. I was about leaving the room, resigned to sleep in the open air, and now bent only upon getting under the lee of some bulkhead that would protect me against the wind.

'In passing out I kept my arms stretched forward to feel my way in

269

the dark, but my feet came in contact with a heavy iron lid; I stumbled and, as I fell, struck one of my hands into the "manhole" (I think this was the name he gave to the oval-shaped opening in the head of the boiler), through which the smith had entered to make his repairs. I fell with my arm thrust so far into the aperture that I received a pretty smart blow in the face as it came in contact with the head of the boiler, and I did not hesitate to drag my body after it the moment I recovered from this stunning effect, and ascertained my whereabouts. In a word, I crept into the boiler, resolved to pass the rest of the night there. The place was dry and sheltered. Had my bed been softer I would have had all that man could desire; as it was, I slept, and slept soundly.

'I should mention though, that, before closing my eyes, I several times shifted my position. I had gone first to the farthest end of the boiler, then again I had crawled back to the manhole, to put my hand out and feel that it was really still open. The warmest place was at the far end, where I finally established myself, and that I knew from the first. It was foolish in me to think that the opening through which I had just entered could be closed without my hearing it, and that, too, when no one was astir but myself; but the blow on the side of my face made me a little nervous perhaps; besides, I never could bear to be shut up in any place—it always gives a wild-like feeling about the head.

'You may laugh, stranger, but I believe I should suffocate in an empty church if I once felt that I was so shut up in it that I could not get out. I have met men afore now just like me, or worse rather, much worse—men that it made sort of furious to be tied down to anything, yet so soft-like and contradictory in their natures that you might lead them anywhere so long as they didn't feel the string. Stranger, it takes all sorts of people to make a world; and we may have a good many of the worst kind of white men here out west.

'But I have seen folks upon this river—quiet-looking chaps, too, as ever you see—who were so teetotally *carankterankterous* that they'd shoot the doctor who'd tell them they couldn't live when ailing, and make a die of it, just out of spite, when told they *must* get well. Yes, fellows as fond of the good things of earth as you and I, yet who'd rush like mad right over the gangplank of life if once brought to believe that they had to stay in this world whether they wanted to leave it or not. Thunder and bees! If such a fellow as that had heard the cocks crow as I did—awakened to find darkness about him—darkness so thick you might cut it with a knife—heard other sounds, too, to tell that it was morning, and scrambling to fumble for that manhole, found it, too, black—closed—black and even as the rest of the iron coffin around him, closed, with not a rivet-hole to let God's light and air in—why—why—he'd a *swounded* right down on the spot, as I did, and I ain't ashamed to own it to no white man.'

The big drops actually stood upon the poor fellow's brow, as he now paused for a moment in the recital of his terrible story. He passed his hand over his rough features, and resumed it with less agitation.

'How long I may have remained there senseless I don't know. The doctors have since told me it must have been a sort of fit—more like an apoplexy than a swoon, for the attack finally passed off in sleep. Yes, I slept; I know *that*, for I dreamed—dreamed a heap o' things afore I awoke: there is but one dream, however, that I have ever been able to recall distinctly, and that must have come on shortly before I recovered my consciousness. My resting-place through the night had been, as I have told you, at the far end of the boiler. Well, I now dreamed that the manhole was still open, and, what seems curious, rather than laughable, if you take it in connection with other things, I fancied that my legs had been so stretched in the long walk I had taken the evening before that they now reached the whole length of the boiler, and extended through the opening.

'At first (in my dreaming reflections) it was a comfortable thought, that no one could now shut up the manhole without awakening me. But soon it seemed as if my feet, which were on the outside, were becoming drenched in the storm which had originally driven me to seek this shelter. I felt the chilling rain upon my extremities. They grew colder and colder, and their numbness gradually extended upward to other parts of my body. It seemed, however, that it was only the under side of my person that was thus strangely visited. I lay upon my back, and it must have been a species of nightmare that afflicted me, for I knew at last that I was dreaming, yet felt it impossible to rouse myself. A violent fit of coughing restored at last my powers of volition. The water, which had been slowly rising around me, had rushed into my mouth; I awoke to hear the rapid strokes of the pump which was driving it into the boiler!

'My whole condition—no—not all of it—not yet—my *present* condition flashed with new horror upon me. But I did not again swoon. The choking sensation which had made me faint when I first discovered how I was entombed gave way to a livelier though less overpowering emotion. I shrieked even as I started from my slumber. The previous discovery of the closed aperture, with the instant oblivion that followed, seemed only a part of my dream, and I threw my arms about and looked eagerly for the opening by which I had entered the horrid place—yes, looked for it, and felt for it, though it was the terrible conviction that it was closed—a second time brought home to me—which prompted my frenzied cry. Every sense seemed to have tenfold acuteness, yet not one to act in unison with another. I shrieked again and again—imploringly—desperately—savagely. I filled the hollow chamber with my cries, till its iron walls seemed to tingle around me. The dull strokes of the accursed pump seemed only to mock at, while they deadened, my screams.

'At last I gave myself up. It is the struggle against our fate which frenzies the mind. We cease to fear when we cease to hope. I gave myself up, and then I grew calm!

'I was resigned to die—resigned even to my mode of death. It was not, I thought, so very new after all, as to awaken unwonted horror in a man. Thousands have been sunk to the bottom of the ocean shut up in the holds of vessels—beating themselves against the battened hatches—dragged down from the upper world shrieking, not for life, but for death only beneath the eye and amid the breath of heaven. Thousands have endured that appalling kind of suffocation. I would die only as many a better man had died before me. I *could* meet such a death. I said so—I thought so—I felt so—felt so, I mean, for a minute—or more; ten minutes it may have been—or but an instant of time. I know not.

'There *was* a time, then, when I was resigned to my fate. But, heaven! was I resigned to it in the shape in which next it came to appal? Stranger, I felt that water growing hot about my limbs, though it was yet mid-leg deep. I felt it, and in the same moment heard the roar of the furnace that was to turn it into steam before it could get deep enough to drown one!

'You shudder. It was hideous. But did I shrink and shrivel, and crumble down upon that iron floor, and lose my senses in that horrid

272

'I soon succeeded in driving the spike through . . .'

agony of fear? No! Though my brain swam and the life-blood that curdled at my heart seemed about to stagnate there for ever, still *I knew!* I was too hoarse—too hopeless—from my previous efforts, to cry out more. But I struck—feebly at first, and then strongly—frantically with my clenched fist against the sides of the boiler. There were people moving near who *must* hear my blows! Could not I hear the grating of chains, the shuffling of feet, the very rustle of a rope—hear them all, within a few inches of me? I did; but the gurgling water that was growing hotter and hotter around my extremities made more noise within the steaming cauldron than did my frenzied blows.

'Latterly I had hardly changed my position, but now the growing heat of the water made me plash to and fro; lifting myself wholly out of it was impossible, but I could not remain quiet. I stumbled upon something; it was a mallet!—a chance tool the smith had left there by accident. With what wild joy did I seize it—with what eager confidence did I now deal my first blows with it against the walls of my prison! But scarce had I intermitted them for a moment when I heard the clang of the iron door as the fireman flung it wide to feed the flames that were to torture me. My knocking was unheard, though I could hear him toss the sticks into the furnace beneath me, and drive to the door when his infernal oven was fully crammed.

'Had I yet a hope? I had; but it rose in my mind side by side with the fear that I might now become the agent of preparing myself a more frightful death. Yes; when I thought of that furnace with its fresh-fed flames curling beneath the iron upon which I stood—a more frightful death even than that of being boiled alive! Had I discovered that mallet but a short time sooner—but no matter, I would by its aid resort to the only expedient now left.

'It was this. I remembered having a marlin-spike in my pocket, and in less time than I have taken in hinting at the consequences of thus using it, I had made an impression upon the sides of the boiler, and soon succeeded in driving it through. The water gushed through the aperture —would they see it? No; the jet could only play against a wooden partition which must hide the stream from view; it must trickle down upon the decks before the leakage would be discovered. Should I drive another hole to make that leakage greater? Why the water within seemed already to be sensibly diminished, so hot had become that which remained; should more escape, would I not hear a bubble and hiss upon the fiery plates of iron that were already scorching the soles of my feet?

'Ah! there is a movement—voices—I hear them calling for a crow-bar. The bulkhead cracks as they pry off the planking. They have seen the leak—they are trying to get at it! Good God! why do they not first dampen the fire? why do they call for the—the——

'Stranger, look at that finger: it can never regain its natural size; but it has already done all the service that man could expect from so humble a member. Sir, that hole would have been plugged up on the instant *unless* I had jammed my finger through!

'I heard the cry of horror as they saw it without—the shout to drown the fire—the first stroke of the cold-water pump. They say, too, that I was conscious when they took me out—but I—I remember nothing more till they brought a julep to my bedside arterwards, And that *julep!*'

'Cooling, was it?'

'Strannger!!'

Ben turned away his head and wept. He could no more.

274

MOWGLI AND THE BANDAR-LOG

Rudyard Kipling

Mowgli, the boy growing up in the jungle with the Seeonee wolf-pack, has as his tutors and friends Baloo, the bear, and Bagheera, the black panther.

One day the shiftless Bandar-log *(Monkey People) abduct him and take him to Cold Lairs, a deserted city in the jungle. Baloo and Bagheera enlist the help of Kaa, the giant python, and go off to Mowgli's rescue.*

In the Cold Lairs the Monkey-People were not thinking of Mowgli's friends at all. They had brought the boy to the Lost City, and were very pleased with themselves for the time. Mowgli had never seen an Indian city before, and though this was almost a heap of ruins, it seemed very wonderful and splendid. Some king had built it long ago on a little hill. You could still trace the stone causeways that led up to the ruined gates where the last splinters of wood hung to the worn, rusted hinges. Trees had grown into and out of the walls; the battlements were tumbled down and decayed, and wild creepers hung out of the windows of the towers on the walls in bushy hanging clumps.

A great roofless palace crowned the hill, and the marble of the court-yards and the fountains was split, and stained with red and green, and the very cobblestones in the courtyard where the king's elephants used to live had been thrust up and apart by grasses and young trees. From the palace you could see the rows and rows of roofless houses that made up the city looking like empty honeycombs filled with blackness; the shapeless block of stone that had been an idol, in the square where four roads met; the pits and dimples at street-corners where the public wells once stood, and the shattered domes of temples with wild figs sprouting on their sides. The monkeys called the place their city, and pretended to despise the Jungle-People because they lived in the Forest. And yet they never knew what the buildings were made for nor how to use them. They would sit in circles on the hall of the king's council chamber, and scratch for fleas and pretend to be men; or they would run in and out of the roofless houses and collect pieces of plaster and old bricks in a corner, and forget where they had hidden them, and fight and cry in scuffling crowds, and then break off to play up and down the terraces of the king's garden, where they would shake the rose trees and the oranges in sport to see the fruit and flowers fall.

They explored all the passages and dark tunnels in the palace and the hundreds of little dark rooms, but they never remembered what they had seen and what they had not; and so drifted about in ones and twos or crowds telling each other that they were doing as men did. They drank at the tanks and made the water all muddy, and then they fought over it, and then they would all rush together in mobs and shout: 'There is no one in the jungle so wise and good and clever and strong and gentle as the *Bandar-log*.' Then all would begin again till they grew tired of the city and went back to the tree-tops, hoping the Jungle-People would notice them.

Mowgli, who had been trained under the Law of the Jungle, did not like or understand this kind of life. The monkeys dragged him into the Cold Lairs late in the afternoon, and instead of going to sleep, as Mowgli would have done after a long journey, they joined hands and danced about and sang their foolish songs. One of the monkeys made a speech and told his companions that Mowgli's capture marked a new thing in the history of the *Bandar-log*, for Mowgli was going to show them how to weave sticks and canes together as a protection against rain and cold. Mowgli picked up some creepers and began to work them in and out, and the monkeys tried to imitate; but in a very few minutes they lost interest and began to pull their friends' tails or jump up and down on all fours, coughing.

'I wish to eat,' said Mowgli. 'I am a stranger in this part of the jungle. Bring me food, or give me leave to hunt here.'

Twenty or thirty monkeys bounded away to bring him nuts and wild pawpaws; but they fell to fighting on the road, and it was too much trouble to go back with what was left of the fruit. Mowgli was sore and angry as well as hungry, and he roamed through the empty city giving the Strangers' Hunting Call from time to time, but no one answered him, and Mowgli felt that he had reached a very bad place indeed. 'All that Baloo has said about the *Bandar-log* is true,' he thought to himself. 'They have no Law, no Hunting Call, and no leaders— nothing but foolish words and little picking thievish hands. So if I am starved or killed here, it will be all my own fault. But I must try to return to my own jungle. Baloo will surely beat me, but that is better than chasing silly rose leaves with the *Bandar-log*.'

No sooner had he walked to the city wall than the monkeys pulled him back, telling him that he did not know how happy he was, and pinching him to make him grateful. He set his teeth and said nothing, but went with the shouting monkeys to a terrace above the red sand-stone reservoirs that were half-full of rain-water. There was a ruined summer-house of white marble in the centre of the terrace, built for queens dead a hundred years ago. The domed roof had half fallen in and blocked up the underground passage from the palace by which the queens used to enter; but the walls were made of screens of marble tracery—beautiful milk-white fretwork, set with agates and cornelians and jasper and lapis lazuli, and as the moon came up behind the hill it shone through the open-work, casting shadows on the ground like black velvet embroidery.

Sore, sleepy, and hungry as he was, Mowgli could not help laughing when the *Bandar-log* began, twenty at a time, to tell him how great and wise and strong and gentle they were, and how foolish he was to wish to leave them. 'We are great. We are free. We are wonderful. We are the most wonderful people in all the jungle! We all say so, and so it must be true,' they shouted. 'Now as you are a new listener and can carry our words back to the Jungle-People so that they may notice us in future, we will tell you all about our most excellent selves.' Mowgli made no objection, and the monkeys gathered by hundreds and hundreds on the terrace to listen to their own speakers singing the praises of the *Bandar-log*, and whenever a speaker stopped for want of breath they would all shout together: 'This is true; we all say so.' Mowgli nodded and blinked, and said 'Yes' when they asked him a question, and his head spun with the noise. 'Tabaqui, the Jackal, must have bitten all these people,' he

277

said to himself, 'and now they have the madness. Certainly this is *dewanee*, the madness. Do they never go to sleep? Now there is a cloud coming to cover the moon. If it were only a big enough cloud I might try to run away in the darkness. But I am tired.'

That same cloud was being watched by two good friends in the ruined ditch below the city wall, for Bagheera and Kaa, knowing well how dangerous the Monkey-People were in large numbers, did not wish to run any risks. The monkeys never fight unless they are a hundred to one, and few in the jungle care for those odds.

'I will go to the west wall,' Kaa whispered, 'and come down swiftly with the slope of the ground in my favour. They will not throw themselves upon *my* back in their hundreds, but——'

'I know it,' said Bagheera. 'Would that Baloo were here; but we must do what we can. When that cloud covers the moon I shall go to the terrace. They hold some sort of council there over the boy.'

'Good hunting,' said Kaa, grimly, and glided away to the west wall. That happened to be the least ruined of any, and the big snake was delayed awhile before he could find a way up the stones. The cloud hid the moon, and as Mowgli wondered what would come next he heard Bagheera's light feet on the terrace. The Black Panther had raced up the slope almost without a sound and was striking—he knew better than to waste time in biting—right and left among the monkeys, who were seated round Mowgli in circles fifty and sixty deep. There was a howl of fright and rage, and then as Bagheera tripped on the rolling, kicking bodies beneath him, a monkey shouted: 'There is only one here! Kill him! Kill.' A scuffling mass of monkeys, biting, scratching, tearing, and pulling, closed over Bagheera, while five or six laid hold of Mowgli, dragged him up the wall of the summer-house, and pushed him through the hole of the broken dome. A man-trained boy would have been badly bruised, for the fall was a good fifteen feet, but Mowgli fell as Baloo had taught him to fall, and landed on his feet.

'Stay there,' shouted the monkeys, 'till we have killed thy friends, and later we will play with thee—if the Poison-People leave thee alive.'

'We be of one blood, ye and I,' said Mowgli, quickly giving the Snake's Call. He could hear rustling and hissing in the rubbish all round him and gave the Call a second time to make sure.

'Even ssso! Down hoods all!' said half a dozen low voices (every ruin in India becomes sooner or later a dwelling-place of snakes, and the old summer-house was alive with cobras). 'Stand still, Little Brother, for thy feet may do us harm.'

Mowgli stood as quietly as he could, peering through the open-work and listening to the furious din of the fight round the Black Panther— the yells and chatterings and scufflings, and Bagheera's deep, hoarse cough as he backed and bucked and twisted and plunged under the heaps of his enemies. For the first time since he was born, Bagheera was fighting for his life.

'Baloo must be at hand; Bagheera would not have come alone,' Mowgli thought; and then he called aloud: 'To the tank, Bagheera. Roll to the water-tanks. Roll and plunge! Get to the water!'

Bagheera heard, and the cry that told him Mowgli was safe gave him new courage. He worked his way desperately, inch by inch, straight for the reservoirs, hitting in silence. Then from the ruined wall nearest the jungle rose up the rumbling war-shout of Baloo. The old Bear had done his best, but he could not come before. 'Bagheera,' he shouted, 'I am here. I climb! I haste! *Ahuwora!* The stones slip under my feet! Wait my coming, O most infamous *Bandar-log*!' He panted up the terrace only to disappear to the head in a wave of monkeys, but he threw himself squarely on his haunches, and, spreading out his fore-paws, hugged as many as he could hold, and then began to hit with a regular *bat-bat-bat*, like the flipping strokes of a paddle-wheel.

A crash and a splash told Mowgli that Bagheera had fought his way to the tank where the monkeys could not follow. The Panther lay gasping for breath, his head just out of water, while the monkeys stood three deep on the red steps, dancing up and down with rage, ready to spring upon him from all sides if he came out to help Baloo. It was then that Bagheera lifted up his dripping chin, and in despair gave the Snake's Call for protection—'We be of one blood, ye and I'—for he believed that Kaa had turned tail at the last minute. Even Baloo, half smothered under the monkeys on the edge of the terrace, could not help chuckling as he heard the Black Panther asking for help.

Kaa had only just worked his way over the west wall, landing with a wrench that dislodged a coping-stone into the ditch. He had no inten-tion of losing any advantage of the ground, and coiled and uncoiled himself once or twice, to be sure that every foot of his long body was in working order. All that while the fight with Baloo went on, and the monkeys yelled in the tank round Bagheera, and Mang, the Bat, flying to and fro, carried the news of the great battle over the jungle, till even Hathi the Wild Elephant trumpeted, and far away, scattered bands of the Monkey-Folk woke and came leaping along the tree-roads to help their comrades in the Cold Lairs, and the noise of the fight roused all the day-birds for miles round.

Then Kaa came straight, quickly, and anxious to kill. The fighting strength of a python is in the driving blow of his head backed by all the strength and weight of his body. If you can imagine a lance, or a battering-ram, or a hammer weighing nearly half a ton driven by a cool, quiet mind living in the handle of it, you can roughly imagine what Kaa was like when he fought. A python four or five feet long can knock a man down if he hits him fairly in the chest, and Kaa was thirty feet long, as you know. His first stroke was delivered into the heart of the crowd round Baloo—was sent home with shut mouth in silence, and there was no need of a second. The monkeys scattered with cries of 'Kaa! It is Kaa! Run! Run!'

Generations of monkeys had been scared into good behaviour by the stories their elders told them of Kaa, the night-thief, who could slip along the branches as quietly as moss grows, and steal away the strongest monkey that ever lived; of old Kaa, who could make himself look so like a dead branch or a rotten stump that the wisest were deceived, till the branch caught them. Kaa was everything that the monkeys feared in the jungle, for none of them knew the limits of his power, none of them could look him in the face, and none had ever come alive out of his hug. And so they ran, stammering with terror, to the walls and the roofs of the houses, and Baloo drew a deep breath of relief. His fur was much thicker than Bagheera's, but he had suffered sorely in the fight. Then Kaa opened his mouth for the first time and spoke one long hissing word, and the far-away monkeys, hurrying to the defence of the Cold Lairs, stayed where they were, cowering, till the loaded branches bent and crackled under them.

The monkeys on the walls and the empty houses stopped their cries, and in the stillness that fell upon the city Mowgli heard Bagheera shaking his wet sides as he came up from the tank. Then the clamour broke out again. The monkeys leaped higher up the walls; they clung

'I am not sure that they have not pulled me into a hundred little bearlings,' said Baloo gravely.

round the necks of the big stone idols and shrieked as they skipped along the battlements, while Mowgli, dancing in the summer-house, put his eye to the screen-work and hooted owl-fashion between his front teeth, to show his derision and contempt.

'Get the man-cub out of that trap; I can do no more,' Bagheera gasped. 'Let us take the man-cub and go. They may attack again.'

'They will not move until I order them. Stay you ssso!' Kaa hissed, and the city was silent once more. 'I could not come before, Brother, but I *think* I hear thee call'—this was to Bagheera.

'I—I may have cried out in the battle,' Bagheera answered. 'Baloo, art thou hurt?'

'I am not sure that they have not pulled me into a hundred little bearlings,' said Baloo gravely, shaking one leg after the other. 'Wow! I am sore. Kaa, we owe thee, I think, our lives—Bagheera and I.'

'No matter. Where is the manling?'

'Here in a trap. I cannot climb out,' cried Mowgli. The curve of the broken dome was above his head.

'Take him away. He dances like Mao the Peacock, He will crush our young,' said the cobras inside.

'Hah!' said Kaa, with a chuckle, 'he has friends everywhere, this manling. Stand back, Manling; and hide you, O Poison People. I break down the wall.'

Kaa looked carefully till he found a discoloured crack in the marble tracery showing a weak spot, made two or three light taps with his head to get the distance, and then lifting up six feet of his body clear of the ground, sent home half a dozen full-power, smashing blows, nose-first. The screen-work broke and fell away in a cloud of dust and rubbish, and Mowgli leaped through the opening and flung himself between Baloo and Bagheera—an arm round each big neck.

'Art thou hurt?' said Baloo, hugging him softly.

'I am sore, hungry, and not a little bruised; but, oh they have handled ye grievously, my Brothers! Ye bleed.'

'Others also,' said Bagheera, licking his lips, and looking at the monkey-dead on the terrace and round the tank.

'It is nothing, it is nothing, if thou art safe, O my pride of all little frogs!' whimpered Baloo.

'Of that we shall judge later,' said Bagheera, in a dry voice that

Mowgli did not at all like. 'But here is Kaa, to whom we owe the battle and thou owest thy life. Thank him according to our customs, Mowgli.'

Mowgli turned and saw the great python's head swaying a foot above his own.

'So this is the manling,' said Kaa. 'Very soft is his skin, and he is not so unlike the *Bandar-log*. Have a care, Manling, that I do not mistake thee for a monkey some twilight when I have newly changed my coat.'

'We be of one blood, thou and I,' Mowgli answered. 'I take my life from thee, tonight. My kill shall be thy kill if ever thou art hungry, O Kaa.'

'All thanks, Little Brother,' said Kaa, though his eyes twinkled. 'And what may so bold a hunter kill? I ask that I may follow when next he goes abroad.'

'I kill nothing—I am too little, but I drive goats towards such as can use them. When thou art empty come to me and see if I speak the truth. I have some skill in these (he held out his hands), and if ever thou art in a trap, I may pay the debt which I owe to thee, to Bagheera, and to Baloo, here. Good hunting to ye all, my masters.'

'Well said,' growled Baloo, for Mowgli had returned thanks very prettily. The python dropped his head lightly for a minute on Mowgli's shoulder. 'A brave heart and a courteous tongue,' said he. 'They shall carry thee far through the jungle, Manling. But now go hence quickly with thy friends. Go and sleep, for the moon sets, and what follows it is not well that thou shouldst see.'

The moon was sinking behind the hills, and the lines of trembling monkeys huddled together on the walls and battlements looked like ragged, shaky fringes of things. Baloo went down to the tank for a drink, and Bagheera began to put his fur in order, as Kaa glided out into the centre of the terrace and brought his jaws together with a ringing snap that drew all the monkeys' eyes.

'The moon sets,' he said. 'Is there yet light to see?'

From the walls came a moan like the wind in the tree-tops: 'We see, O Kaa.'

'Good. Begins now the Dance—the Dance of the Hunger of Kaa. Sit still and watch.'

He turned twice or thrice in a big circle, weaving his head from right to left. Then he began making loops and figures of eight with his body,

283

and soft, oozy triangles that melted into squares and five-sided figures, and coiled mounds, never resting, never hurrying, and never stopping his low, humming song. It grew darker and darker, till at last the dragging, shifting coils disappeared, but they could hear the rustle of the scales.

Baloo and Bagheera stood still as stone, growling in their throats, their neck-hair bristling, and Mowgli watched and wondered.

'*Bandar-log*,' said the voice of Kaa at last, 'can ye stir foot or hand without my order? Speak!'

'Without thy order we cannot stir foot or hand, O Kaa!'

'Good! Come all one pace closer to me.'

The lines of the monkeys swayed forward helplessly, and Baloo and Bagheera took one stiff step forward with them.

'Closer!' hissed Kaa, and they all moved again.

Mowgli laid his hands on Baloo and Bagheera to get them away, and the two great beasts started as though they had been waked from a dream.

'Keep thy hand on my shoulder,' Bagheera whispered. 'Keep it there, or I must go back—must go back to Kaa. Aah!'

'It is only old Kaa making circles on the dust,' said Mowgli, 'let us go'; and the three slipped off through a gap in the walls to the jungle.

'*Whoof!*' said Baloo, when he stood under the still trees again. 'Never more will I make an ally of Kaa,' and he shook himself all over.

'He knows more than we,' said Bagheera, trembling. 'In a little time, had I stayed, I should have walked down his throat.'

'Many will walk by that road before the moon rises again,' said Baloo. 'He will have good hunting—after his own fashion.'

'But what was the meaning of it all?' said Mowgli, who did not know anything of a python's powers of fascination. 'I saw no more than a big snake making foolish circles till the dark came. And his nose was all sore. Ho! Ho!'

'Mowgli,' said Bagheera angrily, 'his nose was sore on *thy* account; as my ears and sides and paws and Baloo's neck and shoulders are bitten on *thy* account. Neither Baloo nor Bagheera will be able to hunt with pleasure for many days.'

'It is nothing,' said Baloo: 'we have the man-cub again.'

'True; but he has cost us heavily in time which might have been spent

in good hunting, in wounds, in hair—I am half plucked along my back
—and last of all, in honour. For, remember, Mowgli, I, who am the
Black Panther, was forced to call upon Kaa for protection, and Baloo
and I were both made stupid as little birds by the Hunger-Dance. All
this, Man-cub, came of thy playing with the *Bandar-log*.'

'True; it is true,' said Mowgli sorrowfully. 'I am an evil man-cub, and
my stomach is sad in me.'

'*Mf!* What says the Law of the Jungle, Baloo?'

Baloo did not wish to bring Mowgli into any more trouble, but he
could not tamper with the Law, so he mumbled: 'Sorrow never stays
punishment. But remember, Bagheera, he is very little.'

'I will remember; but he has done mischief, and blows must be dealt
now. Mowgli, hast thou anything to say?'

'Nothing. I did wrong. Baloo and thou are wounded. It is just.'

Bagheera gave him half a dozen love-taps; from a panther's point of
view they would hardly have waked one of his own cubs, but for a
seven-year-old boy they amounted to as severe a beating as you could
wish to avoid. When it was all over Mowgli sneezed, and picked himself up without a word.

'Now,' said Bagheera, 'jump on my back, Little Brother, and we will
go home.'

One of the beauties of Jungle Law is that punishment settles all scores.
There is no nagging afterwards.

Mowgli laid his head down on Bagheera's back and slept so deeply
that he never waked when he was put down by Mother Wolf's side in
the home-cave.

TO BUILD A FIRE

Jack London

Day had broken cold and grey, exceedingly cold and grey, when the man turned aside from the main Yukon trail and climbed the high earth-bank, where a dim and little-travelled trail led eastward through the fat spruce timberland. It was a steep bank, and he paused for breath at the top, excusing the act to himself by looking at his watch. It was nine o'clock. There was no sun nor hint of sun, though there was not a cloud in the sky. It was a clear day, and yet there seemed an intangible pall over the face of things, a subtle gloom that made the day dark, and that was due to the absence of sun. This did not worry the man. He was used to the lack of sun. It had been days since he had seen the sun, and he knew that a few more days must pass before that cheerful orb, due south, would just peep above the skyline and dip immediately from view.

The man flung a look back along the way he had come. The Yukon lay a mile wide and hidden under three feet of ice. On top of this ice were as many feet of snow. It was all pure white, rolling in gentle undulations where the ice-jams of the freeze-up had formed. North and south, as far as his eye could see, it was unbroken white, save for a dark hair-line that curved and twisted from around the spruce-covered island to the south, and that curved and twisted away into the north, where it disappeared behind another spruce-covered island. This dark hair-line was the trail—the main trail—that led south five hundred miles to the Chilcoot Pass, Dyea, and salt water; and that led north seventy miles to Dawson, and still on to the north a thousand miles to Nulato, and finally to St Michael on Bering Sea, a thousand miles and half a thousand more.

But all this—the mysterious, far-reaching hair-line trail, the absence of sun from the sky, the tremendous cold, and the strangeness and weirdness of it all—made no impression on the man. It was not because he was long used to it. He was a newcomer in the land, a *chechaquo*, and this was his first winter. The trouble with him was that he was without imagination. He was quick and alert in the things of life, but only in the things, and not in the significances. Fifty degrees below zero meant eighty-odd degrees of frost.

Such fact impressed him as being cold and uncomfortable, and that was all. It did not lead him to meditate upon his frailty as a creature of temperature, and upon man's frailty in general, able only to live within certain narrow limits of heat and cold; and from there on it did not lead him to the conjectural field of immortality and man's place in the universe. Fifty degrees below zero stood for a bite of frost that hurt and that must be guarded against by the use of mittens, ear-flaps, warm moccasins and thick socks. Fifty degrees below zero was to him just precisely fifty degrees below zero. That there should be anything more to it than that was a thought that never entered his head.

As he turned to go on, he spat speculatively. There was a sharp, explosive crackle that startled him. He spat again. And again, in the air, before it could fall to the snow, the spittle crackled. He knew that at fifty below spittle crackled on the snow, but this spittle had crackled in the air. Undoubtedly it was colder than fifty below—how much colder he did not know.

But the temperature did not matter. He was bound for the old claim on the left fork of Henderson Creek, where the boys were already. They had come over across the divide from the Indian Creek country, while he had come the roundabout way to take a look at the possibilities of getting out logs in the spring from the islands in the Yukon. He would

287

be in to camp by six o'clock; a bit after dark, it was true, but the boys would be there, a fire would be going, and a hot supper would be ready. As for lunch, he pressed his hand against the protruding bundle under his jacket. It was also under his shirt, wrapped up in a handkerchief and lying against the naked skin. It was the only way to keep the biscuits from freezing. He smiled agreeably to himself as he thought of those biscuits, each cut open and sopped in bacon grease, and each enclosing a generous slice of fried bacon.

He plunged in among the big spruce trees. The trail was faint. A foot of snow had fallen since the last sled had passed over, and he was glad he was without a sled, travelling light. In fact, he carried nothing but the lunch wrapped in the handkerchief. He was surprised, however, at the cold. It certainly was cold, he concluded, as he rubbed his numb nose and cheek-bones with his mittened hand. He was a warm-whiskered man, but the hair on his face did not protect the high cheek-bones and the eager nose that thrust itself aggressively into the frosty air.

At the man's heels trotted a dog, a big native husky, the proper wolf-dog, grey-coated and without any visible or temperamental difference from its brother, the wild wolf. The animal was depressed by the tremendous cold. It knew that it was no time for travelling. Its instinct told it a truer tale than was told to the man by the man's judgement. In reality, it was not merely colder than fifty below zero; it was colder than sixty below, than seventy below. It was seventy-five below zero. Since the freezing point is thirty-two *above* zero, it meant that one hundred and seven degrees of frost obtained.

The dog did not know anything about thermometers. Possibly in its brain there was no sharp consciousness of a condition of very cold such as was in the man's brain. But the brute had its instinct. It experienced a vague but menacing apprehension that subdued it and made it slink along at the man's heels, and that made it question eagerly every unwonted movement of the man as if expecting him to go into camp or to seek shelter somewhere and build a fire. The dog had learned fire, and it wanted fire, or else to burrow under the snow and cuddle its warmth away from the air.

The frozen moisture of its breathing had settled on its fur in a fine powder of frost, and especially were its jowls, muzzle, and eyelashes whitened by its crystalled breath. The man's red beard and moustache were likewise frosted, but more solidly, the deposit taking the form of ice and increasing with every warm, moist breath he exhaled.

Also, the man was chewing tobacco, and the muzzle of ice held his lips so rigidly that he was unable to clear his chin when he expelled the juice. The result was that a crystal beard of the colour and solidity of amber was increasing its length on his chin. If he fell down it would shatter itself, like glass, into brittle fragments. But he did not mind the appendage. It was the penalty all tobacco-chewers paid in that country, and he had been out before in two cold snaps. They had not been so cold as this, he knew, but by the spirit thermometer at Sixty Mile he knew they had been registered at fifty below and at fifty-five.

He held on through the level stretch of woods for several miles, crossed a wide flat of nigger-heads, and dropped down a bank to the frozen bed of a small stream. This was Henderson Creek, and he knew he was ten miles from the forks. He looked at his watch. It was ten o'clock. He was making four miles an hour, and he calculated that he would arrive at the forks at half-past twelve. He decided to celebrate that event by eating his lunch there.

The dog dropped in again at his heels, with a tail drooping discouragement, as the man swung along the creek-bed. The furrow of the old sled-trail was plainly visible, but a dozen inches of snow covered the marks of the last runners. In a month no man had come up or down that silent creek. The man held steadily on. He was not much given to thinking, and just then particularly he had nothing to think about save that he would eat lunch at the forks and that at six o'clock he would be in camp with the boys. There was nobody to talk to; and, had there been, speech would have been impossible because of the ice-muzzle on his mouth. So he continued monotonously to chew tobacco and to increase the length of his amber beard.

Once in a while the thought reiterated itself that it was very cold and that he had never experienced such cold. As he walked along he rubbed his cheek-bones and nose with the back of his mittened hand. He did this automatically, now and again changing hands. But rub as he would, the instant he stopped his cheek-bones went numb, and the following instant the end of his nose went numb. He was sure to frost his cheeks; he knew that, and experienced a pang of regret that he had not devised a nose-strap of the sort Bud wore in cold snaps. Such a strap passed

289

across the cheeks, as well, and saved them. But it didn't matter much, after all. What were frosted cheeks? A bit painful, that was all; they were never serious.

Empty as the man's mind was of thoughts, he was keenly observant, and he noticed the changes in the creek, the curves and bends and timber-jams, and always he sharply noted where he placed his feet. Once, coming around a bend, he shied abruptly, like a startled horse, curved away from the place where he had been walking, and retreated several paces back along the trail. The creek he knew was frozen clear to the bottom—no creek could contain water in that Arctic winter—but he knew also that there were springs that bubbled out from the hillsides and ran along under the snow and on top the ice of the creek. He knew that the coldest snaps never froze these springs, and he knew likewise their danger.

They were traps. They hid pools of water under the snow that might be three inches deep, or three feet. Sometimes a skin of ice half an inch thick covered them, and in turn was covered by the snow. Sometimes there were alternate layers of water and ice-skin, so that when one broke through he kept on breaking through for a while, sometimes wetting himself to the waist.

That was why he had shied in such panic. He had felt the give under his feet and heard the crackle of a snow-hidden ice-skin. And to get his feet wet in such a temperature meant trouble and danger. At the very least it meant delay, for he would be forced to stop and build a fire, and under its protection to bare his feet while he dried his socks and moccasins. He stood and studied the creek-bed and its banks, and decided that the flow of water came from the right. He reflected a while, rubbing his nose and cheeks, then skirted to the left, stepping gingerly and testing the footing for each step. Once clear of the danger, he took a fresh chew of tobacco and swung along at his four-mile gait.

In the course of the next two hours he came upon several similar traps. Usually the snow above the hidden pools had a sunken, candied appearance that advertised the danger. Once again, however, he had a close call; and once, suspecting danger, he compelled the dog to go on in front. The dog did not want to go. It hung back until the man shoved it forward, and then it went quickly across the white, unbroken surface. Suddenly it broke through, floundered to one side, and got away to

290

firmer footing. It had wet its forefeet and legs, and almost immediately the water that clung to it turned to ice. It made quick efforts to lick the ice off its legs, then dropped down in the snow and began to bite out the ice that had formed between the toes. This was a matter of instinct. To permit the ice to remain would mean sore feet. It did not know this, it merely obeyed the mysterious prompting that arose from the deep crypts of its being. But the man knew, having achieved a judgment on the subject, and he removed the mitten from his right hand and helped tear out the ice-particles. He did not expose his fingers more than a minute, and was astonished at the swift numbness that smote them. It certainly was cold. He pulled on the mitten hastily, and beat the hand savagely across his chest.

At twelve o'clock the day was at its brightest. Yet the sun was too far south on its winter journey to clear the horizon. The bulge of the earth intervened between it and Henderson Creek, where the man walked under clear sky at noon and cast no shadow. At half-past twelve, to the minute, he arrived at the forks of the creek. He was pleased at the speed he had made. If he kept it up, he would certainly be with the boys by six. He unbuttoned his jacket and shirt and drew forth his lunch. The action consumed no more than a quarter of a minute, yet in that brief moment the numbness laid hold of the exposed fingers. He did not put the mitten on, but instead struck the fingers a dozen sharp smashes against his leg.

Then he sat down on a snow-covered lot to eat. The sting that followed upon the striking of his fingers against his leg ceased so quickly that he was startled. He had had no chance to take a bite of biscuit. He struck the fingers repeatedly and returned them to the mitten, baring the other hand for the purpose of eating. He tried to take a mouthful, but the ice-muzzle prevented. He had forgotten to build a fire and thaw out. He chuckled at his foolishness, and as he chuckled he noted the numbness creeping into the exposed fingers. Also, he noted that the stinging which had first come to his toes when he sat down was already passing away. He wondered whether the toes were warm or numb. He moved them inside the moccasins and decided that they were numb.

He pulled the mitten on hurriedly and stood up. He was a bit frightened. He stamped up and down until the stinging returned into the feet. It certainly was cold, was his thought. That man from Sulphur Creek had spoken the truth when telling how cold it sometimes got in the country. And he had laughed at him at the time! That showed one must not be too sure of things. There was no mistake about it, it *was* cold. He strode up and down, stamping his feet and threshing his arms, until reassured by the returning warmth.

Then he got out matches and proceeded to make a fire. From the undergrowth, where high water of the previous spring had lodged a supply of seasoned twigs, he got his firewood. Working carefully from a small beginning, he soon had a roaring fire, over which he thawed the ice from his face and in the protection of which he ate his biscuits. For the moment the cold of space was outwitted. The dog took satisfaction in the fire, stretching out close enough for warmth and far enough away to escape being singed.

When the man had finished, he filled his pipe and took his comfortable time over a smoke. Then he pulled on his mittens, settled the earflaps of his cap firmly about his ears, and took the creek trail up the left fork. The dog was disappointed and yearned back toward the fire. This man did not know cold. Possibly all the generations of his ancestry had been ignorant of cold, of real cold, of cold one hundred and seven degrees below freezing point. But the dog knew; all its ancestry knew, and it had inherited the knowledge. And it knew that it was not good to walk abroad in such fearful cold. It was the time to lie snug in a hole in the snow and wait for a curtain of cloud to be drawn across the face of outer space whence this cold came.

On the other hand, there was no keen intimacy between the dog and the man. The one was the toil-slave of the other, and the only caresses it had ever received were the caresses of the whiplash and of harsh and menacing throat-sounds that threatened the whiplash. So the dog made no effort to communicate its apprehension to the man. It was not concerned in the welfare of the man; it was for its own sake that it yearned back toward the fire. But the man whistled, and spoke to it with the sound of whiplashes, and the dog swung in at the man's heel and followed after.

The man took a chew of tobacco and proceeded to start a new amber beard. Also, his moist breath quickly powdered with white his moustache, eyebrows, and lashes. There did not seem to be so many springs on the left fork of the Henderson, and for half an hour the man saw no signs of any. And then it happened. At a place where there were no signs, where the soft, unbroken snow seemed to advertise solidity beneath, the man broke through. It was not deep. He wet himself halfway to the knees before he floundered out to the firm crust.

He was angry, and cursed his luck aloud. He had hoped to get into camp with the boys at six o'clock, and this would delay him an hour, for he would have to build a fire and dry out his foot-gear. This was imperative at that low temperature—he knew that much; and he turned aside to the bank, which he climbed. On top, tangled in the underbrush about the trunks of several small spruce trees, was a high-water deposit of dry firewood—sticks and twigs, principally, but also larger portions of seasoned branches and fine, dry, last year's grasses. He threw down several large pieces on top of the snow. This served for a foundation and prevented the young flame from drowning itself in the snow it otherwise would melt. The flame he got by touching a match to a small shred of birch bark that he took from his pocket. This burned even more readily than paper. Placing it on the foundation, he fed the young flame with wisps of dry grass and with the tiniest dry twigs.

He worked slowly and carefully, keenly aware of his danger. Gradually, as the flame grew stronger, he increased the size of the twigs with which he fed it. He squatted in the snow, pulling the twigs out from their entanglement in the brush and feeding directly to the flame. He knew there must be no failure. When it is seventy-five below zero, a man must not fail in his first attempt to build a fire—that is, if his feet are wet. If his feet are dry, and he fails, he can run along the trail for half a mile and restore his circulation. But the circulation of wet and freezing feet cannot be restored by running when it is seventy-five below. No matter how fast he runs, the wet feet will freeze the harder.

All this the man knew. The old-timer on Sulphur Creek had told him about it, and now he was appreciating the advice. Already all sensation had gone out of his feet. To build the fire he had been forced to remove his mittens, and the fingers had quickly gone numb. His pace of four miles an hour had kept his heart pumping blood to the surface of his body and to all the extremities. But the instant he stopped, the action of the pump eased down. The cold of space smote the unprotected tip of the planet, and he, being on that unprotected tip, received the full force of the blow. The blood of his body recoiled before it.

293

The blood was alive, like the dog, and like the dog it wanted to hide away and cover itself up from the fearful cold. So long as he walked four miles an hour, he pumped that blood to the surface; but now, it ebbed away and sank down into the recesses of his body. The extremities were the first to feel its absence. His wet feet froze the faster, and his exposed fingers numbed the faster; though they had not yet begun to freeze. Nose and cheeks were already freezing, while the skin of all his body chilled as it lost its blood.

But he was safe. Toes and nose and cheeks would be only touched by the frost, for the fire was beginning to burn with strength. He was feeding it with twigs the size of his finger. In another minute he would be able to feed it with branches the size of his wrist, and then he could remove his wet foot-gear and, while it dried, he could keep his naked feet warm by the fire, rubbing them at first, of course, with snow. The fire was a success. He was safe.

He remembered the advice of the old-timer on Sulphur Creek, and smiled. The old-timer had been very serious in laying down the law that no man must travel alone in the Klondike after fifty below. Well, here he was; he had had the accident; he was alone; and he had saved himself. Those old-timers were rather womanish, some of them, he thought. All a man had to do was to keep his head; and he was all right. Any man who was a man could travel alone. But it was surprising, the rapidity with which his cheeks and nose were freezing. And he had not thought his fingers could go lifeless in so short a time. Lifeless they were, for he could scarcely make them move together to grip a twig, and they seemed remote from his body and from him. When he touched a twig, he had to look and see whether or not he had hold of it. The wires were pretty well down between him and his finger-ends.

All of which counted for little. There was the fire, snapping and crackling and promising life with every dancing flame. He started to untie his moccasins. They were coated with ice; the thick German socks were like sheaths of iron halfway to the knees; and the moccasin strings were like rods of steel all twisted and knotted as by some conflagration. For a moment he tugged with his numb fingers, then, realizing the folly of it, he drew his sheath-knife.

But before he could cut the strings, it happened. It was his own fault or, rather, his mistake. He should not have built the fire under the spruce

294

tree. He should have built it in the open. But it had been easier to pull the twigs from the brush and drop them directly on the fire. Now the tree under which he had done this carried a weight of snow on its boughs. No wind had blown for weeks, and each bough was fully freighted. Each time he had pulled a twig he had communicated a slight agitation to the tree—an imperceptible agitation, so far as he was concerned, but an agitation sufficient to bring about the disaster. High up in the tree one bough capsized its load of snow. This fell on the boughs beneath, capsizing them. This process continued, spreading out and involving the whole tree. It grew like an avalanche, and it descended without warning upon the man and the fire—and the fire was blotted out! Where it had burned was a mantle of fresh and disordered snow.

The man was shocked. It was as though he had just heard his own sentence of death. For a moment he sat and stared at the spot where the fire had been. Then he grew very calm. Perhaps the old-timer on Sulphur Creek was right. If he had only had a trail-mate he would have been in no danger now. The trail-mate could have built the fire. Well, it was up to him to build the fire over again, and this second time there must be no failure. Even if he succeeded, he would most likely lose some toes. His feet must be badly frozen by now, and there would be some time before the second fire was ready.

Such were his thoughts, but he did not sit and think them. He was busy all the time they were passing through his mind. He made a new foundation for a fire, this time in the open, where no treacherous tree could blot it out. Next, he gathered dry grasses and tiny twigs from the high-water flotsam. He could not bring his fingers together to pull them out, but he was able to gather them by the handful. In this way he got many rotten twigs and bits of green moss that were undesirable, but it was the best he could do. He worked methodically, even collecting an armful of the larger branches to be used later when the fire gathered strength. And all the while the dog sat and watched him, a certain yearning wistfulness in its eyes, for it looked upon him as the fire-provider, and the fire was slow in coming.

When all was ready, the man reached in his pocket for a second piece of birch bark. He knew the bark was there, and, though he could not feel it with his fingers, he could hear its crisp rustling as he fumbled for it. Try as he would, he could not clutch hold of it. And all the time, in his

The snow descended without warning on the man and the fire . . .

consciousness, was the knowledge that each instant his feet were freezing. This thought tended to put him in a panic, but he fought against it and kept calm.

He pulled on his mittens with his teeth, and threshed his arms back and forth, beating his hands with all his might against his sides. He did this sitting down, and he stood up to do it; and all the while the dog sat in the snow, its wolf-brush of a tail curled around warmly over its forefeet, its sharp wolf-ears pricked forward intently as it watched the man. And the man, as he beat and threshed with his arms and hands, felt a great surge of envy as he regarded the creature that was warm and secure in its natural covering.

After a time he was aware of the first faraway signals of sensation in his beaten fingers. The faint tingling grew stronger till it evolved into a stinging ache that was excruciating, but which the man hailed with satisfaction. He stripped the mitten from his right hand and fetched forth the birch bark. The exposed fingers were quickly going numb again. Next he brought out his bunch of sulphur matches. But the tremendous cold had already driven the life out of his fingers. In his effort to separate one match from the others, the whole bunch fell in the snow. He tried to pick it out of the snow, but failed.

The dead fingers could neither touch nor clutch. He was very careful. He drove the thought of his freezing feet, and nose, and cheeks, out of his mind, devoting his whole soul to the matches. He watched, using the sense of vision in place of touch, and when he saw his fingers on each side the bunch, he closed them—that is, he willed to close them, for the wires were down, and the fingers did not obey. He pulled the mitten on the right hand, and beat it fiercely against his knee. Then, with both mittened hands he scooped the bunch of matches, along with much snow, into his lap. Yet he was no better off.

After some manipulation he managed to get the bunch between the heels of his mittened hands. In this fashion he carried it to his mouth. The ice crackled and snapped when by a violent effort he opened his mouth. He drew the lower jaw in, curled the upper lip out of the way, and scraped the bunch with his upper teeth in order to separate a match. He succeeded in getting one, which he dropped on his lap. He was no better off. He could not pick it up. Then he devised a way. He picked it up in his teeth and scratched it on his leg. Twenty times he scratched before he succeeded in lighting it. As it flamed he held it with his teeth to the birch bark. But the burning brimstone went up his nostrils and into his lungs, causing him to cough spasmodically. The match fell into the snow and went out.

The old-timer on Sulphur Creek was right, he thought in the moment of controlled despair that ensued: after fifty below, a man should travel with a partner. He beat his hands, but failed in exciting any sensation. Suddenly he bared both hands, removing the mittens with his teeth. He caught the whole bunch between the heels of his hands. His arm muscles not being frozen enabled him to press the hand-heels tightly against the matches. Then he scratched the bunch along his leg. It flared into flame, seventy sulphur matches at once! There was no wind to blow them out. He kept his head to one side to escape the strangling fumes, and held the blazing bunch to the birch bark. As he so held it, he became aware of sensation in his hand. His flesh was burning! He could smell it. Deep down below the surface he could feel it. The sensation developed into pain that grew acute. And still he endured it, holding the flame of the matches clumsily to the bark that would not light readily because his own burning hands were in the way, absorbing most of the flame.

At last, when he could endure no more, he jerked his hands apart. The blazing matches fell sizzling into the snow, but the birch bark was alight. He began laying dry grasses and the tiniest twigs on the flame. He could not pick and choose, for he had to lift the fuel between the heels of his hands. Small pieces of rotten wood and green moss clung to the twigs, and he bit them off as well as he could with his teeth. He cherished the flame carefully and awkwardly. It meant life, and it must not perish.

The withdrawal of blood from the surface of his body now made him begin to shiver, and he grew more awkward. A large piece of green moss fell squarely on the little fire. He tried to poke it out with his fingers, but his shivering frame made him poke too far, and he disrupted the nucleus of the fire, the burning grasses and tiny twigs separating and scattering. He tried to poke them together again, but in spite of the tenseness of the effort, his shivering got away with him, and the twigs were hopelessly scattered. Each twig gushed a puff of smoke and went out.

The fire-provider had failed. As he looked apathetically about him, his eyes chanced on the dog, sitting across the ruins of the fire from him, in the snow, making restless, hunching movements, slightly lifting one forefoot and then the other, shifting its weight back and forth on them with wistful eagerness.

The sight of the dog put a wild idea into his head. He remembered the tale of the man, caught in a blizzard, who killed a steer and crawled inside the carcass, and so was saved. He would kill the dog and bury his hands in the warm body until the numbness went out of them. Then he could build another fire. He spoke to the dog, calling it to him; but in his voice was a strange note of fear that frightened the animal, who had never known the man to speak in such way before. Something was the matter, and its suspicious nature sensed danger—it knew not what danger, but somewhere, somehow, in its brain arose an apprehension of the man. It flattened its ears down at the sound of the man's voice, and its restless, hunching movements and the liftings and shiftings of its forefeet became more pronounced; but it would not come to the man. He got on his hands and knees and crawled towards the dog. This unusual posture again excited suspicion, and the animal sidled mincingly away.

The man sat up in the snow for a moment and struggled for calmness. Then he pulled on his mittens, by means of his teeth, and got upon his feet. He glanced down at first in order to assure himself that he was really standing up, for the absence of sensation in his feet left him unrelated to the earth. His erect position in itself started to drive the webs of suspicion from the dog's mind; and when he spoke peremptorily, with the sound of whiplashes in his voice, the dog rendered its customary allegiance and came to him.

As it came within reaching distance, the man lost his control. His arms flashed out to the dog, and he experienced genuine surprise when he discovered that his hands could not clutch, that there was neither bend nor feeling in the fingers. He had forgotten for the moment that they were frozen and that they were freezing more and more. All this happened quickly, and before the animal could get away, he encircled its body with his arms. He sat down in the snow, and in this fashion held the dog, while it snarled and whined and struggled.

But it was all he could do, hold its body encircled in his arms and sit there. He realized that he could not kill the dog. There was no way to do it. With his helpless hands he could neither draw nor hold his sheath-knife, nor throttle the animal. He released it, and it plunged wildly away, with tail between its legs, and still snarling. It halted forty feet away and surveyed him curiously, with ears sharply pricked forward.

The man looked down at his hands in order to locate them, and found them hanging on the ends of his arms. It struck him as curious that one should have to use his eyes in order to find out where his hands were. He began threshing his arms back and forth, beating the mittened hands against his sides. He did this for five minutes, violently, and his heart pumped enough blood up to the surface to put a stop to his shivering. But no sensation was aroused in the hands. He had an impression that they hung like weights on the ends of his arms, but when he tried to run the impression down, he could not find it.

A certain fear of death, dull and oppressive, came to him. This fear quickly became poignant as he realized that it was no longer a mere matter of freezing his fingers and toes, or of losing his hands and feet, but that it was a matter of life and death with the chances against him. This threw him into a panic, and he turned and ran up the creek-bed along the old, dim trail. The dog joined in behind and kept up with him. He ran blindly, without intention, in fear such as he had never known in his life. Slowly, as he ploughed and floundered through the snow, he began to see things again—the banks of the creeks, the old timber-jams, the leafless aspens, and the sky.

The running made him feel better. He did not shiver. Maybe, if he ran on, his feet would thaw out; and, anyway, if he ran far enough, he would reach camp and the boys. Without doubt he would lose some fingers and toes and some of his face; but the boys would take care of him, and save the rest of him when he got there. And at the same time there was another thought in his mind that said he would never get to the camp and the boys; that it was too many miles away, that the freezing had too great a start on him, and that he would soon be stiff and dead. This thought he kept in the background and refused to consider. Sometimes it pushed itself forward and demanded to be heard, but he thrust it back and strove to think of other things.

It struck him as curious that he could run at all on feet so frozen that he could not feel them when they struck the earth and took the weight

But it was all he could do, hold the dog's body in his arms.

of his body. He seemed to himself to skim along the surface, and to have no connection with the earth. Somewhere he had once seen a winged Mercury, and he wondered if Mercury felt as he felt when skimming over the earth.

His theory of running until he reached camp and the boys had one flaw in it: he lacked the endurance. Several times he stumbled, and finally he tottered, crumpled up, and fell. When he tried to rise, he failed. He must sit and rest, he decided, and next time he would merely walk and keep on going. As he sat and regained his breath, he noted that he was feeling quite warm and comfortable. He was not shivering, and it even seemed that a warm glow had come to his chest and trunk. And yet, when he touched his nose or cheeks, there was no sensation. Running would not thaw them out. Nor would it thaw out his hands and feet.

Then the thought came to him that the frozen portions of his body must be extending. He tried to keep this thought down, to forget it, to think of something else; he was aware of the panicky feeling that it caused, and he was afraid of the panic. But the thought asserted itself,

301

and persisted, until it produced a vision of his body totally frozen. This was too much, and he made another wild run along the trail. Once he slowed down to a walk, but the thought of the freezing extending itself made him run again.

And all the time the dog ran with him, at his heels. When he fell down a second time, it curled its tail over its forefeet and sat in front of him, facing him, curiously eager and intent. The warmth and security of the animal angered him, and he cursed it till it flattened down its ears appeasingly. This time the shivering came more quickly upon the man. He was losing in his battle with the frost. It was creeping into his body from all sides. The thought of it drove him on, but he ran no more than a hundred feet, when he staggered and pitched headlong.

It was his last panic. When he had recovered his breath and control, he sat up and entertained in his mind the conception of meeting death with dignity. However, the conception did not come to him in such terms. His idea of it was that he had been making a fool of himself, running around like a chicken with its head cut off—such was the simile that occurred to him. Well, he was bound to freeze anyway, and he might as well take it decently. With this new-found peace of mind came the first glimmerings of drowsiness. A good idea, he thought, to sleep off to death. It was like taking an anaesthetic. Freezing was not so bad as people thought. There were lots worse ways to die.

He pictured the boys finding his body next day. Suddenly he found himself with them, coming along the trail and looking for himself. And, still with them, he came around a turn in the trail and found himself lying in the snow. He did not belong with himself any more, for even then he was out of himself, standing with the boys and looking at himself in the snow. It certainly was cold, was his thought. When he got back to the States he could tell the folks what real cold was. He drifted on from this to a vision of the old-timer on Sulphur Creek. He could see him quite clearly, warm and comfortable, and smoking a pipe.

'You were right, old hoss; you were right,' the man mumbled to the old-timer of Sulphur Creek.

Then the man drowsed off into what seemed to him the most comfortable and satisfying sleep he had ever known. The dog sat facing him and waiting. The brief day drew to a close in a long, slow twilight. There were no signs of a fire to be made, and, besides, never in the dog's experience had it known a man to sit like that in the snow and make no fire. As the twilight drew on, its eager yearning for the fire mastered it, and with a great lifting and shifting of forefeet, it whined softly, then flattened its ears down in anticipation of being scolded by the man.

But the man remained silent. Later, the dog whined loudly. And still later it crept close to the man and caught the scent of death. This made the animal bristle and back away. A little longer it delayed, howling under the stars that leaped and danced and shone brightly in the cold sky. Then it turned and trotted up the trail in the direction of the camp it knew, where were the other food-providers and fire-providers.

THE Q-SHIPS

Graeme Cook

The 'U-boat menace' was perhaps the greatest threat to Britain and her Allies during the First World War. German submarines lurked along the North Atlantic shipping lanes and wrought havoc among the merchant ships bringing Britain her vital war supplies from North America. Losses among these merchantmen reached astronomical proportions and indeed, at one point, the situation was so critical and the U-boats so successful that the First Sea Lord, Lord Jellicoe, estimated that Britain had only enough foodstuffs to last her for six weeks. If something were not done—and quickly—she would be forced to sue for peace.

Even in the very early stages of the war, the threat of the U-boat was recognized when one of them sank three cruisers in a single action. Such losses could not be tolerated, even taking into consideration that the Royal Navy was the largest maritime force in the world.

Many ways were devised of combatting the U-boat but perhaps the most ingenious was the invention of the 'Q-ship'. These Q-ships were invariably ordinary tramp steamers of the sort U-boat commanders were used to seeing plying the oceans' shipping lanes. But behind their seemingly innocent and often dull exteriors lay a deadly sting. Outwardly they were no different from any other tramp but, by a skilful method of camouflage, they hid guns, torpedo tubes and sometimes depth charges.

These ships were manned by Royal Navy personnel but they operated just as if they were legitimate tramp steamers. The idea behind them was simple—but dangerous. They presented themselves as easy targets and so lured German submarines into attacking them. When the attack began, either by torpedo or gunfire, a 'panic party', as it was known, would be seen by the U-boat commander to abandon ship and take to the boats, rowing madly away from the 'doomed' vessel. But in reality, there was still on board the ship's real captain and a sufficiently large crew to man the guns and torpedo tubes. When the U-boat closed on the ship to discover her cargo before sinking her by shell-fire, the Q-boat captain would bring his guns crew into action. The dummy bulwarks would fall away to reveal guns that flashed into life, pounding the U-boat with shells. This basically was the plan of action, but as we shall see it did not always work out that way . . .

The greatest exponent of the art of Q-ship warfare was Captain (later Vice-Admiral) Gordon Campbell. During his time as a Q-ship commander, he won the Victoria Cross, the DSO and two bars, the French Croix de Guerre and the Legion of Honour, which gives a fair indication of his skill and daring.

In September 1915, Campbell, then a lieutenant, was given command of the 2,050-ton Q-ship *Farnborough*. She had been commandeered by the Admiralty and was in the process of conversion when Campbell took command. Her main armament was three twelve-pounder guns, hidden behind cunningly contrived camouflage. (Later she had two twelve-pounders and two six-pounders added).

The completion of her fitting out was a lengthy process and it was not until late October that she was finally ready for sea. Campbell and his crew were in buoyant mood as *Farnborough* put out from Plymouth and headed for the shipping lanes. But in spite of the fact that they laid themselves wide open to attack, not a single U-boat took the bait. And their bad luck continued for a further six months. It seems hardly credible that not a single U-boat attacked these sitting ducks.

Campbell could see during this 'phoney war' of theirs that his men were becoming bored, and to combat this he organized daily rehearsals of 'panic' drill. If their ruse was to work when the real thing came, then this drill had to be done to perfection. The actions of the ship's 'crew' had to be seen by the U-boat commander as exactly those of men panicking under the threat of sinking. Then, one fine spring morning, the alarm bells clanged and the crew raced into action, darting to their action stations to await further orders. But this time it was no practice run—this was the real thing.

Moments earlier, a lookout on the bridge had spotted the bubbling wake of a torpedo lancing through the water towards *Farnborough*. Luckily, it narrowly missed the ship's bow. The atmosphere on the *Farnborough* was tense as everyone on board waited for the captain's orders. The 'panic party' was spread about the ship, ready to put on their theatrical act, while the real crew was poised at action stations. From a slit in the bridge, Campbell scanned the sea for a sight of the submarine and then she appeared, first her conning tower breaking water and then her flat deck top.

He watched as the submarine's gun crew spilled out of the conning tower and manned the deck gun. Moments later it flashed and a shell splashed into the water ahead of *Farnborough*. This was the sign to halt and Campbell brought *Farnborough*'s engines to 'stop'. He then ordered the 'panic party' into action. Men darted here and there, gathering their possessions, releasing the lifeboat and generally giving their impression of being in a real state of panic. The process took some time but this was exactly what Campbell wanted, for while it was going on, the U-boat slid closer to the ship. The submarine's gun flashed again and another shell hit the water close by the Q-ship. Then the U-boat put on a burst of speed and darted towards the *Farnborough*.

The order to 'stand by' was passed to the gun crews, who waited eagerly for the word to go. Meanwhile the lifeboats were almost ready to put off from the ship, along with the navigating officer who was the phoney captain. The U-boat commander, obviously not suspecting that anything was amiss, brought his boat in closer. Then the time came and Campbell bellowed, 'Let go!'

In an instant the camouflage flaps were down and the guns roaring into action. Shells slammed into the U-boat, severely damaging her.

Her crew made a frantic dash for the conning tower as the order to take her down was given, but they were just not quick enough. The shells thudded into the submarine, ripping and tearing the pressure hull. The German tried to squirm away but he was firmly caught and the U-boat sank by the stern and disappeared.

Campbell brought *Farnborough* to the U-boat's last position and dropped a depth charge which heaved up a great waterspout. A moment later the stricken submarine's bows appeared vertically out of the water and the *Farnborough*'s gun crews opened up again, piercing it several times with shells before it finally sank. Even then Campbell was not content with his handiwork and dropped two more depth charges before leaving the scene. *Farnborough* had caught her first U-boat and there were to be more in a highly successful career. She remained in service as a Q-ship until 1917 when, still under Campbell's command, she took part in her final action.

Farnborough was cruising to the south-west of Ireland on 17 February 1917 when the incident occurred. On that day, the officer of the watch caught sight of a torpedo trail slicing through the water towards the ship. It was too late to take evasive action and before Campbell could reach the bridge, the torpedo slammed into the ship's side abreast of the number three hatch and exploded. The detonation shook the whole ship, throwing men to the deck, and tore a great hole in the side. Had it not been for her cargo of timber *Farnborough* would certainly have sunk there and then, but mercifully she stayed afloat. Luckily the guns had remained in one piece and were still serviceable.

Campbell scrambled to the bridge and began issuing orders. The panic party swung into action with enthusiasm. Water poured into the engine-room by the ton as the lifeboats with the panic party pushed off from the ship putting on their usual skilful performance. From his spy-hole on the bridge, Campbell kept a careful watch. Soon he sighted the submarine's periscope on the starboard quarter not far from the ship. It was obvious that the U-boat commander was observing the *Farnborough* closely; the Germans were aware of the Q-boat ruse and were taking no chances. The slightest hint that all was not what it should be would mean the end of the *Farnborough*.

The lifeboats were well away from the *Farnborough* when the submarine, still submerged, eased herself down the ship's side with her commander scanning the decks, looking for any hint that might tell him she was a Q-ship. Campbell was tempted to let fly then and blast the submarine out of the water, but she was too close and travelling at speed. There would be time for only one shot, and if it missed, the submarine would reply with a torpedo. Campbell had to resist the temptation and wait for the right moment.

The submarine rounded the *Farnborough's* bows and proceeded to cruise down her port side before finally coming to the surface on the port quarter. Campbell ordered the gun crew to stand by; then, when *Farnborough* had drifted into a suitable position, he threw off his disguise and the white ensign fluttered out at the mast-head.

The flaps fell away and the guns roared. The U-boat commander had been taken completely by surprise and was not ready for the fusillade of shells that slammed into his boat. In a few moments she was sinking fast and minutes later she was gone forever. With her went all but two of her crew, who were rescued by Campbell.

The battle with the German was over but another equally fierce one was about to begin. *Farnborough* was all but mortally wounded and needed assistance quickly if she was to survive. Campbell sent out urgent messages for help and later a destroyer appeared on the scene to take most of the crew off the crippled ship. Campbell might then have been justified in leaving her to sink but he was made of more determined stuff and he and a handful of men remained on board while *Farnborough* was towed back to Britain. She was no longer fit for Q-ship duties but was repaired and sent back to the Merchant Marine. She remained in service until she was finally broken up, a gallant ship which had served her country well. For his part in the action, Campbell was awarded the Victoria Cross.

One spring evening in 1917, Count Spiegel, commander of the German submarine U-93, scanned the Atlantic horizon through his periscope as his U-boat nosed along just beneath the surface. Suddenly he stopped and focused on a schooner under full sail. A modest prize, he thought, but nevertheless one which he could not let slip through his fingers. The schooner, small as it was and apparently unarmed, did not merit a torpedo, so he surfaced and fired three shots across her bows. Immediately the schooner came to a halt and Spiegel could clearly see the crew taking to the boats. He laughed and turned to a grim-faced man standing beside him in the conning tower.

'This one will be easy,' Spiegel said.

The man beside him wore the uniform of a captain of the British Merchant Marine. He was Captain Burroughs, whose ship Spiegel had sunk some days earlier off the Canadian coast. Burroughs did not share Spiegel's enthusiasm for the easy kill. He watched the schooner's crew desperately pull away from the ship to allow the German captain to get on with his work. He was tempted to avert his eyes but he could not help watching this majestic sailing ship in the last few minutes of her life.

'Fire!' Spiegel's yell echoed from the conning tower and the U-boat's gun roared, hurtling a shell through the air. It smashed into the target followed by more shells until the schooner was on fire. Spiegel, in his eagerness, ordered his boat closer to the schooner and she edged forward. But as she did so, Spiegel uttered a cry . . .

'Mein Gott!' he bellowed as a white ensign unfurled at the top of the main mast. A split second later, the bulwarks fell away and Spiegel found himself staring into the muzzles of two twelve-pounder guns and two Lewis guns.

'It's a trap!' Spiegel shouted, horror-struck. He did not get the opportunity to order the sub to crash-dive, for all four guns on board the schooner opened up, plastering the U-boat's conning tower with shells and raking it with machine-gun fire. In an instant men were mown down while others were blasted clean off the U-boat's casing. Burroughs dived headlong down into the conning tower while Spiegel was thrown into the air as another shell exploded near the tower.

Spiegel thrashed about in the water, cursing himself for falling into the trap as more shells whistled over his head and crashed into the U-boat. He was to be even angrier when the lifeboat launched from the schooner picked him up and he discovered the schooner was none other than HMS Prize—a German ship which had been captured by the British shortly after the outbreak of the war. The man behind the guns on Prize was Lieutenant Sanders and he and his guns crew kept up the barrage of fire until U-93 managed to limp away into the darkness.

As the U-boat disappeared, Sanders and his men dashed from the guns to stem the tide of flames that was engulfing the ship and plug the

The schooner opened up, plastering the U-boat's conning tower . . .

holes through which the sea was rushing into her hold. After a frantic battle against sea and flame they finally succeeded in preventing the schooner from sinking and Spiegel and the other survivors from U-93 were hauled aboard. In spite of his fury at being tricked, Spiegel could not help but admire the courage of the young lieutenant for holding his fire so long, and taking the full force of the German gunfire until the time for his attack was right.

Both the *Prize* and U-93 managed to limp back to their home bases. From the *Prize* Count Spiegel went to spend the remainder of the war in a prisoner-of-war camp in England, while Captain Burroughs did likewise in Germany. But before Count Spiegel was incarcerated he went to great lengths to sing the praises of Lieutenant Sanders for his courage, and even went to the extent of suggesting that he should be awarded the country's highest award for gallantry. This was done, Lieutenant Sanders being decorated with the Victoria Cross.

After a refit, *Prize* put to sea once more, this time with Sanders promoted to Lieutenant-Commander, but alas, she was later sunk by a German U-boat and lost with all hands.

On 7 June 1917, Campbell was at sea again, this time in command of the Q-ship *Pargust*, sailing off the coast of Ireland, when a U-boat slid towards him at periscope depth. The U-boat commander was in a quandary. The ship he saw through his periscope certainly looked like a tramp steamer and it mounted a small gun which two seamen were busily polishing. (This 'gun' was in fact a dummy which Campbell had mounted on deck in the hope that it might make the enemy less suspicious of the guns that lay hidden.)

But the U-boat commander was still not satisfied that the tramp was genuine. He had heard too many stories of his comrades falling victim to British trickery and, deciding to take no chances, he fired a torpedo at the *Pargust*. It struck the Q-ship and exploded, tearing a forty-foot hole in the ship's side just above the water-line and killing one of the crew. As the ship rocked in the waves, tons of water flooded in through the gash and it seemed that she was doomed. But Campbell was determined that the U-boat should not get away with its attack. He swung into action, ordering the 'dummy-crew' to abandon ship. The U-boat commander soon saw men rushing for the lifeboats while the crew on the fake deck-gun acted out the loading procedure, then they too 'panicked' and ran for the boats.

Within a few minutes the boats were pulling away from the *Pargust*. But while they were doing so Campbell and his real crew were lying flat on the decks ready to man the guns when the time came. Through a slit in the bulwarks Campbell could see the 'eye' of the periscope peering just above the surface. He knew that, if the German had the slightest suspicion that the tramp was anything but deserted, he would finish the job with another torpedo. Then, at last, after an agonizing wait, the U-boat surfaced but no one appeared on her conning tower. Still the German was not sure.

Campbell had to have the U-boat's crew on deck before he would chance firing. By doing that, he would make sure that, with her hatches open, the sub would find it difficult to crash-dive quickly. But suddenly he realized that the lifeboats were drifting between the *Pargust* and the U-boat. When he did open up his own men would be in the line of fire. Luckily the same idea occurred to the men in the lifeboats and they rowed out of the way. A few moments later the U-boat commander appeared on the conning tower. Now was Campbell's chance to strike.

311

The bulwarks fell away: the guns blazed. His first salvo smashed the conning tower, leaving it a twisted tangle of jagged metal. More shells thudded into the submarine, puncturing the casing as some of the crew scrambled on to the deck, raising their arms in surrender. When Campbell caught sight of them he yelled.

'Cease fire!'

But no sooner had the guns fallen silent than the submarine made a dash to escape and, as she did so, the men on the outer-casing were washed into the sea. In an instant *Pargust*'s guns opened up once more, lashing the submarine with fire. Then a shell ripped through the U-boat and hit the load of mines she was carrying. The resulting explosion tore the submarine apart and she sank. The battle was over and *Pargust* had won the day. Only two men survived from the U-boat.

Pargust was so badly damaged that she had to radio for help and was towed to port, where she underwent repairs. When the Admiralty heard of the courage of Campbell and his men they made an award of £1,000 to the entire crew. But there was more to follow. It was decided that two VCs would be awarded to the ship's company and a ballot was held to decide who should receive them on behalf of the crew. They chose Lieutenant R. N. Stuart and Seaman William Williams. It was Williams who, after the torpedo had struck the *Pargust* and dislodged a huge plate hiding one of the guns, held that plate in position until Campbell gave the order to fire. Had Williams failed, *Pargust*'s secret would have been revealed and the result of the battle might have been very different.

ONE OF THE MISSING

Ambrose Bierce

Jerome Searing, a private soldier of General Sherman's army, then confronting the enemy at and about Kenesaw Mountain, Georgia, turned his back upon a small group of officers, with whom he had been talking in low tones, stepped across a light line of earthworks, and disappeared in a forest. None of the men in line behind the works had said a word to him, nor had he so much as nodded to them in passing, but all who saw understood that this brave man had been intrusted with some perilous duty. Jerome Searing, though a private, did not serve in the ranks; he was detailed for service at division headquarters, being borne upon the rolls as an orderly. 'Orderly' is a word covering a multitude of duties. An orderly may be a messenger, a clerk, an officer's servant—anything. He may perform services for which no provision is made in orders and army regulations. Their nature may depend upon his aptitude, upon favour, upon accident.

Private Searing, an incomparable marksman, young—it is surprising how young we all were in those days—hardy, intelligent, and insensible to fear, was a scout. The general commanding his division was not content to obey orders blindly without knowing what was in his front, even when his command was not on detached service, but formed a fraction of the line of the army; nor was he satisfied to receive his knowledge of his *vis-à-vis* through the customary channels; he wanted to know more than he was told by the corps commander and the collisions of pickets and skirmishers. Hence Jerome Searing—with his extraordinary daring, his woodcraft, his sharp eyes and truthful tongue. On this occasion his instructions were simple: to get as near the enemy's lines as possible and learn all that he could.

In a few moments he had arrived at the picket line, the men on duty there lying in groups of from two to four behind little banks of earth scooped out of the slight depression in which they lay, their rifles protruding from the green boughs with which they had masked their small defences. The forest extended without a break toward the front, so solemn and silent that only by an effort of the imagination could it be conceived as populous with armed men, alert and vigilant—a forest formidable with possibilities of battle. Pausing a moment in one of the rifle pits to inform the men of his intention, Searing crept stealthily forward on his hands and knees and was soon lost to view in a dense thicket of underbrush.

'That's the last of him' said one of the men; 'I wish I had his rifle; those fellows will hurt some of us with it.'

Searing crept on, taking advantage of every accident of ground and growth to give himself better cover. His eyes penetrated everywhere, his ears took note of every sound. He stilled his breathing, and at the cracking of a twig beneath his knee stopped his progress and hugged the earth. It was slow work, but not tedious; the danger made it exciting, but by no physical signs was the excitement manifest. His pulse was as regular, his nerves were as steady, as if he were trying to trap a sparrow.

'It seems a long time,' he thought, 'but I cannot have come very far; I'm still alive.'

He smiled at his own method of estimating distance, and crept forward. A moment later he suddenly flattened himself upon the earth and lay motionless, minute after minute. Through a narrow opening in the bushes he had caught sight of a small mound of yellow clay—one of the enemy's rifle pits. After some little time he cautiously raised his head, inch by inch, then his body upon his hands, spread out on each side of him, all the while intently regarding the hillock of clay. In another moment he was upon his feet, rifle in hand, striding rapidly forward with little attempt at concealment. He had rightly interpreted the signs, whatever they were; the enemy was gone.

To assure himself beyond a doubt before going back to report upon so important a matter, Searing pushed forward across the line of abandoned pits, running from cover to cover in the more open forest, his eyes vigilant to discover possible stragglers. He came to the edge of a plantation—one of those forlorn, deserted homesteads of the last years of the war, upgrown with brambles, ugly with broken fences, and desolate with vacant buildings having blank apertures in place of doors and windows. After a keen reconnaissance from the safe seclusion of a clump of young pines, Searing ran lightly across a field and through an orchard to a small structure which stood apart from the other farm buildings, on a slight elevation, which he thought would enable him to overlook a large scope of country in the direction that he supposed the enemy to have taken in withdrawing.

This building, which had originally consisted of a single room, elevated upon four posts about ten feet high, was now little more than a roof; the floor had fallen away, the joists and planks loosely piled on the ground below or resting on end at various angles, not wholly torn from their fastenings above. The supporting posts were themselves no longer vertical. It looked as if the whole edifice would go down at the touch of a finger. Concealing himself in the debris of joists and flooring, Searing looked across the open ground between his point of view and a spur of Kenesaw Mountain, a half-mile away. A road leading up and across this spur was crowded with troops—the rear-guard of the retiring enemy, their gun barrels gleaming in the morning sunlight.

Searing had now learned all that he could hope to know. It was his duty to return to his own command with all possible speed and report his discovery. But the grey column of infantry toiling up the mountain road was singularly tempting. His rifle—an ordinary Springfield, but fitted with a globe sight and hair trigger—would easily send its ounce and a quarter of lead hissing into their midst. That would probably not affect the duration and result of the war, but it is the business of a soldier to kill. It is also his pleasure if he is a good soldier. Searing cocked his rifle and set the trigger.

But it was decreed from the beginning of time that Private Searing was not to murder anybody that bright summer morning, nor was the Confederate retreat to be announced by him. For countless ages events had been so matching themselves together in that wondrous mosaic to some parts of which, dimly discernible, we give the name of history, that the acts which he had in will would have marred the harmony of the pattern.

Some twenty-five years previously the power charged with the execution of the work according to the design had provided against that mischance by causing the birth of a certain male child in a little village at the foot of the Carpathian Mountains, had carefully reared it, supervised its education, directed its desires into a military channel, and in due time made it an officer of artillery. But the concurrence of an infinite number of favouring influences and their preponderance over an infinite number of opposing ones, this officer of artillery had been made to commit a breach of discipline and fly from his native country to avoid punishment.

He had been directed to New Orleans (instead of New York), where a recruiting officer awaited him on the wharf. He was enlisted and promoted, and things were so ordered that he now commanded a Confederate battery some three miles along the line from where Jerome Searing, the Federal scout, stood cocking his rifle. Nothing had been neglected—at every step in the progress of both these men's lives, and in the lives of their ancestors and contemporaries, and of the lives of the contemporaries of their ancestors—the right thing had been done to bring about the desired result. Had anything in all this vast con- catenation been overlooked, Private Searing might have fired on the retreating Confederates that morning, and would perhaps have missed. As it fell out, a captain of artillery, having nothing better to do while awaiting his turn to pull out and be off, amused himself by sighting a field piece obliquely to his right at what he took to be some Federal officers on the crest of a hill, and discharged it. The shot flew high of its mark.

As Jerome Searing drew back the hammer of his rifle, and, with his eyes upon the distant Confederates, considered where he could plant his shot with the best hope of making a widow or an orphan or a child- less mother—perhaps all three, for Private Searing, although he had repeatedly refused promotion, was not without a certain kind of ambition—he heard a rushing sound in the air, like that made by the wings of a great bird swooping down upon its prey. More quickly than he could apprehend the gradation, it increased to a hoarse and horrible roar, as the missile that made it sprang at him out of the sky, striking with a deafening impact one of the posts supporting the confusion of timbers above him, smashing it into matchwood, and bringing down the crazy edifice with a loud clatter, in clouds of blinding dust!

Lieutenant Adrian Searing, in command of the picket guard on that part of the line through which his brother Jerome had passed on his mission, sat with attentive ears in his breastwork behind the line. Not the faintest sound escaped him; the cry of a bird, the barking of a squirrel, the noise of the wind among the pines—all were anxiously noted by his overstrained sense. Suddenly, directly in front of his line, he heard a faint, confused rumble, like the clatter of a falling building translated by distance. At the same moment an officer approached him on foot from the rear and saluted.

'Lieutenant,' said the aide, 'the colonel directs you to move forward your line and feel the enemy if you find him. If not, continue the advance until directed to halt. There is reason to think that the enemy has retreated.'

The lieutenant nodded and said nothing; the other officer retired. In a moment the men, informed of their duty by the non-commissioned officers in low tones, had deployed from their rifle pits and were moving forward in skirmishing order, with set teeth and beating hearts. The lieutenant looked at his watch. Six o'clock and eighteen minutes.

When Jerome Searing recovered consciousness, he did not at once understand what had occurred. It was, indeed, some time before he opened his eyes. For a while he believed that he had died and been buried, and he tried to recall some portions of the burial service. He thought that his wife was kneeling upon his grave, adding her weight to that of the earth upon his chest. The two of them, widow and earth, had crushed his coffin. Unless the children should persuade her to go home, he would not much longer be able to breathe. He felt a sense of wrong. 'I cannot speak to her,' he thought; 'the dead have no voice; and if I open my eyes I shall get them full of earth.'

He opened his eyes—a great expanse of blue sky, rising from a fringe of the tops of trees. In the foreground, shutting out some of the trees, a high, dun mound, angular in outline and crossed by an intricate, patternless system of straight lines; in the centre a bright ring of metal— the whole an immeasurable distance away—a distance so inconceivably great that it fatigued him, and he closed his eyes. The moment that he did so he was conscious of an insufferable light. A sound was in his ears like the low, rhythmic thunder of a distant sea breaking in successive waves upon the beach, and out of this noise, seeming a part of it, or possibly coming from beyond it, and intermingled with its ceaseless undertone, came the articulate words: 'Jerome Searing, you are caught like a rat in a trap—in a trap, trap, trap.'

Suddenly there fell a great silence, a black darkness, an infinite tranquillity, and Jerome Searing, perfectly conscious of his rathood, and well assured of the trap that he was in, remembered all, and nowise alarmed, again opened his eyes to reconnoitre, to note the strength of his enemy, to plan his defence.

He was caught in a reclining posture, his back firmly supported by a solid beam. Another lay across his breast, but he had been able to shrink a little way from it so that it no longer oppressed him, though it was immovable. A brace joining it at an angle had wedged him against a pile of boards on his left, fastening the arm on that side. His legs, slightly parted and straight along the ground, were covered upward to the knees with a mass of debris which towered above his narrow horizon. His head was as rigidly fixed as in a vice; he could move his eyes, his chin—no more. Only his right arm was partly free. 'You must help us out of this,' he said to it. But he could not get it from under the heavy timber across his chest, nor move it outward more than six inches at the elbow.

Searing was not seriously injured, nor did he suffer pain. A smart rap on the head from a flying fragment of the splintered post, incurred simultaneously with the frightfully sudden shock to the nervous system, had momentarily dazed him. His term of unconsciousness, including the period of recovery, during which he had had the strange fancies, had probably not exceeded a few seconds, for the dust of the wreck had not wholly cleared away as he began an intelligent survey of the situation.

With his partly free right hand he now tried to get hold of the beam which lay across, but not quite against, his breast. In no way could he do so. He was unable to depress the shoulder so as to push the elbow beyond that edge of the timber which was nearest his knees; failing in that, he could not raise the forearm and hand to grasp the beam. The brace that made an angle with it downward and backward prevented him from doing anything in that direction, and between it and his body the space was not half as wide as the length of his forearm. Obviously he could not get his hand under the beam nor over it; he could not, in fact, touch it at all. Having demonstrated his inability, he desisted, and began to think if he could reach any of the debris piled upon his legs.

In surveying the mass with a view to determining that point, his attention was arrested by what seemed to be a ring of shining metal immediately in front of his eyes. It appeared to him at first to surround some perfectly black substance, and it was somewhat more than a half inch in diameter. It suddenly occurred to his mind that the blackness was simply shadow, and that the ring was in fact the muzzle of his rifle protruding from the pile of debris. He was not long in satisfying himself that this was so—if it was a satisfaction. By closing either eye he could look a little way along the barrel—to the point where it was hidden by the rubbish that held it. He could see the one side, with the corresponding eye, at apparently the same angle as the other side with the other eye. Looking with the right eye, the weapon seemed to be directed at a point to the left of his head, and *vice versa*. He was unable to see the upper surface of the barrel, but could see the under surface of the stock at a slight angle. The piece was, in fact, aimed at the exact centre of his forehead.

In the perception of this circumstance, in the recollection that just previously to the mischance of which this uncomfortable situation was the result, he had cocked the gun and set the trigger so that a touch would discharge it, Private Searing was affected with a feeling of uneasiness. But that was as far as possible from fear; he was a brave man, somewhat familiar with the aspect of rifles from that point of view, and of cannon, too; and now he recalled, with something like amusement, an incident of his experience at the storming of Missionary Ridge, where, walking up to one of the enemy's emplacements from which he had seen a heavy gun throw charge after charge of grape among the

319

assailants, he thought for a moment that the piece had been withdrawn; he could see nothing in the opening but a brazen circle. What that was he had understood just in time to step aside as it pitched another peck of iron down that swarming slope. To face firearms is one of the commonest incidents in a soldier's life—firearms, too, with malevolent eyes blazing behind them. That is what a soldier is for. Still, Private Searing did not altogether relish the situation, and turned away his eyes.

After groping, aimless, with his right hand for a time, he made an ineffectual attempt to release his left. Then he tried to disengage his head, the fixity of which was the more annoying from his ignorance of what held it. Next he tried to free his feet, but while exerting the powerful muscles of his legs for that purpose it occurred to him that a disturbance of the rubbish which held them might discharge the rifle; how it could have endured what had already befallen it he could not understand, although memory assisted him with various instances in point.

One in particular he recalled, in which, in a moment of mental abstraction, he had clubbed his rifle and beaten out another gentleman's brains, observing afterward that the weapon which he had been diligently swinging by the muzzle was loaded, capped, and at full cock —knowledge of which circumstance would doubtless have cheered his antagonist to longer endurance. He had always smiled in recalling that blunder of his 'green and salad days' as a soldier, but now he did not smile. He turned his eyes again to the muzzle of the gun, and for a moment fancied that it had moved; it seemed somewhat nearer.

Again he looked away. The tops of the distant trees beyond the bounds of the plantation interested him; he had not before observed how light and feathery they seemed, nor how darkly blue the sky was, even among their branches, where they somewhat paled it with their green; above him it appeared almost black. 'It will be uncomfortably hot here,' he thought, 'as the day advances. I wonder which way I am looking.'

Judging by such shadows as he could see, he decided that his face was due north; he would at least not have the sun in his eyes, and north— well, that was toward his wife and children.

'Bah!' he exclaimed aloud, 'what have they to do with it?'

He closed his eyes. 'As I can't get out, I may as well go to sleep. The rebels are gone, and some of our fellows are sure to stray out here foraging. They'll find me.'

But he did not sleep. Gradually he became sensible of a pain in his forehead—a dull ache, hardly perceptible at first, but growing more and more uncomfortable. He opened his eyes and it was gone; he closed them and it returned. 'The devil!' he said irrelevantly, and stared again at the sky. He heard the singing of birds, the strange metallic note of the meadow lark, suggesting the clash of vibrant blades.

He fell into pleasant memories of his childhood, played again with his brother and sister, raced across the fields, shouting to alarm the sitting larks, entered the sombre forest beyond, and with timid steps followed the faint path to Ghost Rock, standing at last with audible heart-throbs before Dead Man's Cave and seeking to penetrate its awful mystery. For the first time he observed that the opening of the haunted cavern was encircled by a ring of metal.

Then all else vanished, and left him gazing into the barrel of his rifle as before. But whereas before it had seemed nearer, it now seemed an inconceivable distance away, and all the more sinister for that. He cried out, and startled by something in his own voice—the note of fear—lied to himself in denial: 'If I don't sing out I may stay here till I die.'

He now made no further attempt to evade the menacing stare of the gun barrel. If he turned away his eyes an instant it was to look for assistance (although he could not see the ground on either side the ruin), and he permitted them to return, obedient to the imperative fascination. If he closed them, it was from weariness, and instantly the poignant pain in his forehead—the prophecy and menace of the bullet—forced him to reopen them.

The tension of nerve and brain was too severe; nature came to his relief with intervals of unconsciousness. Reviving from one of these, he became sensible of a sharp, smarting pain in his right hand, and when he worked his fingers together, or rubbed his palm with them, he could feel that they were wet and slippery. He could not see the hand, but he knew the sensation; it was running blood. In his delirium he had beaten it against the jagged fragments of the wreck, had clutched it full of splinters. He resolved that he would meet his fate more manly. He was a plain, common soldier, had no religion and not much philosophy; he could not die like a hero, with great and wise last words, even if there

The thought flashed into his bewildered mind that the rats might touch the trigger of his rifle.

were someone to hear them, but he could die 'game', and he would. But if he could only know when to expect the shot!

Some rats which had probably inhabited the shed came sneaking and scampering about. One of them mounted the pile of debris that held the rifle; another followed, and another. Searing regarded them at first with indifference, then with friendly interest; then, as the thought flashed into his bewildered mind that they might touch the trigger of his rifle, he screamed at them to go away. 'It is no business of yours,' he cried.

The creatures left; they would return later, attack his face, gnaw away his nose, cut his throat—he knew that, but he hoped by that time to be dead.

Nothing could now unfix his gaze from the little ring of metal with its black interior. The pain in his forehead was fierce and constant. He felt it gradually penetrating the brain more and more deeply, until at last its progress was arrested by the wood at the back of his head. It grew momentarily more insufferable; he began wantonly beating his

lacerated hand against the splinters again to counteract that horrible ache. It seemed to throb with a slow, regular, recurrence, each pulsation sharper than the preceding, and sometimes he cried out, thinking he felt the fatal bullet. No thoughts of home, of wife and children, of country, of glory. The whole record of memory was erased. The world had passed away—not a vestige remained. Here, in this confusion of timbers and boards, is the sole universe. Here is immortality in time—each pain an everlasting life. The throbs tick off eternities.

Jerome Searing, the man of courage, the formidable enemy, the strong, resolute warrior, was as pale as a ghost. His jaw was fallen; his eyes protruded; he trembled in every fibre; a cold sweat bathed his entire body; he screamed with fear. He was not insane—he was terrified.

In groping about with his torn and bleeding hand he seized at last a strip of board, and, pulling, felt it give way. It lay parallel with his body, and by bending his elbow as much as the contracted space would permit, he could draw it a few inches at a time. Finally it was altogether loosened from the wreckage covering his legs; he could lift it clear of the ground its whole length. A great hope came into his mind: perhaps he could work it upward, that is to say backward, far enough to lift the

323

end and push aside the rifle; or, if that were too tightly wedged, so hold the strip of board as to deflect the bullet.

With this object he passed it backward inch by inch, hardly daring to breathe, lest that act somehow defeat his intent, and more than ever unable to remove his eyes from the rifle, which might perhaps now hasten to improve its waning opportunity. Something at least had been gained; in the occupation of his mind in this attempt at self-defence he was less sensible of the pain in his head and had ceased to scream. But he was still dreadfully frightened, and his teeth rattled like castanets.

The strip of board ceased to move to the urging of his hand. He tugged at it with all his strength, changed the direction of its length all he could, but it had met some extended obstruction behind him, and the end in front was still too far away to clear the pile of debris and reach the muzzle of the gun. It extended, indeed, nearly as far as the trigger-guard, which, uncovered by the rubbish, he could imperfectly see with his right eye. He tried to break the strip with his hand, but had no leverage. Perceiving his defeat, all his terror returned, augmented tenfold. The black aperture of the rifle appeared to threaten a sharper and more imminent death in punishment of his rebellion. The track of the bullet through his head ached with more intense anguish. He began to tremble again.

Suddenly he became composed. His tremor subsided. He clinched his teeth and drew down his eyebrows. He had not exhausted his means of defence; a new design had shaped itself in his mind—another plan of battle. Raising the front end of the strip of board, he carefully pushed it forward through the wreckage at the side of the rifle until it pressed against the trigger guard. Then he moved the end slowly outward until he could feel that it had cleared it, then, closing his eyes, thrust it against the trigger with all his strength! There was no explosion; the rifle had been discharged as it dropped from his hand when the building fell. But Jerome Searing was dead.

A line of Federal skirmishes swept across the plantation toward the mountain. They passed on both sides of the wrecked building, observing nothing. At a short distance in their rear came their commander, Lieutenant Adrian Searing. He casts his eyes curiously upon the ruin and sees a dead body half buried in boards and timbers. It is so covered

324

with dust that its clothing is Confederate grey. Its face is yellowish white; the cheeks are fallen in, the temples sunken, too, with sharp ridges about them, making the forehead forbiddingly narrow; the upper lip, slightly lifted, shows the white teeth, rigidly clinched. The hair is heavy with moisture, the face as wet as the dewy grass all about. From his point of view the officer does not observe the rifle; the man was apparently killed by the fall of the building.

'Dead a week,' said the officer curtly, moving on, mechanically pulling out his watch as if to verify his estimate of time. Six o'clock and forty minutes.

THE CHICKEN-SWITCH

Elleston Trevor

As soon as I arrived the guards handed me over to a courteous young Air Force captain, and he escorted me along corridors where warning notices became more and more blunt in their phrasing: *If you do not have Special Pass A-Q 6, you are already in trouble! You are entering the Top Security Zone—obey your escort without hesitation!* And so on. But I was unmoved: I did have my Special Pass A-Q 6, and my escort was treating me more as a privileged guest than a doughboy on duty. I even had a signed note from the chief-of-project himself. Despite this, my nerves were playing up a little, because this was my tenth special assignment for Associated Eastern Press, and it was always at this stage of a news-story (nearing completion) that I began to wonder whether the stuff I had written was really any good after all.

Well, it would just have to be. Today, Monday, I was here to observe the start of an isolation test, and a week later I would be here again, to see it end.

The young captain led me past other notices, where doors were let into the long perspective of the passages: *Chief of Test Laboratory. Strictly No Admittance. Monitor Room. Red Light Means Off Limits.* And so on. But I was used to this atmosphere of distrust; it had been the same at the other places—the Aero-Medical Establishment, the Research and Development Centre, the Missile Flight-Plan Headquarters. They had shown me everything—everything, perhaps, except those few top-secret details that maybe only the President himself had access to. I had watched the teams of guinea-pigs—young, fit, cheerful men at their training inside the echoless chambers and the claustrophobic booths. I had watched them pulling their bodies out of the dreadful spins and gyrations of the multiple-axis apparatus for Project Mercury. I had watched their willing subjection to black-out, grey-out, red-out, as the blood was drained from the brain or forced back into it by the centrifuges and the other machines devised by man for the testing of his own kind, designed to simulate every known condition of manned rocket flight. Now there was this last mission to observe; and already I was shaping out the introduction in my head, from long habit. Something, perhaps, like this:

On this fine June morning I am two hundred and fifty feet below ground level in the hermetically-sealed super-beehive known more formally as the Aero-Medical Psychological-Stress Research Laboratory for Man-High Project III . . . I am here to meet one man. It may be that within the year he will become one of the men whose names make up the signposts of human history, for if plans go right, he and his team of astronauts will be leaving us, bound for the unknown. His name is Charles J. Loomis . . .

My thoughts on the article were interrupted. The young Air Force captain had led me into the test room. It was small, high, clinically clean and mortuary-calm.

My escort spoke softly: 'Major Loomis, this is Mr Robert Jasen of Associated Eastern Press, here to observe your entry into the capsule.'

'Nice to have you around,' said Loomis. He looked like other men, ordinary men: a young, pink-skinned face, level eyes, a crew-cut. Only his clothes were strange. He was being helped into them as he answered my few questions, so that, as we talked, the aluminium space-suit and its complicated accessories gradually took away his identity—or lent him a new one, not of this earth.

It was, he said, the fifteenth time he would have been sealed inside the big metal capsule, each time for a longer period, to get him used to prolonged isolation. Yes, this was the actual nose-cone that would be fitted to the big Atlas-D missile when they made the big shoot. 'I wouldn't,' he said with a smile, 'be keen to go out there in anything strange. This capsule's already become my home-from-home, I'm that used to it.'

I looked up at the capsule behind him; it loomed coldly, a tomb, a tower. Home . . . for this one man. He went on answering my questions calmly, cheerfully.

'That's right, this trip is for seven days—around the time it takes to hit the moon and bounce back. No, the capsule won't even move from this room during that time—but all they are testing is my resistance to claustrophobia. For the next seven days I shan't see another soul, or hear another voice. Maybe it doesn't sound very hard to do.'

I said it sounded just awful. I even told him—such was the ease with which he invited confidence—of the time I'd been shut by accident in a cupboard, for just one hour, and suffered nightmares about it years after.

The space-doctor came into the room and began studying Major Loomis unobtrusively while he talked to me and looked steadily into my eyes, appraising me—I thought with a tremor—as if I were going into that capsule with him, as if he had to measure my worth, as a companion under stress.

Had he anything, I asked him, to occupy his time in there, for seven days and seven nights? He shrugged.

'I have routine checks to report—reading instruments and compiling data. But no incoming radio: no voices. And no television panel: no faces. The sense of isolation has to be complete. All I have in there to help me,' he said with his eyes steadily on mine, 'is my own brain. And my gimmick.'

'What gimmick is that, Major Loomis?'

'Maybe I'll let you know, Mr Jasen, a week from now when we have our next date: noon, Monday.'

This 'gimmick' of his intrigued me, but I didn't persist. The trained dressing-crew were securing the white-studded cylinder over his head —the space-helmet. Now they connected the straps and intricate network of electrical leads. I reached for one of the skin-tight wired gloves and shook it, almost surprised to feel a human hand inside.

'Good luck!' I mouthed at the face-panel, and the big white helmet nodded. Then they helped him inside the capsule, and a minute later the test director spoke to him by radio; and I knew that this was the last human voice he would hear for a week.

'Stand by, Major: we're disconnecting you!'

An operator moved his hands on a panel, cutting a switch. There was silence in the room. An amber light on the panel flicked out, as finally as death closing an eye. As I walked out with the crew I wanted to shout to them, 'But you can't just leave him in there alone, sealed up for seven days!'

I controlled my fears for him. This was what had been arranged, meticulously planned. This was what had to be.

On my way to ground level, I asked the young Air Force captain, 'Did you ever go inside that thing yourself?'

'Sure,' he said, 'I held out for almost five hours—then I had to flip the chicken-switch and tell them to get me out. I don't aim to try it again.'

I said: 'Can Major Loomis use the chicken-switch, if he wants?'

'Oh, sure. But I guess he won't do that. He's peak-trained now, and he has a very special kind of mind.'

Outside in the free world of grass and trees and people, I felt the sunshine had lost its warmth. I couldn't stop thinking of Loomis, down there alone, entombed for seven days.

Monday night—the first night—was normal, but I found Tuesday less easy to bear. I couldn't get him out of my mind. The third day, Wednesday, I skipped lunch because I had no appetite. That night I took a couple of sleeping pills. Next day, Thursday, my wife Dorothy tried to talk me out of my acute depression, but all I could think about was what the space-doctor had told me at the Research Base:

'The technical boys are ready for the big shoot, and now there's only the human factor to beat. When we send our first cosmonaut on a trip as far as the moon, he'll be entering a new element, and that hasn't happened, you know, since the time when man crawled out of the primeval slime and learned to breathe air. Right down at the root of our cosmonaut's brain there's going to be opposition to this enormous change we're forcing upon it. The most serious psychological barrier working against him is what we call the break-off effect, and it's comparable with the shock undergone by every infant at the moment of

329

its birth; it is the reason why it cries, and knows fear for the first time: fear of the unknown. In these "guinea-pig tests" we've had a grown man scream, for that same reason. He was convinced he was losing touch with his mother: his mother-earth.'

The words of the space-doctor were still in my mind as if written there, etched in acid. Would Major Loomis, in that isolated coffin of his, be screaming now? If so, nobody would hear him.

Friday, the fifth day, I was like a rag doll. I tried to tell Dorothy how I felt, and she understood, I thought; but her reasoning didn't help. She said, 'Look, Jay, this test is for him, not you. It's only bad for *him*.' She was right: and now I had an added fear—that I was somehow losing my own identity in that of Loomis's.

We tried going to a movie but I had to come out halfway through, because the cinema was full, and I felt the beginnings of claustrophobia. We couldn't even take a cab home, though it was raining: the cab had foam-rubber seats on a tubular frame, just as the pilot's seat was made, in that capsule where *he* was.

Saturday was very bad, and Dorothy called in Doc Jones, who gave me some pills; but my induced sleep was nightmare-ridden. I was in that capsule, alone, sealed up, cut off; and the umbilical cord between the known and the unknown worlds had snapped. When I woke, I became half-aware of how crazy I was acting—shouting at people as if I were so far off they couldn't hear unless I yelled. Sunday I was calmer, because of Doc Jones's pills; but Dorothy had left the apartment to stay at her sister's. She wasn't safe with me any more. The doc had moved in a male nurse who gave me shots when I began shaking and looking around for the chicken-switch ... my only hope. I couldn't seem to find it, and I kept yelling for it. The only time the male nurse left me, I had a bad turn. In my complete isolation I fought it out with the telephone, trying to strangle the thing with my bare hands. I thought I was through to the Research Centre. I was shouting, 'Tell him to flip the chicken-switch—you hear me? You just get him out of there!' Nobody answered. Nobody heard.

Monday I was pretty weak, because of the shots I was being given. Doc Jones came for me and we drove out to the Research Centre for my date with Major Loomis. The doc said I'd be all right again, once I'd seen Loomis, safe and sound. We were checked in and escorted to

'Tell him to flip the chicken-switch—just get him out of there!'

the test chamber, just before noon. It was crowded with technicians and medical men, waiting to let the guinea-pig out and vet him. The blade of the wall-clock quietly carved the air, cutting off the last of the minutes—and suddenly it was noon. Noon, Monday. The technical crew got to work. The amber light came on, and a voice intoned: 'Release-pressure zero, sir. Air-balance negative. Both relay-equalizers running. Ready now.'

'Tell him,' the test-director said. The mike was cut in, and a man said gently, 'Major Loomis . . . we are opening up. Stand by, please.' Two men moved to the levers on the hatch-door of the capsule and the door swung open. They stood back. What happens, I thought, to a man in there, alone for seven days? We all waited. In a couple of minutes Loomis came out—and I felt Doc Jones's hand on my arm. 'Steady up,' he said quietly.

'I'm okay,' I said. 'I'm okay now, Doc.'

They took the white space-helmet off, and Loomis looked around him. His face was pale, but his tone easy. 'The old place hasn't changed,' he said.

In an hour, after the doctors had examined him, I was allowed my interview. Lamely I began, 'Well, Major, you made it.'

'I guess I did.' He smiled. 'Wasn't so bad, though. The gimmick worked.'

I nodded, making notes. 'This "gimmick",' I said. 'You told me you might explain that to me, today.'

'Sure, Mr Jasen.' It surprised me—that he'd remembered my name, the name of a stranger, after that prolonged and dreadful isolation-test. 'For what it's worth,' he went on, 'anyone can try it. It's like this: when I'm inside there, and I start losing emotional equilibrium, and get the urge to flip that chicken-switch, I just project my thoughts—and my fears—outside the capsule. I make myself imagine I'm in the normal world again—you know, seeing a movie, eating a good steak, talking to my wife—everyday things like that. And it works. I've put the burden on someone else, outside.'

I wanted to get this right. 'On someone else?' I asked him. 'You mean on one *particular* person?'

He nodded calmly. 'That's right. Nobody in this place, of course—I know they're all working, and not seeing a movie or anything. I choose someone whose face I've taken a good hard look at before going into the capsule, so I can remember him easily.' His grey eyes gazed at me steadily, just as they had a week ago today. 'A stranger is best, Mr Jasen . . . Someone like you.'

THE TOUGHEST RACE IN THE WORLD

Stirling Moss

Until an accident in 1962, when serious injuries forced him to retire from motor racing, Stirling Moss was the best of British racing drivers, some said the finest in the world. He drove in hundreds of races and came first in forty-three per cent of them, a fantastic record. He was much admired for his skill, his charm, his patriotism and, as one newspaper editor explained, for his dogged determination: 'He was a knight in armour, rushing out of the castle to do battle in foreign lands, and coming back, sometimes with blood on his shield and sometimes not —but always in a hurry to get back and have another bash.' Here he describes a great battle, in a story specially written for this book.

Of all the races I ever drove in, the most frightening and possibly the most fascinating was the thousand-mile race over ordinary roads in Italy, called the 'Mille Miglia'. There was every kind of driving there— long straights where you could roar along at 170 miles an hour, snaking S-bends, sharp turns, mountain zigzags and great cities like Rome or Florence where the traffic had been cleared and you dashed across squares, level-crossings, up side-streets, down tree-lined avenues. The road surface changed continually, too, from smooth to bumpy as the back of a lizard, from greasy to gritty with clouds of dust, quite apart from those treacherous patches, common to all racing circuits, of oil and rubber from competitors' tyres, which could send the car into an uncontrollable skid. The Mille Miglia offered variety, excitement, a gruelling endurance test—and plenty of danger.

For drivers who came from any country except Italy there was a snag, and having competed three times already in the Mille Miglia I knew it well enough. Italians could be expected to know the route exactly. After all it was their country. But for others like myself we could not hope to memorize and produce from memory at just the right moment what lay ahead after every hump-backed bridge, after every blind corner. Did the road go straight on or were there hidden twists to come? It was all-important to know this when driving at high speed and there were hundreds of such places which no one man could hope to register. Yet a single mistake could be fatal.

Yet once again I was determined to have another go at the Mille Miglia. No Englishman had won it since the race was first held in 1927—and it was now late in 1954. For the 1955 race I had been offered a magnificent two-seater sports car, a three-litre, eight-cylinder Mercedes-Benz which developed over 304 b.h.p. at the peak number of revolutions of 7,000 per minute, which meant 117 revolutions of the crankshaft *per second*. At this rate the car was capable of over 170 m.p.h. But there was still the big question: how to get to know the whole route not just well but perfectly, a route which was some 360 miles longer than the whole distance as the crow flies from the south-western tip of Cornwall to the north of Scotland.

I knew I could not do it alone, so—and then the answer struck me. Of course! The car was a two-seater and under the rules I could take someone with me. He would have to be the navigator. Before the race we would go over the whole course together several times, note down every single bump, turn, bridge, level-crossing, then in the race he would give me hand-signals to show what was coming next—signals because, even if he yelled, I would not be able to hear over the roar of the engine. This is what we would do, and I knew the perfect man for the job: Denis Jenkinson, former motor-cycle sidecar champion of the world, intelligent, mad about racing and as cool as a cucumber.

When I phoned Denis just before Christmas he said 'yes' immediately, so then we got together and made our plan. We would go over the course and make detailed notes for every mile, every inch of the way, starting from Brescia, west of Lake Garda in northern Italy, then down across the plain towards the east side of the peninsula skirting the Adriatic Sea, through the foothills of the Apennines over mountainous roads and many river bridges, then west across high valleys in a wide semi-circle towards Rome.

After Rome the route led north towards Florence—a really tough stretch this, over high mountain passes with few straights. From Florence we would be roaring eventually down the mountain slopes of the Futa Pass, towards Bologna, where we would be on the plain once more, heading in a big zigzag north again back to Brescia. Seen on the map the whole route took in the northern half of Italy and looked like a dented box.

First Denis and I made a careful note in writing of all the places which might break something in the car—the suspension, for instance, or the steering—or might lead at high speed to a serious accident if we did not know of them in advance. Then we did the same for all the difficult corners, grading them as 'saucy', 'dodgy' or 'very dangerous'. Last, we pinpointed the different road surfaces and then worked out the different hand-signals that Denis would give me for each.

On these trial runs we had to go fast, otherwise the notes would have been unrealistic. Something entirely safe at 50 m.p.h. could mean death at 150 and it was always in my mind that we would be up against the strongest opposition to be found anywhere—men who would be going as fast as their skills would take them—up to what we called 'ten-tenths motoring', the point, very tricky to judge, where on corners all four tyres would lose adhesion to the road and go into an uncontrollable slide.

When we had done all this Denis wrote out his notes on a special strip of paper over twenty feet long. We then had a holder made with two rollers so that during the race he could unwind the notes from the lower to the upper one and read them off—not easy at high speed— through a small perspex window. During practice I kept on reminding him that the notes had to be one hundred per cent correct, otherwise . . . But his retort was always the same, and fair enough, I thought: 'Remember, Stirling, if you go into the ditch I shall be there, too, so you needn't worry!'

We knew there was an enormous entry for the race, ranging from touring cars to the sports-racing variety. They were to start from Brescia, not in a bunch (which would have been impossible) but at half-minute and one-minute intervals, beginning at 9 p.m. on Saturday, 30 April. Our start was to be at 7.22 a.m. on the following morning, by which time all the lighter stuff would be on its way. The winner would be the car that clocked the shortest time over the whole course, whether or not it was first over the finishing line, and such was the competition that there might be a difference of seconds between first and second.

So it was seconds we had to think of—how to save them if we had to change a wheel on the road, or stop to repair a fault, or when we took in petrol at one of the Mercedes pits located round the route, or get a card stamped at one of the official control points set up to make sure each driver stuck to the proper course. We would take spares with us and we practised breakdowns, learning to change wheels quickly in eighty-five seconds. Mercedes had gone to no end of trouble to give us a fast reliable car, even having the seats tailored to our shapes to lessen fatigue. But in all races there will be plenty of things you cannot foresee, and one of these is the weather. Would it be shine or rain?

The day for our start, Sunday, 1 May, dawned happily with clear skies and the promise of dry roads, which meant that the race would be really fast. We had reckoned to do an average of 90 m.p.h. for the course, which would have been two better than the existing record. But now, in these near-perfect conditions, we would have to go even faster. Looking at the starting list we saw that world champion Juan Fangio was due to go twenty-four minutes behind us, so throughout the race we would never catch up with him on the ground. Also behind us would come a bunch of Italian Ferrari drivers, including the car-punishing Castellotti and the master tactician Taruffi, all sworn to beat the German Mercedes. These were the boys we would have to watch, and if any nipped past us it would be tough going to overtake them. There and then, as we waited for our start, I decided to really try from the beginning, to drive to the limit.

The mechanics pushed the car up on to the starting platform, Denis and I climbed in, I put on my goggles, started the engine and a cloud of smoke blew out from the side exhaust pipes. Then the starter's flag fell and with a roar we were off slowly down the ramp and then to maximum revs in first, second and third gears—there were five forward gears in all—weaving our way past spectators packing the sides of the road. The sun came up, but as it rose in the sky, getting hotter and hotter, the dazzle would get less, and at least I was grateful for bone-dry roads.

Denis twiddled his fingers to indicate a gentle S-bend through a village which I took on full throttle in fourth gear, then went into top to climb up to 150 m.p.h. In less than five minutes we had covered ten miles and there ahead was a red blob which had started two minutes before us, the first of the Ferraris to be overtaken. As in all continental motoring, my steering wheel was on the left and in a few seconds I slipped past him on a left-hand curve while Denis gave a blare on the horn and flashed the lights.

Over long straights then we went even faster, touching 170, and I found myself hurtling over blind brows with complete confidence in Denis's navigation, even though I could not see a yard beyond them. With the heat of the sun and the heat in the cockpit we were beginning to sweat heavily, and Denis kept feeding me boiled sweets to keep my saliva going. Between Verona and Vicenza, north-west of Venice, we began to sail past Austin-Healeys touring along at around 115 m.p.h. Then, as we headed south alongside the Adriatic Sea, I glanced in the rear mirror and saw something red behind us, and gaining. Castellotti in the most powerful of the Ferraris! We had been going fast but he had been faster and was now almost on our tail.

Into Padua I roared, trying to shake him off, down the main street towards a right-angle corner at the end—too fast, as it turned out. I stood on the brakes, then we slid across the road, hit some straw bales by the side, bounced off into the middle—and at that moment Castellotti nipped past with a grin on the inside and shot away like a rocket, throwing up clouds of dust and gravel. We screamed after him along a very fast stretch of road, but although the Mercedes was going flat out, we could not catch up.

But then came more corners and, watching closely, Denis saw Castellotti driving like a maniac, slicing into the gravel and rough stuff on the edges of the road while rubber poured off his rear tyres. At that rate he couldn't and wouldn't last long. Meanwhile it was my job not to get too close in case we suddenly came on him bouncing off a bank or stalled across the road. Finally, sure enough, we did come across him, at the first control point in Ravenna—out of the race with some trouble.

But there was still Fangio, 'The Master', behind us and Taruffi, 'The King of the Mountains' as his fans called him. How were they doing? We had no idea. But one thing was certain: there was not a second to lose. So down we went, flat out along the long coastal strip skirting the Adriatic, through the eastern foothills of the Apennines over many switch-backs and river bridges. What with the sun, heat from the gear-box, engine fumes, brake lining smells and continual buffeting to and fro, Denis's stomach finally revolted and he leant over the side to be

337

sick—at 150 m.p.h. In a flash his glasses had gone and we could have been in a nasty mess, with no more note-reading. But he whipped out a spare pair and carried on, not missing one signal.

We were passing a lot of earlier numbers now, some going very slowly: Italian Maseratis, British Triumphs chugging along in convoy and quite a few wrecked cars by the roadside—we couldn't tell what had happened to the drivers. Then came a dodgy moment. We made for a short cut round a level-crossing marked in our notes to find it blocked by straw bales. It was too late to turn back, so we went straight through them, crashed head on, and felt lucky to hit nothing more solid. We brushed more bales as we skated right across the road with all four wheels sliding into the town of Pescara, the second control point and our first pit stop. Here a superbly drilled Mercedes team poured eighteen gallons of fuel into the tank, cleaned the windscreen thick with flies, handed us coffee, chocolate and peeled bananas, handed Denis a sheet of paper and sent us on our way in just twenty-eight seconds. What was on the paper? I heard Denis yell in my ear: 'Second! Fifteen seconds behind Taruffi!' And Fangio was lying fifth in time.

'We slid across the road, hit some straw bales, bounced off into

It was said that the next stretch, westwards, right across Italy to Rome, was the one Taruffi knew best, so if we were to beat his time here again we had to do some flat-out motoring. We had another slight crisis getting out of Pescara, where there were some more straw bales to cushion the impact if drivers went off the road and I had to drive into them to avoid another car swinging in front of us. However, we got away again quickly and swept on, switch-backing at full speed over blind hummocks, twisting our way through valleys, then up into the mountains sliding round hairpin bends, and so down towards Rome, passing more cars on the way. At one point we hit a level-crossing merely marked on our notes as 'bumpy' with such a thud that we both shot clean out of our seats into the airstream, then landed again with a crash. But nothing was broken and we hurtled on into the city.

The last six miles were a nightmare with dense crowds packing the roadside, so close we could barely get through except by weaving to and fro to make them jump back, while Denis blared the horn and flashed the lights. Here was another pit stop and for the first time since leaving Brescia the engine was switched off. Again a devoted team took

the middle— and Castellotti nipped past in the Ferrari . . .'

charge and before we knew what was happening the car was jacked up, the rear wheels were being changed, fifty-eight gallons of petrol were pouring into the tank, food and drink was being offered and again a hand held out a sheet of paper to Denis: 'Moss, Taruffi'—and the times showed we had a lead of nearly two minutes. So we were ahead of the Mountain King on his home ground!

But there were many more miles to go, and anything could happen. In less than a minute we were off again, to find another Mercedes wrecked by the roadside, someone who had started twenty minutes ahead of us. A thumbs-up sign told us the driver was all right. And now we had a superstition to beat, current among veterans of the race, which said: 'He who leads at Rome never leads home.' Well, we would see about that . . .

We were now heading north, on the west side of Italy, on a very difficult section, over hillocks and hump-backed bridges, up and down mountain passes. There was, too, the continual hazard of passing slower cars. Yet we had no time to dawdle anywhere, but slithered and slid while I went through the corners flat out, judging from experience how much I could demand of the car without losing control.

All the same we had incidents—you can never foresee everything in a race. Once, over a sharp hump, the car took off completely and was airborne for around 200 feet before landing safely on all four wheels. Once, on a right-hand bend down a mountain side, the car suddenly spun without warning and slid into a ditch from which, after a bit of backing and filling, I was able to drive out. And once, only once in the entire race, Denis missed a hand signal when surge from the fuel tank suddenly sprayed his back with petrol. We stayed in one piece because I knew the section well. But where were Taruffi and Fangio? How were they doing?

Soon we had driven nearly 700 miles under a blazing sun. The car that had been gleaming and spotless at Brescia was now as dirty and oil-stained as we were and at one spot Denis saw a bunch of spectators, Italian peasant women, dash away in terror as they saw us roar up to a corner. We must have looked like demons from hell!

Over the high mountain passes and down towards the northern plain the going was very tricky owing to oil and tyre rubber left on the road by other competitors. Also, after many hours driving coupled with the heat and fumes from the engine I was getting tired, and this was dangerous. Fatigue could induce just that little bit of over-confidence, a relaxation of careful judgment, sending me twenty m.p.h. too fast into some corner with fatal results for the car, and possibly us as well.

But still all went swimmingly as we surged down towards Florence, bouncing and leaping over rough roads into the city streets at 120, over the great river bridge, broadside across a square into another control point where another bit of paper was shoved at Denis—from which he gathered we were still in the lead.

This news gave me a big heart for what was to come—more mountain climbs over roads even more slippery from melted tar now as well. Up we screamed over more passes, where enormous crowds waved frantically at us as we shot past. One big man, a friend of mine, I recognized jumping up and down like a maniac. Then we plunged down the other side in a long series of deliberate slides, then into Bologna, another check-point where our route card was stamped while we were still on the move, off again and into fast straights at 170 leading to more towns—and at this point Denis spotted an aeroplane above us which we were actually overtaking.

Once more now we were on the northern plain south-west of Brescia, still passing other competitors and all out for the finish. Just one more control point and one more tricky moment on some melted tar when we nearly hit a concrete wall, and then, for the last few miles, the engine was singing all the way. Denis put away his roller-map and I thought 'By heaven, after four attempts at the Mille Miglia, when I didn't even finish, at last I'm going to make it!'

It was just before 5.30 p.m. when we crossed the line at Brescia in one last long slide at over 100 m.p.h. But then came the anti-climax. We had finished, yes——but had we won? What about Fangio and Taruffi? Minutes later in the official garage they gave us the answer, when at last the news got through: Taruffi was out with a broken oil pump and Fangio was still in Florence with fuel injection trouble. The race was ours and we had broken all the records, averaging nearly 98 m.p.h. over the whole course in a total time of 10 hours, 7 minutes and 48 seconds. And we were the first, the very first British team ever to win the Mille Miglia.

341

THE PIT AND THE PENDULUM

Edgar Allan Poe

I was sick—sick unto death with that long agony; and when they at length unbound me, and I was permitted to sit, I felt that my senses were leaving me. The sentence—the dread sentence of death—was the last of distinct accentuation which reached my ears. After that, the sound of the Inquisitorial voices seemed merged in one dreamy indeterminate hum. It conveyed to my soul the idea of *revolution*—perhaps from its association in fancy with the burr of a mill-wheel. This only for a brief period; for presently I heard no more.

Yet, for a while, I saw; but with how terrible an exaggeration! I saw the lips of the black-robed judges. They appeared to me white—whiter than the sheet upon which I trace these words—and thin even to grotesqueness; thin with the intensity of their expression of firmness—of immovable resolution—of stern contempt of human torture. I saw that the decrees of what to me was Fate were still issuing from those lips. I saw them writhe with a deadly locution. I saw them fashion the syllables of my name; and I shuddered because no sound succeeded. I saw, too, for a few moments of delirious horror, the soft and nearly imperceptible waving of the sable draperies which enwrapped the walls of the apartment. And then my vision fell upon the seven tall candles upon the table. At first they wore the aspect of charity, and seemed white slender angels who would save me; but then, all at once, there came a most deadly nausea over my spirit, and I felt every fibre in my frame thrill as if I had touched the wire of a galvanic battery, while the angel forms became meaningless spectres, with heads of flame, and I saw that from them there would be no help.

And then there stole into my fancy, like a rich musical note, the thought of what sweet rest there must be in the grave. The thought came gently and stealthily, and it seemed long before it attained full appreciation; but just as my spirit came at length properly to feel and entertain it, the figures of the judges vanished, as if magically, from before me; the tall candles sank into nothingness; their flames went out utterly; the blackness of darkness supervened; all sensations appeared swallowed up in a mad rushing descent as of the soul into Hades. Then silence, and stillness, and night were the universe.

I had swooned; but still will not say that all of consciousness was lost. Amid frequent and thoughtful endeavours to remember; amid earnest struggles to regather some token of the state of seeming nothingness into which my soul had lapsed, there have been moments when I have dreamed of success; there have been brief, very brief periods when I have conjured up remembrances which the lucid reason of a later epoch assures me could have had reference only to that condition of seeming unconsciousness. These shadows of memory tell, indistinctly, of tall figures that lifted and bore me in silence down—down—still down— till a hideous dizziness oppressed me at the mere idea of the interminable-ness of the descent. They tell also of a vague horror at my heart, on account of that heart's unnatural stillness. Then comes a sense of sudden motionlessness throughout all things; as if those who bore me (a ghastly train!) had outrun, in their descent, the limits of the limitless, and paused from the wearisomeness of their toil. After this I call to mind flatness and dampness; and then all is *madness*—the madness of a memory which busies itself among forbidden things.

So far, I had not opened my eyes. I felt that I lay upon my back, un-bound. I reached out my hand, and it fell heavily upon something damp and hard. There I suffered it to remain for many minutes, while I strove to imagine where and *what* I could be. I longed, yet dared not, to employ

343

my vision. I dreaded the first glance at objects around me. It was not that I feared to look upon things horrible, but that I grew aghast lest there should be *nothing* to see. At length, with a wild desperation at heart, I quickly unclosed my eyes. My worst thoughts, then, were confirmed. The blackness of eternal night encompassed me. I struggled for breath. The intensity of the darkness seemed to oppress and stifle me. The atmosphere was intolerably close. I still lay quietly, and made effort to exercise my reason. I brought to mind the Inquisitorial proceedings, and attempted from that point to deduce my real condition. The sentence had passed; and it appeared to me that a very long interval of time had since elapsed. Yet not for a moment did I suppose myself actually dead. Such a supposition, notwithstanding what we read in fiction, is altogether inconsistent with real existence—but where and in what state was I?

A fearful idea now suddenly drove the blood in torrents upon my heart, and for a brief period I once more relapsed into insensibility. Upon recovering, I at once started to my feet, trembling convulsively in every fibre. I thrust my arms wildly above and around me in all directions. I felt nothing; yet dreaded to move a step, lest I should be impeded by the walls of a *tomb*. Perspiration burst from every pore, and stood in cold beads upon my forehead. The agony of suspense grew at length intolerable, and I cautiously moved forward, with my arms extended, and my eyes straining from their sockets, in the hope of catching some faint ray of light. I proceeded for many paces; but still all was blackness and vacancy. I breathed more freely. It seemed evident that mine was not, at least, the most hideous of fates.

And now, as I still continued to step cautiously onward, there came thronging upon my recollection a thousand vague rumours of the horrors of Toledo. Of the dungeons there had been strange things narrated—fables I had always deemed them—but yet strange, and too ghastly to repeat, save in a whisper. Was I left to perish of starvation in this subterranean world of darkness; or what fate, perhaps even more fearful, awaited me? That the result would be death, and a death of more than customary bitterness, I knew too well the character of my judges to doubt. The mode and the hour were all that occupied or distracted me.

My outstretched hands at length encountered some solid obstruction.

It was a wall, seemingly of stone masonry—very smooth, slimy, and cold. I followed it up, stepping with all the careful distrust with which certain antique narratives had inspired me. This process, however, afforded me no means of ascertaining the dimensions of my dungeon, as I might make its circuit, and return to the point whence I set out, without being aware of the fact, so perfectly uniform seemed the wall. I therefore sought the knife which had been in my pocket, when led into the inquisitorial chamber, but it was gone; my clothes had been exchanged for a wrapper of coarse serge. I had thought of forcing the blade in some minute crevice of the masonry, so as to identify my point of departure. The difficulty, nevertheless, was but trivial; although, in the disorder of my fancy, it seemed at first insuperable. I tore a part of the hem from the robe and placed the fragment at full length, and at right-angles to the wall. In groping my way around the prison, I could not fail to encounter this rag upon completing the circuit. So, at least, I thought; but I had not counted upon the extent of the dungeon, or upon my own weakness. The ground was moist and slippery. I staggered onward for some time, when I stumbled and fell. My excessive fatigue induced me to remain prostrate; and sleep soon overtook me as I lay.

Upon awaking, and stretching forth an arm, I found beside me a loaf and a pitcher with water. I was too much exhausted to reflect upon this circumstance, but ate and drank with avidity. Shortly afterward I resumed my tour around the prison, and, with much toil, came at last upon the fragment of the serge. Up to the period when I fell, I had counted fifty-two paces, and, upon resuming my walk, I had counted forty-eight more—when I arrived at the rag. There were in all, then, a hundred paces; and, admitting two paces to the yard, I presumed the dungeon to be fifty yards in circuit. I had met, however, with many angles in the wall, and thus I could form no guess at the shape of the vault; for vault I could not help supposing it to be.

I had little object—certainly no hope—in these researches; but a vague curiosity prompted me to continue them. Quitting the wall, I resolved to cross the area of the enclosure. At first, I proceeded with extreme caution, for the floor, although seemingly of solid material, was treacherous with slime. At length, however, I took courage, and did not hesitate to step firmly—endeavouring to cross in as direct a line as possible. I had advanced some ten or twelve paces in this manner, when the remnant of the torn hem of my robe became entangled between my legs. I stepped on it, and fell violently on my face.

In the confusion attending my fall, I did not immediately apprehend a somewhat startling circumstance, which yet, in a few seconds afterward, and while I still lay prostrate, arrested my attention. It was this: my chin rested upon the floor of the prison, but my lips, and the upper portion of my head, already seemingly at a less elevation than the chin, touched nothing. At the same time, my forehead seemed bathed in a clammy vapour, and the peculiar smell of decayed fungus arose to my nostrils. I put forward my arm, and shuddered to find that I had fallen at the very brink of a circular pit, whose extent, of course, I had no means of ascertaining at the moment. Groping about the masonry just below the margin, I succeeded in dislodging a small fragment, and let it fall into the abyss. For many seconds I hearkened to its reverberations as it dashed against the sides of the chasm in its descent. At length, there was a sullen plunge into water, succeeded by loud echoes. At the same moment, there came a sound resembling the quick opening, and as rapid closing, of a door overhead, while a faint gleam of light flashed suddenly through the gloom, and as suddenly faded away.

I saw clearly the doom which had been prepared for me, and congratulated myself upon the timely accident by which I had escaped. Another step before my fall, and the world had seen me no more. And the death just avoided was of that very character which I had regarded as fabulous and frivolous in the tales respecting the Inquisition. To the victims of its tyranny, there was the choice of death with its direst physical agonies, or death with its most hideous moral horrors. I had been reserved for the latter. By long suffering my nerves had been unstrung, until I trembled at the sound of my own voice, and had become in every respect a fitting subject for the species of torture which awaited me.

Shaking in every limb, I groped my way back to the wall—resolving there to perish rather than risk the terrors of the wells, of which my imagination now pictured many in various positions about the dungeon. In other conditions of mind, I might have had courage to end my misery at once, by a plunge into one of these abysses; but now I was the veriest of cowards. Neither could I forget what I had read of these pits—that the *sudden* extinction of life formed no part of their most horrible plan.

Agitation of spirit kept me awake for many long hours; but at length I again slumbered. Upon arousing, I found by my side, as before, a loaf and a pitcher of water. A burning thirst consumed me, and I emptied the vessel at a draught. It must have been drugged—for scarcely had I drunk before I became irresistibly drowsy. A deep sleep fell upon me—a sleep like that of death. How long it lasted, of course, I know not; but when, once again, I unclosed my eyes, the objects around me were visible. By a wild, sulphurous lustre, the origin of which I could not at first determine, I was enabled to see the extent and aspect of the prison.

In its size I had been greatly mistaken. The whole circuit of its walls did not exceed twenty-five yards. For some minutes this fact occasioned me a world of vain trouble; vain indeed—for what could be of less importance, under the terrible circumstances which environed me, than the mere dimensions of my dungeon? But my soul took a wild interest in trifles, and I busied myself in endeavours to account for the error I had committed in my measurement. The truth at length flashed upon me. In my first attempt at exploration I had counted fifty-two paces, up to the period when I fell; I must then have been within a pace or two of the fragment of serge; in fact, I had nearly performed the circuit of the vault. I then slept—and, upon awaking, I must have returned upon my steps—thus supposing the circuit nearly double what it actually was. My confusion of mind prevented me from observing that I began my tour with the wall to the left, and ended it with the wall to the right.

I had been deceived, too, in respect to the shape of the enclosure. In feeling my way, I had found many angles, and thus deduced an idea of great irregularity; so potent is the effect of total darkness upon one arousing from lethargy or sleep! The angles were simply those of a few slight depressions, or niches, at odd intervals. The general shape of the prison was square. What I had taken for masonry seemed now to be iron, or some other metal, in huge plates, whose sutures or joints occasioned the depression. The entire surface of this metallic enclosure was rudely daubed in all the hideous and repulsive devices to which the charnel superstition of the monks has given rise. The figures of fiends in aspects of menace, with skeleton forms, and other more really fearful images, overspread and disfigured the walls. I observed that the outlines

347

of these monstrosities were sufficiently distinct, but that the colours seemed faded and blurred, as if from the effects of a damp atmosphere. I now noticed the floor, too, which was of stone. In the centre yawned the circular pit from whose jaws I had escaped; but it was the only one in the dungeon.

All this I saw indistinctly and by much effort—for my personal condition had been greatly changed during slumber. I now lay upon my back, and at full length, on a species of low framework of wood. To this I was securely bound by a long strap resembling a surcingle. It passed in many convolutions about my limbs and body, leaving at liberty only my head and my left arm to such extent that I could, by dint of much exertion, supply myself with food from an earthen dish which lay by my side on the floor. I saw, to my horror, that the pitcher had been removed. I say, to my horror—for I was consumed with intolerable thirst. This thirst it appeared to be the design of my persecutors to stimulate—for the food in the dish was meat pungently seasoned.

Looking upward, I surveyed the ceiling of my prison. It was some thirty or forty feet overhead, and constructed much as the side walls. In one of its panels a very singular figure riveted my whole attention. It was the painted figure of Time as he is commonly represented, save that, in lieu of a scythe, he held what, at a casual glance, I supposed to be the pictured image of a huge pendulum, such as we see on antique clocks. There was something, however, in the appearance of this machine which caused me to regard it more attentively. While I gazed directly upward at it (for its position was immediately over my own), I fancied that I saw it in motion. In an instant afterward the fancy was confirmed. Its sweep was brief, and, of course, slow. I watched it for some minutes, somewhat in fear, but more in wonder. Wearied at length with observing its dull movement, I turned my eyes upon the other objects in the cell.

A slight noise attracted my notice, and looking to the floor, I saw several enormous rats traversing it. They had issued from the well, which lay just within view to my right. Even then, while I gazed, they came up in troops, hurriedly, with ravenous eyes, allured by the scent of the meat. From this it required much effort and attention to scare them away.

It might have been half an hour, perhaps even an hour (for I could take but imperfect note of time) before I again cast my eyes upward. What I then saw confounded and amazed me. The sweep of the pendulum had increased in extent by nearly a yard. As a natural consequence, its velocity was also much greater. But what mainly disturbed me was the idea that it had perceptibly *descended*. I now observed—with what horror it is needless to say—that its nether extremity was formed of a crescent of glittering steel, about a foot in length from horn to horn; the horns upward, and the under edge evidently as keen as that of a razor. Like a razor also, it seemed massy and heavy, tapering from the edge into a solid and broad structure above. It was appended to a weighty rod of brass, and the whole hissed as it swung through the air.

I could no longer doubt the doom prepared for me by monkish ingenuity in torture. My awareness of the pit had become known to the inquisitorial agents—*the pit* whose horrors had been destined for so bold a recusant as myself—*the pit*, typical of hell, and regarded by rumour as the Ultima Thule of all their punishments. The plunge into this pit I had avoided by the merest of accidents, and I knew that surprise, or entrapment into torment, formed an important portion of all the grotesqueries of these dungeon deaths. Having failed to fall, it was no part of the demon plan to hurl me into the abyss; and thus (there being no alternative) a different and a milder destruction awaited me. Milder! I half smiled in my agony as I thought of such application of such a term.

What boots it to tell of the long, long hours of horror more than mortal, during which I counted the rushing oscillations of the steel! Inch by inch—line by line—with a descent only appreciable at intervals that seemed ages—down and still down it came! Days passed—it might have been that many days passed—ere it swept so closely over me as to fan me with its acrid breath. The odour of the sharp steel forced itself into my nostrils. I prayed—I wearied heaven with my prayer for its more speedy descent. I grew frantically mad, and struggled to force myself upward against the sweep of the fearful scimitar. And then I fell suddenly calm, and lay smiling at the glittering death, as a child at some rare bauble.

There was another interval of utter insensibility; it was brief, for upon again lapsing into life, there had been no perceptible descent in the pendulum. But it might have been long—for I knew there were demons

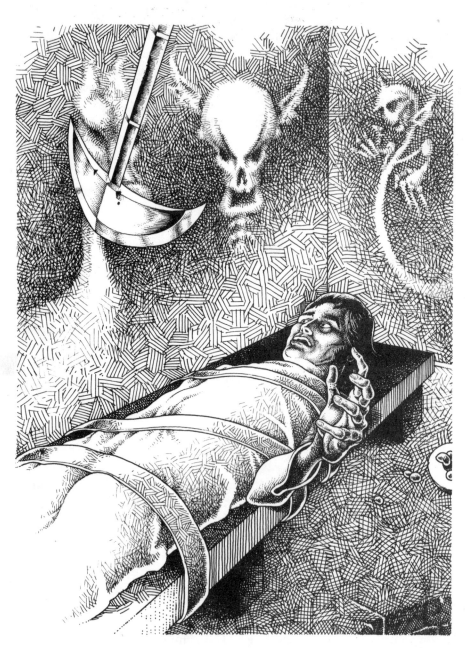

'*Down, relentlessly down! I shrank convulsively at its every sweep.*'

who took note of my swoon, and who could have arrested the vibration at pleasure.

Upon my recovery, too, I felt very—oh, inexpressibly—sick and weak, as if through long starvation. Even amid the agonies of that period the human nature craved food. With painful effort I outstretched my left arm as far as my bonds permitted, and took possession of the small remnant which had been spared me by the rats. As I put a portion of it within my lips, there rushed to my mind a half-formed thought of joy—of hope. Yet what business had *I* with hope? It was, as I say, a half-formed thought—man has many such, which are never completed. I felt that it was of joy—of hope; but I felt also that it had perished in its formation. In vain I struggled to perfect—to regain it. Long suffering had nearly annihilated all my ordinary powers of mind. I was an imbecile—an idiot.

The vibration of the pendulum was at right-angles to my length. I saw that the crescent was designed to cross the region of the heart. It would fray the serge of my robe—it would return and repeat its operations—again—and again. Notwithstanding its terrifically wide sweep (some thirty feet or more), and the hissing vigour of its descent, sufficient to sunder these very walls of iron, still the fraying of my robe would be all that, for several minutes, it would accomplish. And at this thought I paused. I dared not go farther than this reflection. I dwelt upon it with a persistent attention—as if, in so dwelling, I could arrest *here* the descent of the steel. I forced myself to ponder upon the sound of the crescent as it should pass across the garment—upon the peculiar thrilling sensation which the friction of cloth produces on the nerves. I pondered upon all this frivolity until my teeth were on edge.

Down—steadily down it crept. I took a frenzied pleasure in contrasting its downward with its lateral velocity. To the right—to the left—far and wide—with the shriek of a damned spirit! To my heart, with the stealthy pace of the tiger! I alternately laughed and howled, as the one or the other idea grew predominant.

Down—certainly, relentlessly down! It vibrated within three inches of my bosom! I struggled violently—furiously—to free my left arm. This was free only from the elbow to the hand. I could reach the latter, from the platter beside me, to my mouth, with great effort, but no farther. Could I have broken the fastenings above the elbow, I would have seized and attempted to arrest the pendulum. I might as well have attempted to arrest an avalanche!

Down—still unceasingly—still inevitably down! I gasped and struggled at each vibration. I shrank convulsively at its every sweep. My eyes followed its outward or upward whirls with the eagerness of the most unmeaning despair; they closed themselves spasmodically at the descent, although death would have been a relief, oh, how unspeakable! Still I quivered in every nerve to think how slight a sinking of the machinery would precipitate that keen, glistening axe upon my bosom. It was *hope* that prompted the nerve to quiver—the frame to shrink. It was *hope*—the hope that triumphs on the rack—that whispers to the death-condemned even in the dungeons of the Inquisition.

I saw that some ten or twelve vibrations would bring the steel in actual contact with my robe—and with this observation there suddenly came over my spirit all the keen, collected calmness of despair. For the first time during many hours—or perhaps days—I *thought*. It now occurred to me that the bandage, or surcingle, which enveloped me, was *unique*. I was tied by no separate cord. The first stroke of the razor-like crescent athwart any portion of the band would so detach it that it might be unwound from my person by means of my left hand. But how fearful, in that case, the proximity of the steel! The result of the slightest struggle, how deadly! Was it likely, moreover, that the minions of the torturer had not foreseen and provided for this possibility! Was it probable that the bandage crossed my bosom in the track of the pendulum? Dreading to find my faint, and, as it seemed, my last hope frustrated, I so far elevated my head as to obtain a distinct view of my breast. The surcingle enveloped my limbs and body close in all directions—*save in the path of the destroying crescent.*

Scarcely had I dropped my head back into its original position, when there flashed upon my mind what I cannot better describe than as the unformed half of that idea of deliverance to which I have previously alluded, and of which a part only floated indeterminately through my brain when I raised food to my burning lips. The whole thought was now present—feeble, scarcely sane, scarcely definite—but still entire. I proceeded at once, with the nervous energy of despair, to attempt its execution.

For many hours the immediate vicinity of the low framework upon which I lay, had been literally swarming with rats. They were wild, bold, ravenous—their red eyes glaring upon me as if they waited but for motionlessness on my part to make me their prey. 'To what food,' I thought, 'have they been accustomed in the well?'

They had devoured, in spite of all my efforts to prevent them, all but a small remnant of the contents of the dish. I had fallen into an habitual see-saw, or wave of the hand, about the platter; and at length the unconscious uniformity of the movement deprived it of effect. In their voracity, the vermin frequently fastened their sharp fangs in my fingers. With the particles of the oil and spicy food which now remained, I thoroughly rubbed the bandage wherever I could reach it; then, raising my hand from the floor, I lay breathlessly still.

At first, the ravenous animals were startled and terrified at the change—at the cessation of movement. They shrank alarmedly back; many sought the well. But this was only for a moment. I had not counted in vain upon their voracity. Observing that I remained without motion, one or two of the boldest leaped upon the framework, and smelt at the surcingle. This seemed the signal for a general rush. Forth from the well they hurried in fresh troops. They clung to the wood—they overran it, and leaped in hundreds upon my person. The measured movement of the pendulum disturbed them not at all. Avoiding its strokes, they busied themselves with the anointed bandage. They pressed—they swarmed upon me in ever accumulating heaps. They writhed upon my throat; their cold lips sought my own; I was half stifled by their thronging pressure; disgust, for which the world has no name, swelled my bosom, and chilled, with a heavy clamminess, my heart. Yet one minute, and I felt that the struggle would be over. Plainly I perceived the loosening of the bandage. I knew that in more than one place it must be already severed. With a more than human resolution I lay still.

Nor had I erred in my calculations—nor had I endured in vain. I at length felt that I was *free*. The surcingle hung in ribands from my body. But the stroke of the pendulum already pressed upon my bosom. It had divided the serge of the robe. It had cut through the linen beneath. Twice again it swung, and a sharp sense of pain shot through every nerve. But the moment of escape had arrived. At a wave of my hand my deliverers hurried tumultuously away. With a steady movement—

cautious, sidelong, shrinking, and slow—I slid from the embrace of the bandage and beyond the reach of the scimitar. For the moment, at least, *I was free.*

Free!—and in the grasp of the Inquisition! I had scarcely stepped from my wooden bed of horror upon the stone floor of the prison, when the motion of the hellish machine ceased, and I beheld it drawn up, by some invisible force, through the ceiling. This was a lesson which I took desperately to heart. My every motion was undoubtedly watched. Free!—I had but escaped death in one form of agony, to be delivered unto worse than death in some other. With that thought I rolled my eyes nervously around on the barriers of iron that hemmed me in. Something unusual—some change which, at first, I could not appreciate distinctly—it was obvious, had taken place in the apartment. For many minutes of a dreamy and trembling abstraction, I busied myself in vain, unconnected conjecture.

During this period, I became aware, for the first time, of the origin of the sulphurous light which illumined the cell. It proceeded from a fissure, about half an inch in width, extending entirely around the prison at the base of the walls, which thus appeared, and were completely separated from the floor. I endeavoured, but of course in vain, to look through the aperture.

As I arose from the attempt, the mystery of the alteration in the chamber broke at once upon my understanding. I have observed that, although the outlines of the figures upon the walls were sufficiently distinct, yet the colours seemed blurred and indefinite. These colours had now assumed, and were momentarily assuming, a startling and most intense brilliancy, that gave to the spectral and fiendish portraitures an aspect that might have thrilled even firmer nerves than my own. Demon eyes, of a wild and ghastly vivacity, glared upon me in a thousand directions, where none had been visible before, and gleamed with the lurid lustre of a fire that I could not force my imagination to regard as unreal.

Unreal! Even while I breathed there came to my nostrils the breath of the vapour of heated iron! A suffocating odour pervaded the prison! A deeper glow settled each moment in the eyes that glared at my agonies! A richer tint of crimson diffused itself over the pictured horrors of blood. I panted! I gasped for breath! There could be no doubt of the design of my tormentors. Oh! most unrelenting! Oh! most demoniac of men! I shrank from the glowing metal to the centre of the cell. Amid the thought of the fiery destruction that impended, the idea of the coolness of the well came over my soul like balm. I rushed to its deadly brink. I threw my straining vision below. The glare from the enkindled roof illumined its inmost recesses. Yet, for a wild moment, did my spirit refuse to comprehend the meaning of what I saw. At length it forced—it wrestled its way into my soul—it burned itself in upon my shuddering reason. Oh! for a voice to speak! Oh! horror! Oh! any horror but this! With a shriek, I rushed from the margin, and buried my face in my hands—weeping bitterly.

The heat rapidly increased, and once again I looked up, shuddering as with a fit of the fever. There had been a second change in the cell—and now the change was obviously in the *form*. As before, it was in vain that I at first endeavoured to appreciate or understand what was taking place. But not long was I left in doubt. The Inquisitorial vengeance had been hurried by my twofold escape, and there was to be no more dallying with the King of Terrors. The room had been square. I saw that two of its iron angles were now acute—two, consequently, obtuse. The fearful difference quickly increased with a low rumbling or moaning sound. In an instant the apartment had shifted its form into that of a lozenge. But the alteration stopped not here—I neither hoped nor desired it to stop. I could have clasped the red walls to my bosom as a garment of eternal peace. 'Death,' I said, 'any death but that of the pit!' Fool! Might I not have known that *into the pit* it was the object of the burning iron to urge me? Could I resist its glow? Or, if even that, could I withstand its pressure?

And now, flatter and flatter grew the lozenge, with a rapidity that left me no time for contemplation. Its centre, and of course, its greatest width, came just over the yawning gulf. I shrank back—but the closing walls pressed me resistlessly onward. At length for my seared and writhing body there was no longer an inch of foothold on the firm floor of the prison. I struggled no more, but the agony of my soul found vent in one loud, long, and final scream of despair. I felt that I tottered upon the brink—I averted my eyes ——

There was a discordant hum of human voices! There was a loud blast as of many trumpets! There was a harsh grating as of a thousand

355

thunders! The fiery walls rushed back! An outstretched arm caught my own as I fell, fainting, into the abyss. It was that of General Lasalle. The French Army had entered Toledo. The Inquisition was in the hands of its enemies.

THE LITTLE SARDINIAN DRUMMER

Edmondo De Amicis

On 24 July 1848, the first day of the Battle of Custoza, sixty soldiers belonging to an Italian regiment of infantry were ordered to garrison a lonely house on a height near by. But they were suddenly attacked by two companies of Austrians, who, assaulting them on several sides, scarcely gave them time to take refuge within the house and barricade the door, leaving their dead and wounded on the field.

The door being well secured, the Italian soldiers hastened to the windows on the ground floor and upper floor, and opened a deadly fire on the besiegers, who replied vigorously as they slowly approached in the form of a semi-circle.

The sixty Italian soldiers were commanded by two subaltern officers, and by a tall, silent, grim old captain, with white hair and whiskers.

With them was a little Sardinian drummer, a boy scarcely more than fourteen years old, but who did not look even twelve, with his dark, olive skin, and black, deep-set eyes with fire in them.

From a room on the upper storey the captain directed the defence, every order sounding like a pistol shot, his iron countenance showing not the slightest emotion.

The little drummer, pale, but with his feet firmly planted on the table, and holding fast to the walls, stretched out his head and neck to look from the window, and saw through the smoke the Austrians steadily advancing over the fields.

The house was near the top of a very steep hillside, so that only one small high window in the upper floor looked out over the crest. The Austrians did not threaten that side, nor was there anybody on the hill-top. The fire was directed against the front and the two sides.

The firing was infernal—a close, heavy hailstorm of balls rained upon the walls and through the broken roof, tearing out the ceiling, shattering the beams, doors, furniture, filling the air with fragments, plaster, and clouds of lime and dust, utensils and broken glass whizzing, clattering on their heads, rebounding from the walls with a terrifying noise and clash.

Now and then a soldier stationed at the windows fell inward, and was pushed to one side; others staggered from room to room, staunching their wounds with their hands. In the kitchen lay one soldier, pierced through the forehead. The enemy was closing in. At last the captain, until then impassive, began to show signs of uneasiness, and hurriedly left the room, followed by a sergeant. In a few moments the sergeant came rushing back, called the drummer, telling him to follow.

The boy raced up the stairs after him, and entered a dilapidated garret, in which he saw the captain with pencil and paper in hand, leaning on the window-sill, and lying on the ground at his feet was a rope belonging to the well.

The captain folded the paper, and, fixing on the boy those cold, grey eyes before which every soldier trembled, said abruptly:

'Drummer!'

The little drummer's hand went up to his cap.

'Thou art brave,' said the captain.

The boy's eyes flashed. 'Yes, captain,' he answered.

'Look down yonder,' said the captain, taking him to the window, 'on the ground, near the house of Villafranca, where those bayonets glisten. There is our regiment, motionless. Take this paper, grasp this rope, let yourself down from the window, cross the hill like lightning, rush through the fields, reach our men, and give this paper to the first officer you see. Take off your belt and knapsack.'

The drummer took off his belt and knapsack, and hid the paper in his breast pocket; the sergeant threw out the rope, holding fast one end; the captain helped the boy to jump through the window, his back towards the fields.

'Be careful,' said he, 'the salvation of this detachment depends on thy valour and thy legs.'

'Trust me, captain,' said the drummer, sliding down.

'Crouch low on dropping,' warned the captain, taking hold of the rope.

'Have no fear.'

'God speed thee!'

In a few moments the boy was on the ground, the sergeant drew up the rope and disappeared, while the captain hastened to the little window and saw the drummer racing down the hill. He now hoped he would escape unseen, but five or six little clouds of dust rising from the ground warned him that the boy had been discovered by the Austrians, who were firing down from the top of the hill. Those little clouds were the earth torn up by the balls. But the drummer continued running at full speed. After a while the captain exclaimed in consternation: 'Dead!' but scarcely was the word out of his mouth when he saw the little drummer rise.

'Ah, it was but a fall!' said he, and breathed again.

The drummer again ran on, but he limped.

'He has sprained his foot,' said the captain.

A little cloud of dust rose here and there around the boy, but always farther from him.

He was beyond their reach. The captain uttered a cry of triumph; but his eyes followed him, for it was a question of minutes. If he did not soon reach the regiment with the note, asking for immediate help, all his soldiers would be killed, or he would be obliged to surrender and become a prisoner of war.

The boy ran for a while rapidly, then he stopped to limp; again he ran on, but every few seconds he stopped to limp.

'Perhaps a ball has bruised his foot,' thought the captain, and he noted all his movements, and in his excitement he talked to the drummer as if he could hear him. Every moment his eyes measured the distance between the boy and the bayonets that glistened below on the

359

plain, in the midst of the golden wheat-fields.

Meantime he heard the whistling and the crash of the balls in the rooms below, the voice of command, the shouts of rage of the officers and sergeants; the sharp cries of the wounded, and the noise of broken furniture and crumbling plaster.

'Courage! Valour!' he cried, his eyes following the drummer in the distance. 'Forward! Run! Curse it! He stops! Ah, he is up again, forward!'

An officer out of breath comes to tell him that the enemy, without ceasing fire, wave a white handkerchief, demanding their surrender.

'Let no one answer!' shouts the captain, without taking his eyes from the boy, who was now in the valley, but who no longer ran, and who seemed hopeless of reaching the regiment.

'Forward! Run!' cried the captain with teeth and fists clenched. 'Bleed to death, die, unfortunate boy, but reach your destination!' Then he uttered a horrible oath. 'Ah, the idler has sat down!'

In fact, the boy's head, all that could be seen above the wheat, now disappeared as if he had fallen. After a moment his head was again seen, then he was lost behind the wheat-field, and the captain saw him no more.

Then he hurried downstairs. The balls rained, the rooms were full of wounded, some of whom rolled over like drunken men, clutching at the furniture; the walls and floors were covered with blood. Dead bodies lay across the threshold; the lieutenant's arm was broken by a ball. Smoke and powder filled the rooms.

'Courage!' shouted the captain. 'Stand to your post! Help is coming! Courage a little longer!'

The Austrians had approached closer. Their disfigured faces could be seen through the smoke. Through the crash of balls could be heard the savage cries insulting them, demanding their surrender, and threatening to cut their throats. A soldier, terrified, withdrew from the window, and the sergeant again pushed him forward.

The fire of the besieged slackened. Discouragement showed on every face; resistance seemed no longer possible. The moment came when the Austrians redoubled their efforts, and a voice thundered, at first in German, then in Italian: 'Surrender!'

'No!' shouted the captain from a window. The fire became more deadly, more furious on both sides. Other soldiers fell. There was more than one window without defenders. The fatal moment was imminent. The captain's voice died away in his throat as he exclaimed: 'They do not come! They do not come!'

And he ran furiously from side to side, brandishing his sabre convulsively, ready to die. Then a sergeant, rushing down from the garret, shouted: 'They come!'

'Ah, they come!' shouted the captain joyfully.

On hearing that cry all—the well, the wounded, sergeants and officers—crowded to the windows and again the fierceness of the defence was redoubled. Soon the defenders noticed among the enemy the beginning of disorder. Nevertheless, the captain had to gather the survivors on the lower floor to resist with fixed bayonets a final attack by the Austrians.

Then he went upstairs. Scarcely had he mounted when he heard the sound of hurried footsteps, accompanied by a formidable 'Hurrah!' and the pointed hats of the Italian carbineers appeared through the smoke, a squadron at double-quick, a brilliant flash of swords whirled through the air above their heads, their shoulders, their backs; then out charged the little detachment, with fixed bayonets. The enemy wavered, rallied, then at last began to retreat. The position was saved, and shortly after two battalions of Italian infantry and two cannon occupied the height.

The captain and the surviving soldiers rejoined their regiment, fought again, and the captain was slightly wounded in the hand by a spent ball during the last bayonet charge. The victory on that day was won by the Italians.

But the following day the battle continued. The Italians were beaten, in spite of heroic resistance, by superior numbers, and on the morning of 26 July they were in full retreat toward the Mincio.

The captain marched at the head of his company, weary and silent, arriving at sunset at Goito on the Mincio. He immediately sought his lieutenant, who, with his arm broken, had been picked up by the ambulance, and who must have arrived before he did. They pointed out to him a church in which the field hospital had been installed. He went there and found the church filled with the wounded lying in two rows of cots. Two physicians and several practitioners were busily coming and going, and nothing was heard but groans and stifled cries.

The captain heard his name called faintly. It was the little drummer.

Scarcely had the captain entered when he stopped and glanced around in search of his subordinate.

At that moment he heard, near by, his name called faintly:

'Captain!'

He turned. It was the little drummer. He was stretched upon a wooden cot, covered up to the neck with a coarse old red and white check window curtain, his arms lying outside, pale and thin, but with his eyes burning like two coals of fire.

'What! Is it thou?' asked the captain in a surprised, abrupt manner. 'Bravo, thou hast fulfilled thy duty.'

'I did all that was possible,' replied the drummer.

'Art thou wounded?' asked the captain, glancing around at the beds in search of his lieutenant.

'What could you expect?' replied the boy, who was eager to speak of the honour of being wounded for the first time, else he would not have dared to open his lips before his captain.

'I ran as long as I could with my head down, but, though I crouched, the Austrians saw me immediately. I would have arrived twenty

362

minutes earlier had they not wounded me. Fortunately I met a captain of the general's staff, to whom I gave the note. But it was with great effort I got along after that. I was dying with thirst. I was afraid I could not arrive in time. I cried with rage, thinking that every minute's delay sent one of our men to the other world. But I did all I could. I am content. But look, captain, and excuse me, you are bleeding!'

In fact, from the palm of the badly bandaged hand the blood was flowing.

'Do you wish me to tighten the bandage, captain? Let me have it for a moment.'

The captain gave him his left hand, and stretched out his right hand to help tie the knot; but scarcely had the little fellow risen from the pillow when he turned pale, and had to lie back again.

'Enough! Enough!' said the captain, looking at him and withdrawing his bandaged hand, which the drummer wished to retain. 'Take care of yourself instead of thinking of others, for slight wounds, if neglected, may have grave consequences.'

The little drummer shook his head.

'But thou,' said the captain, looking attentively at him, 'thou must have lost much blood to be so weak.'

'Lost much blood?' repeated the boy smiling. 'Something more than blood. Look!' and he threw down the coverlet. The captain drew back in horror.

The boy had but one leg; the left leg had been amputated above the knee. The stump was wrapped in bloody cloths.

Just then a small, fat army physician in shirt-sleeves passed.

'Ah, captain,' said he rapidly, pointing out the little drummer; 'there is an unfortunate case. That leg could have been easily saved had he not forced it so much, caused inflammation; it was necessary to amputate it. But he is brave, I assure you. He did not shed a tear or utter a cry. I was proud, while operating, to think he was an Italian boy, my word of honour! Faith, he comes of good stock!'

And he went on his way.

The captain wrinkled his bushy white eyebrows, and looked fixedly at the little drummer while covering him with the coverlet. Then, slowly, almost unconsciously, yet still looking at him, his hand went to his cap, which he took off.

'Captain!' exclaimed the astonished boy. 'What, captain, for me?'

The rough old soldier, who had never spoken a gentle word to an inferior, replied in a soft and exceedingly affectionate voice:

'I am but a captain; thou art a hero!'

Then he threw his arms about the little drummer and kissed him with all his heart.

CONDEMNED TO DEATH

André Devigny

André Devigny was a member of the French Underground operating in Nice. On 17 April 1943 he was arrested by the Gestapo and taken to Montluc military prison in Lyons, where he was brutally beaten up, condemned to death, handcuffed and placed in solitary confinement awaiting execution.

At first the small cell with its solid oak door seemed to offer no opportunities for escape. Then, with a pin given to him by one of his fellow-prisoners, Devigny learned how to pick the lock on his handcuffs so that he could take them off and put them on at will. This gave him freedom within the confines of his cell.

Next he noticed that although the door was constructed of thick oak boards these were fastened together by tongues of softer wood. By grinding the handle of his iron spoon on the stone of the cell floor the prisoner managed to make himself a joiner's chisel with which, after many days of patient work, he was able to remove first one, then several of the boards. This gave him access to the corridor outside, but he was still far from free. He knew that his cell was high up in the building and that his only escape route lay upwards to the roof.

With infinite patience Devigny began to twist himself a rope from strips torn from his bedding and reinforced with wire taken from his mattress. When his supply was exhausted he used his clothing—everything he could lay hands on. At last he had made sixty-five feet of rope.

Devigny's plan was to climb through a skylight in the ceiling of the corridor outside his cell, cross the roof of the building and lower himself to an inner courtyard. From here he would climb to the roof of another building, cross this and throw his rope to the outer wall of the prison. To make this feat possible he needed grappling-irons on the end of the rope. These he made from the metal frame which surrounded the electric light in his cell.

*Just as Devigny was ready to make his attempt another prisoner
named Gimenez was put in to share his cell. Devigny knew that should
he escape and leave Gimenez behind in the cell the boy, only eighteen
years of age, would be shot for not giving the alarm. The only thing
was to take him along too . . .*

Gimenez took the boards from me one after the other and stacked them
away. In the half-light we could just see the faint, barred outline of
the gallery rails; it was too dark to make out the cell doors on the other
side. I put out my head and listened. Only the creaking of beds as
sleepers turned over, and occasionally a bucket scraping along the
floor, broke the silence—that hostile silence against which we had to
struggle for what seemed like a century.

For two long minutes I remained motionless. Then I pushed one arm
out into the corridor, turned on one side, and crawled forward like a
snake. I stood up cautiously. The light was on down below; but, as
usual, its feeble rays were swallowed up in the vast gloom of the hall.

Gimenez passed me the light rope, which I at once took over to the
latrines. It was followed by the rest of our equipment. I went back to
the cell door to help Giminez. We both stood there for a moment,
listening. All was still. Slowly we moved towards our starting point.

I tied one end of the light rope round my waist—the end, that is,
which had no grappling-iron attached to it. Three steps, and we were
standing by the metal rod. The rope would pay out as I climbed; I left
it coiled loosely on the ground. Gimenez braced himself against the
wall and gave me a leg up. I stood on his shoulders, both hands gripping
the rod, and tried to reach the edge of the skylight. I pulled myself up
slowly, with all the strength I had. But it proved too much of an effort;
I had to come down again.

The weeks of confinement I had undergone since my previous
successful attempt must have sapped my strength more than I thought.
We went back to the latrines to give me a few moments' rest. I inhaled
deeply, waiting till I got my breath back before making a second
attempt.

I had to get up there, whatever happened.

Jaws clenched, I began to climb. I got my feet from Gimenez's
hands to his shoulders, and then to his head. My fingers gripped the

366

metal rod convulsively. Somehow I went on, inch by inch; at last my fingers found the frame of the skylight, and I got my legs over the horizontal rod, which shook in its rings as my weight hung from it. I got round the ratchet supporting the skylight without touching it. I was sweating and panting like a man struggling out of a quicksand, or a shipwrecked sailor clinging desperately to a reef. Eyes dilated, every muscle cracking, I gradually worked my way through the opening. Then I stopped for a minute to get my strength back. I had managed to preserve absolute silence from start to finish.

A few lights twinkled in the distance. The fresh night air cooled my damp face. It was very still. Slowly my breathing became normal again. Carefully I put out one hand on the gritty surface of the flat roof, taking care to avoid touching the fragile glass in the skylight itself; this done, I hauled myself up a little further and got my other hand into a similar position. With a final effort I completed the operation, and found myself standing upright on the roof, dazed by the clear splendour of the night sky. The silence drummed in my ears.

For a moment I remained motionless. Then I knelt down and slowly pulled up the rope. The shoes were dangling in their bundle at the end of it. I let it down again and brought up our coats. The third time I salvaged the big rope; it was a difficult job to squeeze it through the narrow opening.

Go slowly, I thought. Don't hurry. You've got plenty of time.

I unhooked the parcel and put it aside. Then I paid out the rope once more. We had agreed that Gimenez should tie it round his waist so that I could take up the slack and make his ascent easier. I waited a little, and then felt a gentle tug. I pulled steadily, hand over hand, taking care not to let the rope bear heavily on the metal edge of the skylight. We could not risk any noise. I heard the rods creaking under his weight; then, a moment later, two hands came up and got a grip on the sill. Slowly Gimenez's face and shoulders appeared.

I bent down and whispered: 'Don't hurry. Take a rest.'

He breathed in the fresh air, gulping and panting.

My mouth still close to his ear, I said: 'Be careful how you pull yourself up. Don't put your hands on the glass.'

He seemed as exhausted as I was.

I untied the rope from my waist, and he followed suit. I coiled it

367

up carefully, took a piece of string out of my pocket, and ran a bowline round the middle of the coil.

There we both stood, side by side, in absolute silence. Gradually my breathing slowed down to its normal rate, and I began to recover my strength. It was hard to get used to this immense, seemingly limitless space all around me. The glass penthouse (of which the sky-light formed a part) stood out from the roof and vanished in darkness only a few feet away. I made out one or two small chimney-cowls here and there. The courtyard and the perimeter were hidden from us by the parapet. We could walk upright without being seen.

I felt the shingle grit under my feet at the least move I made.

I took a coil of rope in each hand and picked them up with great care. Gimenez did the same with the shoes and coats.

We stood there waiting for a train: it was five perhaps even ten minutes coming.

Gimenez became impatient. I was just about to move when the sound of a locomotive reached us from the distance. It grew louder and louder; presently the train steamed past on the nearby track. We managed to get ten feet forward before it vanished into the distance again. The stretch of line which runs past Montluc joins the two main stations of Lyons. As a result it carries very heavy traffic, which had hardly slackened off even at this stage of the war.

We had nearly reached the middle of the roof now. We found ourselves standing by the far end of the penthouse. A little farther on a second penthouse appeared, which stretched away towards the other side of the roof. My eyes were beginning to get accustomed to the dark. I could see the large glass dome above the penthouse; that meant we were standing above the central well. I thought then for a moment of our friends below in their cells: some asleep, lost in wonderful dreams; others, who knew of our plan, awake, waiting in frightful suspense, ears straining for any suspicious noises.

We had advanced with extreme care, putting each foot down as lightly as possible, bent double as if the weight of our apprehension and of the dangers we had to face was too heavy to be supported. Gimenez kept close behind me. I could hear his slow, regular breathing, and glimpse his dark silhouette against the night sky. We had to wait some time before another train came to our assistance. But this time it was a slow goods train. It enabled us to reach our objective—the side of the roof opposite the infirmary—in one quick move.

We put down our various packages. I turned back and whispered to Gimenez: 'Lie down and wait for me here. Don't move.'

'Where are you going?'

'To see what's happening.'

Gimenez obediently dropped to his knees, and remained as motionless as the equipment stacked round him. I crept slowly round the corner of the roof, raised myself cautiously, and peered over the parapet. Below me I could see the stretch of the perimeter which flanked the Rue du Dauphiné. I lifted my head a little farther, and quickly drew it back again at the sight of a sentry. He was standing in one corner near the wash-house. I had known he would be there; yet in my present situation he scared me nearly out of my wits.

Of course, he could not see me. I told myself not to be a fool.

I pressed my cheek against the rough concrete surface and slowly raised my head once more. Unfortunately, the wide shelf outside the parapet cut off my view of the part of the courtyard immediately below. As this was where we would have to climb down, it was essential to find a better observation-post.

But before moving I took another quick look at the soldier in the far corner. He seemed very wide awake. Soon a second sentry walked over to join him—probably the one who guarded the wooden barrack-block on the other side. I saw the glowing tips of their cigarettes. The lamps in the courtyard gave off so weak a light that the men themselves were mere shadows against the surrounding gloom.

Occasionally a twinkling reflection from buckle or bayonet hinted at their movements. I knew that the best way of remaining unseen was to keep absolutely still. If I had to move, it must be done as slowly as possible, with long and frequent pauses. It took me some time to get back to Gimenez, tell him to stay put, climb over the parapet, and crawl along the outer cat-walk till I was once more opposite the infirmary. A train passed by at exactly the right moment; I scrambled along as fast as I could to the corner of the wall. A loose piece of shingle, even a little sand going over the edge would have given me away. I would feel ahead with my hands, then slowly pull myself forward like a slug, breathing through my mouth.

369

In front of me the perimeter was clearly visible. Beyond it the tobacco factory and the buildings of the military court formed a broken outline against the horizon. Above them the stars shone out in a moonless sky. After a little I could just make out the roof of the covered gallery over which we had to pass. Gradually our whole route became visible. I spotted a familiar landmark—the fanlight of my old cell—and then, on the left, the workshop and women's quarters. Close by was the low wall between the infirmary and the courtyard. Soon, I thought, we should be climbing that wall. One room in the infirmary was still lit up; the light shone behind the wall in the direction of the covered gallery. I was, I realized, directly above cell 45, where my first few weeks of detention had been spent.

I wriggled forward inch by inch, so as to reach the outer edge of the cat-walk and get into a position from which I could observe the whole area of the courtyard. The two sentries were now out of sight round the corner of the block, smoking and chatting. I could see no one below me. The way was clear. My heart beat excitedly. A little further and I would be certain. My face against the rough surface, I peered cautiously over the edge.

I was horrified at the gulf stretching down below me; I could not help feeling that my rope must be too short.

Nothing was stirring. I examined every danger-point in turn—the shadowy corners by the wash-house and workshop, the women's quarters, the alley between the infirmary wall and the main block, the half-open doors leading from court to court, every conceivable hole or corner where a sentry might be lurking. Nothing. The cell windows were patterned on the façade like black squares in a crossword puzzle. Occasionally the sound of a cough drifted out from one or other of them. This, and the recurrent trains, alone broke the silence. Farther down, on the left, some of the windows seemed to be open. The stillness was almost tangible.

Still I scrutinized the courtyard with minute care. Suddenly a dark shape caught my eye, in a corner near the door of the main block. I stared closely at it. After a moment I realized it was a sentry, asleep on the steps. The weight of this alarming discovery filled me with a sudden vast depression. How on earth were we to get past him? How could we even be certain he was asleep? How—in the last resort—

could we surprise him without being seen?

At this point the sentry sat up and lit a cigarette. The flame from his lighter gave me a quick glimpse of his steel helmet and the sub-machine gun he carried. He got up, walked a little way in the direction of the infirmary, and then came back again.

Midnight struck.

It must have been the time when the guard was changed. The soldier passed directly beneath me, between the infirmary and the main block, and vanished in the direction of the guard-house. Four or five minutes later his relief appeared. His footsteps crunched grimly over the cobbles.

A frightful inner conflict racked me as I studied his every movement, like a wild beast stalking its prey. We could not retreat. The way had to be cleared.

The sentry's beat took him away into the shadows at the far end of the court, then back to the main door, where the lamp shone for a moment on his helmet and the barrel of his sub-machine gun.

I watched him for nearly an hour, memorizing the pattern of his movements. Then I raised myself on knees and elbows, climbed quietly over the parapet, and returned to Gimenez.

He was asleep. I woke him gently. 'Time to move on,' I said.

He got up without making any noise. I was busy untying the knot of the string lashed round the big rope.

'All set now,' I whispered. 'As soon as a train comes, we'll lower the rope.'

I stood with one foot on the roof and the other on the cat-walk, the low parapet between my legs. This way I could control the rope with both hands and pay it out without it touching the edge. I left Gimenez to control the coil and see the rope was free from entanglements.

An eternity of time seemed to pass before the train came. At the first distant panting of the engine I began to lower away, slowly at first, then with increasing speed. When I felt the reinforced stretch near the end passing through my fingers I stopped, and lowered the rope on to the concrete. Then I hooked the grappling-iron on to the inner side of the parapet. It seemed to hold firm enough. The rope stretched away into the darkness below us.

Gimenez would sling the parcels containing our shoes and coats round his neck, and follow me down when I gave him the signal. I knew that the moment I swung out from the roof into open space the last irrevocable decision would have been taken. By so doing I would either clinch my victory or sign my own death-warrant. While I remained on the roof it was still possible to return to my cell. Once I had begun the descent there was no way back. Despite the cool night air, my face and shirt were soaked with sweat.

'Hold on to the grappling-iron while I'm going down,' I told Gimenez. I took hold of his hands and set them in position.

Then I crouched down on the outer ledge, facing him, ready to go down the rope at the first possible moment, and waited for a train to pass. Gimenez leant over and hissed nervously in my ear: 'There's someone down below!'

'Don't worry.'

Then I looked at the sky and the stars and prayed that the rope might be strong enough, that the German sentry would not come round the corner at the wrong moment, that I would not make any accidental noise.

The waiting strained my nerves horribly. Once I began my descent there would be no more hesitation, I knew; but dear God, I thought, let that train come quickly, let me begin my descent into the abyss now, at once, before my strength fails me.

The stroke of one o'clock cut through the stillness like an axe.

Had an hour passed so quickly? The sentries' footsteps echoing up to us with monotonous regularity, seemed to be counting out the seconds. There could not be so very many trains at this time of night.

Gimenez was showing signs of impatience. I told him to keep still. The words were hardly out of my mouth when a distant whistle broke the silence. Quickly it swelled in volume.

'This is it,' I said.

I shuffled back towards the edge of the cat-walk. Then, holding my breath, I slid myself over, gripping the rope between my knees, and holding the ledge with both hands to steady myself. At last I let go. The rope whirred upwards under my feet, the wire binding tore at my hands. I went down as fast as I could, not even using my legs.

As soon as I touched the ground I grabbed the parcel containing the second rope, and doubled across the courtyard to the low wall. I released the rope, swung the grappling-iron up, hauled myself over, and dropped down on the other side, behind the doorway, leaving the rope behind for Gimenez.

The train was fading away into the distance now, towards the station. The drumming of its wheels seemed to be echoed in my heaving chest. I opened my mouth and breathed deeply to ease the pressure on my lungs. Above me I saw the dark swinging line of rope, and the sharp outline of the roof against the sky.

I stood motionless, getting my breath back and accustoming my eyes to the darkness. The sentry's footsteps rang out behind the wall, scarcely six feet away. They passed on, only to return a moment later. I pressed both hands against my beating heart. When all was quiet again I worked round to the doorway, and flattened myself against it. I felt all my human reactions being swallowed up by pure animal instinct, the instinct for self-preservation which quickens the reflexes and gives one fresh reserves of strength.

It was my life or his.

As his footsteps approached I tried to press myself into the wood against which my back was resting. Then, when I heard him change direction, I risked a quick glance out of my hiding-place to see exactly where he was.

He did exactly the same thing twice, and still I waited.

I got a good grip on the ground with my heels; I could not afford to slip. The footsteps moved in my direction, grew louder. The sentry began to turn . . .

I sprang out of my recess like a panther, and got my hands round his throat in a deadly grip. With frantic violence I began to throttle him. I was no longer a man, but a wild animal. I squeezed and squeezed, with the terrible strength of desperation. My teeth were gritting against each other, my eyes bursting out of my head. I threw back my head to exert extra pressure, and felt my fingers bite deep into his neck. Already half-strangled, the muscles of his throat torn and engorged, only held upright by my vice-like grip, the sentry still feebly raised his arms as if to defend himself; but an instant later they fell back, inert. But this did not make me let go. For perhaps three minutes longer I maintained my pressure on his throat, as if afraid that one last cry, or even the death-rattle, might give me away. Then, slowly, I loosened my blood-

373

'*I drew the bayonet and plunged it down with one straight, hard stroke into the sentry's back . . .*'

stained fingers, ready to close them again at the least movement; but the body remained slack and lifeless. I lowered it gently to the ground.

I stared down at the steel helmet which, fortunately perhaps, concealed the sentry's face; at the dark hunched shape of the body itself, at the sub-machine gun and the bayonet. I thought for a moment, then quickly drew the bayonet from its scabbard, gripped it by the hilt in both hands, and plunged it down with one straight, hard stroke into the sentry's back.

I raised my head, and saw that I was standing immediately below the window of cell 45. Old memories fireworked up in my mind: hunger and thirst, the beatings I had suffered, the handcuffs, the condemned man in the next cell, Fränzel spitting in my face.

I went back to the doorway, near the infirmary, and whistled twice, very softly. A dark shape slid down the rope. It creaked under his weight. I went to meet him. Gimenez climbed the low wall, detached the light rope with its grappling-iron, passed them down to me, and jumped. In his excitement, or nervousness, he had left our coats and shoes on the roof. At the time I said nothing about this. Clearly his long wait had depressed him; he was shivering all over. He gave a violent start when he saw the corpse stretched out near our feet.

I clapped him on the back. 'You'll really have something to shiver about in a moment. Come on, quick.'

Our troubles had only begun. We still had to cross the courtyard in order to reach the wall between it and the infirmary. Then there was the roof of the covered gallery to surmount, and, finally, the crossing of the perimeter walls.

I carried the rope and the fixed grappling-iron; Gimenez had the loose one. We doubled across to the wall. It was essential for us to get up here as quickly as possible. The light left on in the infirmary was shining in our direction, and a guard could easily have spotted us from a first-floor window of the central block as we made our way towards the inner wall of the perimeter.

Gimenez gave me a leg up, and I managed to reach the top of the wall and hang on. But I was quite incapable by now of pulling myself up; all my strength had drained away. I came down again, wiped my forehead and regained my breath. If I had been alone I should in all probability have stuck at this point. As it was, I bent down against the wall in my turn, and Gimenez got up without any trouble. I undid the bundle of rope and passed him the end with the grappling-iron attached. He fixed it securely. Then I tried again, with the rope to help me this time. Somehow I scrambled up, using hands, knees and feet, thrusting and straining in one last desperate effort. Gimenez lay down flat on his belly to give himself more purchase, and managed to grasp me under the arms. Eventually I made it.

My heart was hammering against my ribs and my chest felt as if it was going to burst. My shirt clung damply to my body. But there was not a minute to lose. We coiled up the rope again and crawled along to the covered gallery. From here it was a short climb up the tiles to the ridge of the roof. We had to hurry because of that damned light; once we had got over the other side of the roof we were in shadow again.

Unfortunately I made a noise. Two tiles knocked against each other under the sliding pressure of my knee. Gimenez reproved me sharply.

'For God's sake take care what you're doing!' he hissed.

'It wasn't my fault——'

'I haven't the least desire to be caught, even if you have!'

Since this was a sloping roof, we only needed to climb a little way down the far side to be completely hidden. If we stood upright we could easily see over the wall. Soon we were both crouching in position at the end of the covered gallery, our equipment beside us.

I was not acquainted with the exact details of the patrols in the perimeter. When I went out to be interrogated, I had observed a sentry-box in each corner, but these were always unoccupied. Perhaps the guards used them at night, however: it was vital to find out. We already knew that one guard rode around and round the whole time on a bicycle; he passed us every two or three minutes, his pedals squeaking.

We listened carefully. Gimenez was just saying that the cyclist must be alone when the sound of voices reached us. We had to think again.

Perhaps there was a sentry posted at each corner of the square, in the angle formed by the outer wall. If this turned out to be so, it would be extremely difficult to get across; nothing but complete darkness would give us a chance. That meant we must cut the electric cable, which ran about two feet below the top of the inner wall, on the perimeter side.

I half rose from my cramped position and took a quick look. The walls seemed much higher from here, and the lighting system enhanced this impression. A wave of despair swept over me. Surely we could never surmount this obstacle?

From the roof it had all looked very different. The yawning gulf had been hidden. But the perimeter was well lit, and the sight of it—deep as hell and bright as daylight—almost crushed my exhausted determination.

I craned forward a little further. The sentry-box below on our left was empty. I ducked back quickly as the cyclist approached. He ground round the corner and started another circuit. A moment later I was enormously relieved to hear him talking to himself; it was this curious monologue we had intercepted a moment earlier. He was alone, after all.

Behind us rose the dark shape of the main block. We had come a long way since ten o'clock. Another six yards, and we were free. Yet what risks still remained to be run!

Little by little determination flowed back into me. One more effort would do it. Don't look back, I thought. Keep your eyes in front of you till it's all over.

Bitter experience had taught me that over-hastiness could be fatal; that every precipitate action was liable to bring disaster in its train. Gimenez was eager to get on and finish the operation, but I firmly held him back. I was as well aware as he was of the dangers that threatened us; I knew that every moment we delayed increased our risk of re-capture. I thought of the open cell, the rope we had left hanging from the wall, the dead sentry in the courtyard, the possibility of his body being discovered by a patrol or his relief. Nevertheless, I spent more than a quarter of an hour watching that cyclist. Every four or five circuits he turned round and went the other way. We were well placed in our corner: he was busy taking the bend, and never looked up. We were additionally protected by the three shaded lights fixed on each wall. All their radiance was thrown down into the perimeter itself, leaving us in shadow. We could watch him without fear of discovery.

Three o'clock.

Gimenez was becoming desperate. At last I decided to move. Holding the end of the rope firmly in one hand, I coiled it across my left arm like a lasso. With the other hand I grasped the grappling-iron. As soon as the sentry had pedalled past, I threw the line as hard as I could

377

towards the opposite wall. The rope snaked up and out, and the grappling-iron fell behind the parapet. I tugged very gently on it, trying to let it find a natural anchorage. Apparently I had been successful; it held firm. A strand of barbed wire, which I had not previously noticed, rattled alarmingly as the rope jerked over it. After a little, however, it was pressed down to the level of the wall.

I gave one violent pull, but the rope did not budge. It had caught first time. I breathed again.

'Give me the other hook,' I muttered to Gimenez. I could feel him trembling.

The cyclist was coming round again now. I froze abruptly. For the first time he passed actually under the rope. When he had gone I threaded the rope through the wire loop and we pulled it as tight as we could. While Gimenez held it firm to prevent it slipping, I knotted it tightly, and fixed the grappling-iron in a crevice on the near side of the parapet. In my fear of running things too fine I had actually over-calculated the amount of rope necessary; over six feet were left trailing loose on the roof. That thin line stretching across the perimeter looked hardly less fragile than the telephone wires which followed a similar route a few yards away.

I made several further tests when the cyclist was round the other side. I unanchored the grappling-iron on our side, and then we both of us pulled on the rope as hard as we could to try out its strength.

If the truth must be told, I was horribly afraid that it would snap, and I would be left crippled in the perimeter. When I pulled on it with all my strength I could feel it stretch. One last little effort and the whole thing would be over; but I had reached the absolute end of my courage, physical endurance, and will-power alike. All the time the cyclist continued to ride around beneath us.

Four o'clock struck.

In the distance, towards the station, the red lights on the railway line still shone out. But the first glimmer of dawn was already creeping up over the horizon, and the lights showed less bright every moment. We could wait no longer.

'Over you go, Gimenez. You're lighter than I am.'

'No, You go first.'

'It's your turn.'

378

'I won't.'

'Go on, it's up to you.'

'No,' he said desperately, 'I can't do it.'

The cyclist turned the corner again. I shook Gimenez desperately, my fingers itching to hit him.

'Are you going, yes or no?'

'No,' he cried, 'no, *no*!'

'Shut up, for God's sake!' I said. I could not conquer his fear; I said no more. Still the German pedalled round his beat. Once he stopped almost directly beneath us, got off his machine, and urinated against the wall. It was at once a comic and terrifying sight. As time passed and the dawn approached, our chances of success grew steadily less. I knew it, yet I still hesitated. Gimenez shivered in silence.

Abruptly, as the sentry passed us yet again, I stooped forward, gripped the rope with both hands, swung out into space, and got my legs up into position. Hand over hand, my back hanging exposed above the void, I pulled myself across with desperate speed. I reached the far wall, got one arm over it, and scrambled up.

I had done it. I had escaped.

A delirious feeling of triumph swept over me. I forgot how exhausted I was; I almost forgot Gimenez, who was still waiting for the sentry to pass under him again before following me. I was oblivious to my thudding heart and hoarse breath; my knees might tremble, my face be dripping with sweat, my hands scored and bleeding, my throat choked, my head bursting, but I neither knew nor cared. All I was conscious of was the smell of life, the freedom I had won against such desperate odds. I uttered a quick and thankful prayer to God for bringing me through safely.

I moved along the top of the wall towards the court-house buildings, where it lost height considerably. I stopped just short of a small gateway. Workmen were going past in the street outside, and I waited a few moments before jumping down. This gave Gimenez time to catch up with me.

At five o'clock we were walking down the street in our socks and shirt-sleeves—free men . . .

INTO THE SNAKE PIT

Gerald Durrell

When people discover my job for the first time, they always ask me for details of the many adventures they assume I have had in what they will persist in calling the 'jungle'.

I returned to England after my first West African trip and described with enthusiasm the hundreds of square miles of rain-forest I had lived and worked in for eight months. I said that in this forest I had spent many happy days, and during all this time I never had one experience that could, with any justification be called 'hair-raising', but when I told people this they decided that I was either exceptionally modest or a charlatan.

On my way out to West Africa for the second time, I met on board ship a young Irishman called MacTootle who was going out to a job on a banana plantation in the Cameroons. He confessed to me that he had never before left England and he was quite convinced that Africa was the most dangerous place imaginable. His chief fear seemed to be that the entire snake population of the continent was going to be assembled on the docks to meet him. In order to relieve his mind, I told him that in all the months I had spent in the forest I had seen precisely five snakes, and these had run away so fast that I had been unable to capture them. He asked me if it was a dangerous job to catch a snake, and I replied, quite truthfully, that the majority of snakes were extremely easy to capture, if you kept your head and knew your snake and its habits. All this soothed MacTootle considerably, and when he landed he swore that, before I returned to England, he would obtain some rare specimens for me; I thanked him and promptly forgot all about it.

Five months later I was ready to leave for England with a collection of about two hundred creatures, ranging from grasshoppers to chimpanzees. Very late on the night the ship was due to sail, a small van drew up with screeching brakes outside my camp and my young Irishman alighted, together with several friends of his. He explained with great glee that he had got me the specimens he had promised. Apparently he had discovered a large hole or pit, somewhere on the plantation he was working on, which had presumably been dug to act as a drainage sump. This pit, he said, was full of snakes, and they were all mine—providing I went and got them.

He was so delighted at the thought of all those specimens he had found for me that I had not the heart to point out that crawling about in a pit full of snakes at twelve o'clock at night was not my idea of a pleasurable occupation, enthusiastic naturalist though I was. Furthermore, he had obviously been boasting about my powers to his friends, and he had brought them all along to see my snake-catching methods. So, with considerable reluctance, I said I would go and catch reptiles; I have rarely regretted a decision more.

I collected a large canvas snake-bag, and a stick with a Y-shaped fork of brass at one end; then I squeezed into the van with my excited audience and we drove off. At half-past twelve we reached my friend's bungalow, and we stopped there for a drink before walking through the plantation to the pit.

'You'll be wanting some rope, will you not?' asked MacTootle.

'Rope?' I said. 'What for?'

'Why, to lower yourself into the hole, of course,' he said cheerfully. I began to feel an unpleasant sensation in the pit of my stomach. I asked for a description of the pit. It was apparently some twenty-five feet long, four feet wide and twelve feet deep. Everyone assured me that I could not get down there without a rope. While my friend went off to look for one which I hoped very much he would not find, I had another quick drink and wondered how I could have been foolish enough to get myself mixed up in this fantastic snake-hunt. Snakes in trees, on the ground or in shallow ditches were fairly easy to manage, but an un-specified number of them at the bottom of a pit so deep that you had to be lowered into it on the end of a rope did not sound at all inviting. I thought that I had an opportunity of backing out gracefully when the question of lighting arose, and it was discovered that none of us had a torch. My friend, who had now returned with the rope, was quite determined that nothing was going to interfere with his plans: he solved the lighting question by tying a big paraffin pressure-lamp on to the end of a length of cord, and informed the company that he personally would lower it into the pit for me. I thanked him in what I hoped was a steady voice.

'That's all right,' he said, 'I'm determined you'll have your fun. This lamp's much better than a torch, and you'll need all the light you can get, for there's any number of the little devils down there.'

We then had to wait a while for the arrival of my friend's brother and sister-in-law: he had asked them to come along, he explained, because they would probably never get another chance to see anyone capturing snakes, and he did not want them to miss it.

Eventually eight of us wended our way through the banana planta-tion and seven of us were laughing and chattering excitedly at the thought of the treat in store. It suddenly occurred to me that I was wear-ing the most inadequate clothing for snake-hunting: thin tropical trousers and a pair of plimsoll shoes. Even the most puny reptiles would have no difficulty in penetrating to my skin with one bite. However, before I could explain this we arrived at the edge of the pit, and in the lamplight it looked to me like nothing more nor less than an extremely large grave. My friend's description of it had been accurate enough, but what he had failed to tell me was that the sides of the pit consisted of dry, crumbling earth, honeycombed with cracks and holes that offered plenty of hiding-places for any number of snakes. While I crouched down on the edge of the pit, the lamp was solemnly lowered into the depths so that I might spy out the land and try to identify the snakes. Up to that moment I had cheered myself with the thought that, after all, the snakes might turn out to be a harmless variety, but when the light reached the bottom this hope was shattered, for I saw that the pit was simply crawling with young Gaboon vipers, one of the most deadly snakes in the world.

During the daytime these snakes are very sluggish and it is quite a simple job to capture them, but at night, when they wake up and hunt for their food, they can be unpleasantly quick. These young ones in the pit were each about two feet long and a couple of inches in diameter, and they were all, as far as I could judge, very much awake. They wriggled round and round the pit with great rapidity, and kept lifting their heavy, arrow-shaped heads and contemplating the lamp, flicking their tongues in and out in a most suggestive manner.

I counted eight Gaboon vipers in the pit, but their coloration matched the leaf-mould so beautifully that I could not be sure I was not counting some of them twice. Just at that moment my friend trod heavily on the edge of the pit, and a large lump of earth fell among the reptiles, who all looked up and hissed loudly. Everyone backed away hastily, and I thought it a very suitable opportunity to explain the point about my clothing. My friend, with typical Irish generosity, offered to lend me his trousers, which were of stout twill, and the strong pair of shoes he was wearing. Now the last of my excuses was gone and I had not the nerve to protest further. We went discreetly behind a bush and exchanged trousers and shoes. My friend was built on more generous lines than I, and the clothes were not exactly a snug fit; however, as he rightly pointed out, the bit of trouser-leg I had to turn up at the bottom would act as additional protection for my ankles.

Drearily I approached the pit. My audience was clustered round, twittering in delicious anticipation. I tied the rope round my waist with what I very soon discovered to be a slip-knot, and crawled to the edge. My descent had not got the airy grace of a pantomime fairy: the sides of the pit were so crumbly that every time I tried to gain a foothold I dislodged large quantities of earth, and as this fell among the snakes it was greeted with peevish hisses. I had to dangle in mid-air, being gently lowered by my companions, while the slip-knot grasped me ever tighter round the waist. Eventually I looked down and I saw that my feet were about a yard from the ground. I shouted to my friends to stop lowering me, as I wanted to examine the ground I was to land on and make sure there were no snakes lying there. After a careful inspection I could not

383

see any reptiles directly under me, so I shouted 'Lower away' in what I sincerely hoped was an intrepid tone of voice. As I started on my descent again, two things happened at once: firstly, one of my borrowed shoes fell off and, secondly, the lamp, which none of us had remembered to pump up, died away to a faint glow of light, rather like a plump cigar-end. At that precise moment I touched ground with my bare foot, and I cannot remember ever having been so frightened, before or since.

I stood motionless, sweating with great freedom, while the lamp was hastily hauled up to the surface, pumped up, and lowered down again. I have never been so glad to see a humble pressure-lamp. Now the pit was once more flooded with lamplight I began to feel a little braver. I retrieved my shoe and put it on, and this made me feel even better. I grasped my stick in a moist hand and approached the nearest snake. I pinned it to the ground with the forked end of the stick, picked it up and put it in the bag. This part of the procedure gave me no qualms, for it was simple enough and not dangerous provided you exercised a certain care. The idea is to pin the reptile across the head with the fork and then get a good firm grip on its neck before picking it up. What worried me was the fact that while my attention was occupied with one snake, all the others were wriggling round frantically, and I had to keep a cautious eye open in case one got behind me and I stepped back on it. They were beautifully marked with an intricate pattern of brown, silver, pink and cream blotches, and when they remained still this coloration made them extremely hard to see; they just melted into the background. As soon as I pinned one to the ground, it would start to hiss like a kettle, and all the others would hiss in sympathy—a most unpleasant sound.

There was one nasty moment when I bent down to pick up one of the reptiles and heard a loud hissing apparently coming from somewhere horribly close to my ear. I straightened up and found myself staring into a pair of angry silver-coloured eyes approximately a foot away. After considerable juggling I managed to get this snake down on to the ground and pin him beneath my stick. On the whole, the reptiles were just as scared of me as I was of them, and they did their best to get out of my way. It was only when I had them cornered that they fought and struck viciously at the stick, but bounced off the brass fork with a reassuring ping. However, one of them must have been more experienced, for he ignored the brass fork and bit instead at the wood. He got a good grip and hung on like a bulldog; he would not let go even when I lifted him clear of the ground. Eventually I had to shake the stick really hard, and the snake sailed through the air, hit the side of the pit and fell to the ground, hissing furiously. When I approached him with the stick again, he refused to bite and I had no difficulty in picking him up.

I was down in the pit for about half an hour, and during that time I caught twelve Gaboon vipers; I was not sure, even then, that I had captured all of them, but I felt it would be tempting fate to stay down there any longer. My companions hauled me out, hot, dirty and streaming with sweat, clutching in one hand a bag full of loudly hissing snakes.

'There, now,' said my friend triumphantly, while I was recovering my breath, 'I told you I'd get you some specimens, did I not?'

I just nodded; by that time I was beyond speech. I sat on the ground, smoking a much-needed cigarette and trying to steady my trembling hands. Now that the danger was over I began to realize for the first time how extremely stupid I had been to go into the pit in the first place, and how exceptionally lucky I was to have come out of it alive. I made a mental note that in future, if anyone asked me if animal-collecting was a dangerous occupation, I would reply that it was only as dangerous as your own stupidity allowed it to be. When I had recovered slightly, I looked about and discovered that one of my audience was missing.

'Where's your brother got to?' I asked my friend.

'Oh him,' said MacTootle with fine scorn, 'he couldn't watch any more—he said it made him feel sick. He's waiting over there for us. You'll have to excuse him—he couldn't take it. Sure, and it required some guts to watch you down there with all them wretched reptiles.'

ESCAPE OF THE ORZEL

Commander John Kerans

As the golden dawn of 1 September 1939, over the Polish port of Gdynia [Danzig] began to throb with the sound of distant planes, the crew of the submarine *Orzel* knew the war was upon them at last. Soon the sky in the west was black with the Heinkels, Dorniers and the JU 87s of the Luftwaffe, filling the air with the opening roar of Hitler's oft-threatened *Blitzkreig*. 'Action stations!' the alarm bells shrilled through the great submarine that was the pride of the Polish Navy. She slid beneath the smooth sea even as the crooked-winged Stukas came howling down erupting red fire and quaking destruction among Gdynia's docks and homes.

The *Orzel*—she was named 'Eagle' to honour Poland's national emblem—was more than the pride of their tiny navy. She was symbolic of the rebirth of the nation from the holocaust of the First World War, a renaissance that had given Poland a seaport on the Baltic once more. *Orzel* had, in fact, sailed into Gdynia harbour on 10 February that year, the twentieth anniversary of the new Poland's rejoining to the sea, and it had been an event for proud and joyous celebrations. The submarine had been built from plans of Polish engineers in the docks at Vlissingen, Holland, and nationwide public subscription had paid most of the cost.

As it disappeared beneath the Baltic before the plunging black Stukas, *Orzel* was not running away. Her captain, Commander Kloczkowski, and his hand-picked, highly-trained crew, had long anticipated just such a treacherous, undeclared beginning to the war. They were aware the German Navy overwhelmingly outnumbered Poland's small fleet of four destroyers, five submarines and two gun-boats and that the Luftwaffe would dominate the skies. *Orzel's* role could only be that of selling their lives as dearly as possible. As Commander Kloczkowski took the great submarine down beneath the waves, every one of her sixty men was resolutely prepared to do just that. Their standing orders were to execute underwater patrols along with the other four submarines. And within a few hours of the first German hammer blows from sky, sea and land these were the only warships remaining to Poland.

For four days and nights *Orzel* haunted the perilous waters of the Baltic in the Bay of Danzig, watching for a chance of revenge. Commander Kloczkowski was operating within a wide network of mines the Polish Navy had laid before the Germans struck, a screen which, until the enemy mine-sweepers could clear it, would keep out the heavier German warships. Tears of anger and bitterness burned behind the eyes of the officers and men as in turn they watched through the periscope the ruthless destruction by the Nazi war machine. For as far as they could see along Poland's coast, wherever there were buildings or dock installations, wave after wave of the great air armada bombed and blasted remorselessly at ten-minute intervals.

Although *Orzel's* radio was constantly manned, ominous silence foreboded the wiping out of all Polish bases and warships. Only one faint message, terse and desperate: 'Have been attacked by German anti-submarine boats and require immediate assistance,' identified as from a sister submarine, did they pick up. With engines at full revolutions they raced to the rescue but found nothing, and heard no more.

Then it was *Orzel's* turn to be discovered and attacked. As the looming bombers peeled off to roar down upon her, the water erupted with the fury of high explosive. The submarine dived deep and lay on the bottom of the sea. Soon shattering blows and the muffled thunder

387

of underwater explosions shook her stout steel hull. She was being depth-charged from all directions, for a whole cordon of German submarine hunters had spread across the Gulf of Danzig after her. There was only one thing to do—slip out through the minefields to the wider waters of the Baltic.

The hunting German warships swiftly spread the news there was still one remaining enemy beneath the sea. Warships and planes hurried in from all directions, quartering sea and sky in their eagerness to destroy the *Orzel*. Deeper and deeper dived the submarine, her men resolved that if they were to die they would account for as many enemies as possible before doing so. When forced to come up in the middle of the night to replenish air and recharge batteries they were spotted and attacked, for the nights were clear and starry and a full moon illuminated the smooth waters of the Baltic like a dark mirror.

The men of the *Orzel* came to understand with increasing clarity that their only chance to revenge their country was to break out of the Baltic to become part of a powerful force that could meet the German Navy on level terms. Somehow they must get to England.

Inevitably the incessant tension and danger increased the physical and mental weariness of the crew of *Orzel*. It was worse for the officers, particularly for the captain, for whom there could be little if any sleep. Eventually the terrible stress told on him and he became increasingly sick and weak. Yet he would not give in, even though every time he wanted to ascend to the conning tower he had to be pulled up at a rope's end. On the twelfth day Captain Kloczkowski collapsed completely, obviously dangerously ill. Lieutenant-Commander Jan Grudzinski, the sturdy, keen-eyed second-in-command, who took over, decided they would have to put into a neutral port to get the captain and the sick-bay petty officer, who also had fallen desperately ill, away to hospital. 'We'll call in at Tallin, for we are not at war with Estonia and The Hague International Convention permits us to stay for twenty-four hours,' said Grudzinski. *Orzel* set off once more to run the gauntlet through the Baltic, heading for Estonia.

On the morning of 15 September the streamlined conning tower of the *Orzel* rose from the calm waters outside Tallin, soon followed by the long bulk of her hull. They were in neutral waters and not even the ruthless Germans would surely dare attack them there? As the *Orzel* wallowed slowly into the outer harbour and anchored a launch put out from a jetty. Soon it was alongside and two government officials clambered aboard. 'Yes, you may put in for twenty-four hours,' they readily agreed as the captain explained his needs. 'We will give you an escort in.' Not long afterwards two armed Estonian patrol vessels cruised out to them and led them into the inner harbour. The *Orzel* went in with the red and white Polish ensign, emblazoned with its black eagle, proudly streaming from her masthead. It gave the men no little satisfaction to see a German merchant ship beside the jetty hurriedly strike her colours as the submarine approached.

The Estonian escorts took *Orzel* right into the inner basin of the port of Tallin, to moorings as far as they could be from the harbour entrance. Officials there indicated the submarine was to tie up with her stern towards the exit. A feeling of unbounded relief went through the crew as they relaxed for the first time in two weeks of the utmost peril on and beneath the waves. Jan Grudzinski went ashore at once and was readily reassured they were welcome to stay for twenty-four hours and all help would be given, including taking the sick captain and petty officer to hospital. No time was lost in beginning to refuel and re-provision. Dockyard technicians came aboard to repair damaged hydraulic leads. The friendliness of the Estonian authorities appeared to have no bounds and they welcomed the crew ashore and took them along to the municipal baths to enjoy their first hot tub for many days.

So well did the work progress that *Orzel* was ready for sea by nightfall. Captain Grudzinski, as he now was, was just about to issue his orders for sailing when he was called to speak to the Estonian naval officer in charge of the docks. 'I'm afraid you'll have to wait here another six hours,' the officer explained blandly. 'You see, that German merchant ship is about to weigh anchor and international law requires that there should be an interval of six hours between the sailings from a neutral point of belligerent ships.'

Although this caused a measure of uneasiness aboard *Orzel* it did not seem unreasonable. But when the German vessel was still there several hours later, with no apparent intention of sailing, uneasiness became a nagging suspicion. 'Why not let us out first and the Germans six hours after, for they don't seem in a hurry to leave?' asked Grudzinski. 'Oh, don't you worry, they are just about to go,' he was reassured. But still

389

there was no activity to indicate that sailing was imminent.

An hour later the Polish sailors knew for certain there was treachery afoot. From the shadows of nearby dock buildings a detachment of armed Estonian sailors suddenly appeared and jumped down on to the deck of the *Orzel*. 'The Estonian Government has now decided to intern your vessel and all aboard her,' the naval officer in charge tersely explained. 'This is in accordance with an agreement signed between the Baltic States during the first days of the war. One of the clauses says that any submarine belonging to either belligerent caught in territorial waters shall be interned. You are probably not aware of this agreement.'

Captain Grudzinski was most certainly unaware of it, and he had a pretty shrewd idea the Polish Government had never been told about it either. Rage, and then despair, filled the hearts of the officers and men of the *Orzel* when they heard how they had been tricked. It deepened when they were next informed: 'The work of disarming your submarine will commence tomorrow morning.'

Although they wracked their brains for a way out, and plotted and counter-plotted far into the night, they could think of no way of outwitting the treacherous Estonians.

By midday next day the disarming of the *Orzel* was far advanced; sixteen torpedoes had been removed for putting ashore. Ammunition and all charts and nautical manuals had been taken off. The captain, seeing there was apparently no hope, burned all the secret papers and books. Meanwhile, to the rage of the Polish sailors, the German merchant ship, obviously with the connivance of the port authorities, ran up the swastika flag and set sail. 'The swine would never dare do that if we still had breaches in our guns!' growled one of the Poles angrily.

From the fury engendered in the breasts of the men of the *Orzel* there developed a determination to escape and fight on at all costs. When they had been at sea, and there had been a semblance of a chance, this urge had been strong enough; but now, when all seemed lost, it was redoubled. A daring plan was put forward by Lieutenant Andzej Piasecki, a clean-featured, handsome young officer, newly-promoted first lieutenant. He had contrived it with the help of a petty officer and a leading seaman. It was enthusiastically received by the rest of the crew and adopted by the captain without hesitation.

First, a burly but stolid-looking chief petty officer stepped ashore with a fishing rod and dropped his line in the sea near the *Orzel*. For a time he sat patiently awaiting a bite, but when nothing resulted he moved farther along the dockside and tried again. Through most of the day this very good-tempered CPO fished, changing his position many times but never his luck. Some of the Estonian officials who noticed him ribbed him about his great patience and small luck, meanwhile remarking that he seemed to be accepting his captivity phlegmatically. When late that afternoon the Polish sailor eventually gave up, he returned to the *Orzel* without a single fish to improve their diet. But the list of accurate soundings he had taken with his leaded line along the submarine's proposed escape route improved their spirits no end!

While the chief petty officer thus employed his guile along the harbour side, his comrades in the *Orzel* had not been idle. Quietly but steadily the coxswain had sawn through the steal hawsers that fastened the submarine to the dockside and to the Estonian destroyer moored alongside to watch over them. They would now snap if strain were exerted. Meanwhile, in the engine-room, the warrant officer in charge had persuaded the Estonians the engines must be given a final cleaning and greasing before dismantling. At the same time a leading seaman operating the crane had somehow been clumsy enough to snap its steel rope before the last half-dozen torpedoes could be swung out on to the dockside.

The chief petty officer telegraphist ordered to dismantle the wireless set encountered rather more difficulty. He just could not shake off the attentions of his Estonian guard. But he became increasingly friendly with the guard until he had sufficiently won his confidence to ask his help. 'Just hold this wire while I undo the other end would you, please?' he asked amiably. And as the guard complied the telegraphist contrived a short-circuit which produced a dramatic spurt of blue flame and cloud of pungent smoke as well as a shock for the Estonian! 'Oh dear, that must be because I have stripped it wrongly,' he explained, having solicitously examined the shocked guard's tingling hand. 'There is only one thing for it, I shall have to put it all together and start again.' The guard not only agreed but set to work with a will to help. Thus by evening the wireless was in full working order again.

Despite the various mishaps, all seeming quite genuine, the Estonians were pleased with the efforts the Poles had made to comply with the

391

orders to demilitarize the *Orzel*. They had expected a surly 'go slow'. 'You will find life really quite pleasant in the internment camp, you know,' the Estonian naval officer in charge assured Jan Grudzinski. 'In any case, there is nothing you can do any more because the Germans have defeated you completely and Poland is as good as finished.'

'Then maybe it won't be too bad,' was the reply of the *Orzel's* captain, with what he intended to be a resigned smile. But his unspoken thought was: 'That's what you bloody well think!'

At six o'clock that evening Lieutenant Piasecki snapped the switch of the gyro-compass to warm it up, for it had to run several hours before becoming operational. 'What's that?' asked the Estonian officer beside him, suspicious at the steady humming.

'Oh, just the additional night ventilation fan,' Piasecki assured him blandly, adding, 'The men are turning in early tonight as they have done a good day's work.' As if to prove his words a sound of deep breathing and steady snoring could be heard throughout the submarine as the crew relaxed into the innocent expressions of feigned sleep. None looked more innocent than the gunner who nursed beneath his blankets a home-made bomb contrived from hand grenades! This was for the German merchant ship which had flaunted the Nazi ensign before them when it had believed them disarmed.

Deep, slumbering peace aboard the *Orzel* prevailed until 2 a.m. Then, according to plan, a powerfully-built leading seaman stole on stockinged feet up behind the guard on the bridge. Just one despairing gasping shout the man managed before he was throttled into unconsciousness. In the control-room it was heard by the guard manning a telephone through to the dockside guardroom. He sprang to his feet, hand reaching for his gun. 'Drop it!' snapped a voice behind him. He turned to look into the cold black muzzle of a revolver in the firm hand of a Polish petty officer. Such was the grim intent in the Pole's face that the guard dropped down in a dead faint. At that moment the searchlight permanently shining on the *Orzel*, along with all the garish lights on the dockside, went out. One blow of the axe of a Polish seaman, who had earlier reconnoitred the main supply cable, had extinguished them.

In the ensuing pitch darkness all hell was let loose. Amidst it the *Orzel's* great engines roared into life and as she threshed out astern the sabotaged hawsers snapped like threads. From several places machine-

'*Drop it!*' *snapped a voice behind him.*

guns, set on fixed lines to cover the submarine, chattered viciously. All around screamed and ricocheted bullets miraculously near-missing. Several bursts actually swept the bridge, stitching staccato death swathes inches above the captain and helmsman, who were lying down to navigate. Soon *Orzel* was far enough out to manoeuvre around and head strongly seawards.

With a shuddering crash *Orzel* jerked to a stop, flinging men violently down. She had run head on into a sandbank. In a desperate effort to free her the engines were roared full astern, roared until the belching blue-black diesel smoke blanketed her even more deeply than the night. Abruptly, she came free. With her bows slightly damaged *Orzel* headed for the open sea again but, although beyond the machine-gun's fury, now she faced the danger of the big guns of Tallin's defences. All around great white plumes glimmered in the night where massive eleven-inch shells hit the water.

'They're getting too close,' muttered Grudzinski. Then: 'Dive!' he ordered, and the klaxon shrieked one short note, one long. The diesels stopped. Momentarily there was quietness—and then there came the loud rush of water breaking into the ballast tanks. This sound dwindled, dwindled into nothingness. In the great silence that followed the men knew they were diving steeply. The palpitating explosion of shells became minute, distant thumps. Then they, too, faded. Once more the eagle was free!

Although she had escaped from treacherous imprisonment, the submarine was still trapped in the Baltic. In this land-locked northern sea they were, they believed, the very last fighting ship left to challenge the enemy's overwhelming might. How would they get through the great screen of warships, warplanes and minefields with which the Germans would seek unremittingly to trap and destroy them? How indeed, when *Orzel* was not only damaged but had no guns, charts or navigational books of any sort . . .

Captain Grudzinski decided to take a great risk; he put out a radio appeal for charts to a Polish port station he thought might still survive. There was no reply. Grimly he realized the Estonians' assertion that Poland was already defeated must be true. A little later there was a reply from another Polish submarine, the *Rys*. In plain language it stated the badly damaged *Rys* was putting into a Swedish port but would hand over her charts if the *Orzel* could effect a rendezvous. Hemmed in by searching enemies as the *Orzel* was, Grudzinski decided it would be fatal thus to reveal his position. For a time he considered another plan to halt the first merchant ship they encountered and send a boarding party armed with revolvers and knives to seize its charts. It soon became apparent this was impracticable. Then the torpedo officer said he thought he could draw a rough chart of the Baltic from memory, and proceeded to do so on a piece of squared paper. During the four precarious weeks which lay ahead of *Orzel* these memory drawings were to prove faultless.

Because the most obvious escape route was to neutral Sweden (where, had they chosen, they could have been comfortably interned for the duration of the war) *Orzel* first headed northwards. En route a halt was made at Gottland Island where the two captured Estonian guards were landed with bottles of whisky to fortify them and a large sum of money to compensate for their abduction. Surprisingly the two men had by now quite entered into the spirit of the adventure and declared they wanted to remain and join the crew. This could not be, and, still protesting, the Estonians were floated off in the submarine's one small boat on a calm night only a few hundred yards from the island's harbour. The Poles had heard German radio propaganda denouncing them as murderers of the Estonians, so now they again risked breaking radio silence and announced to the world what they had done. To dispel the anxiety of the men's relatives they explained exactly where they had been and how they had been treated.

Orzel, on her twenty-second day since escape, then retraced her course for about a hundred miles to confuse possible pursuers. The weather remained fine and calm, but amidst their searching enemies they only dared surface for brief periods to replenish air and recharge batteries. Day after day, night after night, the great submarine cruised around in the Baltic. Believing themselves the last fighting unit of their martyred country, the Polish sailors grimly sought a chance of revenge before making an attempt at breaking out to join the British Navy.

In this they were unlucky. No enemy target worthy of their torpedoes came their way: only relentlessly searching submarine boats and aircraft.

One night, while briefly on the surface, the submarine was almost run down by a flotilla of German destroyers. Only a crash dive saved them from the lean, grey warships that furiously churned the waters above. For hours they could hear their hunters rushing to and fro and they lost count of the pulverizing explosions of depth charges around them. Yet they survived.

After three weeks of this perilous lurking in the Baltic, water and food were low and all were suffering from varying degrees of physical exhaustion. The only thing that kept them going was the burning urge to fight on and be revenged. Cautiously but steadily *Orzel* worked westwards towards the 'Sund', the straits they must break through to reach the open sea where the British battle fleets would challenge every move German warships were likely to make. Patiently, determinedly, the Poles threaded through the intricate channels of the exit from the Baltic, sometimes grounding to sustain further damage, sometimes missing mines by a hair's breadth, often rocked and concussed by the violence of exploding depth charges. But they arrived at the ultimate channel on 12 October. They found the straits ceaselessly patrolled by a crowd of enemy submarine-hunting vessels and armed trawlers. Their only hope was a dark, moonless night.

For weary, weary hours they waited, right beneath their enemies, and the crew grew weaker and weaker. At the end of two days at last came the black night they needed. 'Surface by hydroplane,' the captain quietly ordered. Men almost too weak to move nevertheless moved controls expertly. The depth-gauge pointers slowly climbed, after a while the pull and sway of the restless upper levels of the sea could be felt, the master blowing valve was opened. Then, as the boatswain prepared to open the remaining ballast valves the captain raised one finger, another, and another . . . and the great submarine wallowed quietly up above the sea's surface. Inside, where all men held their breath, only the hiss of compressed air displacing the last of the water ballast could be heard, and after that just the lap of the waves against the hull.

Grudzinski was just about to order the conning tower open when he glimpsed in the darkness through the periscope the towering hull of a big ship right alongside. At that instant its navigation lights were switched on! 'Dive! Dive! Dive!' shouted Grudzinski. *Orzel* crash-dived sickeningly. For agonizing minutes they rested on the bottom awaiting the shattering impact of depth charges. None came.

'We'll go up and try again,' said Grudzinski after a while. The submarine surfaced to find the night even blacker and a'roar with rain. The ship had vanished. Conditions were never likely to be better. Grudzinski took the *Orzel* in as close to the shore as he dared, risking the minefields, avoiding the sweeping searchlights of the warships guarding the main channel through the straits.

As she slunk along on the surface *Orzel*'s engine-room was manned by volunteers; the rest of the crew were on deck or on the bridge where they could plunge into the sea if sudden disaster overtook them. The swell increased, and with it the pitching and lurching of the submarine as it crept slowly through the net of its hunters. The rain lashed so hard that it beat up a soaking mist from the heaving sea. Tension aboard mounted with every minute. Abruptly the dazzling beam of a search-light sprung out of the darkness ahead and groped menacingly over the black waters towards them. The men held their breaths, bit their lips anticipating the moment when they would stand starkly revealed in the merciless glare. But miraculously the beam snapped out just before reaching them. Almost at once another tunnel of sizzling light opened up behind them, as closely missing their stern as the first had missed their bows. It poised briefly and then began to move away in juddering jerks. By amazing good fortune they were slipping through the narrowest of narrow gaps between the end of one probing searchlight's bearings of search and the beginnings of the next!

'Full ahead!' ordered Captain Grudzinski in a voice full of relief. *Orzel* surged forward into the pitch-black night. She slid in behind a narrow strip of land which shielded her from the hunting ships and then gently settled down on to the bottom of the sea in a channel only ninety feet wide. There they would watch and wait. A looming mass of deeper darkness made them realize they were right alongside a wrecked vessel which they had narrowly missed fouling. It was as safe a hiding place as they were likely to find. All through the next day they lay on the bottom.

With the fall of night *Orzel* cautiously surfaced and cruised into the Kattegat. They were nearly through, nearly safe . . .

Two days later—forty-eight hours of acute tension and spine-chilling suspense—they were out in the North Sea. These were waters

397

the Germans did not dominate, for here they had to contend with the British Navy. But for the *Orzel* the presence of friends as well as foe in the North Sea could actually double the danger. The Germans had claimed the destruction of the Polish submarine; what if they could not now identify themselves to friendly warships. After all the determination and nerve-racking agonies of suspense and exhaustion of their escape from the Baltic trap, to be sunk now by the British did not bear thinking about.

Jan Grudzinski did the only thing he could under the circumstances—he risked all in a faltering call in plain language put out over the damaged radio. On 14 October the British Admiralty were amazed when one of their wireless stations picked up a faint message: 'Escaped Polish submarine begs permission enter port and pilot. Have no chart. *Orzel.*'

A few more taut hours passed and then at last the greyhound shape of a British destroyer breasted the horizon and bore down on them in showers of spray. Joyful greetings were exchanged and the destroyer led the *Orzel*, with her gallant, exhausted crew, into a British port. Word had gone round that the Polish submarine was expected and sailors on British warships cheered as it cruised slowly in. For the first time for forty-five days and nights *Orzel* was safe from the enemies who had hunted her so ruthlessly.

The Royal Navy was proud to welcome the *Orzel* to carry on the fight with them against the common enemy. And soon the courageous Jan Grudzinski was called into the presence of General Sikorski, the Polish Commander-in-Chief, to be decorated with the silver cross *Virtuti Militari*, his country's equivalent to the Victoria Cross.

Acknowledgements

The editor and publishers express their acknowledgements to agents, publishers and literary trustees in permitting use of the following stories and extracts:

HOW I WON THE WORLD TITLE from *The Greatest: My Own Story* by Muhammad Ali with Richard Durham, Hart-Davis MacGibbon/Granada Publishing Limited and Random House Inc.

THE TALKING HEAD from *Birds, Beasts and Relatives* by Gerald Durrell, William Collins Sons and Co. Limited and The Viking Press.

THE HUNTING OF TARKA from *Tarka the Otter* by Henry Williamson, The Bodley Head and A. M. Heath and Company Limited.

SECRET MISSION TO NORTH AFRICA by Frederick C. Painton, A. Watkins Inc. and the Reader's Digest.

THE RUUM by Arthur Porges, Scott Meredith Literary Agency.

I ESCAPE FROM THE BOERS from *My Early Life* by Winston S. Churchill, The Hamlyn Publishing Group Limited.

THE LOST MINES IN THE GREEN HELL abridgement of *The Lost Mines of Muribeca*, chapter 1 of *Exploration Fawcett* by Lt-Col P. H. Fawcett, reprinted by permission of The Hutchinson Publishing Group Limited.

THE RAILWAY RAID IN GEORGIA from *A Book of Escapes and Hurried Journeys* by John Buchan Thomas Nelson and Sons Limited.

RESCUE OF THE COMORIN'S CREW, LAFFEY AND THE KAMIKAZES and ESCAPE OF THE ORZEL from *The World's Greatest Sea Adventures* by Commander John Kerans, by permission of John Kerans and Henry Maule.

THE SMASHING OF THE DAMS from *Enemy Coast Ahead* by Guy Gibson, Michael Joseph Limited.

ANNAPURNA from *Annapurna* by Maurice Herzog, translated by Nea Morin and Jan Adam Smith, Jonathan Cape Limited, and E. P. Dutton and Co. Inc.

THE HAUNTED TUCKSHOP by Frank Richards, Howard Baker Press Limited.

ASSIGNMENT WITH AN OCTOPUS from *A Pattern of Islands* by Arthur Grimble, John Murray (Publishers) Limited.

THE VOYAGE TO SOUTH GEORGIA by Sir Ernest Shackleton from *Small Boat Adventures* edited by Michael Brown, Hamish Hamilton Limited.

ACCESSORY BEFORE THE FACT from *Tales of the Uncanny and Supernatural*, The Estate of the Late Algernon Blackwood and The Hamlyn Publishing Group Limited.

CHICKAMAUGA abridgement from *The Hills Beyond* by Thomas Wolfe © 1935, 1936, 1937, 1939, 1941 by Maxwell Perkins as Executor (US and Canadian rights) © 1937, Estate of Thomas Wolfe © renewed 1965 by Paul Gitlin, Administrator C. T. A. of the Estate of Thomas Wolfe. Reprinted by permission of Harper and Row, Publishers, Inc.

CRATERS OF FIRE abridgement of *Not a Very Sensible Place for a Stroll* from *Craters of Fire* by Haroun Tazieff, translated by Eithne Wilkins © 1952 by Haroun Tazieff. Reprinted by permission of Harper and Row, Publishers, Inc.

MOWGLI AND THE BANDAR-LOG from *The Jungle Book* by Rudyard Kipling, The National Trust and the Macmillan Company of London and Basingstoke.

THE Q-SHIPS from *Sea Adventures* by Graeme Cook, Macdonald and Jane's Publishers Limited.

THE CHICKEN-SWITCH by Elleston Trevor from *The 16th Pan Book of Horror Stories*.

CONDEMNED TO DEATH from *Escape from Montluc* by Andre Devigny and *Great Escape Stories* edited by Eric Williams, Dennis Dobson, Gallimard and Arthur Barker.

INTO THE SNAKE PIT from *Encounters with Animals* by Gerald Durrell, Hart-Davis MacGibbon/ Granada Publishing Limited and John Cushman Associates Inc.

Every effort has been made to clear all copyrights and the publishers trust that their apologies will be accepted for any errors or omissions.

The editor and publishers acknowledge the contributions of the following artists:

David Godfrey 41, 97, 125, 152, 179, 191, 362
Bob Harvey 56, 132, 170, 196, 222, 235, 262, 310, 338, 374, 393
Sandy Nightingale 31, 281
Lee Noel 23, 65, 71, 144, 255, 350
Geoff Taylor 87, 211, 296, 301
Barrie Thorpe 10, 82, 111, 246, 273, 322
(all the above represented by David Lewis)
John Davis 162
José María Miralles 331.

First Published 1978
Reprinted 1979, 1980, 1981 and 1982
Published by Octopus Books Limited
59 Grosvenor Street
London W1

ISBN 0 7064 0692 3

This arrangement © 1978 Octopus Books Limited

Produced by Boondoggle Limited
600A Commercial Road
London E1

Printed in Czechoslovakia
50356/5